GREAT
WESTERNS

from *THE SATURDAY EVENING POST*

GREAT WESTERNS

from THE SATURDAY EVENING POST

EDITED BY JULIE EISENHOWER

THE CURTIS PUBLISHING COMPANY INDIANAPOLIS, INDIANA

In the course of researching over one hundred years of literature in the archives of the *Post*, the following members of *The Saturday Evening Post* staff aided me in finding stories and "missing" authors.

Jep Cadou
Roberts Ehrgott
Rosalyn Fox
Astrid Henkels
Jean White

CONTENTS

INTRODUCTION

In the twentieth century, the name *Saturday Evening Post* is synonymous with excellence in short stories. Each week *Post* editors included love, mystery, humor and, in most cases, Western literature as well. The number of stories which crossed the editors' desks was tremendous. In the decade of the 1950's alone, over 150,000 manuscripts were read annually. As a result, the selections in this anthology are truly representative of the best of an art form unique to the United States—the saga of the old West.

The pages of *Great Westerns* evoke an era when grit and determination, and, most of all, courage were needed simply to survive. An era of closeness to nature and of respect and fear for the elements, whether blizzards, dust storms, floods or droughts. And an era of swift justice when moral questions of right and wrong seemed more easily determined. It is not surprising that the Western has been a favorite story form of many men and women with complex problems or occupations. The image of President Eisenhower unwinding at bedtime with a Western comes immediately to mind. But regardless of one's situation in life, the Western story offers a richness in color, adventure and sheer romance which is unmatched.

The *Post* collection of Westerns includes the well-known names of William Faulkner, Walter D. Edmonds (whose *Drums Along the Mohawk* later became a famous movie), and Conrad Richter. Their stories, and those by some modern masters of the genre—Luke Short and Bill Gulick—demonstrate that the Western cannot be pigeon-holed. On the contrary, there is a wide range in theme and mood in the literature in this volume. For example, Morgan Lewis's Western, "The Hasty Hanging," is a masterfully written murder mystery. The story of Abraham Lincoln's grandfather, "His Name Was Not Forgotten," by Joel Townsley Rogers, is historical drama at its best. Faulkner's Civil War story, "A Mountain Victory," is the moving study of the relationship between a soldier and his black servant. And James Warner Bellah's "Mission With No Record" has as its themes questions of discipline and duty.

It is illuminating to study the lives of the *Post* Western writers. The knowledge that L. Omar Barker wrote over fifteen hundred Westerns is evidence of what an incredibly fertile subject area the West is. One discovers also that many of the writers either grew up on ranches or themselves journeyed west toward the unknown and the unexpected as young men. Ernest Haycox spent his youth in logging camps and on the ranches of Oregon. Eugene Manlove Rhodes was a horse wrangler at thirteen, a government guide at seventeen during the Geronimo uprisings, and, before he turned professional author, a cowboy for twenty-five years who read incessantly "everything from paper classics put out by the Durham Company to railroad maps and labels on Worcestershire bottles." And, finally, Bill Gulick, author of the well-known "Hallelujah Trail," was born in Missouri but progressively moved farther and farther west and finally settled in Walla Walla, Washington.

The West is a land of physical contrasts: mountains and plains, deserts and rolling rivers. It is a land of contrasts in people as well: the adventurer, the missionary, the brash young kid, and the wise trapper. The stories in the *Post* volume are full of these contrasts. When one reads "The Grampus and the Weasel," the sheer exhilaration of conquering new territory and living daily with the unknown is captured. One finds too loneliness and the need for reserves of inner strength portrayed beautifully by Williams Forrest in "The Plainswoman." And the courage and pain of a young boy's struggle to become a man is never more vividly described than against the Western background of "Ride a Golden Horse."

The authors represented in the *Post* Western anthology recreate in words the earthiness, the humor and the sense of wanderlust which the men and women who ventured west seemed to possess in abundance. In so doing, they stimulate curiosity and excitement in the reader which enable him to understand better the famous words "Go West Young Man."

GREAT
WESTERNS
from THE SATURDAY EVENING POST

BAD COMPANY

S. OMAR BARKER

Swaller big, kid," said Chug-
water. "That panther milk will put whiz in your gizzard!" The
straw-haired youngster on a sweaty cow pony hesitated. For two
days he had been out whooping around with this curly-wolf cowboy
from Wyoming and the two Bonnadeen boys, and he had a pretty
good idea what punishment his Uncle Tate would have in store for
him when he got back to the ranch. Uncle Tate was a quiet-spoken,
gristle-necked old bachelor with stern, old-fashioned ideas about
how a boy should be raised, and he had promised this one a
walloping the next time he ran off to "hell around," as he called it,
with Chet and Smoky Bonnadeen.

Willie Shelton knew he would be needing some "whiz in his
gizzard" when he got back to the T 8, but he soberly doubted if the
kind that came in a bottle would help very much. Yet sometimes
nothing can seem more important to a nearly-sixteen-year-old than
not to be tagged as a sissy. Willie leaned his lankness from the saddle
and took the proffered bottle.

"Here's to long ropes and loose hobbles!" he proclaimed. "Let the
he-wolves howl and the pant'ers prowl!"

Big-enough talk, just right for a bold, booted buckaroo. At least
he hoped it sounded that way. He stuck the neck of the bottle inside
his mouth and pretended to swallow a lot more than he actually did.

"Woo-haw!" With a sudden squall, Chet Bonnadeen poked the
chestnut horse in the flank with the butt end of his quirt.

The four of them had spent a good part of the day match-roping

1

on T 8 yearlings over on Potrillow Creek and their horses were pretty well ridden down. But the chestnut pony still had enough life in him to jump almost from under his rider when Chet poked him.

"You get me throwed, you bangtailed buck idiot," said Willie, "and I'll come over you like a bullwhacker's bad dream!"

He made it sound tough, but there was no real anger in it—just the kind of rawhide talk Chet and Smoky were always swapping around. It gave him a swaggery feeling to be able to swap it right back at them.

Chet and Smoky were local cowboys, around nineteen and twenty, with restless black eyes and wildcat ways. In Uncle Tate Murdock's tallybook they were bad companions for the nephew he had taken to raise after an epidemic of typhoid fever had orphaned him some three years before. But Willie, with the disquiet of oncoming manhood in his blood, had lately taken to running with them anyway, just as any high-spirited colt may take to running with the wild bunch. They called him "Bill," not "Willie," and he liked that too.

Chugwater was older, a ruddy, moonfaced cowpoke with a sandy bristle of mustache and yellow-green coyote eyes. He hadn't been around the Black Mesa country more than a few weeks. If he had any name but Chugwater, he had never bothered to mention it. He said he owned a horse ranch up in Wyoming, and was just out on a *pasear* to see what kind of cayuses grew in New Mexico, and maybe kick up his heels a little in fresh pasture. He rode a fancy rig and had money to spend. He carried a long-reach lass-rope and was just as handy with it as he seemed to be with six-gun, rawhide talk and rye whisky. It never occurred to Willie that there might be anything odd about a stranger of Chugwater's age taking up so readily with the much younger Bonnadeens, whooping around with a trio of youngsters as if they were just as much man as he was.

Now, after a couple of days of comparatively harmless high jinks, Willie was headed for home, the others on their way back in to Black Mesa.

When they came in sight of the Otis place on Tusa Creek, Willie challenged Smoky to a race, saddle-stand style, as far as the bridge beyond the Otis house.

"Shucks, you couldn't stand up in a wagon bed!" scoffed Smoky.

So Willie showed him. His chestnut pony was half a length ahead as they fogged past the Otis gate. Willie let out a long-drawn cowboy yell. He couldn't see whether Letha Otis was watching from a window or not, but he couldn't help hoping she was.

Where the road turned off to the T 8, Chugwater offered his bottle again, but Willie shook his head.

"Too close to home base, Chug." His grin had an uneasy look about it. "Uncle Tate'll be mad enough as it is!"

"Here, Bill!" Smoky Bonnadeen handed him a piece of gum. "Chaw that if you're scared the ol' gristle-neck will sniff likker on your wind!"

"Let him sniff," shrugged Willie. "If he gets too rollicky, I'll quit him and take out for Texas!"

"Make it Wyoming," said Chet, with a wink at Chugwater, "and you might have company. I hear that's curly-wolf country up there."

"But tough on pups!" Chugwater batted his coyote eyes at Willie as if sizing him up for caliber.

"You ain't talkin' about me!" Willie batted boyish blue ones right back at him. "I'm a growed he-wolf with a hanker to howl!"

"Then maybe you'd just as well ride on in with us. There ain't no law says you got to check in ever' few minutes, is there?"

Willie sensed challenge in it, but he hesitated only a second. "No law, I reckon," he said. "But I'm goin' to—this time, anyway. So long, you saddle bumpers!"

"So long, gopher gizzard!" Chet poked Willie's chestnut in the flank again. "See you in Wyoming!"

Willie wondered about that Wyoming talk as he rode away from them. Maybe it was all just cowboy hurrawing, maybe it wasn't. He wished he knew. He wondered some about himself, too, trying to remind himself that he ought to be grateful to Uncle Tate for furnishing him with bed, board and a place on the ranch roller towel for the past three years. In those three years Uncle Tate and his right bower, a wizened old *vaquero* named Policarpio Mascarenas, had somehow made him over from a raw kid roustabout into a copper-bradded cow hand, ready and able to ride for the brand. For that he owed them.

But he wished Uncle Tate could get it through his head that he was now old enough, and man enough, to pick his own company—and too old to take a whipping. Not that Uncle Tate had walloped him any more than his own father probably would have if he had lived; five or six times in three years, mostly for bad talk, and all but one of those wallopings had been more than a year ago. That was all right. He'd been just a kid then, and maybe needed that kind of daddying. But Uncle Tate's last application of a doubled lead rope, only three weeks ago, had been for drinking beer with Chet and Smoky Bonnadeen. Willie had wanted mighty bad to warn Uncle Tate right then that the next time he tried it he'd have a fight on his hands. But he had lacked enough courage to get it said.

All right, Uncle Tate. You've got your ideas, and I've got mine. I reckon you might as well find out right now that they don't always tally. That was what he was planning to say this time.

The man waiting by the saddle-shed door with a doubled lead rope in his hand was medium tall, built like a thong of rawhide, with a bony, weather-leathered face. There was little about his appearance to remind Willie of his dead mother except the quiet, steady look that stayed in his deep-set blue eyes, no matter what kind of humor he was in. Right now they looked at the sweat-caked horse more than at the boy.

"Willie," he said, "you been helling around with them no-account Bonnadeens again?"

He didn't raise his voice any more than if he had been asking about some stray cow he'd sent a cow hand out to look for. But Willie knew what was up. He got off and unlaced his saddle without answering. He wished he knew some way to make Uncle Tate understand about the big feeling it gave him to be accepted by Chet and Smoky and Chugwater as their rough, tough, rawhide equal. But it wouldn't be any use to try.

He put up his saddle and started to go turn his pony out.

"Poley will turn out your horse, Willie," said Uncle Tate quietly. "you come here."

"I'll turn out my own horse," said Willie. "I ain't crippled."

He started off with the pony, but old Policarpio came hobbling over from where he was wedging rags into a leak in the water trough and took the reins.

"Take easy, Weellie," he advised. "More queeck you cry, more queeck he don't wheep no more!"

"Cry, my foot!" The boy turned and went back to the saddle shed, flapping his chaps defiantly.

"Willie," said Uncle Tate, so quietly that his voice almost sounded kind despite its sternness, "I promised your mother I'd try and make a man out of you, but I won't never get the job done as long as you slip off and run around with rubbish."

"They ain't rubbish! They're——"

"I know what they are. You want to stand for your whippin' or have I got to hold you?"

"Neither one, Uncle Tate." Willie was tall enough to meet the older man's eyes almost on the level. "I've took my last whippin'. I'm headin' out for Wyoming—and you've lost you a cow hand!"

The look in Uncle Tate's eyes betrayed neither anger nor surprise.

"All right, Willie," he began, "if that's——"

"That's another thing!" the boy broke in hotly. "A man old enough to punch cows don't have to be called 'Willie'!"

"Willie," said Uncle Tate slowly, "I've broke a heap of broncs in my time, but I never did whip a horse except to learn him right from wrong—nor a boy either. Only a whippin' won't do you no good if you don't know you need it." He tossed the rope inside the saddle she. "If that's the way you see it, you might as well saddle you a horse and git goin'!"

"Never mind a horse!" Willie tried to put all the man-sized don't-give-a-hoot into his voice that he could. "I'll make out afoot till I get one!"

"No, by ginger, you won't!" It was the first time Willie had ever heard Uncle Tate sound sure-enough mad. "I never have set a cow hand afoot, and I don't aim to start now! Ol' Gravy's your horse. You take him—and that duckfoot dun to pack your bedroll on if you want him." He fished out a pocket-worn wallet. "Here's fifty dollars due you in wages. I don't give a hoot how you spend it, but I won't have no nephew of mine sneakin' off broke and afoot like a hobo sheepherder! Either you leave the T 8 up in the saddle like a white man, or else you stay and take your whippin'. And remember what I tell you: whatever trail you take from now on out, you've got to pick it yourself!"

Willie wound up by taking Gravy and the fifty dollars, but not the pack-horse. He already had his own saddle.

After Uncle Tate went in the house, old Poley came out to where Willie was saddling up, with some cold biscuits in a flour sack.

"Wyoming putty far place," he said.

"So's the hot place," shrugged the boy, "but I reckon the trail's open!"

"The Ol' Man don't got no keeds hees own, Weellie!"

"Well, that ain't my fault!"

"You be good boy, Weellie. Someday you come back *mucho hombre!*"

"Don't look for me right quick!" Willie managed to put on a good-bye grin. This horse-warped old *mejicano* had been mighty good to him.

Old Boojum Johnson, the cook, and a T 8 cowboy called Tack Akers stood in the cookshack door and watched him bundle his warbag on behind the saddle, but neither of them made any comment.

It was around sundown when Willie came riding past the Otis place. Letha Otis was standing just inside the gate, teasing a pup with a long switch. She kept her back turned to the road, as if she didn't see him. Willie leaned over the gate and gave one of her gold-yellow braids a yank. She whirled around and whacked him, not very hard, with the switch.

"Shame on you, Willie Shelton!" she said. "Don't you ever do that again!"

"Likely I won't, taffy-top," Willie told her. "I'm quittin' the country—for good."

Letha was just a little ranch girl, hardly a day over fourteen, with freckles and a snubby nose, but the surprised way her big blue eyes looked up at him gave Willie's heart a twist.

"Don't talk silly!" she said.

"Silly, my foot! Me and Uncle Tate had a showdown, and I'm on my way!"

"Good riddance!" Letha flipped her braids in a sassy gesture, then abruptly sobered. "Not—not sure 'nough, Bill?"

"Sure as cockleburs on a coyote!" Willie sat straight in the saddle. "A man's got to pick his own trail, Letha, and I'm Wyoming-bound!"

The girl didn't say good-bye, but when he looked back from on down the road, she waved to him.

Chet and Smoky Bonnadeen had folks over on Tejon Creek, but they didn't stay with them much. They had a little shack on the outskirts of Black Mesa where they batched most of the time, and where Chugwater had thrown in with them the past several weeks. Willie felt sure he would be welcome there.

But first he rode into town. At Horseshoe Higgins's store he bought a couple of soogans, a horsehide jacket with fringes on it like the one Chugwater wore, a secondhand .45 in a black leather holster, and some cartridges. Horseshoe Higgins hesitated a little about selling the gun.

"Your uncle know you're buyin' this weepon?" he asked.

Willie shrugged. "He will when you tell him."

"You sure you know which end the bullets come out of?"

"I'm fixin' to study up on it," Willie told him. "You goin' to sell me this pistol, or ain't you?"

The fat storekeeper shrugged and let him have it. Willie added some dry salt pork, sardines, crackers and dried prunes to his purchases. Welcome or not, he didn't intend to sponge on anybody.

He thought about stopping at the Bullhorn Saloon for a bottle of whisky, but he was afraid Brocky Jones might not sell him hard liquor, and there might be cowboys around to josh him about it. Besides, now that he was riding his own trail, with no one to forbid him, he had already decided it might be a good idea not to drink much more than might be necessary to keep from looking like a sissy.

It was dark when he rode up to the Bonnadeen shack. Even with his horse loaded like a sheepherder's burro with soogans and sacks, it gave him a big feeling to arrive well supplied and with a six-shooter on. He reined up and let out what the cowboys call a squall. Both the Bonnadeens came out.

"You holler wicked for a tenderfoot," grinned Smoky. "Fall off your horse, we can drag you in and see how bad you're shot!"

"Woo-haw-w-w-w!" squalled Willie again. He stepped off his horse, drew his new gun and banged away a couple of times in the air.

"You want Constable Ellers rompin' out here to see who's shootin' off firecrackers?" Chet demanded.

Willie waited till he had put up his horse and sat down to biscuits and gravy before he told them how he had slipped his hobbles and come to throw in with them.

"Big feller!" Chet walloped him on the back. "Let's have a drink of bob-wire extract on it!"

Smoky got a jug out from under one of the bunks.

"Here's to the three muskrat ears!" he declaimed. "One for all, all for one—unless he gets caught!"

Brash, breezy talk. Willie liked it, but he made his turn at the jug a light one.

"Chet," he inquired, "where's ol' Chugwater?"

"Gone to the wilderness to look for the ol' gray mare," said Chet. "We're fixin' to meet him at some old corrals at the mouth of Torcido Canyon about Sunday mornin', with our beds all rolled and grub in a sack."

"What about Wyoming?"

"Why? You goin' with us?"

"Try and stop me!"

"All right, but don't go blabbin' it around, you savvy!"

Willie wondered if he ought to tell them that he had already bragged to Uncle Tate and Poley and Letha Otis about being Wyoming-bound, but as long as they hadn't robbed a bank or anything, he couldn't see that it mattered.

He and Chet and Smoky spent part of the next few days shoeing horses, rigging pack saddles, readying gear for packing, and part of it in Black Mesa. No high jinks that would get Constable Ellers after them. Just Junin' around, as the cowboys say.

His first afternoon in town, Willie saw Boojum Johnson with the T 8 supply wagon. On a sudden impulse he helped the old cook load some hundred-pound sacks of salt. For a while Chet and Smoky stood around, hurrawing him for being a flunky, then strutted off, spurs a jingle, to the Bullhorn Saloon.

"I heard you and them two no-accounts had took out to Wyoming, Willie," Boojum grinned. "You back already?"

"You can hear a heap of things when you got big ears," shrugged Willie.

The next morning Willie came across Tack Akers just lighting down at the Bullhorn hitch rack.

"Hi, Tack," Willie said. "How come you townin' on a weekday?"

"I come lookin' for an egg to suck," grinned Tack. "How's Wyoming?"

"A foot wide and open in the middle," Willie breezed back at him. "Same as a cowboy's mouth. How's the ranch?"

"Better," said Tack. "I ain't seen a dirty place on the roller towel since you left. Say, you wouldn't know the whereabouts of a feller called Chugwater, would you?"

"He's gone to the wilderness to look for the old gray mare. You want him for somethin'?"

"Nothin' important," Tack shrugged. "I punched cows up around the Chugwater country one summer. Just wonderin' if he was some jasper I'd met up there. You headin' for Wyoming west of the mountains or east up the flats?"

Willie couldn't think of any reason why Tack might want to pump him, but he remembered what Chet had said about keeping his blab shut.

"Who wants to know?" he asked.

"Not me, Willie." The T 8 cowboy shrugged and went on into the Bullhorn.

That night after supper Chet saddled up and rode away by himself. After he was gone, Willie asked Smoky where Chet was headed for, that he had to ride by night.

"To help Chug look for the ol' gray mare," said Smoky.

"Doggone it, Smoky!" Willie flared up at him. "You talk riddles to me and I'll come over you like a wet saddle blanket! What's all this about the old gray mare?"

"Keep your shirt on," Smoky advised him with a grin. "Chet's gone to help gather some horses Chug's been buying for us to take along to Wyoming, whenever we go."

"Buyin'?"

"What else? You don't think a big ranch owner like Chug would be borrowin' 'em, do you?"

Willie didn't know for sure what to think. But what he did know was that he had thrown in with this outfit of his own free will, and as long as they continued to treat him good, he sure didn't aim to raise a fuss over something that really was none of his business.

"It ain't nothing to me where Chugwater gets his horses," he said. "Let's wander down to Brocky's and shake for the beers."

The next afternoon the two young cowboys met Tate Murdock and old Poley coming out of Horseshoe Higgins's store. Uncle Tate nodded to him as casually as if he were a stranger and walked on down the street. Old Poley didn't even nod.

"Ol' gristle-gut!" shrugged Smoky. "You're lucky you quit him!"

Willie restrained an unaccountable impulse to warn Smoky to mind his tongue where Uncle Tate was concerned.

"Sure," he said, instead. "You ain't heard me cryin' about it, have you?"

He was trying a new saddle blanket on his horse out back of the store a few minutes later when old Poley showed up with a brand-new rope in his hand. Smoky was still inside the store, probably teasing Horseshoe's none-too-pretty daughter.

"How you makin', Weellie?" The old *vaquero's* sharp black eyes seemed to be appraising the boy's new six-shooter in its black leather holster. "Whassamatta you don't went to Gwyoming?"

Willie started to say "None of your business," but something like shame stopped him. This was a man who had never spoken an unkind word to him in his life.

"We'll be pullin' out," he said instead, "as soon as Chugwater finds the ol' gray mare. How's things at the ranch?"

"Joost same. Water trough still leakin'." Poley shrugged, batting wrinkle-bound black eyes. "Señor Chugwater, he's nize man, eh? Geeve you good job in Gwyoming, Weellie?"

One thing sure, Willie didn't want Poley—or anybody else—feeling sorry for him.

"Sure," he said. "On his horse ranch. Forty a month. Same as he's payin' me to help trail a bunch with us. We're fixin' to pick 'em up at Torcido Canyon, Sunday mornin'. I'm my own man now, Poley, and——Hey, what you think you're doin' with that rope?"

Poley finished tying a fine new lariat on Willie's saddle.

"Leetle borthday's present, Weellie," he grinned. "You forget you sixteen years today?"

Willie gulped. "I sure had," he said. "Gosh! Much obliged! I'll sure try to keep the kinks out of it!"

"*Buen cabestro, vaquero honesto!*" Policarpio Mascarenas spoke the words with a certain dignity. "*Adios*, Weellie!"

Good rope, honest cowboy. He don't have any call to preach at me, thought the boy. *I'm grown now, and able to pick my own trail.*

He hadn't meant to blab, but he was tired of getting gigged about still not being gone to Wyoming. Anyhow, why should it matter?

That night he and Smoky got to trying to see which one could do a better job of tilting a jug one-handed, with the result that Willie swallowed a little more barbed-wire extract than he meant to. He woke up the next morning with a ratty taste in his mouth and all his clothes on, and for the first time, stayed away from the two dusty streets of Black Mesa all day.

Both Willie and Smoky were surprised when Chugwater and Chet came riding in late Saturday evening. Chet said they had got the old corrals patched so they would hold the ol' gray mare overnight, so had decided they might as well ride in and help pack out.

Chugwater's ruddy face bristled like a porcupine with a week's growth of sandy whiskers. After a long pull at the jug, he lathered up and shaved them off, including his mustache.

"You look like moonrise over a cowpen, Chug," Willie told him.

"You can't insult me, kid." Chugwater's laugh was short. "I wasn't put together for purty, like you. Chet tells me you've slipped your hobbles an' lookin' for passage to Wyoming."

"You heard him right. From now on, I'm skinnin' my own wolf. You see my new six gun?"

Chugwater took the .45, spun it expertly on his finger and handed it back.

"Totin' a hogleg don't make you a curly wolf, kid. Not till you learn when, where an' how to make it talk for you. You sing the right tune till we git to Wyoming, an' maybe I'll give you a few pointers."

They packed up and pulled out by moonlight, leading three pack horses. From the wrecked condition in which Chet and Smoky left their shack, it looked to Willie as if they were not expecting to come back. Well, neither was he.

It was a twenty-mile ride to where Torcido Canyon twisted its way out of the rimrocks in such poor grass country that nobody had ever bothered to fence it and few stock ever ranged there. Eighteen of those twenty miles were already behind them when sunrise began to spread an orange-red glory over rimrocked buttes and mesas.

Willie had never ridden this far east of the T 8 before, but yonder, westward some fifty miles away, he could recognize La Ceja—the long "eyebrow" of mesa rim that marked off his Uncle Tate's main summer range—with the golden broom of sunrise slowly brushing away its purple haze.

Willie was wondering if sunrise would ever be like this in Wyoming, when, topping a low rise, they came upon a little bunch of loose horses: a mare with a colt, some twos, threes and full-grown geldings. Eleven head, all golden chestnuts but two. Willie didn't have to look twice to recognize them for T 8 horses, some of Uncle Tate's best. What they were doing off here forty miles from T 8 headquarters, thirty from the nearest T 8 fence, Willie had no idea. But here they were.

Tate Murdock had never raised his horses wild. These put up their heads and circled a little, but didn't run. When the four riders came close enough to read brands, Chugwater reined up. He looked as surprised as Willie felt.

"Hell's ahootin'!" he exclaimed. "Where did these nags come from? That T 8's your uncle's brand, ain't it, kid?"

Willie nodded. He took a deep breath, unconsciously straightening a little in the saddle as he remembered what Uncle Tate had said about picking his own trail.

"Boys," he said quietly, "here's where I quit you. I'm goin' to take these strays back where they belong."

Chugwater swung his horse around to face the boy, a coldly calculating squint in his coyotelike eyes.

"I don't know how these strays got here, kid," he said, "but there ain't no sense kickin' luck in the face. They've got the same brand as the horse you're ridin'. What's to keep us from throwin' 'em up the trail, sell 'em an' split the take?"

"Not a damn thing," said Willie, "except that I'm takin' 'em home!"

"Don't be a knucklehead, Bill!" That was Chet. "You've done throwed in with this outfit, and by gulliver——"

"I'll 'tend to this, boys," Chugwater cut in dryly. He turned again to Willie. "I ain't foolin', kid. I want these horses. You goin' to be reasonable, or ain't you?"

Willie stared at the six-shooter that had appeared with sudden ease in Chugwater's hand.

His own gun came out of the holster awkwardly. It shook when he tried to point it.

"You horse thieves can go to hell!" he said, between white, tight lips. "I'm takin' these horses home!"

"You double-crossin' little so-and-so!" said Chet. . . . "let him have it, Chug!"

If I shoot first I'll miss, thought Willie grimly. *And if I don't——*

"Chet," said Chugwater without taking his eyes off the white-faced boy in front of him, "if you think I'm fool enough to put myself on the list for shootin' a pucker-brained pipsqueak, you're crazy! A few horses just ain't worth it! Let's git goin'!"

They went. So did Willie, in the other direction. He was shaking all over. He wondered how Chugwater knew he hadn't been going to shoot unless he had to. He was short a bedroll and some stuff in the departing packs, but it didn't matter. All he wanted now was to get these strays started back to the T 8.

He pushed them up a little draw, then cut back over the next ridge north and found a rimrock from which he could get a good look down at about twenty horses in the old Torcido Canyon corrals. If he saw even one T 8 chestnut among them, he knew he would have to go back down there. He was glad that he saw none.

Willie ran into some rough country getting back to the T 8, but by using his new rope to catch a fresh mount a couple of times and pushing right on by moonlight, he managed to hit headquarters with his strays a little before sunup the next day. Always an early riser, Uncle Tate saw the drive coming and opened the gates. Willie shoved the horses on into the horse trap beyond the corrals.

"Must be some fence down someplace," said Uncle Tate when he came riding back through the trap gate. "Where'd you find 'em?"

He sounded like a man who had sent a cow hand out to look for some strays and was passably glad he'd found them.

"Over east," Willie told him. " 'Bout a mile south of Torcido Canyon."

"You've made a good ride, Bill." Uncle Tate's leathery face looked no different from what it had as he stood there at the saddle shed a few days ago, with a rope in his hand. "Turn out your horse and we'll go in to breakfast."

It was the first time, as far as Willie could remember, that Uncle Tate had ever called him Bill. The man-to-man, matter-of-fact sound of it was in itself a promise and a testimony of new understanding between them.

Still the boy stayed on his horse. Blabbing on those he had so lately counted as friends was not going to be easy. But they had picked their own trail, and now he had picked his.

"Some fellers had a bunch of horses penned in them old corrals, Uncle Tate," he said. "I reckon maybe——"

"Sheriff Ortega's keepin' tabs on 'em," Tate Murdock broke in quietly. "It ain't your fault if everybody can't be honest, Bill."

He didn't say "like you," but Willie knew what he meant. If it turned out that some of those horses were stolen, he hoped the law wouldn't be too hard on Chet and Smoky—especially Smoky.

But now he still had his own gully to jump. He got off his horse and took down the new rope old Poley had given him.

"I'm still due that whippin', Uncle Tate," he said. "Here's a rope."

Uncle Tate didn't take the rope, nor even look at it. It was almost the first time Willie had ever seen anything like a twinkle in his eye.

"Horse or man," he said, "sixteen is too damned old to whip! Let's go in to breakfast. Then you better rest up awhile."

Along toward noon Willie took a notion to ride over to the Otis place and see how Letha was making out with her pup. Old Poley was out there, wedging rags in a water-trough leak when he came out to saddle up.

"How you makin', Beel!" he grinned. "Those new rope ketch putty good?"

"It sure did," said Willie earnestly.

Because now he understood how it was: why Boojum and Tack and Poley had tried to pump him; why those T 8 strays had turned up where they were—not wholly by accident. And when an old gristle-neck like Uncle Tate would risk losing some of his best horses on the chance that a runaway kid's finding them would put him back on the right trail, it sure did give a man a fine, big feeling!

MISSION WITH NO RECORD

JAMES WARNER BELLAH

The Officer of the Guard heard the sound of many wagon wheels echoing up from the Sudro Road. It was almost four in the morning and the dawn wind that carried the sound husked across the Fort Starke parade ground, pelting sand at the pine boards of the Officers' Picket Quarters, lashing the taut halyards in a frenzied tattoo against the flagpole.

The O.G. started running—those wagons were the replacement detail, almost a day ahead of time. He skirted the parade ground and took the short cut past Colonel Massarene's isolated quarters, back toward the guardhouse. Then he stopped stock-still in his tracks, his head cocked to the soft call of a violin—"Samanthe . . . while the moon doth shine . . . Samanthe." Through the lighted window of the C.O.'s quarters, he could see the slender silhouette of Colonel Massarene, head bent, arm crooked to the bow, drawing out a gentle song of lost years and of forgotten candlelight and of jasmine on the night air—"Samanthe——"

For a second, the Officer of the Guard stood listening and staring in utter disbelief. A frigid shadow of a man, D.L. Massarene, living in Capuchin solitude with one chair, one cot, one table. Ruling the West and the regiment with it, with the iron hand of duty. Never a meal with another officer. Never a word of praise or a word for laughter. Alone there and friendless, with the grisly sobbing of his violin to lift the lost years from his soul and give him surcease.

Suddenly to the O.G., it was as if he were peeping—as if he had sneaked into another man's privacy and desecrated it, for in some strange fashion there was the honor of a woman in that song . . . and bitter tears and lonely desperation. In quick embarrassment, he turned and ran again, toward headquarters and the guardhouse and the slow, rocketing sound of the wagon convoy that was rolling onto the post now from the Sudro Road.

The O.G. came up behind Sergeant Shattuck, and the sergeant swung around. "Recruit replacement from Jefferson Barracks, Mr. Topliff; eighteen hours ahead of schedule. General Sheridan rode in with 'em from Elkhorn. He's in post headquarters. A runner's gone for the colonel." D'Arcy Topliff took the headquarters veranda in two long strides. Philip Henry Sheridan, his back to the hanging lamp, was flicking the damper, toeing open the draft, throwing in post oak until the stove roared like a river boat.

"Sheridan, mister"—in a bleak York State twang—"what about coffee?"

"Topliff, Officer of the Guard, sir," and D'Arcy put the duty coffeepot on.

Sheridan stretched out his hands to thaw their numbing chill. He must have looked pinched and blue this way, the morning he galloped in from Winchester to smash Jubal Early, for it can be cold in the early mornings in October in the Shenandoah Valley.

Colonel Massarene, running along the headquarters duckboards, struck the veranda once, lightly, and pushed open the door with a quick insistence that flowed through him easily from head to clicked heels, to voice, "Good morning, general."

Sheridan said, "Seven years, isn't it, Massarene, since we last had coffee together?"

"Seven, sir. Even. On the fifteenth of next month."

Tall, Massarene. Spare, almost to a whisper of pain, but a magnificent animal turned like a fine tool to his job. Colonel of cavalry and nothing more, for there was nothing left to him beyond that. Nor for Sheridan either. But with Sheridan there was a flamboyant touch in mustache and chin whisker, of no depth in their gesture, that the saber blade of his fine nose didn't throw the laugh to.

He said, "Massarene, I'm bringing you an order. I'm giving it to you personally. I'm sending you across the Rio Grande after the Lipans, Kickapoos and the Apaches. I'm tired of hit and run, and diplomatic hide and seek. Cross the border and burn 'em out, and to high hell with the Department of State!"

"Mr. Topliff," Massarene said, "you didn't hear that . . . except officially. Which is not hearing it at all."

Outside, the recruits from Jefferson Barracks were unloading

15

baggage with the dogged sullenness of early morning, thumping it down to the ground, cursing softly, getting the job done, but with no joy in it.

"Do I have a written order for the mission, general?" Massarene asked.

"No." Phil Sheridan shook his head. "Grant and I will take personal responsibility in Washington, but we want no official paper record to exist. My job is to protect Texas. You cross the Rio Grande and smash 'em, Massarene, as Mackenzie smashed 'em!"

Outside, with the wagon train unloaded and the gray first light loping across the prairie like the shadow of a gaunt wolf, Sergeant Shattuck began calling the roll of the replacement detail, "Andrews, Blake, Cattlett, Fink——"

Inside, General Sheridan said, "Too bad about your son, Massarene."

"I beg your pardon, sir?"

"Being found, I mean. Dismissed from the Academy."

"——Heinze, Hooker, Ives, Jacobs——"

"I still don't understand you, general."

"Your son was dismissed from West Point two months ago. Hadn't you heard?"

Headquarters was cold suddenly with the tomb's breath, and the years that had passed over the colonel began to flow suddenly back toward him.

He said, "I have had no news of my son, general, since he was three years old. And I never expect to hear anything about him again——"

"——Lowry, Lutz, Marble, Massarene——"

No one of the three in headquarters moved an eye but it was as if the living fiber of Colonel Massarene had been belly-kicked—as if a shadow, fast moving, had flicked him with physical force.

After a moment, he said, "I shall move out with the regiment, general, at reveille, the day after tomorrow. . . . Mr. Topliff, knock out the adjutant at once." But the sound that hung in the room was the echo of that name "Massarene," like a dead man's coat on a peg.

The news ran through the regiment before morning stable call: "One of the new recruits from Jefferson is the Old Man's son! He failed in mathematics and they kicked him out of the Academy. He enlisted the same day at Highland Falls." And at breakfast in the bachelor officers' mess: "His mother was one of the Fahnestock sisters. Unbelievably beautiful. And the youngster is as handsome as sin, with the Old Man's wiriness. She couldn't take the life, they say. Had her own money. Left Massarene years ago, when he was a lieutenant."

When D'Arcy Topliff saw the paymaster's wagon and inspected the escort for Sheridan's trip to Elkhorn, the general thanked him.

Then as he climbed in, he turned his head. "You married, mister?"

Topliff smiled. "That's hard to come by out here, general."

"When you come by it," Sheridan said, "see that it's an Army girl. One that can cook, sew, ride, shoot, breed and keep her complexion. And remember, I told you, mister."

The men joked about putting chevrons on at Starke with hooks and eyes. They hated Colonel Massarene because he hewed so close to the line that no humanity ever got between, only an immaculate military justice that was machine-made, and as icy as the fingers of death. They hated him because he was ever right, and they hated him because they knew they could never love him. "God, I hope the boy has steel; for the Old Man will break him in his two hands, if he hasn't!"

When Colonel Massarene inspected the recruit detail, he looked straight into his son's eyes, but there was no recognition in either man, no wavering.

"I hope the blood of every one of you ran thick down your legs in the Jefferson riding ring," the Old Man said to the detail. "I hope you're all dry of it, except in your hearts. Desert . . . and I'll find you and rope you and bring you back. Go slack in your duties . . . and I'll stiffen your spines against escort-wagon wheels. In this regiment, it is harder to make corporal than it is for a Hindoo to get into heaven. You're for company duty as of today. . . . Dismiss the detail." And he turned on his heel and walked off.

After guard mount, when Topliff marched off as O.G., the Old Man sent for him to come to headquarters. "Mr. Topliff," he said, "only you and I know where the regiment is going. That's enough tongues to leak it. So we'll have no more tongues—not even the adjutant's—in on it. Chart me three alternate routes. Roughly, I want to move southwest from Starke to the Tablelands, as a diversion, and I want to cross the border somewhere between Peco and San Jacinto by forced night march, leaving the escort wagons behind. The moon is dark in nine days. I'll cross then and I'd like very well to have the regiment think it was crossing the Querhada River, rather than the Rio Grande. . . until the last possible minute. I suppose you understand you may resign your commission? Should General Sheridan die in the midst of this, you'll lose it, and I'll lose mine . . . and everyone else."

"You don't intend to offer resignation to the other officers, sir. You only mention it to me because I was present and know the mission?"

"An order, Mr. Topliff, is an order. I cannot offer it to the others until the Rio Grande is crossed, and then I will not."

Working out the lines of march, D'Arcy Topliff was in the outer office of headquarters when Private Massarene came in. He heard the interview, and it was like the pounding of short in-blows through the partition.

"You sent for me, sir?"

"I did." And a long pause that writhed in the air as the eyes of those two met and whipped at each other like knives. "I sent for you to put it to you straight. That you are my son is merely a matter of official record. For years you have undoubtedly lived with a concept of me, as I have of you. I shall give you my concept of you. It is not pleasant. There are two blood streams coursing in you. One is deeply ingrained in a way of soft and moneyed living—so deeply that pride of oath and commitment is secondary to its continued necessity. That is on your record."

Outside, Topliff could feel in his own cheeks the hot rush of angry blood darkening the boy's handsome face until the lips became white as a new scar. And in his mind Topliff whispered frantically, *Don't answer him. Don't talk back.*

"And it is on your record, too, that you have failed at West Point and been turned out as unfit for a commission. So you have enlisted, in a dramatic gesture, to lacerate yourself by showing your carbine to men you have hazed. Neither the failure nor the attempt to atone for it impresses me. Your other blood stream is mine, but your concept of that is a concept of plumes, parades and band music. Following the lie of their lure, you have rashly and thoughtlessly placed your living upon the table top, and the cards are dealt. I put it to you flatly, that the royal straight flush of glory never comes up in life, and that only fools hope for it. My father shot, for cowardice, at Chapultepec, the officer son of a United States senator with his own hand. I shall not bedevil you, but what comes to other men will only come to you in this regiment through a meticulous, immaculate performance of duty up to the last detail. You have chosen my way of life; I shall see that you attain to it unto its deepest essence or leave your bones to bleach under the prairie moon!"

Topliff, outside, realized that his own hands were clenched so tightly that his arms ached to the elbows. It was the boy's voice—low, even and controlled, like flicked gloves.

"Do I . . . have the privilege of speaking, sir . . . or do I not?"

"Within the strict limitations of decorum."

"I didn't ask to be sent to this regiment, sir, but I wouldn't have it otherwise, now that I'm here. Except for one thing."

18

"And what is that one thing?"

Young Massarene said, "That there might be any faint thought in your mind, sir, that I came to this regiment ever to call you 'father.' "

Jasper! What life can do to people at times, and so uselessly, so wholly without reason.

Young Massarene went to C Company for duty—Lieutenant Cohill's company—but as the way is with things like that, once you've been let in on the inside track, D'Arcy Topliff kept crossing the boy's trail. A lean youngster, lithe and flat in the hips, deep-chested. Loading the regimental escort wagons behind the commissary corral. On the ammunition detail. Post fatigue detachments. Stables. And Topliff watched him closely to see what was there, for there could have been many wrong things.

Because Topliff had gone over to the youngster's side instinctively, when the colonel had flayed him, he stayed over. And without knowing quite how, a part of him got into young Massarene's mind, just as a part of him had got into the colonel's mind when he had heard that violin at four in the morning.

The regiment moved out on schedule and took the long trail down into the southwest country. And sometimes in the days that followed, D'Arcy Topliff rode as young Massarene. Sometimes he rode as the colonel. He was young Massarene when they found the burned-out wagon train and the dead wagoners, with one strapped face downward to a wagon shaft with his tongue cut out, but still alive to the horror of writhing ants. Young Massarene, with the bitter bile in his throat, swallowing as he dug the long grave, swallowing eternally to keep his food down against the green corruption in his nostrils. *White gloves and pipe-clayed cross belts. Varnished boots and brass buttons in the Hudson River sunlight.* Another world away from Sergeant Shattuck, drawing his revolver carefully and putting it in the wagoner's agonized hand. Picking it up again from where it whipped to, in jerking recoil, from the lone shot that brought peace.

But Topliff was the colonel in his mind, when the smoke was high beyond the head of the column, when they rode slowly down into Corinth Wells to the burned-out houses. Women were dead in the yards, and there was a twelve-year-old girl with her mind gone completely and forever to her torn nakedness. "Someone please give me a drink of water and tell me a funny story."

"Cohill," Colonel Massarene said, "take the pursuit. I'll give you twelve hours. Twenty men. Meet me"—he put his finger on his map—"here, at San Jacinto." And Topliff felt it in Colonel Massarene's mind before the colonel said it. Felt it for what the colonel's

19

thinking was, for it is easy to steady recruits with action, but it is the hard way to make them see, and not lash back. It is easy to temper their anger with hot carbines, but it is merciless to hold them in close restraint. And nothing is worse than burying women the Apaches have worked over; nothing is worse than an insane girl digging down again to her mother's dead face in the starlight.

"Don't take the detail from C Company, Mr. Cohill. Take the pickets. And under no circumstances cross the Rio Grande," the colonel said.

Cohill didn't run the hostiles down. They were across the Rio Grande before he hit the river line. Across, as they always were now, safe in formal protocol, reeking with drying blood in the green smoke of their villages, under the theoretic protection of a wreck of empire that had sprawled in disorder since the breeze of Queretaro whipped at the blue smoke of the firing party's rifles and ruffled the blond beard of Maximilian von Habsburg, dead in the dust that rose about his riddled body. "Don't take the detail from C Company, Mr. Cohill."

So it was for days, as Massarene moved the regiment steadily along. Then presently the regiment was a bad joke to itself—a slow-moving buffoon with the clowns who got the laughs, slapsticking in behind it to strike and dashing up ahead to grimace in derision. Almost they seemed to watch from the other side, time the regiment's march and plan their forays to fit the pattern.

Anger burned deep as bowel pain, and still Massarene held the regiment in his two gray hands, watching it as a surgeon watches sickness, listening to its faintest curse and the wire-pulled shadow of anger in faces. It was as if the regiment were a single man to him—Topliff's mind again—a man he would condition by withholding water, by making him sweat in the forced night marches, by shortening rations to empty his belly for the scalpel, by toning his animal instinct to face the shock of the cutting edge. "Under no circumstances will you cross the Rio Grande."

The regiment went cold and silent under the treatment, sullen to a point of meticulous fury in performance. Quick animal fights in the bivouacs, put down quickly with harder fists; and the horses had it, too, in their souls—hoof lashings on the picket ropes, soft and angry screams. And still, like a surgeon, Massarene watched it to the final moment. Then he rolled up his sleeves and strapped on his rubber apron and reached for the scalpel.

He bivouacked that afternoon at three-thirty and grazed wide on the picket pins. He inspected personally—like a pup lieutenant on his first detail to the guard. He fed a hot meal at four-thirty. He made a double ammunition issue, and one short ration and a cantle-roll oat issue, and suddenly, through the command, the thinking was like the cocking of a piece on a frosty night—a leaping question—a cold threat—a resurgence that turned the anger from white to crimson.

When the first darkness came down, Colonel Massarene stood to horse, on passed voice order. No water, except on officer order. No unauthorized eating or feeding. No advance guard. No flank guards. No trumpet calls. Nothing but a long column closely knit, cased in discipline, poised for a javelin cast into the night.

"Mount."

A quick reversal of the day's direction of march, a quick doubling back at a tangent toward the south and east, and at half past eleven that night: "Jasper!"—through the column—"This ain't the Querhada! This is the Rio Grande!" And there it was, with its saffron waters cutting the dust of the march like a double-bitted ax blade, holding it high over the United States while the regiment forded across, in the cold inertia of its movement—forded across and stood sweat-dank under the stars while the Old Man called in his officers.

"Gentlemen," he said, "the direction of march is south by west, magnetic, to Santa Maria. I'm burning out everything in my path— everything Kickapoo, Lipan and Apache, and anything else that the darkness fails to distinguish. I'm going through like a scourge—in column at the gallop, so that the next five hours will be remembered for twenty years to come. If I'm opposed by troops, I'm still going through, for a recrossing at Paredes at six a.m. You will leave your dead, shoot wounded horses and lash your wounded in their saddles. There will be no dismounted action." And then he said the one thing he had to say while his hatred of the necessity twisted across his gray face and left its bitter taste upon his lips: "Gentlemen, I am operating under orders. You are operating under my orders. You need, therefore, have no thought for the consequences of tonight's work. That will be thrashed out thousands of miles away by men who wear clean clothing and sit in comfortable offices." And then he did it, as coldly as the drawing of a saber: "Mr. Cohill, screen me to the southward at a thousand yards' distance and cut me a pathway. Mr. Cohill, take C Company."

There it is. No easy first commitment, no racing fight in daylight across your own terrain with reserves behind you and surgeons to stop your bone-broken screaming. No, you'll watch that from the sidewalk. But this is different. If your mount goes down on this, you're done to get back, unless you catch a free mount. You're out ahead, in this fight, for first contact in darkness, for ambush and barricades and a burst of tearing fire from shadows. If you're hit, you're done, unless a bunkie ties you on. If you break, Cohill will shoot you like a dog. And if you are a hero, no one will see it in the darkness for a cheap reward. "Mr. Cohill, screen me to the southward at a thousand yards' distance and cut me a pathway. Mr. Cohill, take C Company." But the words Topliff seemed to hear were not those words; they were the other ones: "or leave your bones to bleach under the prairie moon."

Strangely, as C Company moved out under Flint Cohill's low word of command, there were not hoofs and creaking leather in it, not shirt sweat and horse dung, but the faint rustle of silken skirts and jasmine on the night air, and the quiet sobbing of a woman, echoing down the lost years.

Topliff saw young Massarene's face as he passed by in the darkness, for there was starlight in the river wash—saw it briefly. Handsome as sin, but a man's face, and a man's body moving in easy oneness with his mount. Only between that and the colonel's face there was a subtlety of difference that was more than years—linen cuffs instead of wool. The turned-up collar of the duelist instead of gray eyes along open sights. Laughter warming the cold word, for humanity. The stamina of insouciance to face a mistake with a fillip and work it down the hard way to a rightful place once more, on the wings of ancient blood.

Harder that way by far, than the ruthless runway of a lifetime of discipline. *Don't try too hard, boy*, Topliff's mind whispered. And the knowledge was on Topliff that there are ways of life for all of us and no man dare criticize another for the pathway that fits his feet, for it is a lonely journey always, and God speaks many tongues.

"Lead out!"

Well, it is in the books—impersonally, with the date and the fact—but it is left there suspended in midair, for two laws crossed each other and diplomacy is manner, not morality. But see the reprisal raid for a red beast in the night, clawing on a forty-seven-mile arc of the world like the devil in white-hot armor. See the spoor of dead in its pathway, hacked open and gaping, and the crimson flowers of flame that burst against the darkness and guttered in the echo of ruthless hoofs.

The breathing in men's throats was drawn wire, tearing at membranes, and there were fear and murder and hope in their minds until they were as raw as clawed flesh.

But one mind wasn't. "Topliff, get after Pennell to close up! Close up!" One mind frozen to the machine, one mind holding it to the job. Even if it vibrated from its bed, it wouldn't cast loose. Lash it. Hold it true. Grab it and keep it functioning even if it tears the fingers from your hands. "Tell Pennell, Tell him I'll shoot him, damn him, if he separates. Keep the column closed up—closed up!"

Seven villages they burned out—Lipan, Kickapoo and Apache—hitting them out of the night on the exact positions the colonel's authenticated information had placed them. Coming down like an avalanche from the darkness, leaving nothing behind but the wail of savage women, halting each time to reform briefly and take up the inexorable march at the walk, and then presently at the trot, and then again, "Right front into line! Gallop! Yo!" all the way to Escobedo, and there in the last darkness and the cold river mists—with the end of it in sight—the word had gone on ahead on the wings of the flames behind or on instinct, and C Company hit the barricade and the running fire that defended it. Horses were down, shrieking in agony, and the command bunched in on itself in the roadway and a ricochet sent the chapel bell tolling briefly overhead. Flames burst high and made the whole thing clear for just a second—not actually to see at the time, but to remember long afterward.

Red knife cuts laced across the night and 'dobe dust spat from the lashed walls. The regiment crushed in on C Company, debouching right and left around the chapel to keep its momentum, dividing—"Go through, Cohill! Damn you, go through!" And Cohill, with his face covered with blood in the flames and white-streaked in dust, a centaur on his bunched horse, leaped over and screamed to C to follow him.

Someone was thrashing in the roadway, his horse down, flaying at him with pain-crazed hoofs—thrashing and screaming, "Mother! Mother!" as they will.

Topliff was knee to knee with the colonel when the other rider cut in front of them, bent low at the gallop and grabbed the man's thrown-up arm, wrenching him to his dragging feet, pulling him to his pommel, just as his own horse pitched forward, throwing both of them to the chapel steps, head over. With one hand young Massarene still held the man he had rescued. With the other he began to fire steadily into the firing, like a man on the pistol range, squeezing off evenly, his handsome lips drawn back in the firelight.

Colonel Massarene threw up his own mount, turned him on his heels and raced back into the murderous firing to a free horse—raced back to the chapel steps.

"Mount, Donald, you fool!" and his son threw on, dragging his bunkie up again.

"Thank you, sir"—as cold as a word passed at whist, not studied, not controlled, but the voice of the man himself—of a competent journeyman, working well at his trade.

Then it was, as the three of them galloped knee to knee, that Topliff heard the bullet strike the Old Man like a rock hurled into mud. Then it was also that he saw young Massarene's shoulder and upper arm torn clean open to the white bones, for the mesquite bushes stood outlined now against the racing dawn.

The colonel was down close to his mount's neck, sweat-drenched and worn thin and broken with pain, but he kept at the gallop until he reached the head of the column and halted it to reform. Then he said, "Mr. Topliff, I can't dismount. Rope me in the saddle."

Topliff tied one of his feet and young Massarene passed the halter under his horse and tied the other foot.

"You're hurt," the colonel said to the boy, and suddenly Topliff knew that the lost years no longer stood between those two like grinning beggars with their hungry hands held out for alms. The essence of affinity was there, as it had always been. The handsome face beside the gray one—that was like a finer metal stamped from the same coin press.

"That doesn't matter, does it, sir?"

And in the broad light of day there was the feeling of soft white hands on D'Arcy Topliff—hands touching him gratefully for his understanding, because what D'Arcy heard was: *I'm sorry, but all my life I knew I would have to show you someday that she wasn't as wrong as you cared to believe her; that I'd have to come out here and prove it to you in the only way you could ever understand, father.*

And the reason Topliff heard those words was that young Massarene grinned when he said, "That doesn't matter, does it, sir?"

The regiment recrossed the Rio Grande at Paredes at six a.m. Colonel Massarene was the last man over, riding between his son and Lieutenant Topliff, lashed still in his saddle.

"Mr. Topliff, pass the word to Major Allshard to take over command. Donald, turn in to the regimental surgeon for that arm, and rejoin your company. When the surgeon is finished with the wounded, send him along. I'll wait here for the escort wagons. Untie me and let me down."

Topliff untied the halter and slid the colonel out of his saddle. Young Massarene, half-circling his mount on the forehand, saluted with his bridle hand, for the other arm was useless, and bowed slightly into the salute. There was infinite grace in the gesture and a gentleness of finer living.

The colonel, one hand pressed tightly into his torn side, returned the courtesy, and whatever stain lay between those two was washed clean. The years they had lost were forgotten and the debt was paid in full.

LAW OF THE LASH

PRENTISS COMBS

Padraic Conmaire was a man with his feet on a road. And a man must follow a road chosen to its end. Boggy or dry, rocky or smooth, level or steep, nor can a man turn from it. He may change his name, his clothes and the place he lives, but the road has a chancy and frightening way to it of appearing beneath a man's feet, no matter what path or highway he walks.

Padraic Conmaire was out of Ballyshannon. A sweet, blond lance of a man, his hair a deep gold and his eyes sea-washed green. He sprang from kings and his smooth face was given the strengthening arch of a high nose, thin and sensitive as a prophet's. He was a maker of songs, and all his songs were of Deirdre, pale and golden, loved and loving, named well for an ancient princess. She was the light of Ballyshannon and all the world to Padraic Conmaire and the lodestone that drew him ever back from the reaches of the land, and he coursing and questing, seeking a kingdom for himself and his queen.

But the face of Ireland lay under the great gray cloak of the bad times and many there were with the deep daft that settles on a man, and he with small ones starving slow before his eyes, and his woman thrusting an empty breast to a small sick face. Every eye in Erin wept, and finally, in all the land, there was no place left to look.

So Padraic whispered a great tale into the lovely ear of Deirdre, "It's to America, then. Three months there and your two fair hands overflowing with the gold I'll send. A short year, no more, and it'll be Squire Padraic Conmaire, plug hat and fine clothes, riding his acres

25

on a blooded horse, and his beautiful wife, Deirdre, clad in jewels, velvet gowns and the mantle of her own man's true love."

It was a thundering tale. Deirdre believed, and worse, so did he. America was not like the tales told. It was a kick here and a curse there and the rough side of every man's tongue for the Irish. Padraic Conmaire was only one of the many who had left the sad land. The weak stayed in cities. But the proud and the driven went west to lay the shining tracks across the mountains and plains. It was the railroad. Hard and tearing work for small pay, but a man had to make a start. The black fit fell on many, and many died, but there were always more.

Now Padraic was a proud man. Could a proud one write to tell his queen that gold didn't lie in the streets? Could he say it would be a year before he had one cent to call his own? He could not. He could no more than clutch his emptiness to himself and work.

On payday there was wild drinking at the way station, and Padraic wet his throat, no more. But there was a huge hulk of a Sligo man with the forward curve to his neck and shoulders like a fighting bull. He fleered his pig eyes at Padraic and gave him the bad word.

"I'll take a fall out of you," he said, "and you not running."

Padraic laughed. It was a fine day, with Deirdre's money in his pocket.

"Ah, you killer," he smiled, "and most of your dead home drinking their victory while you pick yourself up."

"So, that's the way it is," the Sligo man said, stripping his shirt.

"Now, let's see the way of it," Padraic answered reasonably, and off with his own shirt. He stripped clean, with bosses of muscle defining lean and ropy under his golden skin.

The Sligo man was big and quick, and Padraic's back marked the sod more than once. But he rose quickly, smiling palely, and he was skilled. In the end, Padraic fetched him a terrible clout and then closed his eyes in quick fear to see the big man's skull slap one of the rails.

So Deirdre's money went to pay the Sligo man's hospital bills, back at the city. The small bit left, Padraic spent in dark drinking.

Just before the next quarter and payday, a work train came. The last to get off was Michael Noolan, of Ballyshannon. A sad man, ever sour-rinded and thin, his tongue bitter with the acid of his sadness. He was stake thin and his eyes were deep pools of something bad.

"Michael Noolan," Padraic shouted to him in his ringing voice, "you've brought me word?"

"Aye, Padraic Conmaire, I've a word." He said it thinly, his eyes fixed on Padraic.

26

And as Padraic came near, Noolan's blue eyes filled and spilled, and the sound came from him, torn and thin, like the cries of the crones at the wakes, and he said the word, and with the word put the curse on Padraic Conmaire as surely as if he'd been an old warlock.

"Deirdre!" came the word and all the meaning in it.

"Ah, my heart, not dead?" cried Padraic.

"Killed," said Michael Noolan, flatly and remotely, patting the curse. And Padraic had never before dreamed that little Michael Noolan had loved Gold Deirdre. When he went on, Padraic knew that Michael had held her as she died and that Michael was having a triumph.

"Who?" asked Padraic, the madness rising in him.

"The slayers were three, Padraic. Sorrow was one, hunger was the other, and the last was proud Padraic Conmaire. Never a penny, proud Paddy. Never a scratch from a pen and never a penny."

Padraic's face froze to stone. Seeing it, Michael Noolan turned with a sour smile and spat upon the ground. He'd waited long for the day.

Padraic wheeled and started to walk. He walked to rail's end and on to the last of the ties, turning then on his empty road, across the vastness of the plain. By dusk he was no more than a small moving thing almost over the rim of the burning land. He walked on into the night at the same steady pace. By sundown of the next day he was down clawing at the dirt, with his tongue too big for his mouth.

Next, there was the sweetness of water in his mouth, a hand gentle beneath his head and a voice crooning in a strange tongue. Padraic looked up into a face with great sad black eyes and a huge scar running over a ruined nose. He was dark as a Spanish tinker. In a half circle about him were eight or ten horsemen dressed crazily in big hats and much silver. Heading them on a great black stud was a man with the mark of power and evil stamped on him as with a hot iron. Padraic felt a stirring in him and knew this man had a finger in his life, that his name was in the mouths of men, and no word of it good. He was a giant, his length of leg stretching below the black stud's barrel. In his black eyes danced a wild, flickering light. His face was wide, and the bosses and planes were deeply pitted with pox. He snorted as he smiled down at Padraic, as if his strength were too great to be borne still, as a nervous horse must fret and snort.

"Get up and walk, gringo," he said, his voice thick with accent.

Padraic slowly shook his head.

"I'll make you, then."

It was a fine whip. It lay dark and oiled and gleaming in wicked coils over the pommel of the strange saddle. He lifted it off, stroking

27

it through his big hands. He moved the horse back one pace by some trick of his knee, and the whip became a thing alive in his hand, making a big streaking S through the air. The lash licked Padraic's left ankle and then the right. The big man's teeth were yellow and long as he laughed. Padraic, proud Padraic, obeyed the lash, taking four, six, eight steps before he fell. The next blow of the lash came down like a hammer across his face, pounding the lifting arch of his nose and crumpling the ridge. He didn't stir.

He woke dimly with the thrust of a horse's hind leg against his face. He was face down across a horse in motion. A gentle hand patted his back and the same voice crooned. Daylight sometimes, and at others dark. Water forced in his mouth, and him muttering and weeping with his fever.

He awakened in bed. There was a buzzing quiet outside. There was a clay jar of water beside his bed, and he drained it. He slept some more, and when he awakened he was hungry with a healthy hunger.

He walked unsteadily out onto a long, cool corridor. There was a great green square where water ran from a fountain and where there were cool trees, and somewhere the gentle clang of a bell.

Behind him a deep, kind voice spoke, and he turned to see a priest.

"Greetings, Lazarus," the priest said in English. "You have risen, then, from the grave."

He was a tall, thick man, his stomach pushing out his cassock, his brown eyes crinkling in kindness and his thatch of white hair springing wild from his head.

"Is it good to be alive?" the priest asked with a smile.

And Padraic drew a breath and found it was.

"Where am I, and who brought me?" Padraic asked.

"You are in La Mision San Gabriel. Little Eusebio wrought the miracle."

"A small dark man with a scar, he would be."

"Yes. The scar is El Satiro's work. Some call him El Fuete. He's well called. He's Satan himself with whip or women. Eusebio risked his life to bring you in. El Satiro left you to die."

"Is there no law here, then?" Padraic asked.

"This is Mexico, my friend. Here, El Satiro is the law."

The priest looked at Padraic and probed with his kind eyes and asked a question, "Are you hunted?"

Padraic shook his head slowly. "Can a man find himself?" he asked.

And the priest answered the strange question sadly, guessing its meaning, " 'Follow me; and let the dead bury their dead.' "

So Padraic Conmaire took up his life at the mission. His strength came back quickly, but his nose was ruined, and his eyes had changed from the laughing, glimmering eyes of a man of dreams. Now they lay ageless and beyond caring. No formal vows made, no oaths taken, but the fine fire in him had died. The fight with the Sligo man had killed Deirdre as surely as if he had stabbed her. Deep within him was the knowledge that he could never again strike a man in anger.

The months passed easily as they worked and slept, speaking seldom. If El Satiro came to the mission village to drink wine in the night, Padraic left his cell-like room to sleep the night under the stars on the plain. He would fight no man. There went with him, trembling and troubled, little Eusebio, who had held Padraic's life in his hand. Lying there, Padraic looked at the stars and remembered he had never thanked Eusebio.

The mission life moved at an easy rhythm. Mexicans and Indians with light work, long sleeps in the heat of the afternoon, guitars at night stirring old embers and singing. The father was one of those with the understanding heart. He would lay his hand on Padraic's shoulder at these times. Bit by bit, fragment by fragment, he had the story from Padraic. He was a patient man, and he started obliquely and cannily to make Padraic into what he felt him to be.

"Lazaro," he said, calling Padraic the name the village put to him, "I will ask you a favor. Down in the bend of the river there is a bit of land. It is fallow and waste. Would you and Eusebio build a small house there and plant the land to corn and beans?"

Padraic looked at him with his flat eyes and nodded. "All things are the same to me, Father."

The preparing of the soil, the planting of the seed, the wonder as it swells to bursting, the deep singing in a man as he reaps. It can cure many things. There's a demanding thing about becoming a part of the great cycle of the land.

To build a house is a warm thing too. Especially a house made of adobe—mud bricks with straw to bind. Each brick receives the pat of a man's hand. Padraic made the bricks, patting them and molding them, and they dried in the sun. He laid the courses, one atop the other, and as the wall grew, something lifted inside him. The house finished, he and Eusebio made their furniture from willows and rawhide. In the gently lowering dusk the two sat there, smoking and watching the slow rhythm of the life around them—the winking fires, the children playing, the pat-pat-pat of the tortilla makers. It was a balm to Padraic.

The father came in the evenings to smoke a pipe with them, talking slow about small things.

It was not unusual for girls to pass. Mothers sent daughters past the house of Lazaro. He was handsome, for all his scarred face, and a worker. But Padraic did not look, ever.

But one evening a girl passed, and she was a slow-moving poem. She walked with an olla of water balanced on her head. Her bare feet taking that small, smooth step necessary for carrying burdens on the head, straight as a saguaro, breast ajut and her face as still and lovely as the morning.

The father sighed windily. "*Ai, Dios*, there, driven from house to house, beaten and despised. Nobody cares but me. El Satiro put his hands to her on his last visit, and next time he will take her. Take her for a few weeks and then toss her as a scrap to one of his savages. And what can I do?"

He shook his head and fetched that sigh again, and Padraic's fine head raised a trifle on his neck. Deep within, a hackle raised.

The next evening she passed again, and the next; and the father, wrenching his sighs from inside him, shook his head and moaned for her, and her so alone.

Padraic raised his head full, followed the honey-sweet figure of her down the path and asked quietly, "How is she called?"

"Maria de la Luz. Mary of the Light," the priest said quickly. "Her mother was blessed on her christening day, for no other name would suit her. She's the sun to her own day. To think of her in the paws of that beast." He brought out another gusty sigh, filled his cheeks and stole a quick glance at Padraic.

"If some man would wed her, the whole thing would be taken care of. Certainly even El Satiro would feel respect for marriage vows. Ah, the poor, poor small thing."

He grasped Padraic by the arm quickly.

"A Christian favor for charity, Lazaro. Take her into your house. Let the vows be but a farce if need be. But help me keep her from him."

And Padraic shrank. "Father," he said thickly, "and me no more than half a man."

"It's only for charity, man."

And Padraic, not understanding the strange yearnings in him, agreed. It was a wedding with no feasting. As they left the church to walk to Padraic's small house Maria de la Luz fell in behind him, as was meet with women.

Padraic stopped, took her gently by the arm and made her walk beside him. Her smile was shy and gentle and a thing of deep joy.

That was how Padraic Conmaire followed a strange road winding, and took Maria de la Luz into his house. She had a man to protect her, and Padraic had a gentle woman to cook his meals. But there were small things to do for her and to be grateful for, and so it was that he did not spend the day thinking of himself only.

One evening the father went to that house and found something there to make him smile a slow, deep smile. He had not dreamt it would happen so soon. For there was a rhythm and a joy in that small house like deep music. It was not until he saw Padraic lay his hand gently on her shining head that he was really sure. Here was a house with love. Somewhere in the dark softness of a night they had found themselves. The poor, poor things had found the wondrous gift of love. There was a quiet shining about them that was a wonder to see. They were one, and yet the father did not feel unwanted.

Padraic had sworn no vows, had taken no great oaths, but still his deep feelings against violence started to spin a slow winding web, and his feelings were as oaths.

An Indian came into his cornfield and stole corn, and Padraic said no small word. Lazy Emeterio let his cows come in to trample the squash vines and beans, and Padraic said nothing. Antonio borrowed his horse once, and then again and again, taking the animal from the corral and abusing it as if it were his own, and Padraic cast his eyes down and held his peace. A small shadow began to grow in the back of the gentle eyes of Maria de la Luz.

El Satiro came thundering into the village one evening, drink-taken and spirits raging. Little Eusebio was caught in the plaza and the little man was chased from corner to corner, crying as El Satiro howled with laughter and chewed pieces out of him with his whip.

Padraic and Maria de la Luz stood in the shadows.

"Your friend needs help," she said softly.

Padraic's body set up a trembling, and he turned his back, covering his eyes.

El Satiro caught sight of him there, and he kicked his stud over the low wall and laughed down at them.

"Come closer, gringo. Are you growing brave? Why are not you in a hole?"

He laughed, the high, fleeing, half-mad laugh, and flicked out the lash.

"Run, gringo. Find a hole. Run! Run!"

Padraic stood rock still, his hand covering his face, and let the lash bite him. Maria de la Luz stood and watched while the whole village saw her man humiliated.

"A little wedding present from El Satiro." He laughed, coiling the lash. "If I want you, little pigeon, I take you," he said to Maria de la Luz, showing the red point of his tongue.

31

"And you, whom they call Lazaro, another christening." He spat down upon Padraic's bowed head. "Your new name is Gringo Mouse."

Now the whole village knew that the bandit was a madman and a cruel killing beast. But still, they said, a friend is a friend, and pride——

"It would be better to die," some said boldly. It is easy to say such things. But now they no longer called Padraic the affectionate Lazaro, he who had risen from the dead. Some turned their heads and spat as he passed. Small boys, with their great capacity for cruelty, galloped by him, cracking imaginary whips, and the bolder ones shouted the name El Satiro had put to him.

So Padraic's fine little house became like a coffin to him. Little Eusebio came to him, drawn by the ties between them, and Maria de la Luz ran from the house, refusing to hear Eusebio beg forgiveness for her husband's cowardice, her shame making her heart a stone. When she went to market, she hurried, with head cast down. Her life had been so good, and now it was a rock in her breast and ashes in her mouth.

The days passed, and they were sad. Padraic kept to his house and his fields, and sometimes he looked·up at the sky and trembled. His eyes sank in upon themselves and a line was drawn from the bitter curve of his nostril to his mouth.

It was a time of waiting. And the waiting was over one day. El Satiro jumped the plaza wall on his big, foaming, black stud and made it rear in the plaza, roaring for the priest.

"*Olé*, man in skirts!" he bellowed. "Roast a fatted calf and bring wine! You are going to have a wedding! El Satiro will take a wife!"

The priest looked up at him, pale. "Who?"

"The little pigeon of the Gringo Mouse," he laughed.

"She's wed," the priest answered, smiling grimly.

"A widow within the hour," El Satiro promised, patting his gun.

The father sent a small boy pelting to the small house by the river to tell Padraic the words of El Satiro. The small boy, spent and gasping with excitement, saw the two turn toward each other.

"Will I go, then, my man?" Maria de la Luz asked calmly.

And Padraic bent his head and looked at the floor and around him at what had been the peace of his life.

"We will go talk to him," he said finally.

Maria de la Luz bent her own small head and went to pack.

"What are you about, my heart?"

"Taking from this house the things with which I came."

"I said I would talk to him."

"If that is what you will do, then I will need these things."

And Padraic again bowed his fine head, and they went out together, through the rows of their planted fields where they had worked together, and into the mission, and finally they stood in the plaza before El Satiro.

He saw them and laughed and licked his lips with his red tongue. He tossed out the lash so it curled about the small waist of Maria de la Luz. He drew her to him, awkward in the clutch of the lash, up against his leg.

His mad black eyes looked down at her, and his tongue again went out over his lips as he said, laughing, "A man, eh? You will like to be with a man for a while."

She took the lash from her waist and turned proudly to look at Padraic Conmaire and asked one question. "Shall I bring your son back to you, husband?"

Padraic heard her. His smile at her was a thing of great gentleness. He lifted his pale face and answered, speaking remotely, almost to himself, "You will not go, my heart. You gone, and I'm a dead man. What are fears and feelings to a dead man?"

He filled his chest with a deep breath, looking up at the big, dark man on the stallion, and there was the same flickering light behind his eyes that was in El Satiro's. He was smiling palely under his broken nose.

"You've been long in dying. Let us let blood, then. Two killers. My oaths broken and fears gone, and you a dead man." His voice was a kind of singing.

The madman on the stud cut the lash through the air, seeing Padraic changed before him, and he said, "A killer? A mouse. I christened you. I will spank you."

Padraic nodded his head, still smiling. He moved closer to the bulk of the horse.

"Ay, dead man. Me beaten and you dead on the ground with my hands frozen at your throat." Deep inside him was the singing of a man released from all things, and the old sickness wiped from him and the whetting sound of a keen blade sharpened.

He trembled with the power of it, and the dark man, seeing it, spoke again. "Only a small beating now. Don't tremble."

The lash went whirling out, cutting a piece from Padraic's ear, and that man reached one hand up in a kind of wonder and saw the blood on his hand. The singing in him went to a high, rending scream of wildness, and when the lash came next time, he caught it in an iron hand. One quick flash, like catching a fly. The lash in his grip, the sudden rending twist, and the bulk of the man out of the saddle.

El Satiro's hand was at his belt as he fell, rolling, and a small twisting figure ran out from the crowd, and little Eusebio, his ruined face smiling eagerly, picked his spot carefully, kicked the wrist and knocked the gun flying. He picked it up, squatted, panting a little on the fringe of the crowd, and let the barrel waver over the bellies of El Satiro's men. With the fingers of his free hand he felt the seams of the scar on his nose.

So they faced each other. Two men, half mad. One mad with ancient berserkers keening and wailing inside him, giving him the strength of ten men and they all mad. "Blood," the ancient voices wailed, and Padraic moved in, face frozen into a terrible smile, to still their singing. The dark one, evil from his spawning, never beaten, eager to rend and to break to still the wild singing of his own blood lust.

They came together with a shock, and the dark giant felt the smaller man hold firm, and as they gripped each other, trying first this and then that, the black man laughed softly, for this man was strong and the pleasure would be deep.

As they walked around, thighs ridged, loins locked with effort, Padraic smiled coldly, his face frozen and his voice brazen, speaking things softly from the cold bronze trumpet gripped deep in his throat. He spoke the things that men tell men whom they will kill. He held the dark man in his hand and he knew it with a terrible strength of certainty.

Some of the people moaned as they watched the struggle. Some yelled hoarsely as they became animals caught in its ancient grip, and some turned their heads away.

They fought as animals—kicking, kneeing, butting, biting and hitting. There was blood on the ground, and when they grew weak from fighting, they fought on their knees, and when they could no longer stand on their knees in the blood and sweat, they crouched like two snapping, snarling dogs, their teeth naked, their eyes dripping.

Finally the big black man slowly felt fear rise in him. He came to know that no matter what he might do, the little man would still be there, and he remembered the words before the fight began, of how Padraic's fingers would be at his throat and he dead. He knew, suddenly and in a panic, that if he reached with clawed hands and plucked the heart from Padraic's body and held it pulsing in his hand, Padraic would not know it at all, but would go on rending and hacking.

Pacraic caught the man's huge arm in a cruel lock and bent it, arching the bow of his back into the effort. As the giant's arm snapped loud in the silence of pent breaths, the Satyr screamed and rolled free. Padraic crawled toward him with his fingers locked into steel hooks and his glazed eyes fixed on the man's pulsing, swollen throat, and there was nothing but the dread certainty that he would strangle, and who was the man with the courage to tell him no or to put out a hand to stop him?

He reached him, the big man's eyes wide open and the mouth agape to scream, and Padraic raised his red hands and stopped the scream as it started. The hands sank into the throat, and Maria de la Luz came from the crowd and sank beside him. She pressed her lips close to his ear and whispered and crooned, and one small hand tugged at his wrist.

"Come back to me, heart of my heart and love of my love, and don't kill the swine. As I love you, I beg you. His corpse will be a thing between us, and I yearn to bear your son so he will be all there is between us."

Padraic's frozen face wavered, his breaths came in great torn gasps, and he turned to look at her without loosening his terrible grip. Maria de la Luz looked full at him, and all her love and gentleness shone there in her eyes. As El Satiro's eyes bulged and his face became black, Padraic Conmaire knew his wife from the depths of his madness and his grip relaxed.

He rose to his feet, straightened, looked around at his new world, and then fell with a terrible weariness, and she had his head in her arms and his ruined face against her breast and her crooning in his ears before he hit the ground. She stayed there, her lovely face reflecting the agony of the terrible game she had played and won, and there was a peace, too, on Padraic's face.

They were beautiful to see. It was the end of a road for Padraic Conmaire, and he had ended his coursing and questing for he had found his kingdom.

TRAIL TRAP

MERLE CONSTINER

When his father was shot, Shelby was standing by his side. There was nothing he could do about it when it happened, it happened so swiftly, and there was nothing he could do about it afterward, either, with that big six-pistol waving in the lamplight, just begging for more blood. It happened at the counter of Chapman's Store, and the people present were Shelby and his father, Mr. Fales, old Mr. Chapman and the mad-dog stranger. Chapman's Store was a lonely but famous station on the great trail. Shelby's Texas home was three hundred miles to the south; the Kansas railroad yet four hundred miles to the north. With the herd bed-grounded for the night nearby, his father had ridden over for tobacco. Mr. Fales had come along for the sociability.

This was Shelby's first drive. He was seventeen, soft-voiced, and suspicious of everything that didn't have four legs and a tail. He was already a top-notch stockman, but he was being further educated. He was intensely suspicious of the stranger the minute he entered, but it wasn't his place to show it.

The stranger was a squat man, odorous and foul, with a cameo breastpin on his hatband as an ornament. He nodded almost imperceptibly, drew off horsehide gauntlets and thrust them in his belt. At the counter he bought crackers and a can of peaches and ate wolfishly.

When he had finished, he turned to Shelby's father and said, "Why, it's Sheriff Back-shootin' Phillips, from Milk River, Montana. Where's that big posse o' your'n now?"

36

"I've never been in Montana in my life," said Shelby's father quietly. "My name is Stearns Davis. I'm driving cattle up out of Texas."

"Then maybe you can prove it," said the squat man.

"I can, but I won't," said Shelby's father, husky with anger.

The squat man drew and shot. Shelby had never seen such effortless speed. His father crumpled.

"It's only his leg; I didn't kill him," said the gunman. "Though I should have. He's no good. Look at him. He's too sneaky even to wear his badge."

When Shelby tensed, the gunman said savagely, "Hold it, bird-shot. You're outclassed." Then he was gone.

From the night outside, they could hear his horse in a frenzied gallop.

They took Shelby's father back into a storeroom and laid him on a cot. The storekeeper dressed the wound. He was an old friend, and his fingers were deft and gentle. "Well, Stearns," he said at last. "You're going to be bedfast for about two weeks."

"We're moving three thousand cows," said Shelby's father. "Up in Kansas they might come to upward of sixty thousand dollars. And I'm the trail boss."

"You was the trail boss," said the storekeeper. "Now you're just a sorry ole checker player."

"Charley," said Shelby's father. Mr. Fales stepped forward.

He was a small man, middle-aged, stern and decisive. Shelby's ranch was the big owner in the drive, owning about a third of the herd. Mr. Fales's cows were few, but magnificent. The great bulk of the herd was owned by a hodgepodge of neighbors and kin, small ranchers. Mr. Fales, a neighbor, was the only other owner along on the drive.

"Ride back to camp and get Picketwire and Yaqui," said Shelby's father, closing his eyes. These were the most reliable and mature men among the crew. Mr. Fales nodded and left.

"Well, son," said the storekeeper affectionately. "Looks like you're suddenly a trail boss. Can you handle it?"

"Yes, sir," said Shelby softly. "I can handle it."

An hour later Mr. Fales returned with Yaqui and Picketwire. Smoldering and silent, they gathered about the cot.

Shelby's father, his face drawn with pain, took from his blouse a wallet knotted with beeswaxed string. This wallet, Shelby knew, contained the miscellany of papers which legalized the drive: bills of sale, powers of attorney, assignments of interest.

He handed the wallet to Mr. Fales. "Boys," he said, "Charley

Fales is your new boss. I'd like to give you Shelby, but I daren't.
Shelby's a good man, and we all know it, but he just isn't trail-
seasoned. Too many folks at home, poor folks, are depending on us.
The worst is yet to come, and those cows got to be delivered."

"They'll be delivered," said Mr. Fales grimly.

"One thing more, Charley," said Shelby's father. "You've been
drawing hand's wage, thirty dollars. Now you draw boss wages, one
hundred dollars."

"Not me," rasped Mr. Fales. "I ain't no money grabber. But thank
you kindly."

As they left the room, Shelby said, "Good-bye, dad."

His father smiled. "Just do what Mr. Fales says, and everything
will be all right."

The herd crept northward. The crew flinched a little beneath their
new boss, but accepted him. He was a hard driver, hard on others,
hard on himself. In the choking dust of the prairie he seemed a man
alone, dedicated, tireless, obsessed. One day, riding with Picketwire,
Shelby said, "He'll get the herd through all right, and in good shape."

"But will he get me through, and in good shape?" said Picketwire.
"I ain't worth twenty dollars at the chutes, and I bet he knows it."

Working, always mercilessly working, they crossed the Red,
passed through Comanche country, through the shadowy menace of
white renegades. The parched miles unrolled behind them; Mr. Fales
grew harsher, more decisive, more efficient. Then it came, the first
sign of disaster.

At sunset one evening a man in a buckboard drove into camp. He
was withered and garbed in the clothes of a small rancher headed for
town. He was bound for the Santa Fe Railway just as they were, it
turned out, and he was excited and happy. He was going to the
railroad to buy a starter herd.

"My wife's brother has an office job in the stockyards in Chi-
cago," he said. "There's a panic setting in, he writes, and it's going to
be worse than the panic of 'Seventy-three. The cattle market is
already beginning to collapse, and she's due to really bust come any
day. Nothing can stop her. Cows will be piling up at the steel, and
nobody wanting them. A fellow can pick up a top-grade starter herd
for the price of their hides. I'm sorry for folks like you all, naturally,
but these things happen."

Mr. Fales looked faintly amused.

When their visitor had departed, Yaqui said, "Whoof!"

"The things a man will believe," said Mr. Fales scornfully.

Then, three days later, they ran into the speculator.

The herd was still two rough weeks south of the railroad. Just ahead, about twenty miles, was the first real town, a notorious hellhole named Tuckerville. Shelby was working swing, and Mr. Fales was with him, when the speculator rode out of a cedar brake and joined them. He danced his horse to a stop, introduced himself as Mr. Rhodes and stated his business.

He was gaunt, travel-worn and heavily armed. It would be his custom to go heavily armed, Shelby knew, because at times he would carry large sums in gold. His money at the moment, though, would probably be in a saloon or bank in Tuckerville. These speculators, Shelby had heard, fanned down from the railroad, sometimes at great distances, and tried to buy trail herds for cash. They gambled on their knowledge of the markets, and were experts in finance. "I'm selling these cows at the railroad," said Mr. Fales arrogantly. "And at the railroad only."

"Then I won't waste your time," said Mr. Rhodes. "I'll just get along to Tuckerville."

"What kind of a price did you have in mind?" said Shelby curiously. "If you don't object to saying?"

"Not at all," said Mr. Rhodes. "The going price at the railroad, the last I heard, was seven dollars a head. But these look to be special fine, and I'm willing to take a chance, so I'll offer ten."

Shelby was stunned. A speculator would cheat you, but he wouldn't lie to you. The railroad's price, seven, came to twenty-one thousand. Mr. Rhodes's came to a little more, thirty thousand. But where had that hoped-for twenty dollars a head—that sixty thousand dollars—gone?

Mr. Fales looked numb and shocked. From a man of stone he crumbled to a man of sand. "We heard there was a panic," he mumbled. "We heard it, but we didn't believe it."

"It's no panic," said Mr. Rhodes. "Money is my business, and if there was a panic, I'd know about it. And I certainly wouldn't be buying. It's just a fluctuation. A bad one, I grant you, but it'll straighten out."

"How soon?" asked Shelby.

"Longer than you can afford to wait, I'm afraid," said Mr. Rhodes. He nodded formally, wheeled his mount and loped away.

"You heard him," said Mr. Fales, moistening his lips. "Who knows the most about the market, him or that suet-headed rancher in the buckboard? It's going to straighten itself out. We'll speed up, and we'll make it. We got nothing to worry about."

This sounded so muddled to Shelby, he didn't bother to answer.

That was what Mr. Fales had said then. Next morning he had something different to say. Red-eyed, looking as if he'd had a sleepless night, he made an announcement. "Shelby and Picketwire are riding into Tuckerville with me. Yaqui, you hold the herd right here for a couple of days."

After a moment of silence Shelby said, "You're selling to Mr. Rhodes."

"I'm doing the best as I see it," said Mr. Fales. "I don't expect no thanks, but I ain't in no condition for no argument either."

Shelby had scarcely been in Tuckerville ten minutes when he met the girl. She looked beautiful to him; of course, she would look beautiful to anybody, but he was so tired and worried he hardly paid her any heed.

The three of them—Mr. Fales, Picketwire and Shelby—reached town about nine that night. Sooty shadows swathed the sheet-iron shanties and false-fronted stores of Main Street, and watery lamplight from grimy windows mottled their wiry mounts. The place looked as mean as its reputation. There was a feeling about it, a feeling of utter lawlessness. Picketwire took the horses to the livery stable, Mr. Fales set out to inquire for Mr. Rhodes, and Shelby looked up a hotel for lodgings.

Midway down the first block, tilted letters on a blank door said, HOTEL. He entered, climbed dark steps and came out in a dim cubbyhole. A girl sat by a desk, doing sums with slate and slate pencil. She was about his age, and there was a cloud of loveliness about her. Clearing his throat, he said, "Is this a hotel lobby?"

She bridled, gave him a hard look, and said, "In my opinion, yes."

"I got a couple of friends coming along later," he said politely. "I'd like to hire three beds."

He noticed her shoes; they were frayed. Patches of tin had been tacked to the floor, to keep out rats. There was a feeling of poverty about the place, of stubbornness and courage and struggle.

"Three rooms will be three dollars," she said, and took a key from a board. He paid her. Clumsily he signed a register.

They went down a narrow hall. A door was open and the room lighted, and as they passed, he glanced in. He saw a little room like a horse stall, an iron bed, a washstand with a pair of gloves on it and a shuck-bottomed chair. She said disapprovingly, "Number Five is down on Main Street somewhere, having supper. He was drunk when he left, but that is no excuse to leave a lamp burning. Burning lamps are dangerous."

"And expensive," said Shelby, trying to be sympathetic.

She bridled again and gave him another hard look.

His room was Number Nine. She entered, lighted a lamp, and he followed her inside. It was exactly like Number Five.

Standing there by her side, idly remembering Number Five, he suddenly went ice cold. In his mind's eye he saw the washstand, and something he had scarcely noticed at the moment—the gloves. They were gauntlets, and their cuffs were ornamented in nailheads in a pattern of interlacing diamonds. They were the gauntlets of the gunman who had shot down his father in Chapman's Store. It was an instant before he could speak.

"Who is the man in Number Five?" he asked.

"I don't know. He's been too ugly and drunk to sign the register."

"Does he wear a cameo pin on his hatband?"

"Yes."

"Could you let me know when he comes in? If it isn't too much trouble? I've got a little private business with him."

Then smoothly, because she was too interested, he changed the subject. He learned that her uncle was the proprietor, but that he was out in the country with a sick kinsman. He learned her name was Cynthia Sperry.

She had been gone for some time, and he was sitting on the edge of his bed, thinking of his wounded father, when Mr. Fales and Picketwire came into the room.

"I found Rhodes, all right," said Mr. Fales. "He was watching faro in a skunky little saloon called The Shamrock. We got our deal set up. He tried to whip me down to twenty-five thousand, but I held him to his thirty. He keeps his money in The Shamrock safe. We meet there tomorrow at ten, in the back room, and pass money and papers."

I didn't hear nothing about any panic," said Picketwire. "The market is a little unsteady, but they say it gits that way sometimes. I asked some keerful questions."

"Of who did you ask 'em?" said Mr. Fales.

"Of fellers I met on the street, loafers and such. Who else?"

"You're doing the wrong thing, Mr. Fales," said Shelby.

"There comes times," said Mr. Fales calmly, "when a man don't have nothing in the world to fall back on but his judgment. If my judgment said run those cows into a gulch and dynamite them, I'd do it. It tells me to sell them for thirty thousand, and quick."

Then, in his velvet voice, Shelby told them about the gauntlets in Room Five. There was a moment of appalled silence.

"What are we going to do about it?" asked Picketwire.

"You're not going to do anything," said Shelby. "I'm going to. I'm going to face him. He can't go around shooting down decent people no-show, like he did in Chapman's Store."

"You saw him in action," said Mr. Fales tonelessly. "But you ain't old enough or been around enough to know what you really saw. They ain't many better."

"That can't be helped," said Shelby.

"Back in Texas," said Mr. Fales, "your nearest neighbor is a old widow named Mrs. Hackett. She sent along twenty-two cows. Last winter the only sugar she had in her house was some molasses she boiled down from pumpkins. You know that?"

"Yes, sir."

"Ordinarily, I'd say if you wanted to get yourself killed, that was your affair. But I won't have no trouble with the law, nor anybody else, until I get those cows sold. What was the last thing your daddy told you?"

"To do as you say."

"Then simmer down."

There was a knock on the door. Shelby opened it. Miss Sperry was standing on the threshold.

"Did you see the man in Room Five?" she asked.

"No," said Shelby. "When?"

"About a half an hour ago. He came in and I told him you wanted to see him. He looked in the register, to get your name straight, then came back here, down the hall. I just noticed his saddlebags and things are gone from his room, though. It looks like he's gone without telling me. Is everything all right?"

"You bet everything's all right," said Picketwire. "That's the best news I've heard for a long time. Thank you, ma'am."

When she had left, Mr. Fales said "By now he's really long gone. But it wasn't you he was afraid of, boy, it was of our whole crew. Maybe our luck is changing. Let's go to bed."

Next morning, after breakfast, Mr. Fales explained his plan. Usually a cattle sale was just a cattle sale, money and papers being exchanged, but now—with the big moment at hand—he was as nervous as a cat. Mr. Rhodes, it seemed, had dropped a word of warning; a casual warning that might mean nothing at all, or might mean last-minute disaster. No matter how hard you tried, Mr. Rhodes had told Mr. Fales, you weren't going to keep the sale quiet. The money was coming out of The Shamrock safe, and the proprietor would have to open the safe himself, and there it was out. He might tell anybody, and Tuckerville was crawling with human wolves just slavering for such information. It was one thing getting the money in your hands, said Mr. Fales to Shelby and Picketwire, and another getting out of town with it. So he had worked out a foolproof plan to baffle any robbers.

It was a pretty good plan at that, Shelby and Picketwire decided.

This was the way they would work it. Mr. Fales, of course, as trail boss, would be the marked man. He would buy a new valise, and enter The Shamrock through the front door. Shelby and Picketwire would be in the alley behind The Shamrock, waiting. In the back room, Mr. Fales would receive the money from Mr. Rhodes; he would put it not in the valise but in a grain bag he would be carrying under his coat. He would take the grain bag to the back door and hand it to Shelby; Shelby and Picketwire would then ride like hell for camp.

In the meantime, Mr. Fales would just sit there in the back room of the saloon and hold Mr. Rhodes in idle conversation. For a half hour, say. Mr. Rhodes seemed perfectly trustworthy, but you couldn't afford to take a chance, and this would keep Mr. Rhodes himself from any mischief. When Mr. Fales left the Shamrock, he would leave by the front door, and from then on anyone who wanted that empty valise could have it.

Up until now, Shelby had thought that ranching itself was just about the roughest punishment that mortal man could take—sleet, plague, rustlers, drought; the business of bringing a calf to good beef. But now this new world, the world of the trail, almost had him reeling—gunmen, speculators, panics, robbers. Now, as they sat in Mr. Fales's room in the hotel, he said as much.

"We've had our troubles," said Mr. Fales, sweating a little, showing signs of strain. "But we'll handle 'em like I used to handle corn when I was a boy back in Illinois. We just shucked one ear at a time."

He got up and left the room, and Picketwire, a little later, followed. Shelby waited about ten minutes, according to the plan, and also left.

Miss Cynthia Sperry was at her desk in the lobby, sorting buttons. The little cubbyhole was windowless and dim, and she worked in a wisp of candlelight. *She spends most of her life here, shut up in this little box,* Shelby thought. *Once, just once, she should see the swales and sage bowls and rich bottomlands of my father's ranch.* As he passed her he smiled gravely, and she smiled as gravely in return.

Impulsively, apropos of nothing, he said, "Do you like calves?"

"We've never kept one," she said. "But I'm attracted to their general appearance."

"Is that so?" he said warmly. "Well, so am I, and always have been. To feed a sick calf, you get it warm and break a raw egg in its mouth. You want to know something? I've wondered and wondered why that wouldn't work on babies?"

"No," she said firmly. "I don't think it would work on babies."

He went down the stairs and out onto Main Street. He was

embarrassed and wondered what had come over him, talking to a perfect stranger about such personal things.

A half block down Main Street he turned into an alley. Behind him, at a rack before a store, were the horses, his sorrel and Picketwire's black, saddled and ready to go. His big nickel watch on its leather thong said one minute to ten. After a dozen yards, he turned once more, left, into a narrow passage, and came out into a weedy courtyard. All about him were the backs of shops and offices, ramshackle and sun-scorched, making a little quadrangle. Picketwire stood just within the passage mouth, and joined him silently as he passed.

On the far side of the court was a drab two-storied building with a rickety outside staircase angling upward across it. Beneath the staircase were two doors, one of raw pine, one spick-and-span with glossy green paint. The pine door, they knew, led into an empty storeroom; the green door was the back door of The Shamrock, and this was their station. They took up their position under the overhang of the staircase and waited. Shelby watched the door, and Picketwire watched the passage mouth.

Ten minutes went by, then ten more. There was nothing but the searing sun, and the swarming flies, and the tinkle of a distant anvil.

Suddenly the door opened, and Mr. Fales appeared, smiling. Under his breath he said, "He's one hard trader. He tried to belt me down, but I held him to his offer. Tell the boys at camp he'll be sending out his own crew tomorrow to take over."

He thrust the bulky grain bag into Shelby's hand. "Now git!" He withdrew, and the door closed.

Almost instantly the pine door swung inward, and a man stood in the opening, with a Colt forty-five in his fist.

He was a withered man, and they recognized him instantly. The man back on the trail, the man in the buckboard. He'd looked excited and foolish then; but he didn't look that way now, he looked vicious and professional.

"I kill when I have to," he said tonelessly. "Now unbuckle them gunbelts and toss them yonder. . . .Right. Now hand me that bag. . . .Right. Now turn around."

They faced about, with their backs to him. They heard the door shut, and a bolt being slammed. Shelby vaulted for his weapon. Picketwire threw himself against the pine panel, but it was like iron.

"By now he's on Main Street, and on his way," said Shelby, panting.

Picketwire said, "I'm gettin' to loathe and despise that man."

That night, about eleven o'clock, Mr. Fales, Shelby and Picketwire sat in Mr. Fales's room at the hotel. It had been a terrible twelve hours. All day Main Street had been a hive of rumors, and all day posses had pushed out from town like wagon spokes, but nothing whatever had been accomplished. Mr. Fales looked like a man in a nightmare.

"First the herd, and now the money," said Picketwire.

"We'll get it back," said Mr. Fales hoarsely. "There's a law against stealing."

They averted their eyes from him.

"I'm bone tired," said Mr. Fales. "I ain't had a good night's sleep in three weeks, though I figger it makes no difference to nobody."

"Not to me, anyways," said Picketwire. "Let's go, Shelby."

"I ain't blaming you boys for handing it over," said Mr. Fales. "But you didn't even put up a little tussle."

"I didn't want to take no advantage of him," said Picketwire. "It wouldn't have been fair, him weighted down that way with such a big pistol."

With Shelby at his elbow, he left the room. As they walked down the dark hall, Shelby said, "Hold up a minute," and knocked softly on a door. This room, he knew, was Miss Sperry's bedroom. There were rustlings from within, a hinge squeaked, and they could feel her presence in the blackness before them. "It's me," said Shelby. "The buckaroo from Texas. We're going out for a while."

"Did you get your money back?" she asked.

"No," said Picketwire. "But it's only stole, so we ain't worrying."

"What I want to ask you is this," said Shelby. "Could he be staying here, right in this very hotel? I mean Mr. Rhodes."

"Mr. Rhodes, the speculator?"

"You know him?"

"I had him pointed out to me on the street today. No, he's not here. They say he's staying at The Shamrock."

"That's a new one on me," said Shelby. "Bedding in a saloon. I don't think I'd care for that."

"Not in the saloon—above it. There's a little upstairs room they sometimes rent. You get to it through the alley."

"I hope we didn't wake you up," said Shelby. "Good night, ma'am."

"You sound mighty soft talking and dangerous," she said. "I don't want you to go out and get yourself hurt. This is a bad town. Take care of him, Picketrope."

"Yes, ma'am," said Picketwire. "By setting him a good example."

They went through the lobby, down the stairs and out onto the boardwalk. The town was deserted and mostly dark. They stood for a moment in the black shadows, letting the night coolness touch their cheeks.

"I just got a idee," said Picketwire. "I won't say I got it before you did, but I will say I got it. It's this. Maybe we was took by a swindle—worked by Mr. Rhodes himself and the feller in the buckboard. The feller hits us back on the trail, baits us with a scare of panic and shoos us right into Mr. Rhodes's arms. Then Mr. Rhodes makes us just the right kind of a smart proposition to convince us. We was never supposed to keep the money. It was to be took from us right after, which was did. Did you have something like that in mind?"

"Yes," said Shelby. "And it's my guess, too, that Mr. Rhodes isn't even a genuine speculator. I'm a slow thinker, and it only came to me about eight minutes ago."

"Then that would explain how the robber got away," said Picketwire. "He just waited inside until we were gone, then come out again and went up them outside stairs to Mr. Rhodes's room. He's been there all day. He's there now!"

"Let's hope so," said Shelby. "If we catch them together, they're finished. And if we're right on the rest, they'll be together, they have to be."

They turned down the alley, down the passage and came into the court. The darkness here was utter; it was like being in a well of ink. "I'll get us inside," Shelby said. "Inside, use your own judgment. It's likely to be rough."

They crossed the court, located the staircase and ascended silently to the landing. Their weapons were in their hands. The keyhole threw a pencil of light on Shelby's cartridge belt; from within came the sound of muffled voices. "Now," said Shelby softly, and knocked.

He knocked loud and excitedly. The wood of the door clamored and rattled beneath his knuckles.

The conversation beyond the door stopped instantly. After a pause, Mr. Rhodes called out, "Who is it?"

"It's me, Henry Lawrence," said Shelby. Henry Lawrence was the stableman at the livery barn. "That bay o' your'n is having a monstrous fit, frothing and foaming and smashing her stall. But we don't want to exterminate her without your say-so."

The door was swung open.

For an instant things moved with lightning rapidity. The man who opened the door held a pistol at the half-ready, but he was unsuspecting and light blinded, and almost before he could blink, Shelby's gun muzzle was in the hollow of his throat, pressing him inward. He dropped his pistol and splayed his fingers in frantic surrender. Picketwire came past them in a rush and slowed to a stop in the middle of the room, his rusty gun barrel level and eager.

Mr. Rhodes sat on a chair by a kitchen table; the holdup man sat on the edge of the bed. Neither was armed; both were stupefied. Now, in the lamplight, Shelby got his first good look at the man he had captured. It was the man with the cameo on his hatband, the gunman who had shot down his father.

For a moment the silence was tomblike. In a corner of the room was the grain bag.

Mr. Rhodes's gaunt face was a mask of terror. When he spoke, however, his voice was reasonably steady. He said, "What do you aim to do?"

"I don't know," said Shelby.

From a pocket of his dusty frock coat Mr. Rhodes took the wallet which belonged to Shelby's father, and handed it to Shelby.

Shelby laid it on the table by the lamp, spread out its papers and checked them. He checked them slowly, meticulously, expressionlessly. "The bill of sale, from Mr. Fales to you," he said.

Mr. Rhodes produced a final paper. "That's all," he said. "Now what are you going to do?"

Shelby seemed in a trance. "I'm thinking about my father," he said at last. "I'm wondering if he has gangrene."

When no one spoke, he said to the gunman with the cameo, "This is going to make me sick to my stummick, you unarmed and all, but I got to shoot you in the leg to even it up."

"No," said the gunman, flinching. "No."

"To Mr. Rhodes, Picketwire said, "Give me fifty cents."

Mr. Rhodes dug into his trousers and complied.

"Now, Shelby," said Picketwire, when he had stowed the coin in his pocket. "After what we been through, that won't even up nothing. We'll shoot 'em all in the leg, or better yet, both legs."

"Boys," said Mr. Rhodes, "Hold steady."

Even the hard-bitten man in the canvas vest showed stark fear.

"We got what we wanted," said Shelby. "I guess we better go."

When they were on Main Street, heading for the hotel, Picketwire said, "Well, we're just back where we started."

"No," said Shelby. "We're considerably ahead. I bet we make our sixty thousand yet."

After a bit he said, "Trouble with you, Picketwire, is that when you spin a tale you really run hog wild. Shooting three men in six legs."

"They believed it, didn't they?"

"They would have believed anything."

"Truth is, I half believed it myself. Why do you think I hit Mr. Rhodes for that fifty cents? Because if it really come to such a waste of ammunition, I was durned if I was going to pay for my own cartridges."

Shelby shot him an uneasy glance. They climbed the stairs and crossed the lobby. As they went down the hall, Shelby said, "We got our cows back, which was the main thing. This is outlaw country, new country, and we're the strangers here, not them. It would have been long, discouraging, and probably impossible to jail them."

"Unless we'd brought along our own jail, which was shorely an oversight," said Picketwire. "But we aged 'em ten years, and that's about what they'd have got from a judge."

Mr. Fales had been asleep. He was in his drawers. He let them in, lighted a lamp and blinked at them, red-eyed.

"We went to Mr. Rhodes's room and got the wallet back," said Shelby, taking it from his blouse. "It was all a swindle. Mr. Rhodes was there, and the man who shot my father, and the man who robbed us. They didn't give us any argument whatever."

For a moment Mr. Fales looked dazed. Then he smiled slowly, smugly. "I been saying everything would come out all right," he said. He reached for the wallet.

"No," said Shelby. "And furthermore, you're fired."

"Fired?" said Mr. Fales. "A hand can't fire his boss."

"I'm the new boss," said Shelby. "Cut your mangy cows out of the rest of the stuff by noon tomorrow, or send somebody to do it." Picketwire gaped.

Mr. Fales said tonelessly, "You think I was in on it?"

"I know you was in on it. I think you was the head of it. Here's the way you worked it. You got my father shot, well knowing he'd make you boss. Then come the man in the buckboard to yell panic, Mr. Rhodes to make you an offer and the imitation robbery. The panic part, by the way, was mighty clever. It was to give you an excuse to sell to Mr. Rhodes. It didn't have to be a sensible excuse, just an excuse. When you got back home you could say, 'I might have made a mistake, but I did my best.' You'd look foolish, but not criminal."

"I'll tell you one thing," said Picketwire. "He shore fooled me with Widow Hackett and her pumpkin molasses, and all that homey talk about how to shuck corn."

Mr. Fales said nothing.

"The man with the cameo," said Shelby. "He saw my name in the hotel register and left. But he wasn't supposed to know my name.

When he shot my father in Chapman's Store, it was supposed to be a mistake."

After a pause, Mr. Fales said, "Anything else give you the idea I was in on it?"

"The grain bag," said Shelby. "The grain bag proved it. It was there in the corner of the room, still tied. If it had had thirty thousand dollars in it—money that was supposed to be counted in your presence—don't you think the money would have been removed? Picketwire and I were robbed of a dummy package."

"I don't think the law will touch me," sneered Mr. Fales.

"If I was in your place, I wouldn't be worrying about the law," said Shelby. "You own a fine little ranch in Texas. You either got to sell it at sacrifice prices, or live among people who will know you have betrayed them. I'd rather be dead, myself."

Next morning, as Shelby and Picketwire came into the lobby with their saddlebags, Miss Sperry was at her desk. Shelby stared at her. He had never seen anything so lovely. He had a nervous sort of feeling that he had dreamed about her all night, but he couldn't quite remember. Her eyes were misty and miserable, and she said, "In a hotel people always go. The bad ones and the nice ones."

"If you're talking about Mr. Fales," said Shelby, "he looked nice, but he was really one of the bad ones."

"They claim you got your money back or something," she said. "But mostly I'm glad you didn't get hurt. You're more important than money."

They touched their hats in farewell and went down the stairs.

Outside, on the boardwalk, Shelby said suddenly, "Me, more important than money. Now what did she mean by that?"

"Being of a contrary opinion, I haven't no idee," said Picketwire.

"Maybe I'd better find out," said Shelby.

He turned and raced back up the steps.

A GUNMAN
CAME TO TOWN

WILL COOK

Grizzly Springs had **really** only
one street; the rest were lanes that led to private residences. All the
stores and shops and the one saloon and hotel fronted Apache
Street, named after the small band of Mimbrenos who had been
camped where the stable now stood.

Every morning just before seven when Fritz Bruner walked the
length of it to open his small shop, the street was totally deserted,
except for Bruner and Crippled Jake, who always swept the saloon
porch just to keep things tidy. A bland sun brightened the adobe
buildings; and no wind stirred, so that if a man walked a dozen steps
down the middle of the street he could stop and turn and see the
small rises of dust left by his passage, slowly settling.

Bruner put the key in the lock and opened the door, and as he did
so he saw Pete Graves, the town marshal, making rapid way from the
telegraph office. It wasn't often that Graves hurried about anything,
and this made Bruner curious. Graves stopped on the saloon porch
and took Crippled Jake by the arm and made him stop sweeping.
Then he waved a telegram and spoke, but Bruner could not hear the
words, so he went on into his shop. As a boy in Germany he had
learned his trade well from an elderly *Meisterschuhmacher*, who
made a splendid shoemaker of him, but failed to make him humble
by caning him nightly. The trouble was, Bruner thought, the passing
years had not taught him either. He could not recall an exact image
of the old master, but he could still summon a resentment at the

50

canings. This bothered him—this remembering so strongly the wrongs done against him, and after thirty years too.

Bruner was not a young man, yet he possessed a wiry strength, an agile mind and a strong sense of independence. He lived with his wife in a small house near the edge of town, and his life was very regimented, with one day very much like any other. He liked it.

Before he set to work Bruner took a box of horehound candy from beneath the counter and filled a glass bowl sitting on top. He was doing this when Pete Graves walked in. Graves was a serious-minded young man who took his job home every night and worried all the time about the things he should have done and the things he should have done differently.

"How many pounds of candy do you think two generations of kids have eaten, Fritz?" He dipped into the bowl, dropped a few pieces into his shirt pocket and put another in his mouth.

"Some never grow up," Bruner said. He studied the young man over the rims of his glasses. "For a man who is getting married Saturday night, you have a glum face."

Young Graves plunked his hands flat on the counter and leaned on his stiffened arms. "Fritz, do you believe lightning can strike the same place twice?"

Bruner puffed his cheeks and made his dense mustache bristle. "When my mother carried me lightning struck our house; a nurse who lived down the road said I'd be marked. But I wasn't. When I was ten lightning struck again, but burned only the barn. *Ja*, I would say that it could."

Pete Graves blew out his breath and shifted from one foot to the other. He took the candy from his pocket and put it in his mouth and stood there, crunching it as though he needed something to do. Fritz Bruner smiled and put a handful in the marshal's pocket. Then he wiped his sleeve across the star. "Pete, you should keep that shiny so that people will respect it. A policeman's badge is like a man's boots; they both should shine and tell the world that he cares about the little things."

"Right now I'd trade this badge for a ticket to Prescott," Graves said. "Fritz, what makes bad news so hard to tell?"

"What bad news?"

"Here, read it for yourself," Graves said, handing him the telegram. The old man adjusted his glasses and, as he read, Graves watched his face, watched the expression change from gentleness to a hard, unforgotten anger.

Then Bruner threw the telegram on the counter. "Ah, so he comes back! After eight years he comes back!" He quickly bent his head forward and brushed the hair aside to show Graves the deep scars there. "Jim Pardee put these on my head with the barrel of his pistol, as payment for the boots I worked four days on." He tossed his gray hair in place and looked defiantly at Pete Graves. "So he comes back to this town. Does he come back to kill me—or Jake, who walks with smashed hips Pardee's bullet left as a remembrance?"

"He's running from the law again," Graves said. "Less than three weeks ago he shot three men and escaped from Fort Yuma, where he was being held to hang. The last report is that he's coming this way. Trying to get to Mexico, I guess." He picked up the telegram and read it again, as though he couldn't really believe what it said. "The Arizona rangers are hot after him, and I guess they sent these to every city marshal along the way, hoping someone will stop him until they get here."

"They want more than hope," Bruner said flatly. "It is plainly written; they want *you* to stop him." His eyes were hard beneath the gray thickets of eyebrows. "Pete, the rangers want you to hold him here. You must do this thing then."

"How?" Graves asked. "I'm not good enough to go up against a killer like Pardee. Hell, look what he did to the town eight years ago. He ran everyone clean off the streets for four days."

"Except me," Bruner said proudly. "I bow to no man, Pete."

Graves nodded and smiled fondly. "Yes, I know, Fritz. You were too proud to bow, and Jake just didn't have better sense. And Pardee left you bleeding in the street too. You didn't know your name for nearly three days." He wiped a hand across his mouth and drew the flesh down tightly against his cheekbones. "You want to know the truth? I'm scared. I don't want to be, but I am."

"It carries no shame," Bruner said, "to fear a man like Pardee."

"Sure," Graves said, turning toward the door. "But I'm the marshal and I'm paid not to be scared."

He went out and down the street, and Bruner began his day's work; yet his mind was sharply focused on Jim Pardee. He could recall every line in the man's face, every intonation of his voice, every movement he had made, and resentment was a bright flood in his mind.

Schoolchildren came by in a noisy flock and paused before his door as they always did. A girl of eight came in and curtsied. "How are you, Mr. Bruner?" one asked in German. "I'm just fine, little one," he replied in kind.

The children laughed, and the girl took candy for all of them; then they ran noisily down the street as the first bell sounded for school.

At noon Bruner's wife brought the hot lunch for him to eat, then sat and talked with him until one o'clock; he could see that she knew nothing of Jim Pardee, and he did not trouble her by mentioning it. As soon as she left the shop he deserted his cobbler's bench, for there was an acid in his spleen now, and his mind would not focus on work. He stood in the doorway and observed the activity on the street. The town sat on a bed of rimrock above the desert floor, high, where the sun was more intense, the sky a deeper, purer shade of blue. A bake-oven heat lay over the town, and in the distance the badlands danced ashimmer, so that it hurt his eyes to look long at it. Dust lay on the boardwalks, and the adobe buildings were pale in the hard sunlight. The walls were three feet thick at the base; each building was a fort unto itself, for this had once been Apache country where raids were commonplace.

From the way people moved around, or stood in groups to talk, Bruner knew that the word was out about Pardee coming back, and he searched his own mind for what course of action he would follow. His master had once caned him regularly because he was strong, and because he was the master; Bruner had been helpless to change that. And he had been helpless when Pardee whipped him with his pistol to prove, Bruner believed, that Pardee was strong and that he was humble. *Well*, he thought, *I am a proud man.* The only trouble was, he could never act like it—not to a man like Pardee.

A group stood on the bank corner, talking, and Bruner left his shop to cross over. Abe Murchison was waving his hands and saying, "No, no, no! I'm not going to take a chance on Pardee robbing my bank. Charley, it's none of your business where I'm going to take the money. It'll be safe." Then he saw Bruner, who had been a steady depositor for twenty years. "Fritz, come here a minute. Let me ask you—do you think it's safe to leave the money in the bank with Pardee on his way here?" The others started talking all at once, but he held up his hand for silence. "Now I'm asking Fritz, so let him answer."

Everyone looked at Bruner while the old man scratched his head. "It seems to me that with Pardee in so much of a hurry to get away from the rangers who're chasing him, he wouldn't take the time to blow open the vault."

"Now that's what I said," Lem Harris put in. "Are we going to be afraid of one man?"

"We were eight years ago," Murchison said. "And I don't see where any of us have suddenly got more courage." He looked at Fritz Bruner. "You ought to go home and stay there until this blows over. If those boots you made Pardee ever pinched his feet, he's likely to kill you for it. That's the way he is."

"They were the best pair of boots I ever made," Bruner said proudly. He chided himself for this display of pride; he simply could not pretend humility when it was not there to begin with. Bad man or not, pistol whipping or not, he was proud of the boots he had made for Jim Pardee.

"Well, I'm not going to stand around and end up like Crippled Jake," Lem Harris said. "Or get my head busted open either."

"Somebody ought to get on one of the buildings and shoot him as he rides into town," Herb Manners said. He ran the hay-and-feed store at the end of the block and it was an ideal spot for an ambush.

"Would you shoot him?" Bruner asked.

"No, because I've never shot anyone," Manners said. "He's not harmed me. But you've got a reason, Fritz. It would not be hard for you. As I recall, you put three years in the German Army, didn't you?"

"*Ja*," Bruner said, smiling, "but fixing the officers' boots." He shrugged. "I could not shoot a rabbit. In my family it has been over four hundred years since arms were taken up. They have always been tradesmen."

"Well, my business is being closed until Pardee is clear to hell and gone," Manners said.

"Same here," Harris said.

Bruner left them and walked to the saloon. Crippled Jake was sitting on the porch, his chair leaned back against the adobe wall. He was in his fifties, hard used by life and half abandoned by it.

Jake said, "Eight years don't seem so long now, does it, Fritz?"

"Like yesterday," Bruner admitted. He had no secrets from this man; few people did. "What are we to do, Jake? The same mistakes all over again?"

"What can we do? Walkin' vexes me, so I guess I'll sit here. See more that way. And what I see, I can relate; and if I see somethin' good, I can tell it over and over for ten years. Can't rightly say how many free drinks that'll fetch me, but I reckon it'll be plenty." He squinted at Bruner, then spoke more softly and with a new seriousness. "Fritz, stop thinkin' about the headache he gave you. I guess I'd like to gut-shoot him just to hear him moan, but I won't. I'll sit here and try to keep out of his mean way. Livin's mighty sweet when the time nears for dyin'."

"I can't help think what a shame that a man like Pardee could come twice through our lives, and we do nothing about it."

"What can you do? He kills for the fun of it; he don't need a reason." He waved a hand at the street; the merchants were closing their shops, barring the doors. "They've been thinkin', and it's got 'em stirred up like chickens with a fox in their midst. All they want is a hole to jump in so they can pull it in after 'em." He squinted at Fritz Bruner. "I'd go home, was I you. You won't lose much business today."

"People do not deserve to be frightened," Bruner said. "When I was a boy in Germany the wolves would come in the winter. We'd have to stay inside until the hunters came and killed them."

Jake laughed without humor. "Germany ain't so different from Arizona after all, is it?"

Pete Graves came down the walk then, his long legs measuring an even stride. "Business is kind of dead," he said and laughed hollowly. He kept shifting his pistol holster on his hip as though he couldn't decide where he wanted to carry it.

Crippled Jake said, "There wouldn't be a man in town who'd blame you if you carried that in your hand, son."

Young Graves colored, and Bruner, watching him, thought, *He has that pride too, and it is what kills men.*

Graves said, "Jake, you've lived in tough towns. Is a marshal supposed to handle anything, or are there some things so big a man can't stand up under them?"

"It depends on how far a man can back down and still live with himself. Any man's got to stop there."

"I don't know how far that is," Graves said, genuinely troubled. He looked at Fritz Bruner. "How do I stop him?"

"I don't know," Bruner said. "I would like to stop him myself, but I don't know how. I have never fought." He looked at Graves and felt sorry for the young man. "Keep yourself safe."

"How? By being hard to find when he gets here?" He shook his head. "I've heard of marshals like Masterson and Earp who've been hard to find from time to time, but they have a big reputation to take the stink off afterward. So I guess I'll be here when Pardee shows up."

So saying, he turned and walked back up the street.

Fritz Bruner went back to his shop, thinking about Graves; unless the young man was very careful, there might not be a wedding on Saturday. He had work to do, but his hands moved mechanically and he kept sounding his mind for some satisfactory no man's land between his inability to extract justice for himself and his burning desire for it. Something that would allow him to think of himself as a man who had conducted himself proudly.

While he worked he thought of the boots he had made for Jim Pardee. They had been sewn of the finest, softest leathers—with a delicate, but strong sole and a solid, well-made arch. He had molded them around each irregularity in Pardee's foot, so that he would know comfort afoot or in the saddle. Many shoemakers ignored this last element of their craft, for a horseman needs to support his weight in the stirrups, and a badly fitted boot can raise blisters and fire tempers.

It was nearly five o'clock when Bruner heard a solitary horseman ride down the main street; the silence was so profound that he could hear dry saddle leather protest when the man dismounted. Bruner could not see from his shop and he did not leave his bench to have a look; his ears picked up the man's step, and eight years passed as nothing as he recognized Jim Pardee's stride.

The man walked up and down the walk on the other side, then turned into the saloon. The street was silent again, and Bruner worked on, although he felt the sweat start on his forehead and upper lip.

A slight noise at the rear of his shop drew his attention and he got up and unbolted the back door; Pete Graves stood there, his manner bleak.

"Come in," Bruner said.

Graves sighed. "I'm just trying to get up my nerve, that's all." He wet his lips, then unbuckled his gunbelt and laid it on Bruner's counter. "I thought you'd close up, Fritz. You know, I was ready to run and hide until I saw your shop still open. So I'm going over to the saloon and talk to him, ask him to leave town with no more fuss. Just fill his canteen, take a sack of the free lunch off the bar and leave."

He was, Bruner knew, trying to justify to himself his course of action, just as Bruner sat at his bench pretending he had so much work he couldn't even look out the door at Pardee. The truth was, Bruner had to admit, that he was afraid to look. He was afraid he'd look and remember the days of semiconsciousness and the pain, and just run like the genuinely frightened man he was.

"We should walk over together," Bruner said calmly. "I've been working hard and a beer would taste good."

"You don't have to go," Graves said. "Fritz, that must be wonderful, not having to go." He said it as though he was almost jealous; then Bruner took off his apron.

"As long as these scars remain, Pete, I have to go."

He turned to the door and stopped there, and after a hesitation Pete Graves walked across with him.

Crippled Jake was not in his chair, and when they stepped inside they saw him down at the end of the bar, his hands idle on the polished walnut. Jenner was tending bar, and Jim Pardee turned to look at the men who had intruded on his privacy. He was a tall man, heavy through the shoulders, and his face was unchanged from what Fritz Bruner remembered; it was rather handsome, broad through the forehead, with a straight nose and full lips. But Pardee's eyes were a dull gray, like old glass beads neglected in the bottom of a sewing basket, dull with age. He wore a pistol on each hip, but he did not touch them; he had no fear of those around him, and Bruner supposed the man lacked the emotion completely.

To Graves he said, "Are you going to arrest me?"

"No. . . .A couple of beers here, Jenner." He turned to face Pardee, and it was not an easy thing for him to do. "I want you to water up, grub up and leave. There'll be no trouble."

"I know that," Pardee said. He looked closely at Bruner, as though he were trying to place him. "Wasn't you here before when I came through? Sure. You made me these boots." He held one leg out as though to admire them. They were in very bad shape, split at the seams, with run-over heels and large curls along the edges of the soles, which spoke of holes in the bottoms.

"You paid him by pistol-whipping him," Graves said boldly.

"So I did," Pardee said, remembering. "Well, you took too danged long." Then he smiled. "The best pair of boots I ever owned. One fella tried to back-shoot me for 'em, and a cheap Wyoming sheriff tried to take 'em away from me. Yes, sir, the best boots I ever had." He pushed away from the bar and moved over beside Bruner, who had to fight hard not to move a pace backward. "If I swore on a stack of Bibles I wouldn't lay a gun on you again, would you make me another pair?"

"It would take two days," Bruner said. "I don't think you can wait that long."

Pardee laughed. "Are those doggoned rangers still chasin' me? They don't know when to give up." His laughter faded. "Which one of you gents is going to stop me until they get here?" He was standing with his back to Crippled Jake and he jerked a thumb in that direction. "He'd like to kill me, but his nerve's gone. The bartender there, he keeps thinking of that shotgun down a ways. . . . Don't you, bartender?"

"I'm not going to give you any trouble," Jenner said.

"And the law ain't even carryin' a gun," Pardee pointed out. He slapped the bar, then peeled off one of his boots and shifted his weight to the other leg to take off the other. Then he threw them at Bruner, who grunted when they hit him in the stomach; his hands came up automatically to catch them and there was a fleeting fire in the old man's eyes, which he banked quickly enough. "Now you go over there to your shop and fix them boots up proper, old man. I'll give you a couple hours."

"That isn't much time," Bruner said. "They're in bad shape."

"Don't tell me how bad they are. They're so threadbare I can't ride another mile." He reached out and gave Bruner a shove backward. "And to show you how much I appreciate it, I'll only kill one of you before I leave."

"Why kill anybody?" Graves asked flatly.

"To show you I can if I want," Pardee said, swinging his head around to look at the marshal. "Ain't that a good reason?"

"It's no reason at all," Graves said.

Bruner edged his voice in between them. "Two hours is not much. I'll have to get right to work." He started to back away, like he was in the presence of royalty, then his pride took hold and he turned and walked out with his head high.

In his shop he bent over his bench and tried to piece together the frayed bits of leather into a wearable whole. He thought about Jim Pardee while he hammered and sewed, and seeing the man again was not the terrible experience he had imagined. He felt a measure of resolution return; he was not foolish enough to imagine it was courage, and he began to feel good inside and strong and clean—and he worked with a new determination.

There was so much to be done on the boots; the soles were gone, and the instep had to be rebuilt on both. As the end of the two-hour period neared, Bruner was not quite finished. Pardee came to the porch and yelled into the empty street.

"Where's my boots, old man? Ten minutes! I give you that!"

It would be enough, Bruner decided, and worked until the sweat poured down his cheeks. He ran his hands inside the boots and inspected them carefully, then left his shop and carried them to the saloon. Jim Pardee came out, pushing Jake and Graves and Jenner ahead of him.

He took the boots, turned them over admiringly, then slipped into them. He stamped around to settle them, then said, "By golly, that's some job. But they feel a little funny though."

"You have let them get into bad shape," Bruner explained. "And your feet are so used to the broken arches, good arches feel strange now. In a few hours you'll feel a great difference, I promise you."

"I guess you know your business," Pardee said. He took out a five-dollar gold piece and handed it to Bruner.

"I have no change," Bruner said. "Besides, I intended to charge nothing."

"I pay for what I get, one way or another," Pardee said. He stepped down to where his horse was tied. A full canteen and a bag of grub hung from the saddle-horn. "I guess I'll be on my way, gents." He went into the saddle. "When those rangers get here, tell 'em I'll send 'em a postcard from Mexico." Then his amusement vanished like a puff of wood smoke. His hard eyes settled on them. "I've been thinkin'. Which one of you is the most worthless?" He gave his decision away when he looked at Pete Graves, and the young man had that much warning, enough to make a long jump for the saloon door as Pardee drew his portside gun. The bullet chipped wood, and Graves made it inside; Pardee started to swing down, irritated because he had missed and determined to finish the job.

Then glass crashed as Graves pawed under the bar for the shotgun, and this was enough to make Pardee change his mind completely. He kicked his horse into motion and stormed out of town, leaving behind a choking pall of dust.

"Thank God it's over," Jenner said.

Graves came out with the shotgun; he fingered his badge as though wondering whether or not he should be touching it. "I guess I'm through," he said. "Jake? Fritz? Am I through?"

"One thing for sure," Jake said dryly. "You got an answer for anyone who says anything. You met him face to face, which is more'n they can claim."

"Yes," Graves said dully. "That's something, isn't it?" Then he turned and walked rapidly down the street.

Crippled Jake watched him leave, then said, "A good boy there, but suddenly the job turned out bigger'n a hog's dream."

Fritz Bruner, who had remained silent, said, "I should have told him to speak to the rangers when they get here. Pardee will not be far away."

Jenner stared, then laughed. "With Mexico only fifty miles away, he'll be there by morning!" He frowned. "You don't make sense, Fritz."

"That's possible," Bruner said and walked to his shop.

The rangers arrived in town after sundown, and the captain did not blame Graves for letting Pardee pass on. The lawmen watered their horses, ate standing up at Jenner's bar, then went on, eight determined men with a long hard ride ahead of them.

Fritz Bruner ate his supper, smoked a pipe, and sat on the porch after his wife went to bed; she never stayed up after ten o'clock, and could not understand why he wanted to. Bruner kept thinking about Pardee and the country he would have to ride through and the time it would take him, and at eleven he went uptown. Young Graves walked the streets, his expression sober, and Bruner hoped he was not doing private penance, yet he knew he was; it was the fate of sensitive men.

He misjudged the return of the rangers by thirty-five minutes, but he was standing on Jenner's porch when they came back, Pardee with them, hands bound, legs roped to the stirrups. He was a weary pathetic man bound for the hangman's rope, and as soon as the news spread, everyone came to Apache Street to see him. They wanted to look at the man who had put so much fear in them; yet when he glared at them now, they showed no fear, for he was just an animal in a cage.

Crippled Jake saw something peculiar and asked the ranger captain about it. "Where's his boots?"

"Right here," he said, taking them from his saddle bag.

Everyone was asking questions: "How did you capture him?"

"We came across him in the badlands," the captain said. He was a polite man, accustomed to dealing with a fickle public. "Pardee was sitting on a rock, rubbing his feet. We took him by surprise, threw down on him, and he surrendered. No man wants to draw when a dozen guns have the drop on him."

Fritz Bruner elbowed his way to Pardee's horse. He took the gold piece from his pocket and gave it back. "My work was free this time, same as before." There was a strong pride in his voice. "How far did you go before they hurt your feet?"

The ranger captain caught this and edged his horse around. "What's this about sore feet? Did you fix his boots?"

"I made the boots eight years ago, and he beat me for it. This time I repaired them, but inside, beneath the lining, I placed a small string of leather thong. He would not notice it at first, but after ten miles of riding, this little thing would bruise his feet so badly he would have to dismount and sit. He would be unable to ride or walk." He took the boots from the ranger and examined them critically. "Yes, they are the best boots I have ever made, an example of my finest work. Even my old *Meisterschuhmacher* would have been proud to hang them in his shop."

"Well, if you'd be so kind," the captain said, "I'd like to buy them off you and hang them in *my* 'shop.' "

"Accept them as a gift," Fritz Bruner said. "I have already been repaid."

Then he excused himself and left the crowd, hurrying home because never in twenty years had he been able to sneak into the house undetected, and Emma would fuss at breakfast until he presented a proper excuse. And he wondered if he had one.

OPEN WINTER

H. L. DAVIS

The drying east wind, which always brought hard luck to Eastern Oregon at whatever season it blew, had combed down the plateau grasslands through so much of the winter that it was hard to see any sign of grass ever having grown on them. Even though March had come, it still blew, drying the ground deep, shrinking the watercourses, beating back the clouds that might have delivered rain, and grinding coarse dust against the fifty-odd head of work horses that Pop Apling, with young Beech Cartwright helping, had brought down from his homestead to turn back into their home pasture while there was still something left of them.

The two men, one past sixty and the other around sixteen, shouldered the horses through the gate of the home pasture about dark, with lights beginning to shine out from the little freighting town across Three Notch Valley, and then they rode for the ranch house, knowing even before they drew up outside the yard that they had picked the wrong time to come. The house was too dark, and the corrals and outbuildings too still, for a place that anybody lived in.

There were sounds, but they were of shingles flapping in the wind, a windmill running loose and sucking noisily at a well that it had already pumped empty, a door that kept banging shut and dragging open again. The haystacks were gone, the stackyard fence had dwindled to a few naked posts, and the entire pasture was as bare and as hard as a floor all the way down into the valley.

The prospect looked so hopeless that the herd horses refused even to explore it, and merely stood with their tails turned to the wind, waiting to see what was to happen to them next.

Old Apling went poking inside the house, thinking somebody might have left a note or that the men might have run down to the saloon in town for an hour or two. He came back, having used up all his matches and stopped the door from banging, and said the place appeared to have been handed back to the Government, or maybe the mortgage company.

"You can trust old Ream Gervais not to be any place where anybody wants him," Beech said. He had hired out to herd for Ream Gervais over the winter. That entitled him to be more critical than old Apling, who had merely contracted to supply the horse herd with feed and pasture for the season at so much per head. "Well, my job was to help herd these steeds while you had 'em, and to help deliver 'em back when you got through with 'em, and here they are. I've put in a week on 'em that I won't ever git paid for, and it won't help anything to set around and watch 'em try to live on fence pickets. Let's git out."

Old Apling looked at the huddle of horses, at the naked slope with a glimmer of light still on it, and at the lights of the town twinkling in the wind. He said it wasn't his place to tell any man what to do, but that he wouldn't feel quite right to dump the horses and leave.

"I agreed to see that they got delivered back here, and I'd feel better about it if I could locate somebody to deliver 'em to," he said. "I'd like to ride across to town yonder, and see if there ain't somebody that knows something about 'em. You could hold 'em together here till I git back. We ought to look the fences over before we pull out, and you can wait here as well as anywhere else."

"I can't, but go ahead," Beech said. "I don't like to have 'em stand around and look at me when I can't do anything to help 'em out. They'd have been better off if we'd turned 'em out of your homestead and let 'em run loose on the country. There was more grass up there than there is here."

"There wasn't enough to feed 'em, and I'd have had all my neighbors down on me for it," old Apling said. "You'll find out one of these days that if a man aims to live in this world he's got to git along with the people in it. I'd start a fire and thaw out a little and git that pack horse unloaded, if I was you."

He rode down the slope, leaning into the wind to ease the drag of the wind on his tired horse. Beech heard the sound of the road gate being let down and put up again, the beat of hoofs in the hard road, and then nothing but the noises around him as the wind went through its usual process of easing down for the night to make room for the frost. Loose boards settled into place, the windmill clacked to a stop and began to drip water into a puddle, and the herd horses shifted around facing Beech, as if anxious not to miss anything he did.

He pulled off some fence pickets and built a fire, unsaddled his pony and unloaded the pack horse, and got out what was left of a sack of grain and fed them both, standing the herd horses off with a fence picket until they had finished eating.

That was strictly fair, for the pack horse and the saddle pony had worked harder and carried more weight than any of the herd animals, and the grain was little enough to even them up for it. Nevertheless, he felt mean at having to club animals away from food when they were hungry, and they crowded back and eyed the grain sack so wistfully that he carried it inside the yard and stored it down in the root cellar behind the house, so it wouldn't prey on their minds. Then he dumped another armload of fence pickets onto the fire and sat down to wait for old Apling.

The original mistake, he reflected, had been when old Apling took the Gervais horses to feed at the beginning of winter. Contracting to feed them had been well enough, for he had nursed up a stand of bunch grass on his homestead that would have carried an ordinary pack of horses with only a little extra feeding to help out in the roughest weather. But the Gervais horses were all big harness stock, they had pulled in half starved, and they had taken not much over three weeks to clean off the pasture that old Apling had expected would last them at least two months. Nobody would have blamed him for backing out on his agreement then, since he had only undertaken to feed the horses, not to treat them for malnutrition.

Beech wanted him to back out of it, but he refused to, said the stockmen had enough troubles without having that added to them, and started feeding out his hay and insisting that the dry wind couldn't possibly keep up much longer, because it wasn't in Nature.

By the time it became clear that Nature had decided to take in a little extra territory, the hay was all fed out, and, since there couldn't be any accommodation about letting the horses starve to death, he consented to throw the contract over and bring them back where they belonged.

The trouble with most of old Apling's efforts to be accommodating was that they did nobody any good. His neighbors would have been spared all their uneasiness if he had never brought in the horses to begin with. Gervais wouldn't have been any worse off, since he stood to lose them anyway; the horses could have starved to death as gracefully in November as in March, and old Apling would have been ahead a great deal of carefully accumulated bunch grass and two big stacks of extortionately valuable hay. Nobody had gained by his chivalrousness; he had lost by it, and yet he liked it so well that he couldn't stand to leave the horses until he had raked the country for somebody to hand the worthless brutes over to.

Beech fed sticks into the fire and felt out of patience with a man who could stick to his mistakes even after he had been cleaned out by them. He heard the road gate open and shut, and he knew by the draggy-sounding plod of old Apling's horse that the news from town was going to be bad.

Old Apling rode past the fire and over to the picket fence, got off as if he was trying to make it last, tied his horse carefully as if he expected the knot to last a month, and unsaddled and did up his latigo and folded his saddle blanket as if he was fixing them to put in a show window. He remarked that his horse had been given a bait of grain in town and wouldn't need feeding again, and then he began to work down to what he had found out.

"If you think things look bad along this road, you ought to see that town," he said. "All the sheep gone and all the ranches deserted and no trade to run on and their water threatenin' to give out. They've got a little herd of milk cows that they keep up for their children, and to hear 'em talk you'd think it was an ammunition supply that they expected to stand off hostile Indians with. They said Gervais pulled out of here around a month ago. All his men quit him, so he bunched his sheep and took 'em down to the railroad, where he could ship in hay for 'em. Sheep will be a price this year, and you won't be able to buy a lamb for under twelve dollars except at a fire sale. Horses ain't in much demand. There's been a lot of 'em turned out wild, and everybody wants to git rid of 'em."

"I didn't drive this bunch of pelters any eighty miles against the wind to git a market report," Beech said. "You didn't find anybody to turn 'em over to, and Gervais didn't leave any word about what he wanted done with 'em. You've probably got it figured out that you ought to trail 'em a hundred and eighty miles to the railroad, so his feelings won't be hurt, and you're probably tryin' to study how you can work me in on it, and you might as well save your time. I've helped you with your accommodation jobs long enough. I've quit, and it would have been a whole lot better for you if I'd quit sooner."

Old Apling said he could understand that state of feeling, which didn't mean that he shared it.

"It wouldn't be as much of a trick to trail down to the railroad as a man might think," he said, merely to settle a question of fact. "We couldn't make it by the road in a starve-out year like this, but there's

64

old Indian trails back on the ridge where any man has got a right to take livestock whenever he feels like it. Still, as long as you're set against it, I'll meet you halfway. We'll trail these horses down the ridge to a grass patch where I used to corral cattle when I was in the business, and we'll leave 'em there. It'll be enough so they won't starve, and I'll ride on down and notify Gervais where they are, and you can go where you please. It wouldn't be fair to do less than that, to my notion."

"Ream Gervais triggered me out of a week's pay," Beech said. "It ain't much, but he swindled you on that pasture contract too. If you expect me to trail his broken-down horses ninety miles down this ridge when they ain't worth anything, you've turned in a poor guess. You'll have to think of a better argument than that if you aim to gain any ground with me."

"Ream Gervais don't count on this," old Apling said. "What does he care about these horses, when he ain't even left word what he wants done with 'em? What counts is you, and I don't have to think up any better argument, because I've already got one. You may not realize it, but you and me are responsible for these horses till they're delivered to their owner, and if we turn 'em loose here to bust fences and overrun that town and starve to death in the middle of it, we'll land in the pen. It's against the law to let horses starve to death, did you know that? If you pull out of here I'll pull out right along with you, and I'll have every man in that town after you before the week's out. You'll have a chance to git some action on that pistol of yours, if you're careful."

Beech said he wasn't intimidated by that kind of talk, and threw a couple of handfuls of dirt on the fire, so it wouldn't look so conspicuous. His pistol was an old single-action relic with its grips tied on with fish line and no trigger, so that it had to be operated by flipping the hammer. The spring was weak, so that sometimes it took several flips to get off one shot. Suggesting that he might use such a thing to stand off any pack of grim-faced pursuers was about the same as saying that he was simple-minded. As far as he could see, his stand was entirely sensible, and even humane.

"It ain't that I don't feel sorry for these horses, but they ain't fit to travel," he said. "They wouldn't last twenty miles. I don't see how it's any worse to let 'em stay here than to walk 'em to death down that ridge."

"They make less trouble for people if you keep 'em on the move," old Apling said. "It's something you can't be cinched for in court, and it makes you feel better afterward to know that you tried everything you could. Suit yourself about it, though. I ain't beggin'

65

you to do it. If you'd sooner pull out and stand the consequences, it's you for it. Before you go, what did you do with that grain?"

Beech had half a notion to leave, just to see how much of that dark threatening would come to pass. He decided that it wouldn't be worth it. "I'll help you trail the blamed skates as far as they'll last, if you've got to be childish about it," he said. "I put the grain in a root cellar behind the house, so the rats wouldn't git into it. It looked like the only safe place around here. There was about a half a ton of old sprouted potatoes ricked up in it that didn't look like they'd been bothered for twenty years. They had sprouts on 'em——" He stopped, noticing that old Apling kept staring at him as if something was wrong. "Good Lord, potatoes ain't good for horse feed, are they? They had sprouts on 'em a foot long!"

Old Apling shook his head resignedly and got up. "We wouldn't ever find anything if it wasn't for you," he said. "We wouldn't ever git any good out of it if it wasn't for me, so maybe we make a team. Show me where that root cellar is, and we'll pack them spuds out and spread 'em around so the horses can git started on 'em. We'll git this herd through to grassland yet, and it'll be something you'll never be ashamed of. It ain't everybody your age gits a chance to do a thing like this, and you'll thank me for holdin' you to it before you're through."

II

They climbed up by an Indian trail onto a high stretch of tableland, so stony and scored with rock breaks that nobody had ever tried to cultivate it, but so high that it sometimes caught moisture from the atmosphere that the lower elevations missed. Part of it had been doled out among the Indians as allotment lands, which none of them ever bothered to lay claim to, but the main spread of it belonged to the nation, which was too busy to notice it.

The pasture was thin, though reliable, and it was so scantily watered and so rough and broken that in ordinary years nobody bothered to bring stock onto it. The open winter had spoiled most of that seclusion. There was no part of the trail that didn't have at least a dozen new bed grounds for lambed ewes in plain view, easily picked out of the landscape because of the little white flags stuck up around them to keep sheep from straying out and coyotes from straying in during the night. The sheep were pasturing down the draws out of the wind, where they couldn't be seen. There were no herders visible, not any startling amount of grass, and no water except a mud tank to catch a little spring for one of the camps.

They tried to water the horses in it, but it had taken up the flavor of sheep, so that not a horse in the herd would touch it. It was too near dark to waste time reasoning with them about it, so old Apling headed them down into a long rock break and across it to a tangle of wild cherry and mountain mahogany that lasted for several miles and ended in a grass clearing among some dwarf cottonwoods with a mud puddle in the center of it.

The grass had been grazed over, though not closely, and there were sheep tracks around the puddle that seemed to be fresh, for the horses, after sniffing the water, decided that they could wait a while longer. They spread out to graze, and Beech remarked that he couldn't see where it was any improvement over the ticklegrass homestead.

"The grass may be better, but there ain't as much of it, and the water ain't any good if they won't drink it," he said. "Well, do you intend to leave 'em here, or have you got some wrinkle figured out to make me help trail 'em on down to the railroad?"

Old Apling stood the sarcasm unresistingly. "It would be better to trail 'em to the railroad, now that we've got this far," he said. "I won't ask you to do that much, because it's outside of what you agreed to. This place has changed since I was here last, but we'll make it do, and that water ought to clear up fit to drink before long. You can settle down here for a few days while I ride around and fix it up with the sheep camps to let the horses stay here. We've got to do that, or they're liable to think it's some wild bunch and start shootin' 'em. Somebody's got to stay with 'em, and I can git along with these herders better than you can."

"If you've got any sense, you'll let them sheep outfits alone," Beech said. "They don't like tame horses on this grass any better than they do wild ones, and they won't make any more bones about shootin' 'em if they find out they're in here. It's a hard place to find, and they'll stay close on account of the water, and you'd better pull out and let 'em have it to themselves. That's what I aim to do."

"You've done what you agreed to, and I ain't got any right to hold you any longer," old Apling said. "I wish I could. You're wrong about them sheep outfits. I've got as much right to pasture this ridge as they have, and they know it, and nobody ever lost anything by actin' sociable with people."

"Somebody will before very long," Beech said. "I've got relatives in the sheep business, and I know what they're like. You'll land yourself in trouble, and I don't want to be around when you do it. I'm pullin' out of here in the morning, and if you had any sense you'd pull out along with me."

There were several things that kept Beech from getting much sleep during the night. One was the attachment that the horses showed for his sleeping place; they stuck so close that he could almost feel their breath on him, could hear the soft breaking sound that the grass made as they pulled it, the sound of their swallowing, the jar of the ground under him when one of the horses changed ground, the peaceful regularity of their eating, as if they didn't have to bother about anything so long as they kept old Apling in sight.

Another irritating thing was old Apling's complete freedom from uneasiness. He ought by rights to have felt more worried about the future than Beech did, but he slept, with the hard ground for a bed and his hard saddle for a pillow and the horses almost stepping on him every minute or two, as soundly as if the entire trip had come out exactly to suit him and there was nothing ahead but plain sailing.

His restfulness was so hearty and so unjustifiable that Beech couldn't sleep for feeling indignant about it, and got up and left about daylight to keep from being exposed to any more of it. He left without waking old Apling, because he saw no sense in a leave-taking that would consist merely in repeating his commonsense warnings and having them ignored, and he was so anxious to get clear of the whole layout that he didn't even take along anything to eat. The only thing he took from the pack was his ramshackle old pistol; there was no holster for it, and, in the hope that he might get a chance to use it on a loose quail or prairie chicken, he stowed it in an empty flour sack and hung it on his saddle horn, a good deal like an old squaw heading for the far blue distances with a bundle of diapers.

III

There was never anything recreational about traveling a rock desert at any season of the year, and the combination of spring gales, winter chilliness and summer drought all striking at once brought it fairly close to hard punishment. Beech's saddle pony, being jaded at the start with overwork and underfeeding and no water, broke down in the first couple of miles, and got so feeble and tottery that Beech had to climb off and lead him, searching likely-looking thickets all the way down the gully in the hope of finding some little trickle that he wouldn't be too finicky to drink.

The nearest he came to it was a fair-sized rock sink under some big half-budded cottonwoods that looked, by its dampness and the abundance of fresh animal tracks around it, as if it might have held water recently, but of water there was none, and even digging a hole in the center of the basin failed to fetch a drop.

The work of digging, hill climbing and scrambling through brush piles raised Beech's appetite so powerfully that he could scarcely hold up, and, a little above where the gully opened into the flat sagebrush plateau, he threw away his pride, pistoled himself a jackrabbit, and took it down into the sagebrush to cook, where his fire wouldn't give away which gully old Apling was camped in.

Jackrabbit didn't stand high as a food. It was considered an excellent thing to give men in the last stages of famine, because they weren't likely to injure themselves by eating too much of it, but for ordinary occasions it was looked down on, and Beech covered his trail out of the gully and built his cooking fire in the middle of a high stand of sagebrush, so as not to be embarrassed by inquisitive visitors.

The meat cooked up strong, as it always did, but he ate what he needed of it, and he was wrapping the remainder in his flour sack to take along with him when a couple of men rode past, saw his pony, and turned in to look him over.

They looked him over so closely and with so little concern for his privacy that he felt insulted before they even spoke.

He studied them less openly, judging by their big gallon canteens that they were out on some long scout.

One of them was some sort of hired hand, by his looks; he was broad-faced and gloomy-looking, with a fine white horse, a flower-stamped saddle, an expensive rifle scabbarded under his knee, and a fifteen-dollar saddle blanket, while his own manly form was set off by a yellow hotel blanket and a ninety-cent pair of overalls.

The other man had on a store suit, a plain black hat, fancy stitched boots, and a white shirt and necktie, and rode a burr-tailed Indian pony and an old wrangling saddle with a loose horn. He carried no weapons in sight, but there was a narrow strap across the lower spread of his necktie which indicated the presence of a shoulder holster somewhere within reach.

He opened the conversation by inquiring where Beech had come from, what his business was, where he was going and why he hadn't taken the county road to go there, and why he had to eat jackrabbit when the country was littered with sheep camps where he could get a decent meal by asking for it?

"I come from the upper country," Beech said, being purposely vague about it. "I'm travelin', and I stopped here because my horse give out. He won't drink out of any place that's had sheep in it, and he's gone short of water till he breaks down easy."

"There's a place corralled in for horses to drink at down at my lower camp," the man said, and studied Beech's pony. "There's no reason for you to bum through the country on jackrabbit in a time like this. My herder can take you down to our water hole and see that you get fed and put to work till you can make a stake for yourself. I'll give you a note. That pony looks like he had Ream Gervais's brand on him. Do you know anything about that herd of old workhorses he's been pasturing around?"

"I don't know anything about him," Beech said, sidestepping the actual question while he thought over the offer of employment. He could have used a stake, but the location didn't strike him favorably. It was too close to old Apling's camp, he could see trouble ahead over the horse herd, and he didn't want to be around when it started. "If you'll direct me how to find your water, I'll ride on down there, but I don't need anybody to go with me, and I don't need any stake. I'm travelin'."

The man said there wasn't anybody so well off that he couldn't use a stake, and that it would be hardly any trouble at all for Beech to get one. "I want you to understand how we're situated around here, so you won't think we're any bunch of stranglers," he said. "You can see what kind of a year this has been, when we have to run lambed ewes in a rock patch like this. We've got five thousand lambs in here that we're trying to bring through, and we've had to fight the blamed wild horses for this pasture since the day we moved in. A horse that ain't worth hell room will eat as much as two dozen sheep worth twenty dollars, with the lambs, so you can see how it figures out. We've got 'em pretty well thinned out, but one of my packers found a trail of a new bunch that came up from around Three Notch within the last day or two, and we don't want them to feel as if we'd neglected them. We'd like to find out where they lit. You wouldn't have any information about 'em?"

"None that would do you any good to know," Beech said. "I know the man with that horse herd, and it ain't any use to let on that I don't, but it wouldn't be any use to try to deal with him. He don't sell out on a man he works for."

"He might be induced to," the man said. "We'll find him anyhow, but I don't like to take too much time to it. Just for instance, now, suppose you knew that pony of yours would have to go thirsty till you gave us a few directions about that horse herd? You'd be stuck here for quite a spell, wouldn't you?"

He was so pleasant about it that it took Beech a full minute to realize that he was being threatened. The heavy-set herder brought that home to him by edging out into a flank position and hoisting his rifle scabbard so it could be reached in a hurry. Beech removed the cooked jackrabbit from his flour sack carefully, a piece at a time, and, with the same mechanical thoughtfulness, brought out his triggerless old pistol, cut down on the pleasant-spoken man, and hauled back on the hammer. He stood there with the pistol poised.

"That herder of yours had better go easy on his rifle," he said, trying to keep his voice from trembling. "This pistol shoots if I don't hold back the hammer, and if he knocks me out I'll have to let go of it. You'd better watch him, if you don't want your tack drove. I won't give you no directions about that horse herd, and this pony of mine won't go thirsty for it, either. Loosen them canteens of yours and let 'em drop on the ground. Drop that rifle scabbard back where it belongs, and unbuckle the straps and let go of it. If either of you tries any funny business, there'll be one of you to pack home, heels first."

The quaver in his voice sounded childish and undignified to him, but it had a more businesslike ring to them than any amount of manly gruffness. The herder unbuckled his rifle scabbard, and they both cast loose their canteen straps, making it last as long as they could while they argued with him, not angrily, but as if he was a dull stripling whom they wanted to save from some foolishness that he was sure to regret. They argued ethics, justice, common sense, his future prospects, and the fact that what he was doing amounted to robbery by force and arms and that it was his first fatal step into a probably unsuccessful career of crime. They worried over him, they explained themselves to him, and they ridiculed him.

They managed to make him feel like several kinds of a fool, and they were so pleasant and concerned about it that they came close to breaking him down. What held him steady was the thought of old Apling waiting up the gully.

"That herder with the horses never sold out on any man, and I won't sell out on him," he said. "You've said your say and I'm tired of holdin' this pistol on cock for you, so move along out of here. Keep to open ground, so I can be sure you're gone, and don't be in too much of a hurry to come back. I've got a lot of things I want to think over, and I want to be let alone while I do it."

IV

He did have some thinking that needed tending to, but he didn't take time for it. When the men were well out of range, he emptied their canteens into his hat and let his pony drink. Then he hung the canteens and the scabbarded rifle on a bush and rode back up the gully where the horse camp was, keeping to shaly ground so as not to leave any tracks. It was harder going up than coming down.

He had turned back from the scene of his run-in with the two sheepmen about noon, and he was still a good two miles from the camp when the sun went down, the wind lulled and the night frost began to bite at him so hard that he dismounted and walked to get warm. That raised his appetite again, and, as if by some special considerateness of Nature, the cottonwoods around him seemed to be alive with jackrabbits heading down into the pitch-dark gully where he had fooled away valuable time trying to find water that morning.

They didn't stimulate his hunger much; for a time they even made him feel less like eating anything. Then his pony gave out and had to rest, and, noticing that the cottonwoods around him were beginning to bud out, he remembered that peeling the bark off in the budding season would fetch out a foamy, sweet-tasting sap which, among children of the plateau country, was considered something of a delicacy.

He cut a blaze on a fair-sized sapling, waited ten minutes or so, and touched his finger to it to see how much sap had accumulated. None had; the blaze was moist to his touch, but scarcely more so than when he had whittled it.

It wasn't important enough to do any bothering about, and yet a whole set of observed things began to draw together in his mind and form themselves into an explanation of something he had puzzled over: the fresh animal tracks he had seen around the rock sink when there wasn't any water; the rabbits going down into the gully; the cottonwoods in which the sap rose enough during the day to produce buds and got driven back at night when the frost set in. During the day, the cottonwoods had drawn the water out of the ground for themselves; at night they stopped drawing it, and it drained out into the rock sink for the rabbits.

It all worked out so simply that he led his pony down into the gully to see how much there was in it, and, losing his footing on the steep slope, coasted down into the rock sink in the dark and landed in water and thin mud up to his knees. He led his pony down into it to drink which seemed little enough to get back for the time he had fooled away on it, and then he headed for the horse camp, which was all too easily discernible by the plume of smoke rising, white and ostentatious, against the dark sky from old Apling's campfire.

He made the same kind of entrance that old Apling usually affected when bringing some important item of news. He rode past the campfire and pulled up at a tree, got off deliberately, knocked an accumulation of dead twigs from his hat, took off his saddle and bridle and balanced them painstakingly in the tree fork, and said it was affecting to see how widespread the shortage of pasture was.

"It generally is," old Apling said. "I had a kind of a notion you'd be back after you'd had time to study things over. I suppose you got

72

into some kind of a rumpus with some of them sheep outfits. What was it? Couldn't you git along with them, or couldn't they hit it off with you?"

"There wasn't any trouble between them and me," Beech said. "The only point we had words over was you. They wanted to know where you was camped, so they could shoot you up, and I didn't think it was right to tell 'em. I had to put a gun on a couple of 'em before they'd believe I meant business, and that was all there was to it. They're out after you now, and they can see the smoke of this fire of yours for twenty miles, so they ought to be along any time now. I thought I'd come back and see you work your sociability on 'em."

"You probably kicked up a squabble with 'em yourself," old Apling said. He looked a little uneasy. "You talked right up to 'em, I'll bet, and slapped their noses with your hat to show 'em that they couldn't run over you. Well, what's done is done. You did come back, and maybe they'd have jumped us anyway. There ain't much that we can do. The horses have got to have water before they can travel, and they won't touch that sheep. It ain't cleared up a particle."

"You can put that fire out, not but what the whole country has probably seen the smoke from it already," Beech said. "If you've got to tag after these horses, you can run 'em off down the draw and keep 'em to the brush where they won't leave a trail. There's some young cottonwood bark that they can eat if they have to, and there's water in a rock sink under some big cottonwood trees. I'll stay here and hold off anybody that shows up, so you'll have time to git your tracks covered."

Old Apling went over and untied the flour-sacked pistol from Beech's saddle, rolled it into his blankets, and sat down on it. "If there's any holdin' off to be done, I'll do it," he said. "You're a little too high-spirited to suit me, and a little too hasty about your conclusions. I looked over that rock sink down the draw today, and there wasn't anything in it but mud, and blamed little of that. Somebody had dug for water, and there wasn't none."

"There is now," Beech said. He tugged off one of his wet boots and poured about a pint of the disputed fluid on the ground. "There wasn't any in the daytime because the cottonwoods took it all. They let up when it turns cold, and it runs back in. I waded in it."

He started to put his boot back on. Old Apling reached out and took it, felt of it inside and out, and handed it over as if performing some ceremonial presentation.

"I'd never have figured out a thing like that in this world," he said. "If we git them horses out of here, it'll be you that done it. We'll bunch 'em and work 'em down there. It won't be no picnic, but we'll make out to handle it somehow. We've got to, after a thing like this."

Beech remembered what had occasioned the discovery, and said he would have to have something to eat first. "I want you to keep in mind that it's you I'm doin' this for," he said. "I don't owe that old groundhog of a Ream Gervais anything. The only thing I hate about this is that it'll look like I'd done him a favor."

"He won't take it for one, I guess," old Apling said. "We've got to git these horses out because it'll be a favor to you. You wouldn't want to have it told around that you'd done a thing like findin' that water, and then have to admit that we'd lost all the horses anyhow. We can't lose 'em. You've acted like a man tonight, and I'll be blamed if I'll let you spoil it for any childish spite."

They got the horses out none too soon. Watering them took a long time, and when they finally did consent to call it enough and climb back up the side hill, Beech and old Apling heard a couple of signal shots from the direction of their old camping place, and saw a big glare mount up into the sky from it as the visitors built up their campfire to look the locality over. The sight was almost comforting; if they had to keep away from a pursuit, it was at least something to know where it was.

V

From then on they followed a grab-and-run policy, scouting ahead before they moved, holding to the draws by day and crossing open ground only after dark, never pasturing over a couple of hours in any one place, and discovering food value in outlandish substances—rock lichens, the sprouts of wild plum and serviceberry, the moss of old trees and the bark of some young ones—that neither they nor the horses had ever considered fit to eat before. When they struck Boulder River Canyon they dropped down and toenailed their way along one side of it where they could find grass and water with less likelihood of having trouble about it.

The breaks of the canyon were too rough to run new-lambed sheep in, and they met with so few signs of occupancy that old Apling got overconfident, neglected his scouting to tie back a break they had been obliged to make in a line fence, and ran the horse herd right over the top of a camp where some men were branding calves, tearing down a cook tent and part of a corral and scattering cattle and bedding from the river all the way to the top of the canyon.

By rights, they should have sustained some damage for that piece of carelessness, but they drove through fast, and they were out of sight around a shoulder of rimrock before any of the men could get themselves picked up. Somebody did throw a couple of shots after them as they were pulling into a thicket of mock orange and chokecherry, but it was only with a pistol, and he probably did it more to relieve his feelings than with any hope of hitting anything.

They were so far out of range that they couldn't even hear where the bullets landed.

Neither of them mentioned that unlucky run-in all the rest of that day. They drove hard, punished the horses savagely when they lagged, and kept them at it until, a long time after dark, they struck an old rope ferry that crossed Boulder River at a place called, in memory of its original founders, Robbers' Roost.

The ferry wasn't a public carrier, and there was not even any main road down to it. It was used by the ranches in the neighborhood as the only means of crossing the river for fifty miles in either direction, and it was tied in to a log with a good solid chain and padlock. It was a way to cross, and neither of them could see anything else but to take it.

Beech favored waiting for daylight for it, pointing out that there was a ranch light half a mile up the slope, and that if anybody caught them hustling a private ferry in the dead of night they would probably be taken for criminals on the dodge. Old Apling said it was altogether likely, and drew Beech's pistol and shot the padlock apart with it.

"They could hear that up at that ranch house," Beech said. "What if they come pokin' down here to see what we're up to?"

Old Apling tossed the fragments of padlock into the river and hung the pistol in the waistband of his trousers. "Let 'em come," he said. "They'll go back again with their fingers in their mouths. This is your trip, and you put in good work on it, and I like to ruined the whole thing stoppin' to patch an eighty-cent fence so some scissor-bill wouldn't have his feelings hurt, and that's the last accommodation anybody gits out of me till this is over with. I can take about six horses at a trip, it looks like. Help me to bunch 'em."

Six horses at a trip proved to be an overestimate. The best they could do was five, and the boat rode so deep with them that Beech refused to risk handling it. He stayed with the herd, and old Apling cut it loose, let the current sweep it across into slack water, and hauled it in to the far bank by winding in its cable on an old homemade capstan. Then he turned the horses into a counting pen and came back for another load.

He worked at it fiercely, as if he had a bet up that he could wear the whole ferry rig out, but it went with infernal slowness, and when the wind began to move for daylight there were a dozen horses still to cross and no place to hide them in case the ferry had other customers.

Beech waited and fidgeted over small noises until, hearing voices and the clatter of hoofs on shale far up the canyon behind him, he gave way, drove the remaining horses into the river, and swam them across, letting himself be towed along by his saddle horn and floating his clothes ahead of him on a board.

He paid for that flurry of nervousness before he got out. The water was so cold it paralyzed him, and so swift it whisked him a mile downstream before he could get his pony turned to breast it. He grounded on a gravel bar in a thicket of dwarf willows, with numbness striking clear to the center of his diaphragm and deadening his arms so he couldn't pick his clothes loose from the bundle to put on. He managed it, by using his teeth and elbows, and warmed himself a little by driving the horses afoot through the brush till he struck the ferry landing.

It had got light enough to see things in outline, and old Apling was getting ready to shove off for another crossing when the procession came lumbering at him out of the shadows. He came ashore, counted the horses into the corral to make sure none had drowned, and laid Beech under all the blankets and built up a fire to limber him out by. He got breakfast and got packed to leave, and he did some rapid expounding about the iniquity of risking the whole trip on such a wild piece of foolhardiness.

"That was the reason I wanted you to work this boat," he said. "I could have stood up to anybody that come projectin' around, and if they wanted trouble I could have filled their order for 'em. They won't bother us now, anyhow; it don't matter how bad they want to."

"I could have stood up to 'em if I'd had anything to do it with," Beech said. "You've got that pistol of mine, and I couldn't see to throw rocks. What makes you think they won't bother us? You know it was that brandin' crew comin' after us, don't you?"

"I expect that's who it was," old Apling agreed. "They ought to be out after the cattle we scattered, but you can trust a bunch of cowboys to pick out the most useless things to tend to first. I've got that pistol of yours because I don't aim for you to git in trouble with it while this trip is on. There won't anybody bother us because I've cut all the cables on the ferry, and it's lodged downstream on a gravel spit. It anybody crosses after us within fifty miles of here, he'll swim, and the people around here ain't as reckless around cold water as you are."

Beech sat up. "We got to git out of here," he said. "There's people on this side of the river that use that ferry, you old fool, and they'll have us up before every grand jury in the country from now on. The horses ain't worth it."

"What the horses is worth ain't everything," old Apling said. "There's a part of this trip ahead that you'll be glad you went through. You're entitled to that much out of it, after the work you've put in, and I aim to see that you git it. It ain't any use tryin' to explain to you what it is. You'll notice it when the time comes."

VI

They worked north, following the breaks of the river canyon, finding the rock breaks hard to travel, but easy to avoid observation in, and the grass fair in stand, but so poor and washy in body that the horses had to spend most of their time eating enough to keep up their strength so they could move.

They struck a series of gorges, too deep and precipitous to be crossed at all, and had to edge back into milder country where there were patches of plowed ground, some being harrowed over for summer fallow and others venturing out with a bright new stand of dark-green wheat.

The pasture was patchy and scoured by the wind, and all the best parts of it were under fence, which they didn't dare cut for fear of getting in trouble with the natives. Visibility was high in that section; the ground lay open to the north as far as they could see, the wind kept the air so clear that it hurt to look at the sky, and they were never out of sight of wheat ranchers harrowing down summer fallow.

A good many of the ranchers pulled up and stared after the horse herd as it went past, and two or three times they waved and rode down toward the road, as if they wanted to make it an excuse for stopping work. Old Apling surmised that they had some warning they wanted to deliver against trespassing, and he drove on without waiting to hear it.

They were unable to find a camping place anywhere among those wheat fields, so they drove clear through to open country and spread down for the night alongside a shallow pond in the middle of some new grass not far enough along to be pastured, though the horses made what they could out of it. There were no trees or shrubs anywhere around, not even sagebrush. Lacking fuel for a fire, they camped without one, and since there was no grass anywhere except around the pond, they left the horses unguarded, rolled in to catch up sleep, and were awakened about daylight by the whole herd stampeding past them at a gallop.

They both got up and moved fast. Beech ran for his pony, which was trying to pull loose from its picket rope to go with the bunch. Old Apling ran out into the dust afoot, waggling the triggerless old pistol and trying to make out objects in the half-light by hard squinting. The herd horses fetched a long circle and came back past him, with a couple of riders clouting along behind trying to turn them back into open country. One of the riders opened up a rope and swung it, the other turned in and slapped the inside flankers with his hat, and old Apling hauled up the old pistol, flipped the hammer a couple of rounds to get it warmed up, and let go at them twice.

The half darkness held noise as if it had been a cellar. The two shots banged monstrously. Beech yelled to old Apling to be careful who he shot at, and the two men shied off sideways and rode away into the open country. One of them yelled something that sounded threatening in tone as they went out of sight, but neither of them seemed in the least inclined to bring on any general engagement. The dust blew clear, the herd horses came back to grass, old Apling looked at the pistol and punched the two exploded shells out of it, and Beech ordered him to hand it over before he got in trouble.

"How do you know but what them men had a right here?" he demanded sternly. "We'd be in a fine jackpot if you'd shot one of 'em and it turned out he owned this land we're on, wouldn't we?"

Old Apling looked at him, holding the old pistol poised as if he was getting ready to lead a band with it. The light strengthened and shed a rose-colored radiance over him, so he looked flushed and joyous and lifted up. With some of the dust knocked off him, he could have filled in easily as a day star and a son of the morning, whiskers and all.

"I wouldn't have shot them men for anything you could buy me!" he said, and faced north to a blue line of bluffs that came up out of the shadows, a blue gleam of water that moved under them, a white steamboat that moved upstream, glittering as the first light struck it. "Them men wasn't here because we was trespassers. Them was horse thieves, boy! We've brought these horses to a place where they're worth stealin', and we've brought 'em through! The railroad is under them bluffs, and that water down there is the old Columbia River!"

They might have made it down to the river that day, but having it in sight and knowing that nothing could stop them from reaching it, there no longer seemed any object in driving so unsparingly. They ate breakfast and talked about starting, and they even got partly packed up for it. Then they got occupied with talking to a couple of wheat ranchers who pulled in to inquire about buying some of the horse herd; the drought had run up wheat prices at a time when the country's livestock had been allowed to run down, and so many horses had been shot and starved out that they were having to take pretty much anything they could get.

Old Apling swapped them a couple of the most jaded herd horses for part of a haystack, referred other applicants to Gervais down at the railroad, and spent the remainder of the day washing, patching clothes and saddlery, and watching the horses get acquainted once more with a conventional diet.

The next morning a rancher dropped off a note from Gervais urging them to come right on down, and adding a kind but firm admonition against running up any feed bills without his express permission. He made it sound as if there might be some hurry about catching the horse market on the rise, so they got ready to leave, and Beech looked back over the road they had come, thinking of all that had happened on it.

"I'd like it better if old Gervais didn't have to work himself in on the end of it," he said. "I'd like to step out on the whole business right now."

"You'd be a fool to do that," old Apling said. "This is outside your work contract, so we can make the old gopher pay you what it's worth. I'll want to go in ahead and see about that and about the money that he owes me and about corral space and feed and one thing and another, so I'll want you to bring 'em in alone. You ain't seen everything there is to a trip like this, and you won't unless you stay with it."

VII

There would be no ending to this story without an understanding of what that little river town looked like at the hour, a little before sundown of a windy spring day, when Beech brought the desert horse herd down into it. On the wharf below town, some men were unloading baled hay from a steamboat, with some passengers watching from the saloon deck, and the river beyond them hoisting into whitecapped peaks that shone and shed dazzling spray over the darkening water.

A switch engine was handling stock cars on a spur track, and the brakeman flagged it to a stop and stood watching the horses, leaning into the wind to keep his balance while the engineer climbed out on the tender to see what was going on.

The street of the town was lined with big leafless poplars that looked as if they hadn't gone short of moisture a day of their lives; the grass under them was bright green, and there were women working around flower beds and pulling up weeds, enough of them so that a horse could have lived on them for two days.

There was a Chinaman clipping grass with a pair of sheep shears to keep it from growing too tall, and there were lawn sprinklers running clean water on the ground in streams. There were stores with windows full of new clothes, and stores with bright hardware, and stores with strings of bananas and piles of oranges, bread and crackers and candy and rows of hams, and there were groups of anxious-faced men sitting around stoves inside who came out to watch Beech pass and told one another hopefully that the back country might make a good year out of it yet, if a youngster could bring that herd of horses through it.

There were women who hauled back their children and cautioned them not to get in the man's way, and there were boys and girls, some near Beech's own age, who watched him and stood looking after him, knowing that he had been through more than they had ever seen and not suspecting that it had taught him something that they didn't know about the things they saw every day. None of them knew what it meant to be in a place where there were delicacies to eat and new clothes to wear and look at, what it meant to be warm and out of the wind for a change, what it could mean merely to have water enough to pour on the ground and grass enough to cut down and throw away.

For the first time, seeing how the youngsters looked at him, he understood what that amounted to. There wasn't a one of them who wouldn't have traded places with him. There wasn't one that he would have traded places with, for all the haberdashery and fancy groceries in town. He turned down to the corrals, and old Apling held the gate open for him and remarked that he hadn't taken much time to it.

"You're sure you had enough of that ridin' through town?" he said. "It ain't the same when you do it a second time, remember."

"It'll last me," Beech said. "I wouldn't have missed it, and I wouldn't want it to be the same again. I'd sooner have things the way they run with us out in the high country. I'd sooner not have anything be the same a second time."

SKANASUNK

WALTER D. EDMONDS

The two children taken captive in the raid on Dygartsbush got over their fear of the Indians almost at once. The boy, Peter Kelly, was more than thirteen; Ellen Mitchel was a month or two younger; they were of an age to forget what they had seen of the raid, and indeed, in Ellen's case, that was little enough. She had gone on an errand to Dygart's for her mother and got twisted in the darkness and lost her way in the woods. She could hear the shooting, the wild high-pitched yells of the Indians, and see the glow of burning cabins through the trees or the glow of the fire against the rainy sky, but instinct had kept her in the woods. She was crouched there on the edge of a clump of bushes when Skanasunk, the Fox, came along, hauling Peter Kelly behind him.

He was a great strapping young brave. Often, in the years following, she was to remember him as he stepped round the bushes. A high leap of the fire in the clearing gave her a clear glimpse of him, all coppery and shining with the rain; the bear on his chest painted in black; the upper part of his face painted red, and his cheeks black with white stripes on them. He looked long-legged and swift, but even then, seeing him in the firelight under the dripping branches, she did not think he looked ugly; just hideous and wild and fierce. She liked those things and she liked the feeling that she belonged to him, especially when she saw the other Indians and the way they abused the women in the line of captives. She did not know that her own family had been wiped out; she thought, when she thought at all

81

about it, that her mother must be with another band of the Indians.

Ellen had a moment of horror the night old Mrs. Staats was killed helping Honus Kelly, Pete's brother and the only man taken captive, escape. Seeing Mrs. Staats's scalp dried and stretched and hooped was somehow different, it having all happened right in front of her. It made her serious, and for several days she kept tight to Pete, so close that he became embarrassed and spoke of her scornfully, calling her a sissy girl. But she accepted his taunts meekly and stuck to him like a leech; and she noticed that even Pete was inclined to stay as near to Skanasunk as possible. On the night after, he went so far as to admit that he was glad it was Skanasunk who had taken them both.

"Why?" she asked, though she echoed him in her heart.

"Aren't you too?" he demanded. "He don't look so full of poison."

"No," she said. It was true. He treated them different; he was always ready to show her how he painted the bear on his chest; he acted proud of it, though she felt she could paint one that would look a whole lot more like a bear. But for her the real reason for being glad was the feeling that she and Pete would be together.

Skanasunk confirmed this the evening after he left the main band on the headwaters of the Chemung. While the three of them hunched round their small fire that evening to watch the thin naked body of a hare give way in the boiling water, he took them into his confidence. He even smiled at them—a broad and big-toothed grin—through his worn paint. He said he was going to adopt them both. That is, he would get his wife to adopt them. Women, he explained, did the adopting in the Indian nations. She was a fine squaw, he said, and she had lost one child by her first husband and another child by him, which made her feel sad. Now that he had two healthy children for her, she would feel better. It would be fine having two healthy children in his house. It made him feel good himself to think of it. They would like it in the Indian village. Pete would not have to work, and Ellen could learn cooking and making skins soft under his wife's guidance.

"Shucks," said Pete. "I never was a hand to work. But I'm good at hunting."

"Teach you hunt," said Skanasunk. "Sometime pretty soon you big man, I buy you gun maybe. Fine gun like mine."

The name of the village was Tecarnohs. It was a small place of half a dozen houses and, perhaps, ten families, and the council house was no more than a small bark cabin in the open land by the bend of the creek. They came overland to it from the Genesee watershed, and looked down at it from one of the steep hills late in the afternoon.

The creek wound down through the narrow valley, catching a sheen from the sunlight where the woods did not shadow it. It had the look of good fishing water, and Pete said, "It appears good country to me," soberly, as his small face turned north and south, and his eyes took in the rough hills and heavy woods.

Skanasunk grunted and stretched a bare arm upstream, to point out a small house. "My house," he said. "Corn patch there. Have garden back of house." He touched Ellen's shoulder with the ball of his thumb. "See Newataquaah."

Looking down, Ellen made out the foreshortened figure of an Indian woman before the entrance of the house. She was dressed in deerskins and she was at the moment bending over a stump mortar to grind corn. Her brown hands worked the pestle steadily and a faint sound of it came up to the "tap, tap, tap," as soft as though it were the tail of the bitch patting the dust in the sunlight close by, while a mess of puppies suckled her like wrestlers. Ellen glanced quickly at Skanasunk, but he was not looking at her but over the valley. He had refreshed his paint that morning after oiling himself. His feather made a moving bar of shadow over one shoulder as it moved in the wind. It was hard to think of him as having feelings, when you looked at him, and yet she felt that he had pointed out his squaw so she would have an interest in the town. It wasn't the kind of thing you expected of an Indian, but she felt sure of it, and her thin brown face softened.

Ellen could not see herself, of course. She hardly ever thought what she looked like. She still had the lanky figure of a girl, with long flat legs that were more likely to break out running than to carry her at a nice walk. Her petticoat, grown ragged from her long journey, showed her ankles scarred and scratched, and the feet bruised, like any little girl's. But there was a suggestion of what Mrs. Staats had called her growing womanish in the slight rounding under her blue-and-white short gown. Except for that short gown, she looked all brown, almost a nut brown—brown hair, brown eyes and a clear, tanned, unfreckled skin.

Glancing at her, Pete irrationally conjured up a vision of a twelve-point buck. She looked kind of pretty, he thought; she had curly hair that showed even with the braids. Both started as Skanasunk cupped his mouth in his hands and let out a high-pitched wavering cry.

Instantly the bitch jumped to her feet, shaking off puppies right and left, and the squaw's hands stopped on the pestle. The barking of dogs broke out here and there along the creek. A couple of old men who had been smoking together in front of a house got up and shaded their eyes. Skanasunk said, "You come now," and started down the hill at an abrupt trot. The two children were hard put to it to keep pace with him.

Later that summer it seemed odd to think that she had been nervous about meeting Newataquaah. She was a small, neat, birdlike woman, not at all like the person Ellen had visualized from Skanasunk's description. Though she was ten years older than her husband, she was neither wrinkled nor bent. As Ellen came to know her better, she even began to think of her as pretty, much prettier than her own mother had been. There was no fear hanging over Newataquaah's life. And though she performed an immense amount of labor in a day, the work never seemed to oppress her and she found time for everything. As soon as she saw Skanasunk or Pete returning from a morning hunt, she would leave her garden patch or cornfield, or stop working her skins, and give them food. It was a thing every woman was expected to do. She did not ask a man if he wanted food when he entered her house; she had the food itself ready for him. She delighted in making them eat.

With Ellen she showed infinite patience. "You are my own daughter now," she would say. "I would have you sew well. You must learn beadwork. All men value a fine beadworker and a woman who tends her house. It is so everywhere." She had a slight, sidelong smile that made her black eyes shine. When Skanasunk praised some of her own handiwork, she would look down and be silent with pleasure for half a day. Ellen, who liked to work, found the life pleasant. She learned that the Indian women did the labor, not because the men made slaves of them, as white people supposed, but because they preferred it so. She also learned that hunting was more arduous than it seemed. A man might be out two days with only a piece of quitcheraw to eat before he brought in meat enough to please his wife. "Let them rest now in summer," said Newataquaah. "It is their easy time while we lay up our winter's corn. When the cold comes, then women sit inside by the fire and the men must hunt in the snow."

Peter Kelly, of course, was in his natural element, without any of his brothers or his drunken old father to order him around. Not that they ever tried to get him to work—they hardly did a lick themselves. But in Tecarnohs a man was meant to hunt and fish, and trap enough to get a couple of bales every year or two to trade for beads, an iron kettle, a gun or a knife. He lorded it over the Indian lads, for even those who were larger than he were not permitted to go out with a gun, and it soon was made evident that Pete was far and away the best shot in the village. Skanasunk made no bones about it, but went around making boasts of his son's prowess.

"It's a queer thing," Peter said one evening to Ellen. "Old Skanasunk, he really does think I'm his son. He told me about his son, and apparently, if he was alive, he'd be four years old now. But I got his name, and it don't make no difference—I just am, the way his heathen mind looks at it. My name's Deawendote. Know what that means? Constant Dawn. Don't they have the craziest ideas? It's the same way with Newataquaah; I bet she figures you're her genuine daughter, the one she had by her first man."

"Yes, she does," Ellen said.

"It's kind of a nuisance, you know," Pete said.

"What do you mean?"

Pete was at work swabbing out the musket. His small dark face was intent upon his job, and when he answered her he used his offhand voice. "Why," he said, "I was talking to Skanasunk about it. I said to him, I said, 'If you really think we're your own children,' I said, 'how are me and Ellen going to get married?' "

Ellen raised her eyes from the legging seam she was stitching with sinew. "You and me marry!"

He had given her one quick look. "Sure," he said. "You want to stay here, don't you? I mean, when are you and me going to get away? White people don't come this way. Why, we might have to stay here four, five years."

"I hadn't thought," she confessed. "But we don't need to get married about it."

Pete crossed his legs. "Do as you're a mind to," he said. "I ain't going to bother you. I can get along with one of them little Indian girls. Some of them are real pretty and no browner than you be. I just thought it'd save you marrying an Indian."

Ellen gasped and stared at him.

"I don't think I'd want to marry an Indian, you know."

Pete nodded.

"That's it, but how can you and me marry if we're brother and sister this way? That's what I said to Skanasunk. First he said we was both too young, but I said no, you was about eighteen now and I was only four, so we'd be doing what him and Newataquaah had done. Then I told him your real ma wanted you to marry me before we turned into Indians."

"You know that's not so, Peter Kelly."

"Well, I bet she'd rather have you marry even me than a greasy Indian. Anyhow, I told him. And he said he'd have to look it up with the Honundeont, whoever she is. Kind of a she preacher, maybe. She lives down on the Genesee somewhere. This town ain't got one—not big enough—and he won't see her for a while, probably." He laid the gun aside and grinned. "Poor old Skanasunk, he's so mixed up with what we're his children and Newataquaah's, and being two white people—which he don't want to admit, but knows is so—and how old we are one way and how old the other, he's fit to scratch the back of his ear with his hind leg. But just the same, White Blanket, I wouldn't mind marrying you."

Ellen flushed. She felt the flush inside her overdress, all over her. She didn't see why she should feel so hot about plain nonsense.

"I guess I've got something to say about that, Master Smart!"

She lifted her chin at him, but he just grinned at her flushed face.

"Oh, no, you haven't. You're just a squaw, or you will be when you argue with me. And squaws don't never argue with their menfolks, either. Just remember that."

Tecarnohs was a peaceful place. No war parties passed through it, for it lay between the large towns of the Genesee, from which war parties always headed against the Mohawk Valley settlements, and those on the Allegheny, whose young braves preferred to strike south. Newataquaah, like the other women, harvested a fair crop of corn and vegetables against the winter, and the hunting continued better than usual.

Toward the middle of October, Skanasunk and Peter, with most of the younger men, struck off down Oil Creek, heading for the Allegheny, which they called the O-hee-yo, and the Ohio lands. For a week beforehand, Newataquaah kept herself and Ellen busy pressing parched corn and maple sugar into cakes of quitcheraw, and dicing smoked deer meat and dried blueberries into pemmican. Extra moccasins had to be made, new brow straps braided from elm fibers, leggings and hunting blouses patched. Ellen made Peter, secretly, a coonskin cap. She thought he was not used to going bareheaded in cold weather, and shaping it for him made her experience a queer sense of motherliness, as if he were a boy she had to look out for. Both of them turned bright red when she presented it the night before they left.

He tried it on in the house, and Newataquaah admired it. Skanasunk said, "Fine white-man hat"; but when the squaw wanted to sit up all night to make one, too, he said, no, he was an Indian. It made Pete act sheepish, but he wore it away in the morning, which happened to be a warm one, and Ellen was content. She and Newataquaah had a quiet two months after the men left, during which they made clothes and visited the women in the other houses and spent half of each day bringing dry wood down off the hills.

The snow mounted quickly in their steep valley, once it began to fall, and soon the village was snowed deep in and the roofs of the houses looked like canoes bottom up upon the crust. The houses themselves became warm and snug. They were laced together by snowshoe trails. Snowshoes were made for the little children, so that they might learn, and Ellen, using them daily, learned why the mothers taught their children to toe in.

The men returned from their hunting early in December. They came in just ahead of the first real blizzard, their packs and clothes white and stiff with the driven icy flakes. They had had fair luck and got plenty of beaver and had killed three deer in a small yard on the way back.

At the single-family house of Skanasunk, Newataquaah's eyes sparkled. "Now we will have fresh meat to cook for our two men," she cried to Ellen, and went, laughing, about her work. Ellen herself had not realized how long they had been without fresh meat. While the men were away, all the women had eaten lightly, conserving every bit of smoked meat and their dried berries and squash. But the heaped pots Newataquaah brought out were like a New Year's feast. Skanasunk and Pete gorged themselves until they had to sleep. While they slept, the woman and the girl went through their packs, exclaiming at the worn-out moccasins and the mending to be done, and showing each other the best pelts. It was a happy time.

The winter passed and spring came with a rush and a white frothing of wild cherry on the hills, while the roar of the creek was a voice that filled the valley day after day. In May, Newataquaah began to watch the growing moon. The day before it filled, she took Ellen to the garden patch and planted her corn and beans in regular spaced hills, five seeds of each, and in the land between the hills she planted squash—the yellow crane-neck squash, and the green round squash, and scalloped squash, the pumpkin and sunflowers. Then every day she visited the patch, watching first the white lobes of the beans, and then the green pencils of the rolled corn leaves, pierce the earth. That day she made a scarecrow out of an old blouse and leggings of Skanasunk's, fashioning a ball of bearskin for the head and fastening a feather to it; and that night she roused Ellen stealthily and beckoned her out to make with her the woman's circle of the crop. Ellen went from curiosity, but the darkness of a starless night filled her with a sense of magic. Newataquaah's hard thin hand with the warm pads on the fingers grasped her own to lead her. They went without light, letting the narrow hard-worn path direct their feet. A little way from the field, Newataquaah stopped and turned to Ellen, placing her finger on her lips first to silence her. Ellen nodded.

Then she felt the hands lift her overdress up over her shoulders and unknot the skirt thong. A moment later, Newataquaah herself undressed. Then she took hands with her again and led the way to the cornfield. Once there, she let go.

Dragging their clothes along the ground behind them, the two made the circuit of the planted ground three times; by the power of their garments, yet warm from their bodies, drawing a ring around the field that would keep off the cutworm, the wireworm that ate the corn roots, the caterpillar and the grasshopper, and insure the fruitfulness of the crop. It was a strange mysterious business to Ellen. Newataquaah had unbraided her hair and let it hang in a loose invisible cloud upon her shoulders. Clouds covered the stars. One could not see—only a darker shadow of surrounding woods against an inky sky. Peepers along the creek, with voices clear above the sound of water, piped with their eternal unconcern; but the woman and the girl went silently, feeling the cold dewy earth between their toes. Once as Ellen, overtaking at a corner of the field, brushed her shoulder against the cool bare skin of the squaw, she was invaded through the touch by a sensation of the power in her body; and when they stole back into the lodge, so quietly that even the dogs were not disturbed, she felt herself mysteriously grown.

But that summer they became aware of the war. Without warning, the Indians from the Allegheny villages passed by Tecarnohs. They came and went in a day, stopping only to be fed. Skanasunk, with the men of the village, held a long council during the afternoon, and once Peter came back to the house to talk to Ellen.

"There's two armies coming," he said. "One's coming up the Allegheny and the other's coming from Tioga." His face was moody and he acted restless. He stared a moment into Ellen's puzzled face. "Maybe we ought to clear out."

"Clear out?" she echoed.

"Yes. We're white. The armies are burning the towns. Maybe the Indians here won't like us so well now."

"Oh," she said. "But Skanasunk and Newataquaah wouldn't do anything to us."

"They ain't the only Indians." He looked at her again. "Don't you want to go home?"

Ellen looked back at him and suddenly shook her head.

"Me neither," he said. "I like it here."

He dug the ground with his toe. "Here I'm as good as anybody.

They think I'm better than most. I am too. Back home, I'm just a Kelly. Everybody but Honus is killed."

She had nothing to say. But she heard his voice tighten:

"Back home you wouldn't want to see me anymore."

"I would too." She blushed, but her brown eyes met his.

"It wouldn't matter," he said. "They wouldn't let you."

Her thin hands made fists.

"I don't think they'd do anything to us. Let's stay."

"I got to look out for you."

"Silly," she said. "They won't hurt me."

He seemed suddenly relieved.

"I'll go back and hang around the council house and see what's going on. But you stay where I can find you."

She promised, and watched him trot away. He did not return till nearly dark. Then he came with Skanasunk.

Skanasunk was serious. "Most people want to go to Niagara—anyway, to Chenandoanes," he said to them. "I do not want to go. I do not think the white army will find our little town. Newataquaah does not want to go. We think Niagara is a bad place for our children. The British would find them and make them white again."

Newataquaah shook her head vigorously.

"Even if all the others leave Tecarnohs," continued Skanasunk, "we can live here. *Hano!*"

He stared round solemnly on all three of them; his big nose, black shiny eyes and flat cheeks like an exaggerated bird's head in the firelight. Way off, a dog was barking, shrill as a fox. For a moment they were silent, listening; then Newataquaah's soft voice unexpectedly broke in: "Maybe our children wish to be white again."

It was the first time Ellen had ever seen Skanasunk show surprise.

He looked so completely taken aback, so upset and so troubled that Ellen felt like crying out, "No, no!" But she drew her breath and looked down modestly at the toes of her moccasins, and left it for Pete to answer.

Pete said, "We both of us like it here. We talked about it this afternoon. But maybe some of the other people won't like us now. Maybe we ought to get out before they get mad at us."

Skanasunk beamed all over, and Newataquaah, with a happy laugh, caught Ellen's hand. "They all like you," Skanasunk said. "They will not hurt you. You are my son." He drew himself up on his hams and announced: "We stay here."

The runners coming in during the third week in August reported the American army of six hundred men at Daudehokto, the village on the bend of the Allegheny only a few miles west. Before night, half the village had packed up and taken the trail to Chenandoanes. The few who still remained stood silent, watching them go: the women toiling ahead up the steep trail, and the men a restless rear guard looking back.

After they were gone, the valley for a while seemed desolate. Night came with a scud of rain and dimmed the hilltops. The remaining men held another council.

Newataquaah, alone in the house with Ellen, confided that it was Skanasunk's plan, if the others left, to take her and Ellen and Pete back into the hills and hide out until the army was out of the country. They would then return, using the caches of parched corn to live on, and building a new house.

But the army did not come. Next morning a solitary Indian with a bullet hole in his left arm came up the valley to inform them that the army had headed back along its trail. They gave the Indian a feast.

After that, the life went on as it had before and the war no more affected them. The women went out to pick the blueberries and the men hunted. There were too few of them to drive deer, even with the children left, and they killed only half a dozen in four days. The wasp nests were built not very high that fall, and Skanasunk predicted a wet bad winter. The corn harvest at Tecarnohs was only fair.

The first snow came in November—a light wet slush that set the small brooks flooding as it melted. Heavy mists hung in the valley, even during the days. The Indians seemed to feel it more than Ellen and Pete; they became silent, there was less laughter when the women visited.

It was during these weeks that Peter's uneasiness returned. He spent more time in the house, keeping Ellen company. His small black-Irish face sharpened. Once when they were alone, he said, "I wish we'd gone back."

Ellen was placid. "Skanasunk and Newataquaah are staying here on account of us. We couldn't leave them if we wanted to. Not rightly, Pete."

"I guess that's so." Pete in his Indian dress looked small and unhappy. Ellen moved impulsively toward him, bent her face and kissed his lips.

She said, "I'll never marry anybody else but you, Pete."

Pete's face went white under the tan.

"You mean that?" he said huskily. And when she nodded, "Honest to God? Cross your heart?" She nodded each time. Her brown braids twitched beside the sharp little points her breasts made under her overdress.

He tried to think of something more to say, and while he fumbled

90

in his mind, he heard Newataquaah returning. Ellen heard her too. They moved apart from each other and faced the door. Newataquaah was coughing.

Newataquaah was sick. As soon as she came through the door, both children realized that. She had been up on the hillsides looking for dry wood. She was wet, and she had a chill. As soon as she laid down her faggot, she huddled beside the fire and asked Ellen to brew her some hemlock tea.

She said she felt better after she had drunk it all, and smiled deprecatingly, as though she had made too much fuss already. "We must cook the food for the men," she said. But she did not look right to Ellen. There was a dark flush in her cheeks and her eyes were too bright. When she put her hand on the woman's forehead, Ellen knew she had fever. Ellen said, "The men can wait. Now you are going to bed. You must take off those wet things and put on dry, and I will heat your blankets." She hung a bearskin on the poles nearest the fire, and several blankets, warming them thoroughly, while Newataquaah undressed in the cubicle.

Newataquaah said several times, "I met Tekhatenhokwa's wife on the hill. She was really sick. I did not think she would get home. I had to carry down her wood."

"And then go back up for your own. I know," Ellen thought, reproaching herself that she had not gone also. One got so used to all the work Newataquaah did that one hardly noticed her. She was sitting down, swaying a little from the waist, forward over her knees. Ellen went quickly to her and pushed her back firmly onto the bearskin. "Peter! Peter!" Peter, who had withdrawn while Newataquaah undressed, poked in his dark face.

"I think you'd better hunt up Skanasunk," Ellen said.

"What do you think she's got?"

"I don't know. I thought it was an ague, but it's some kind of a fever. Her breath sounds queer. I wish you'd go right off, Pete."

"All right," he said. "Don't get scared."

Ellen thought that her mother would know what to do right away. But she didn't even know what was wrong. And lately she had been feeling like a grown-up woman. All at once it came to her that Newataquaah was really the only Indian in the village she knew well. It wasn't the Indian way of living that she liked; it was Newataquaah that made her think she liked it. She longed now for white towels to bathe the woman's face with, for a piece of camphor to keep the air pure, and, above all, for the conveniences of a good log cabin, with shelves and tea kettles and spoons. Sitting on the edge of the cubicle, she was aware of the Indian's brown hand reaching out to pat hers.

"Don't look so afraid. I am a strong woman." The same sidelong smile in the brown face. "This is the first time I was ever sick, so I shall get well fast."

Peter came in with Skanasunk. The latter had been visiting in the village and smelled rank of tobacco. He stalked over and stood beside the cubicle with his arms folded.

"Are you sick?" he asked.

"I am sick." She said it apologetically, and added, "But not very sick."

"I think you are very sick," he replied, looking along his nose at her.

He ate a little from the stew Ellen had ready for him, then got his blanket and hunched himself before the fire. He stayed that way all night. Ellen slept only in spells; whenever she looked up, he was still there, looking down at the fire.

In the morning, however, Newataquaah seemed a little brighter. She called Skanasunk and informed him she had dreamed of a false face. It was not, therefore, a sickness but a demon in her. Skanasunk looked immeasurably relieved. He left the house at once, and as soon as he had gone, Newataquaah, in a hoarse voice, asked Ellen to prepare a feast for two people. "There are only two false faces in Tecarnohs now. They will come when it grows dark again."

Ellen had seen the false faces once visit a girl in the village who had sore eyes, and she was prepared for them. But it seemed fearful to have them come to one's own house. A little after dusk, she and Peter and Skanasunk heard the whisper of their shell rattles through the falling snow, and suddenly they were inside the door, two of them, in wooden masks with great stringy heads of false hair. The hideous faces were real enough in the firelight to have been alive, with the living eyes behind them; and yet they had no life.

They scuttered swiftly toward the fire, raising and lowering their faces with erratic jerks, while the bean seeds rattled softly in the turtle shells. They gathered ashes from the fire and, approaching Newataquaah's cubicle, powdered her with ashes. Then they made a circle of the fire, shaking their rattles here and there.

Suddenly they joined and swooped upon Newataquaah. Ellen opened her mouth to protest as they seized the sick woman and three times forced her round the house between them.

She could not walk and her head wobbled on her shoulders. She tried feebly to follow their erratic steps. The sweat streamed down her face; her eyes were glazed and foolish; and when they finally flung her down on her blankets, her labored breathing sounded like the fading rattles. Before Ellen could cover her, the false faces had gone.

Skanasunk sat with his head covered. Even Pete was wordless. It seemed crazy to Ellen. She did what she could to comb the mess of ashes out of Newataquaah's hair and wash her face. She did not dare undress her, overheated as she was, for the wind had come up and drafts were shaking the flames of the fire. But she reheated the food the false faces had not tasted, and they ate together, without speaking. When she went out into the little vestibule for more wood, she saw that it was snowing heavily.

Newataquaah seemed no better in the morning. After eating, Skanasunk left the house. He was gone all morning. The snow stopped toward noon and a high wind cut through the valley from the north, clearing the pine boughs of white, and humming through the hardwood limbs. Peter hung round the house. He did not speak much except to whisper, "Do you think she's going to die?" Ellen did not know what to answer. She only knew that Newataquaah was desperately sick. Toward dark, Skanasunk returned from a second expedition. He had a snowbird in a little basket. This he hung at the far end of the house; and after it had been there a little while, the bird began to make small twittering notes.

It twittered during the night from time to time. Ellen heard it over the wind. She would have liked to set it free, but Pete told her not to touch it. "I don't know what he wants it for, but I followed him this afternoon. He's been digging a hole."

"He thinks she's going to die!"

"I guess he does. Tekhatenhokwa's squaw died yesterday, and there's a lot more sick. Half the Indians is sick with the same disease, I guess." Pete shivered. After black dark, Ellen felt shivery too. In lulls of the wind she could hear shrill screaming wails of Indian women in the village. Even the bird hushed when they were audible.

Skanasunk sat beside Newataquaah's cubicle. "If it wasn't bad weather, I'd leave here," Pete whispered.

He started suddenly. Ellen got to her feet, walked round Skanasunk and looked into the cubicle. She didn't feel sure. But Skanasunk said, "She is dead." He had not moved.

Ellen gave way. She flung herself into her own cubicle and covered herself with her robes, trying to shut out the Indian house. But it could not be shut out. The smell of the skins covering her was Indian. The smoke was Indian. It was not clean. It was terrifying.

Peter sneaked up to her and touched the mound of blankets.

"Ellen," he whispered.

Her muffled voice answered him: "Leave me alone!"

But he kept his hand on the blankets.

Skanasunk took no notice of her or of Pete. He continued to sit by the fire, unmoving, his big-nosed face like a carved image. In the morning, Pete went to the village and gave the news of Newataquaah's death, and a few Indians came up to the house to condole with the relatives. The women got Ellen aside to weep with them, but she did not want to weep. Newataquaah dead was not the same to her. She was not a human being anymore. She was a dead Indian. The women glanced askance at Ellen for making so little noise. They finally asked her when she was going to dress the body, so it could be buried; but Ellen could not bear to touch it.

The women did the work and left without addressing her. When they had gone, Skanasunk rose and ordered Ellen to bring a kettle of food, uncooked, some burning punk and a little faggot of sticks. He told Peter to carry the bird in the little basket. Then he himself picked up Newataquaah and carried her from the house.

There was no fog that day; a new snow had begun to fall—a cold driving storm of dry hard flakes. Even in the thick grove of hemlocks where the Indian finally stopped, it sifted down with a continual sibilance through the heavy branches.

There was a round hole in the snow, in which Skanasunk placed the body, crouching slightly, the sightless eyes turned eastward. Beside the body he placed the filled kettle. Then he covered the hole with limb wood and piled earth in a mound upon it. He stood still a while when he was done before he took the basket from Pete and opened the cover.

The little snowbird hopped up on the rim, clasping it with his wiry toes. Suddenly, with a soft twitter, it let go and flipped up into the branches. None of them could follow it far in the snow. As soon as it had disappeared, Skanasunk knelt down and started a small fire. They left while it still crackled brightly, a tiny spot of color in the black and white of woods and snow.

Skanasunk had changed. The whole village had changed. As the snow drifted in, it seemed like death made visible. Three of Tekhatenhokwa's children died after the coming of the new year. He died himself two weeks later, and there was no relative to bury him or make a lamentation. The snow had become so deep and the ground so frozen that the bodies could not be buried, but were left on tree platforms in the ancient fashion. The Indians seemed to have no resistance to the disease, but neither Pete nor Ellen caught it. Once an Indian woman stopped Ellen and said, "The Honundeonts have said we were not sick this way before white people came." Ellen did not know what to answer, and hurried home, but she could feel the woman's eyes following her and hear her heavy coughing. None of the Indians laughed anymore. She remembered how Newataquaah, and even Skanasunk, used to laugh. He had changed more than the others. He would sit by the fire, hour after hour, following Ellen's motions with his black eyes. He made her nervous and afraid. She asked Pete to stay nearby one day.

"Why?" asked Pete.

"I don't know. He makes me afraid."

Pete, studying her, suddenly thought he understood. Ellen was growing up faster than he was. But he didn't say so to her. He merely made a point of never going out of call while Skanasunk was in the house. At nights, the two of them sat together on the other side of the fire, whispering to each other if they had anything to say. "Do Indians go crazy?" Ellen asked.

"Everything goes crazy," Pete said "Even hedgehogs do, I guess."

Ellen had to work hard, doing all the work for herself and two men. It left her tired out at nights, and easy to frighten. She shuddered when Pete said that.

"We'll leave here when the snow goes," Pete said. He began turning over plans in his mind.

That night Skanasunk began to cough. He lay in his cubicle for days, or dragged himself out to the fire like a dog and sat huddled close up to it. He hardly ate at all, and the flesh seemed to shrink on his skull, so that his eyes appeared to hang loose in overlarge sockets. It required all the fortitude she could muster for Ellen to nurse him the three days he was sickest, and she had to get Peter to help move him. Skanasunk dreamed of a false face, as Newataquaah had done, but Ellen would not let Pete find the surviving one to come and dance. She thought now that it was the false faces as much as the disease that had killed Newataquaah. She did not know why she worked so hard to save the Indian, but at times she felt that Newataquaah was nearby, watching, and she was afraid not to help him. She had a presentiment of Newataquaah's presence whenever she saw a snowbird. There was one especially that seemed to hang round the house.

Skanasunk survived. The sickness left him so weak, however, that Peter felt he could leave the house safely, and went hunting, staying away all day.

During that day, when Ellen gave him his food, Skanasunk broke his long silence: "Listen to me."

She looked up from her own ladle.

"Yes, *Hanih*." She gave him the Indian name for "father."

"Listen to me," he repeated. She had a strange feeling that the intentness in his black eyes had taken her own and fixed them, so that she could not turn her own away. "Newataquaah is dead. Skanasunk has no wife. Skanasunk has no mother. You have no mother. So Skanasunk must speak himself." He drew his breath so lightly that his chest hardly rose. "Skanasunk is not your *Hanih*. You are white."

As he paused, she at last managed to wrench her eyes away.

"Listen to me. A young girl should marry an old man. It is the ancient law. It is better that way. Skanasunk is not old, but he is a good man. *Hano!*"

Ellen had no idea what she should do or say. She could only cry, "Peter, Peter," silently. She could not answer Skanasunk. She could only stare at his sunken face, which seemed, to her, to have become cruel and ruthless, as cold and flat-cheeked as an eagle's. When, after a while, he said, "I am still sick," she could stand it no longer.

She was like a little girl running out of the house. She caught up her faggot strap from the vestibule as an excuse, and all that afternoon she dawdled on the hillside, watching for Pete's return.

She intercepted him on the hill trail and blurted out her news before he could begin speaking. He had half a doe, cut up, and he listened to her with his face intent and white.

"We can't go now," he said. "The snow's plain slush. It'll be two weeks before we can travel, even if the weather holds warm."

"I want to go now. I can keep up with you. The snow's not so deep."

Pete, with his long mussed hair, looked wild and frightened.

"Stop blatting, can't you? We've got to wait till the snow's gone. Anybody could track us now." He stopped, looking down at the musket. "We've got to wait till we can travel fast. There's only powder for about four shots left. We can't use it hunting."

She hadn't thought of that. Nobody had been out of Tecarnohs to trade since the middle of last summer. "Can't you shoot a bow and arrow?"

"No," he said glumly. "Only Indians are good at that." Then he became practical again: "I've got the other half of this doe hung up. I'll smoke it tomorrow. Maybe in ten days we can start."

The weather held. The late March thawing took the snow from the woods, but left the brooks so high that they made hard crossing. Ellen and Pete had crossed the Genesee on a raft, headed north of the Conhocton, and made the southern circuit of the lakes. At the head of both Seneca and Cayuga they found marks of the Continental Army, and rummaged twice in burned towns, looking for corn.

The trip had taken longer than they had expected. Their venison had given out and their corn was low.

At night Peter cut hemlock boughs with Skanasunk's war hatchet and they slept close together, doubling their blankets. They had encountered the tracks of about forty men, mostly Indians, on the Conhocton, and considering it a war party, Peter had doubled west and north to find a swamp where they could lose their own trail, spending two days in the process.

Ellen followed him, blindly accepting his lead. She felt complete-ly secure in his knowledge of the woods, knowing that as long as she could follow him far enough, he would lead her into the Mohawk Valley. The trouble was to keep walking. They did not talk much, even at nights, when they lay together in their flimsy lean-tos. They were too exhausted and too cold; for, after seeing the track of the war party, Pete refused to build fires.

It was the day after they had crossed the headwaters of the Owego River that they began to feel that they were being followed. By then they were so short of food that the few grains of parched corn that Pete doled out were not enough to warm them. A heavy frost had settled, and finally Pete agreed that they must have a fire.

They built a small one and huddled over it, luxuriating in the strange sensation of outer warmth. Looking across it at Ellen, Pete was struck by her thinness.

Her face looked immeasurably older and gray under the weather burn. It made her brown hair seem darker colored and more heavy. He said suddenly, "You're a pretty good girl, Ellen. You ain't made a fuss at all, even when I got twisted sometimes." She only smiled a little. Her back was slumped and she hugged her knees, resting her chin on them. Her knees had grown knobby as she lost flesh.

Finally she asked, "How much farther is it, do you think?"

"I don't know. I guess it's a week's travel to the Unadilla, maybe."

"Then how far?"

"Two days into German Flats for us."

"Nine days isn't so long a time."

He said abruptly, "If I see a deer tomorrow, I'll take a chance and shoot it."

She started to smile, started to say, "That's wonderful," but suddenly her lips grew wet; and then she buried her face and started crying. It was while she was crying that Pete saw the snowbird, and said, "That's queer."

"What is?"

"That snowbird. It's about dark. I've hardly ever seen one so late in spring either."

She stopped crying to look at the little bird. The sight of it made her remember Newataquaah, and so she thought of Skanasunk. They had slipped out one morning; Pete first, to collect the jerked deer meat; she later, pretending to go for wood, and meeting him on the hill over the village. They had gone down the far side, climbing over rocky places to hide their trail, and then wading a small brook for nearly a mile. By dusk, Pete figured they had had a seven-mile start.

They watched the snowbird hang around for several minutes, and after it was gone, crept under their hemlock lean-to. They could still feel the fire's warmth against their feet. But Ellen woke Pete several times by talking in her sleep about Newataquaah and Skanasunk. She made him uneasy. In the morning he did what he had not done for several days. He scouted round the camp.

He found no tracks that looked human. But he did find a black squirrel dead under a tree, and there was nothing to show how it had died. When he picked it up, he saw that its neck was broken, but he had never heard of a squirrel dying of a broken neck. He carried it back to their camp and they roasted it over a small fire. He told Ellen, however, that he had decided not to shoot that day, as long as they had been so lucky as to find the squirrel.

A little after noon, though, he came on the track of a single Indian, and the track was fresh. Ellen saw it too. It was following a small deer run eastward. Both of them realized then how fortunate it was that they had not tried to hunt a deer.

Pete thought they ought to follow the trail to see where the man was heading. They went very slowly, making no sound, until finally it brought them to a camp site where half a dozen Indians had spent the night. Pete made Ellen stand still off the run while he rummaged round the tracks. When he returned, his face was troubled. "Our man joined up with the others. They broke camp, but he turned back, so he's somewhere back of us now."

The next two days they hurried. But they saw nothing. They began to get desperate for food, so that Ellen kept eyeing even the robins hungrily. Pete looked for hedgehogs, hoping to find one on the ground. But all the hedgehogs they saw were well up in trees, and seemed inclined to stay there. Then, on the third day, as they followed another deer path, they found one lying dead.

They stopped where they were and made a fire and feasted, too hungry even to question their providence until they had done eating. Peter, finally brought to a sense of his own carelessness, dragged Ellen off the path and made her hide under a stony hill while he scouted. Again he found the tracks of one man. They led him due north and then east for nearly a mile, and were lost in a shallow river crossing.

Pete studied the river thoughtfully. The trunk of an enormous hemlock lay out into the ford under water and two huge roots, upended, were joined like praying hands. The queerness of the tree raised an echo of something he had been told. Suddenly he remembered. Honus had said it was the best lower crossing of the Unadilla.

He lay on the bank for a long time, staring across the smooth slide of brown water without seeing anything. After sunset he went back for Ellen and told her they had reached the Unadilla. He led her in a wide sweep northward, telling her they would follow to the mouth of Butternut Creek, head through the Edmeston Patent and go overland west of Andrustown. He knew that way, once he had found Butternut Creek.

Now they could travel at night having a moon. They made fair progress, spotted the Butternut in the gray before dawn. They were going to cross, when an owl began hooting from the far bank.

Pete stood stock-still.

"Listen," he whispered. "That ain't no bird."

Ellen could not tell.

"We better wait. It don't sound right to me."

As they waited, a group of men bunched on the bank above them. Then they lined out again over the river. Their shapes were dark shadows against the water, holding guns above their heads. But even in the darkness, the children could make out that the arms were bare.

"Indians," Pete breathed into her ear. After an hour of silence, they heard an owl hoot again. He said, "That's a natural-sounding owl." It came from the far side of the river. "We'll chance crossing."

It was next morning on the hills south of German Flats that they were sure. Pete had said, "That sounds like a deer ahead." But they did not care. They were only two hours from the forts. They could already see the wide expanse of sky that meant the valley, between the trees ahead.

It was a day of bright sunlight. The naked brow of the hill with the dead winter's grass dry underfoot gave them a view of the forts on each side of the river, the burned sites of settlers' houses, and men plowing the ground while a guard surrounded the field they worked in.

Then, as they stepped over the edge of the hill, they saw a feathered arrow stuck in the ground. Beside it was a blue square of calico, and on the calico were laid two fox ears and a little silver brooch of Indian make.

"It's Newataquaah's," Ellen exclaimed. "What are the fox ears for?"

"It's Skanasunk. So we would know who the brooch was from, if you didn't recognize it."

"You mean he left it for us?"

"I guess. I guess it was him all along."

Pete was lost in thought. Then he set the musket down—the musket he had never fired on all their long journey—with the powder horn beside it. "He's hanging round somewhere. He'll find it all right. But I guess he means for me to take the arrow. I guess he didn't have nothing else for me."

Long after the war, when she had been Mrs. Peter Kelly for many years, Ellen used to like to wear the brooch. The children often humored her by asking why she wore a queer thing like it, and then she would tell them about how she and Mr. Kelly lived among the Indians.

THE LADY
AND THE LASH

HAL G. EVARTS

The first customer had settled in my chair for a shave that morning when the Shafter brothers rode into Wagon Box. I was stropping the old razor just as their horses pulled up out front and spurs jingled on the plank walk. Sim Shafter shouldered through the door, followed close by Con—two big men wearing guns. Guns were common enough in our part of the territory; most cattlemen packed them on the range and in town too. It was the look on Sim's face that sobered me.

He stared at the man in my chair, stared all around the barbershop. Then those gray eyes swung back to me.

"Where is he, Doc?" Sim said quietly.

He was like that, a slow, closemouthed man, thick in the shoulders and muscled like a bull, and just about as hard to stop. You didn't howdy him or pass the time of day. Sim Shafter brushed talk aside like it was a waste of time, and time was cash.

"Where's who?" I said.

"That tintype fellow. The picture taker."

Outside my window the July sun was shining and across Tongue Creek the bare hills shimmered in a heat haze. Another scorcher of a day, but right sudden it seemed cold to me.

"Lee Dowd?" I said. "He cleared out last night."

"I know that. Where to?"

If I had known I wouldn't have told him. In the six years since I'd set up shop in Wagon Box the Shafter boys hadn't spent a dime with

101

me. Did their own barbering on each other. Some people called Sim ambitious and thrifty, a shrewd trader. I'd call him worse. Out of sweat and man-killing work and billy-goat stubbornness he'd built the family's original section into the biggest ranch around. Out of tears and blood, too, I guess, for he drove his sister and his brother like he drove himself. A hard man, Sim Shafter was, with a silver dollar for a soul.

"Didn't tell me where," I said. "He just drifted out."

Sim considered this in his deliberate way, then turned back to the door past Con, who had been standing motionless behind him. Con was his brother's shadow, five years younger, almost as big and stubborn, and maybe slower thinking. But I always had a hunch that at least he wanted to be civil, just didn't know how.

So I said, "What's wrong, Con?"

Con's eyes were troubled. "He run off with Emmie."

I put down my razor. "Lee ran off with your sister?"

Con nodded. "Leastways she wasn't in her room this morning."

Outside, Sim was peering up and down the street, hitching at his shell belt. "Come on, Con," he called. "They can't be far. We'll find 'em." That's when I saw the whip coiled on his saddle horn.

To understand this you have to know about Lee Dowd. I've served all kinds in my chair—cowpokes and drummers, nesters and sheriffs, miners and soldiers, and more than a few on the dodge. But I've never met one like Lee Dowd, and never will again. Different from the common run, but he wasn't crazy, like some folks claimed. A dreamer, maybe that's the word. He must have been to fall in love with Emmie Shafter. I could've told him that was one dream without a future.

It was a sizzling afternoon late in June when he first turned up. I saw this wagon with a saggy top crawling down the street, pulled by one sorry sway-back mule. The driver took a turn through our business district, the whole block of it, and reined up in front of my place. He climbed down from the seat, beat the dust out of his pants and grinned.

"My name's Dowd," he said. "Lee Dowd. From Missouri. And mighty glad to make your acquaintance, sir."

I shook hands and invited him in, mainly out of curiosity, pegging him for some sort of peddler. His raggedy sun-bleached hair curled over his ears, his shirt was patched and faded almost white, and his cracked boots squeaked on my floor. He was tall and skinny, a gangly, awkward-moving man with a hungry look in his soft hound-dog eyes that seemed to say he wanted to make friends with the whole wide world. I didn't figure him for the price of a shave, but he climbed into the chair and handed me a printed card: *Leander T. Dowd, Photographer. Portraiture a Specialty. Family Gatherings, Weddings, Anniversaries, All Occasions.*

"Pretty little town, Wagon Box," he said. "I'm looking for space to do some business the next few days."

"That's one thing we got plenty of in this desert," I said. "Space."

He gave me another grin, sighed and leaned back while I lathered up. "Yes, sir," he said, "she's big all right. I been four days crossing from the mountains. Big and kind of—wonderful."

"Yup," I said. "If you like wind and dust and heat and alkali water, it's paradise."

He got to talking then, and I learned that he traveled about from town to town in his wagon, taking portraits wherever he found a customer, charging a dollar or swapping a picture for his bed and keep. It seemed a strange, shiftless way to live, but he didn't speak like a tramp. He was a queer one for sure, plain peculiar.

Right now he planned to stay in Wagon Box over the Fourth of July and he wanted a likely spot to park his wagon. I owned a vacant lot next door, between my place and Jake Groot's saloon, and I told him he was welcome to camp there and use my back-porch pump. He offered to pay rent, but I said no, that we'd call it square if he took my picture.

I was wiping the soap off his chin when Sim Shafter stepped into the shop. Sim didn't nod or say as much as "Afternoon, Doc," though I hadn't seen him since early spring. He came straight to the point. "Con's got a bellyache," he said.

Emmie Shafter was hanging back timidly by the door, and I smiled at her, thinking she must have pestered her brother to drive in from the ranch.

"If Con's got a bad one," I told Sim, "you better send for the doctor in Chloride."

"I can't spare the time to ride ninety miles over there and back," Sim said.

I'm not a real doctor. Now and again I'm called on to set a bone or pull an aching tooth, because we have no doctor, but I know better than to shrug off a stomach ache. I knew better, too, than to argue with Sim, and I said dryly, "Well, he's your brother, but I've got some pain killer you can try."

"How much?"

I got down a bottle of pills from the shelf where I keep a few medical supplies. "Six bits."

Sim grunted. "That's pretty steep for a few pills."

"Cheaper than a ninety-mile ride to Chloride."

You couldn't embarrass the man or shame him. I knew he was weighing the cost of those pills, not against the chance that Con might die, but against the man-hours lost till Con got well enough to work again. Finally he fished a worn, greasy purse out of his hip pocket, unsnapped it and laid three quarters on my palm.

"These better work," he said.

"They'll work," I told him. "You better pray Con hasn't got a ruptured appendix."

He turned and tramped out with the pills. Lingering in the door, Emmie flushed and said softly, as if to apologize for Sim's gruffness, "Thank you, Doc."

She wasn't looking at me, though, but at Lee Dowd up in the chair, and he was staring back at her with his mouth open.

Nobody would ever call Emmie Shafter pretty. A tall gaunt woman in a shapeless cotton dress, she was maybe twenty-six, with straggly brown hair and red, work-chapped hands, but Sim hadn't quite stomped all the spirit out of her yet. Her chin lifted as she watched Lee, and her plain face lighted up. Then she was gone, following Sim outside.

Something passed between those two. It doesn't happen often, but it happened that day. Nothing so simple as love at first sight. But a feeling, a need, some recognition. I should've read the symptoms because I had to tap Lee three times before he stepped down, but I was too busy grumbling about Sim Shafter's tightfisted contrariness to notice.

That night Lee camped on my lot and pulled out early next morning. Probably decided our town wasn't worth a layover after all, I thought, but he was back again by suppertime. Later I heard him at the pump and went out to see what had changed his mind. He had his shirt peeled off to wash up, and bare-chested like that he looked even scrawnier.

"Those pills did the trick," he said. "Con got over his stomach ache."

"Kill or cure," I said. "But how do you know?"

"I drove out there today."

It seems that Lee had done just that. He'd gone the five miles out to Sim's ranch to drum up a little trade and maybe catch another look at Emmie. Luckily, the boys were off somewhere when he arrived, and Emmie had asked him to stay for dinner. He'd accepted, thinking it mighty special, and it was, too, though not the way he supposed. Afterward he and Emmie sat and talked for quite a spell, and he got out his camera and tripod to take her picture. Just about then Sim and Con rode back into the ranch yard.

"That Sim," Lee said in a hurt, puzzled voice. "What ails him? Why, he ordered me off the place."

It didn't puzzle me any. I remembered how a while back a young cow hand had set out to court Emmie Shafter. Like I say, she was no beauty, but she'd have made a fine wife. Lord knows she had experience—cooking for her brothers and their crew all these years, keeping house, patching clothes, raising chickens, growing vegetables, and with never a hired girl or chore boy to help her. Sim didn't believe in pampering a woman, and I always suspected that's why he never married. Why gamble on a wife when Emmie did the work of three women and expected nothing in return? Anyway, he chased off her only suitor with a rifle, and after that I guess Emmie gave up. It certainly discouraged the other young bucks from calling.

"Money," I told Lee. "That's what ails him. He's a miser."

"But I was going to give her the picture," Lee said. "It wouldn't've cost him a cent."

"That's not the point. Sim's afraid somebody might marry her and leave him short a cook."

Still Lee didn't see it. "This is a free country," he said. "No, sir, no man has a right to treat his sister like that."

"We're not talking about rights," I said. "Emmie's a nice girl, but take my advice and stay away. Else you'll only cause her trouble."

Lee toweled himself off slowly, a sad faraway look in his eyes. Then he let out a breath and said, "Hadn't thought of it like that, Doc. Wouldn't want to put any hardship on her, no, sir."

Next day he was off again, but by now I was getting used to his itchy-footed ways, and sure enough he knocked on my back door after supper. He had some picture he wanted me to see, so I walked over to his wagon, curious for a glimpse inside. It was fitted out like a traveling laboratory, with tanks and stacks of plate holders and rows of bottles and a sour chemical stink on everything. Up front he'd pitched a tent of orange calico on the wagon bed for his darkroom, which left only one corner for his bedroll and personal gear. A sheepherder's wagon had nothing on his for cramped, smelly quarters.

Lee handed me a print that was still damp. "What do you think of that?" he said, his eyes all dancy and shining.

"Indian Butte," I said.

His head bobbed. "I been out there all day, tryin' to catch the light just right. But I surely got it now!"

Indian Butte was just another big cussed pile of rock a few miles down the creek. I'd passed it a hundred times. But somehow in Lee's picture it looked different—the cracks and hollows and shadows and shape of it. It looked almost—I know this sounds crazy—almost like a face you'd got used to and never noticed much, a homely weather-beat face with lines of character worn in bone deep. I turned it this way and that, and the longer I stared the more I wondered at Lee Dowd. Because Indian Butte lay on the north end of the Shafter ranch.

"You better not let Sim catch you out there," I said.

"Don't figure to," Lee said. "Thought I'd send this to Emmie. She might like it."

It seemed an odd present to give a woman, specially when she could look out her window and see that butte every day of her life, but I didn't say so. Lee got out a big album then, full of pictures he'd taken on his wanderings. Pictures of a windmill, an old steer carcass, a busted-down wagon, a homesteader's shack, a nursing colt, an Injun wickiup, and all kinds of rocks and cliffs and trees. Common, ordinary things you wouldn't look at twice.

"You mean people'll buy these things?" I said.

"A few," he said. "Mostly I just keep 'em. I reckon most people are too close to the forest. They don't see the wonders God scattered about in this land."

He sounded cheerful about it, as though the rest of us were more to be pitied than blamed, and he was one of the lucky few. He was excited now, full of his dream, and I let him talk.

He was born and raised in the flatlands of Missouri, a farmer all his life and planning to stay one till he died. And then one day some traveling lecturer turned up in the nearest town with a set of colored lantern slides on the Rocky Mountains. To hear Lee tell it, this was something like a man getting religion on his first trip to church. From that moment on, he had to see those mountains, and beyond them. Until he did he'd never be happy again.

In Denver he stopped long enough to scrape together an outfit with what cash he had, and headed on west, learning his trade as he went. In the four years since, he'd photographed Pikes Peak, the Canyon of Colorado, Yellowstone and a lot of country in between. That was his real love. But portraits were his beans and bacon, and every penny he could spare he plowed back into more expensive equipment. Long ago he'd given up any thought of going home to Missouri. I guess he couldn't help himself.

He knew just one talent he could turn to a profit—mules, skinning mules—and he was proud of that. Lee must've ridden a passel of miles behind a jerk line, hauling freight and ore and Army supplies. Last time had been a ten-span team moving borax to the railroad from Death Valley. If you've ever tried to handle twenty ornery mules you'll know where he got that underfed buggy-whip look. Now he had enough money left to see him through the summer, he said, and come fall he planned to drift south into Sonora. Brand-new country that no photographer had touched.

Finally he talked himself out and put away his album. "Usually I'm not so windy, Doc," he said. "People think I'm a little cracked, so I keep my ideas to myself. But you've been kindly, you and Emmie Shafter."

I tamped some more tobacco into my pipe and waited for the rest, because somehow I had to stop this chuckleheaded fool. He might know all the West, but he didn't know Sim Shafter like I did.

"That talk I had with her yesterday," he said. "We see things alike, me and Emmie. I'm goin' to marry her if she'll have me."

I told him then—told him flat out. "Lee," I said, "this country isn't big enough to hide in if you sneak off with Emmie. Sim'd hunt you down no matter where."

"Who said anything about sneakin' off? When I take her, it'll be right and decent."

"How?" I said disgustedly. "Tell me how you argue with a gun."

His eyes had lost that soft hound look and he drew a breath that filled him out to more than life size.

"I ain't much now," he said. "But I'll come back someday, when I've more than a poky wagon and one fleabit mule. She'll be waiting. Sim can't hold her here forever."

I breathed easier then. That was tall talk, empty talk, the stuff dreams are made of, like the poet says. Someday was a long ways off. I'd come to like this queer lanky specimen of humankind and hated to see him hurt. So I said good night and climbed the stairs to my room, feeling virtuous.

It might have ended there, except for the Fourth of July celebration. The next few days Lee kept to town. He hung out a sign and rigged up his camera beside the wagon in front of a backdrop painted all over with snowy peaks, and there he sat under a striped umbrella, ready for business. All told, he took in three dollars, from a bunch of miners who turned up at Groot's saloon on a payday spree.

By noon of the Fourth, Wagon Box was filling up with folks from all around, come to attend the barbecue and speech-making and horse races and hoedown that night. It's the one day of the year when you can see all your neighbors without riding two hundred miles to do it. Even Sim Shafter drove in, though he wasn't much for sociables. Sim and Con. And Emmie, sitting primly in the back of their spring wagon.

She didn't appear so prim when I saw her again, later that

afternoon. She was sitting in Lee Dowd's chair before the snowy peaks, and Lee was fussing behind his camera under a black cloth, focusing the lens. Her cheeks were pink and her eyes had a sparkle, and her hair was done up in a tidy bun, and she wore a dress that made her look all woman.

For a second you didn't see the squint lines and leathery skin because Emmie's face was shining so. Lee popped out from under his cloth and their eyes met. Then he squeezed the bulb and the shutter clicked.

She must have given Sim the slip, for he wasn't in the nearby crowd, and that worried me. I stepped up, hoping to get her away quick, and said, "Having fun, Miss Emmie?"

She laughed, a laugh that was pure music. "Oh, Doc, if Con hadn't got that stomach cramp——" and blushed as she looked up at Lee.

Lee stared back at her with a worshipful grin. "Yes, sir, Doc," he said, "we've you to thank for this."

I could've kicked his silly butt. How long Emmie had been there I don't know, and it showed what spunk she had to come at all, but I was too late. Sim pushed out of Groot's saloon next door, glanced across the street, then spotted her in Lee's chair. He elbowed through the crowd like a man plowing a furrow, with Con at his heels, and stopped beside the camera.

Emmie stood up and smoothed down her dress, all the glow gone from her eyes.

"Go back to the wagon, Emmie," Sim said in his deep quiet bass.

"He—Mr. Dowd promised to take my picture," she said faintly.

Sim didn't raise his voice. "Emmie," he said.

She gave him a half-scared, half-defiant look; then her shoulders drooped and she walked through the silent ring of onlookers and turned toward the livery stable.

Lee stood there, red in the face, with Sim looming up beside him, stiff and grim and deadly. "Mr. Shafter, sir," he said, "there's no charge for the picture. I'd like for her to have it."

Sim never shifted his flat stare from Lee's face. "No sister of mine," he said, "goes beholden to cheap gypsy trash."

It was Con—big, slow-moving Con—who eased the tension. He edged up between them, one hand in his pocket, and said mildly, "If'n she's got her heart set on it, Sim, I'll buy the thing for her."

Sim gave him one black look and Con moved aside. All the people watching this didn't fluster Sim.

"I warned you once to keep away from her," he said to Lee. "I won't do it again."

He turned and walked off, and he didn't look back. Five minutes later he drove out of town, down the creek road toward his ranch. Sim and Con. And Emmie huddled in the back.

That night I was slicking up for the dance when Lee Dowd tapped on my door for the last time. He didn't mention what had happened that afternoon, but his mouth had a set, stubborn look. His wagon was loaded up and the mule hitched between the shafts. I got mad and a little sick whenever I thought of Emmie. Mad at him, too, for being such a jackass, and I said, "Pulling out?"

"Tonight. But I wanted to show you this first." He handed me a photograph.

It was the one he'd taken of Emmie, fitted in a fancy leather frame.

"She's beautiful," he said.

She was too. She looked like every woman in love ought to look—young and shy and smiling. She was beautiful because a man, one man, had told her so, and she believed him. Her face told the whole story and I thought back to his talk about being too close to the forest, how there was beauty in everything around if you had the eyes to see it. For Emmie, it must've been like opening a window she had thought was boarded up forever, letting sunshine into the dark room where she lived. Looking at that picture made me feel old and useless, because I couldn't help her. Nobody could.

"Don't get any more notions," I said. "Sim'll kill you next time."

"Give it to her for me, will you, Doc?" Lee said.

I told him yes, I could do that much, and because he looked so glum I asked him into Groot's for a drink. He sipped his beer, not saying a word, until we went back outside. He climbed up into his wagon.

"I'll be back," he said. "Tell her that too."

He shook his reins and rolled out into the night.

The next part is hard to tell because I didn't see it happen. But I knew Lee Dowd and how he thought, and I heard some of Emmie's version next morning. Certainly she had no reason to lie. I believed her then, and still do. A few details may be wrong, but the heart of it has to be right. That I'll vouch for.

Lee went south on the Chloride road that night, driving hard and fast, and getting madder every mile. Always before, he'd been content to drift and take his pictures, but Emmie had given him a purpose. He wasn't running out on her. There were mines in Chloride, jobs for a top mule skinner, and he was hell-bent to grab one. He still had some fool noble idea that when he came back with the prospect of a steady job, Sim would change his mind. He was even ready to sell his outfit, camera and all, for the chance to marry

Emmie. But, womanlike, she had more common sense.

When he pulled up at Coyote Spring late to make his camp, Emmie crawled out from under that tent in his wagon, where she'd been hiding all the way from town.

That afternoon when she got home, she told Lee, Sim had locked her in her room. But all the years of suffering finally had taught her. After dark, she climbed out the window and walked into Wagon Box, on her own for the first time in her life. She was terrified that Sim would follow, that Lee would try to fight him. That was her first instinct, to protect Lee, to get him beyond Sim's reach. So, when she saw his wagon was ready to roll, she crawled aboard while Lee was having a farewell drink with me, knowing he'd refuse.

What they said to each other out in the big starlit emptiness of Coyote Spring is anybody's guess. Emmie was frantic to go on. Lee was gentle, but stubborn, just as she'd feared he would be. What they were doing was sneaky and underhanded, he told her, no way to start their life together. He couldn't get it through his thick head that Sim would never give consent. No man, he said, could be that unreasonable. So, with Emmie sobbing and clinging to his arm, he reined that tired old mule around in its tracks and started back for Wagon Box. Emmie Shafter had run away for nothing, because her man was bound and determined to get himself shot.

That's how it was that hot still morning after the Fourth when Sim and Con stepped out of my shop. A couple of punchers were nursing hangovers down by the horse trough and a swamper was brooming the night's debris out of Groot's saloon. The day was so quiet you could hear a breeze rustling the cottonwood leaves. Then we all heard another sound—the squeal of dry axles—and Lee Dowd's battered dusty wagon turned into the far end of the street.

I saw Lee's shoulders stiffen, but he came straight on, Emmie perched up beside him. Opposite the shop he pulled to a halt, set his brake and climbed down slowly. Sim stood there, waiting, thumbs hooked in his shell belt, with Con at his side. Lee gave Emmie a little tight-lipped smile and stepped out to the middle of the street.

"This ain't how I planned it," he said in that soft Missouri twang, "but I'm askin' you for Emmie's hand, sir."

Sim stared at him, his big square face black as ten feet down. Then Emmie cried, "It isn't like you think, Sim! I hid in his wagon! He didn't know till we got to the spring!"

"Get off that wagon," Sim said. "I'll tend to you later."

I thought she'd crawl down, like she'd done before, or burst into tears. Her knuckles showed white where she gripped the seat and her chin was trembling, but she didn't budge. Love had made her bloom, and toughened her fiber too.

"It's true, Sim!" she said. "He didn't run off with me. He could have, but he brought me back instead."

Con put a hand on Sim's arm. "Might be she is tellin' the truth," he said.

Sim shook him off and stepped to his horse. It was awful to see, the slow, brutal way he took that whip from his saddle horn and shook it out, a dozen wicked feet of freshly oiled leather. Trailing the popper in the dust, he moved toward Lee.

Until that very instant, Lee had never realized that Sim intended violence. An almost comic surprise washed across his face, and then a dull red fury. My stomach churned and I let out a yell as Sim cocked his arm and swung the whip, knowing he'd cut Lee to raw meat in seconds. The leather snaked out, black and murderous, and Lee pivoted on his feet, one arm flung up before his face. The whip curled around his forearm with a sickening crack, but he didn't scream. He gave it a vicious lightning twist, before Sim could move, and jerked the whipstock right out of Sim's hand.

Blood trickling down his sleeve, he coiled the leather in and gripped the handle in his big calloused fist. "Sim," he said between his teeth, "never try to whip an old Missouri mule skinner. They'll belt you every time."

With a savage flick of his wrist, Lee sent that lash hissing back at Sim. It popped like a firecracker, bit a scallop out of his hatbrim and scaled it off into the dirt. Sim reared back, growling in his throat, and Lee cocked his arm again.

"You're not fit to live," he said in a thick, choked voice. "You've bullied Emmie and slaved her half to death. You're a skinflint, Sim, mean and ugly to your stingy core." I guess that was the vilest epithet he knew—ugly. "Go on," he said. "Try for your gun now."

Sim looked up at Emmie on the wagon seat, at Lee's cold steady eyes, then at the whip. He was looking at death, and he knew it. The fastest gun slinger living—and Sim was far from that—couldn't outdraw that coiled blacksnake in Lee Dowd's hand. Sim rubbed one palm along his pants, and right there I saw a man shrink down to size, with all his puniness showing through the fear.

"Con!" he called, and it was a bleat for help. "Con!"

Con planted his feet on the walk and his hand brushed his holster. "Emmie," he said, "you want to go with this fellow?"

She swallowed, and nodded weakly.

Slow, patient thoughts stirred across Con's broad face. Maybe he was remembering how Emmie had brought him the pain-killer pills or how he'd been pushed and herded all his own life. Maybe he was seeing how a woman could bring a trifling no-'count kind of man to stand up against a whip and a pair of guns. Or maybe, like me, he saw that proud shine in his sister's eyes.

"Light out then," he said, said it softly too. "Nobody'll foller you."

Sim's face flamed in protest and for a second I was afraid he might draw anyway. Behind him, Con said in a tone of quiet authority, "Leave her be, Sim. She's earned it."

Sim bent stiffly, picked up his hat, jammed it on his head and tramped over to his horse. Lee stared at his rigid back and shook his head. Like a man coming out of a dream, he dropped the whip and turned back to the wagon. He nodded once to Con and climbed up, sitting tall and straight beside Emmie on the seat. She made a soft low sound and clutched his hand, and then they wheeled around in the street.

I remembered the picture then, the one he'd given me for Emmie. I called out, but Lee didn't stop. He didn't need any picture. He had Emmie.

Con and I stood there together, watching them dwindle into the heat haze, into the big, empty desert that for once seemed beautiful.

A MOUNTAIN VICTORY

WILLIAM FAULKNER

Through the cabin window the five people watched the cavalcade toil up the muddy trail and halt at the gate. First came a man on foot, leading a horse. He wore a broad hat low on his face, his body shapeless in a weathered gray cloak from which his left hand emerged, holding the reins. The bridle was silver mounted, the horse a gaunt, mud-splashed Thoroughbred bay, wearing in place of saddle a navy-blue army blanket bound on it by a piece of rope. The second horse was a short-bodied, big-headed scrub sorrel, also mud splashed. It wore a bridle also contrived of rope and wire, and an army saddle in which, perched high above the dangling stirrups, crouched a shapeless something larger than a child, which at that distance appeared to wear no garment or garments known to man.

One of the three men at the cabin window left it quickly. The others, without turning, heard him cross the room swiftly and then return, carrying a long rifle.

"No you don't," one of the other men said.

"Don't you see that cloak," the first said—"that rebel cloak?"

"I won't have it," the second said. "They have surrendered. They have said they were whipped."

Through the window they watched the horses stop at the gate. The gate was of sagging hickory, in a rock fence that straggled down a gaunt slope sharp in relief against the valley and a still farther range dissolving into the low, dissolving sky.

They watched the creature on the second horse descend and hand

113

his reins also into the same left hand of the man in gray which held
the reins of the Thoroughbred. They watched the creature enter the
gate and mount the path and disappear beyond the angle of the
window. Then they heard it cross the porch and knock at the door.
They stood there and heard it knock again.

"Go and see," the second man said.

One of the women turned from the window, her feet making no
sound on the floor. She went to the front door and opened it. The
chill, wet light of the dying April afternoon fell in upon her—upon a
small woman with a gnarled face, in a gray garment. Facing her
across the doorsill was a creature a little larger than a large monkey,
dressed in a voluminous blue overcoat of a private in the Federal
Army, with, tied tentlike over his head and falling about his shoulders, a piece of oilcloth that might have been cut square from the
hood of a sutler's wagon; within the orifice the woman could see
nothing whatever save the whites of two eyes, momentary and
phantomlike, as with a single glance the Negro examined the woman
standing barefooted in her calico garment, and took in the bleak and
barren interior of the cabin hall.

"Marster Major Soshay Weddel send he compliments and say he
wishful for sleeping room for himself and boy and two horses," the
Negro said in a pompous, parrotlike tone. The woman looked at him.
Her face was like a mask. "We been up yonder a piece, fighting them
Yankees," the Negro said. "We done quit now. Gwine back home."

The woman seemed to speak from somewhere behind the mask of
her face, as though behind an effigy or a painted screen: "I'll have to
see."

"We ghy pay you," the Negro said.

"Hit ain't nere a hotel on the mou-tin."

"Don't make no difference. We done stayed the night at worse
places than what this is. We ghy pay you." Then he saw that the
woman was looking past him. He turned and saw the man in the
worn gray cloak already halfway up the path from the gate. He came
on and mounted the porch, removing with his left hand the broad
hat bearing the wreath of a Confederate field officer. He had a dark
face, with dark eyes and black hair, his face at once thick and
arrogant. He was not tall, yet he topped the Negro by five or six
inches. The cloak was weathered, faded about the shoulders where
the light fell strongest. The skirts were bedraggled, frayed, mud-
splashed; the garment had been patched again and again, and
brushed again and again; the nap was completely gone.

"Good day, madam," he said. "Have you stable room for my
horses and shelter for myself and my boy for the night?"

The woman looked at him with a static, musing quality, as though she had seen without alarm an apparition.

"I'll have to see," she said.

"I shall pay," the man said. "I know the times."

"I'll have to see," the woman said. She turned, then stopped. A man came into the hall behind her. He was big, in jean clothes, with a shock of iron-gray hair and pale eyes.

"I am Saucier Weddel," the man in the gray cloak said. "I am on my way home to Mississippi from Virginia. Am I in Tennessee now?"

"You are in Tennessee," the other man said. "Come in."

Weddel turned to the Negro. "Take the horses on to the stable," he said.

The Negro returned to the gate, shapeless in the oilcloth cape and big overcoat, with that swaggering arrogance which he had assumed as soon as he saw the woman's bare feet and the meager and barren interior of the cabin. He took up the two bridle reins and began to shout at the horses with needless and officious vociferation, to which the two horses paid no heed, as though they were long accustomed to him. It was as though the Negro himself paid no attention to his cries, as though the shouting were concomitant to the action of leading the horses out of sight of the door, like an effluvium, by both horses and Negro accepted and relegated in the same instant.

II

Through the kitchen wall the girl could hear the voices of the men in the next room—the room from which her father had sent her when the stranger approached the house. She was about twenty; big girl, with smooth, simple hair and big, smooth hands, standing barefoot in a single garment made out of flour sacking. She stood close to the wall, motionless, her head bent and her eyes quite blank, when she heard the stranger and her father enter the other room.

The kitchen was a plank lean-to built against the log wall of the cabin. From between the logs of the near wall the clay chinking, dried out by the heat of the stove, had fallen away in places. Stooping, her movement slow and lush and soundless as the silent whispering of her bare feet on the floor, she leaned her eye to one of these orifices and looked into the room. She could see a bare table on which sat an earthenware jug and a box of musket cartridges with the letters "U.S. Army" stenciled on the box, and at the table her two brothers were sitting in splint chairs. The older brother was taking the cartridges one by one from the box and crimping them and setting them upright at his hand like a mimic parade of troops. His back was toward the door; he did not look up when the stranger and the father and mother entered.

"Vatch would have shot him," the girl said, breathed to herself, stooping. "I reckon he will yet."

Then she heard the others enter, and saw her mother cross the room toward the door into the kitchen, blotting out the orifice through which she peeped, vacating it again. She did not move when her mother entered the kitchen. The mother went to the stove—a small woman, humped, and began to remove the lids. The girl did not move, stooped to the crack, her breathing regular and deep and unhurried. Then she saw the stranger for the first time. He came within range of her single eye, carrying his hat in his left hand. Vatch did not look up.

"I am Saucier Weddel," the stranger said.

"Soshay Weddel," the girl breathed into the dry chinking, the crumbled and powdery wall. She could see him full length, in his stained and patched and brushed cloak, not tall, black-headed, his face thin, worn and gaunt, swaggering and intolerant, like a knife blade whetted and worn and worn and whetted again.

"Take some whisky," Vatch said. Through the crack the girl could see Vatch's face still bent above his hands, above the cartridge which he was crimping. Breathing quietly into the crack, the girl saw the stranger at the table, looking down, and Vatch, now turned in his chair, looking up at the stranger. She breathed quietly into the wall, the crack, through which their voices came quietly, without particular significance; that dark and smoldering and violent and childlike vanity of men:

"You recognize these, then?"

"Why not? We used them too. We never had the time to stop and make our own cartridges. So we had to use yours."

"Maybe you would know it better if it exploded in your face."

"Vatch"—it was the father's voice. The younger brother was raised a little in his chair, leaning a little forward. He was about seventeen. The stranger stood, looking down at Vatch, his hat clutched against his cloak in his left hand.

"You can show your other hand too," Vatch said. "Don't be afraid to leave your pistol go."

"No," Weddel said, "I am not afraid to show it."

"Take some whisky, then," Vatch said.

"I am obliged," Weddel said. "It's my stomach. For three years I have had to apologize to my stomach; now I must apologize for it. But if I might have a glass for my boy. Even after four years, he cannot stand cold."

"Soshay Weddel," the girl breathed into the dry chinking from beyond which the voices, the vain and subjective conceit of men, came:

"Or maybe behind your back you would know it best of all."

"You, Vatch!"

"Stop, sir. If he was in the army for as long as one year, he has run, too, once. Maybe oftener, if he faced the Army of Virginia."

"Soshay Weddel," the girl said, stooping to the crack. Weddel was now approaching, moving toward the door into the kitchen, his hat crumpled beneath his arm and a thick tumbler half full of what looked like water in his left hand.

"Not that way," Vatch said. The girl ceased to breathe on a single, unhurried inhalation. The stranger paused, turning, looking at Vatch. "Don't you go in there," Vatch said. "You damn nigra."

"So it's my face and not my cloak," Weddel said. His hair was long; it had been trimmed roughly across the back, as though with a knife. His gaunt profile was bronze-colored, wasted and haughty. "And you fought four years to free us."

"I reckon you better go out the front way," the father said. "I reckon you better not go back there."

"Soshay Weddel," the girl said. Behind her the mother clattered at the stove. "Soshay Weddel," the girl said. She did not say it aloud. She breathed again, deep and quiet and slow: "It's like a music. It's like a singing."

III

The Negro was squatting in the hallway of the barn, the sagging and broken stalls of which were empty save for the two horses. Beside him was a worn rucksack, open. He was engaged in polishing a pair of thin dancing slippers with a cloth and a tin of paste, empty save for a thin rim of polish about the circumference of the tin. Beside him on a piece of board sat one finished shoe. The upper was cracked and worn; it had a crude sole nailed recently and crudely on by a clumsy hand.

"Thank the Lord, folks can't see the bottom of your feets," the Negro said. "Thank the Lord, it's just these here mountain trash. I'd even hate for Yankees to see your feets in these things." He rubbed the shoe, squinted at it, breathed upon it, rubbed it again upon his squatting flank.

"Here," Weddel said, extending the tumbler.

The Negro ceased, the shoe and the cloth suspended. "What?" he said. He looked at the glass. "What's that?"

"Drink it," Weddel said.

117

"That's water," the Negro said. "What are you bringing me water for?"

"Take it," Weddel said. "It's not water."

The Negro took the glass gingerly. He held it as though it contained nitroglycerin. He looked at it, blinking, bringing the glass slowly under his nose. He blinked. "Where'd you get this here?" Weddel did not answer. He had taken up the finished slipper, looking at it. The Negro held the glass under his nose. "It smells kind of like it ought to," he said. "But I be dawg if it look like anything. These folks fixing to pizen you." He tilted the glass and sipped gingerly, and lowered the glass, blinking.

"I didn't drink any of it," Weddel said. He set the slipper down.

"You better not," the Negro said. "When here I done been four years trying to take care of you and get you back home like what Mistis told me to do, and here you sleeping at night in folks' barns like a tramp, like a pat-roller nigger——" He put the glass to his lips, tilting the glass and his head in a single jerking motion. He lowered the glass, empty; his eyes were closed; he said, "Whuf!" shaking his head with a violent, shuddering motion. "It smell right, and it act right. But I be dawg if it look right. I reckon you better let it alone, like you started out. When they try to make you drink it you send um to me. I done already stood so much, I reckon I can stand a little more for Mistis' sake."

He took up the shoe and the cloth again. Weddel was stooped above the rucksack.

"I want my pistol," he said.

Again the Negro ceased, the shoe and the cloth poised. "What for?" He leaned forward and looked up the hill toward the house. "Is these folks Yankees?"

"No," Weddel said.

"In Tennessee? You told me we was in Tennessee, where Memphis is, even if ain't nobody told me before it was all this here up-and-down land in the Memphis country. I know I never seed none of it when I went to Memphis. But you says so. And now you telling me them Memphis folks is Yankees?"

"Where is the pistol?" Weddel said. He stooped toward the rucksack.

"I done told you," the Negro said. "Acting like you does. Letting these folks see you come walking up the road, leading Caesar because you think he tired; making me ride while you walk, when I can outwalk you any day you ever lived, and you know it, even if I is forty, you twenty-eight. I ghy tell your maw. I ghy tell um."

Weddel dug into the rucksack with his left hand and took from the rucksack a heavy cap-and-ball revolver and chucked it in his hand, drawing the hammer back and letting it down again; the Negro watching him, crouched like an ape in the Union Army overcoat.

"You put that thing back," the Negro said. "The war is done with They told us at Virginia it was done with. You don't need no pistol now. You put it back."

"I'm going to bathe," Weddel said. "Is my shirt——"

"Bathe where? In what? These folks never seed a bathtub."

"Bathe at the well. Is my shirt ready?"

"What they is of it. . . . You put that pistol back, Marse Soshay. I ghy tell your maw on you. I ghy tell um. I just wish marster was here."

"Go to the kitchen," Weddel said. "Tell them I wish to bathe in the well house. Ask them to draw the curtain on the window." He put the pistol away inside the cloak. He went to the stall where the Thoroughbred was. The horse nuzzled at him, its eyes rolling soft and wild. He patted its nose with his left hand. It whinnied, not loud, its breath sweet and warm.

IV

The Negro entered the kitchen from the rear. He had removed the oilcoth tent and he now wore a blue forage cap, like the overcoat much too large for him, resting upon the top of his head in such a way that the unsupported brim oscillated faintly when he moved, with a movement of its own. He was completely invisible save for his face, between cap and collar like a dried Dyak trophy, almost as small, dusted lightly over as with a thin grayish powder of wood ashes, from the cold. The mother was at the stove. She did not look around when the Negro entered. The girl was standing in the middle of the kitchen. She looked at the Negro, watching him with her slow intent, secret gaze as he crossed the kitchen with that air of swaggering assurance and upturned a log block in the corner between stove and wall, and sat down.

"If this here is the kind of weather yawl has up here all the time," he said, "I don't care if the Yankees does has this country." He opened the overcoat, revealing his lower legs and feet as being wrapped, shapeless and huge, in some muddy and anonymous substance, giving them the appearance of two muddy animals the size of half-grown dogs lying on the floor; moving a little nearer, the girl saw that his feet were wrapped in two pieces of beaver fur, such as might have been cut from a coat. "Yes, sir," the Negro said. "Just let me get home again, and the Yankees can have all the rest of it."

"Where do you-all live?" the girl said.

119

"In Mississippi. On the Domain. Ain't you heard tell of County-maison?"

"Countymaison?"

"That's it. His grandpappy named it Countymaison because it's bigger than a county to ride over. You can't ride across it on a mule betwixt sunup and sundown." He rubbed his hands slowly on his thighs. Already the ashy overlay on his skin had disappeared, leaving his face dead black, wizened, his mouth a little loose, as though the muscles had become slack with usage, like rubber bands—not the eating muscles, the talking ones.

"Countymaison," the girl said. She looked at the Negro. Then she turned her head and looked at the wall, her face perfectly blank, perfectly inscrutable, without haste, with a profound and absorbed deliberation.

"That's it," the Negro said. "Even Yankees is heard about Weddel's Countymaison, and about Francis Weddel. Maybe you all seen um pass in the carriage, time he went to Washndon to tell yawl's President how he never liked the way yawl's President was treating the people. He rid all the way to Washndon in the carriage with two niggers to drive, and the man done went on ahead with a wagon and the extra horses. He must a passed right in front of yawl's house. I reckon your pappy or maybe his pappy seen um pass." He talked on, voluble, in soporific singsong, his face beginning to glisten, to shine a little with the rich heat, while the mother cooked the supper and the girl, motionless, static, her bare feet cupped smooth and close to the rough puncheons, her big, smooth young body cupped soft and richly mammalian in the rough garment, watching the Negro with her pale, unwinking gaze, her mouth open a little.

The Negro talked on, his eyes closed, his voice interminable, singsong, boastful, his air more lazily intolerant than if he, a stable-man, in the domestic hierarchy a man of horses, had been spending the evening in the cabin of field Negroes, until the mother dished the food and left the room, closing the door behind her. He opened his eyes at the sound of the door and looked toward the door, then back to the girl. She was looking at the wall, at the closed door through which the mother had departed.

"Don't they let you eat at the table with um?" the Negro said.

The girl looked at the Negro, unwinking. "Countymaison," she said. "Vatch says he is a nigra too."

"Who? Him? Him a nigger? Which un is Vatch?" The girl looked at him. "That's because yawl ain't been nowhere. Ain't seen nothing. Up here on a hill. Him a nigger? I wish his maw could hear you say that." He looked about the kitchen, wizened, his eyeballs rolling, white, ceaseless, this way and that. The girl watched him.

"Do the girls there wear shoes?" she said.

The Negro looked this way and that about the meager kitchen. "Where does yawl keep that there Tennessee spring water? Back here?"

"Spring water?"

The Negro blinked slowly. "That there drinking kahysene."

"Kahysene?"

"That there light-colored lamp oil that yawl drinks. Ain't you got a little of it back here somewhere?"

"Oh," the girl said. "You mean corn." She went to the corner and lifted a loose board in the floor, the Negro watching her, and drew out a second earthen jug. She filled another thick tumbler and gave it to the Negro and watched him jerk it down his throat, his eyes closed. Again he said, "Whuf!" and drew his back hand across his mouth.

"What was that you asked me?" he said.

"Do the girls down there at Countymaison wear shoes?"

"The ladies does. If they didn't have none, Marse Soshay could sell a hundred niggers and buy em some. . . . Which un is it say Marse Soshay a nigger?"

The girl watched him. "Is he married?"

"Who married? Marse Soshay?" The girl watched him. "How he have time to get married, with us fighting the Yankees for four years? Ain't been home in four years where no ladies to marry is." He looked at the girl, his eye whites a little bloodshot, his skin shining in faint and steady highlights. Thawing, he appeared to have increased a little in size too. "What's that to you, if he married or not?"

They looked at each other. The Negro could hear the girl breathing. Then she was not looking at him at all, though she had not yet even blinked or turned her head. "I don't reckon he'd have any time for a girl that didn't have any shoes," she said. She went to the wall and stooped again to the crack. The Negro watched her. The mother entered and took another dish from the stove and left the room again without having looked at either the Negro or the girl.

V

The four men sat about the supper table. The broken meal lay on thick plates. The knives and forks were iron. On the table the jug sat. Weddel was coatless. He was shaven, his still-damp hair combed back. Upon his bosom the ruffles of the shirt frothed in the lamplight, the right sleeve pinned across the breast with a thin gold pin. Under the table his frail and mended slippers rested among the brogans of the father and Vatch and the bare, splayed feet of the boy.

"Vatch says you are a nigra," the father said.

Weddel was leaning a little back in his chair. "That explains it," he said. "I was thinking he was just congenitally ill-tempered. And having to be a victor too."

"Are you a nigra?" the father said.

"No," Weddel said. He was looking at the boy, his gaunt face a little quizzical. The boy watched him. "As if I might be an apparition," Weddel said to himself. "A hant. Maybe I am. . . . No." he said, "I am not a Negro."

"Who are you?" the father said.

Weddel sat a little sideways, his hand lying on the table. "Do you ask guests who they are in Tennessee?" he said. Vatch was filling a tumbler from the jug. His face was bent, his hands big and hard. His face was hard. Weddel looked at him. "I think I know how you feel," Weddel said. "I expect I felt that way once. But it's hard to keep on feeling any way for four years."

Vatch said something, sudden and harsh. He clapped the tumbler on to the table, splashing some of the liquor out. It looked like water, with a violent dynamic odor. It seemed to possess an inherent volatility which carried a splash of it across the table and on to the foam of frayed yet immaculate linen on Weddel's breast, striking sudden and chill through the cloth against his breast.

"Vatch!" the father said.

"He didn't mean to do that," Weddel said.

"When I do," Vatch said, "it will not look like an accident."

Weddel was looking at Vatch. "I think I told you once," he said. "My name is Saucier Weddel. I am a Mississippian. I live at a place named Contalmaison. My father was a Choctaw chief named Francis Weddel, of whom you have probably not heard. He was the son of a Choctaw woman and a French emigre of New Orleans, a general of Napoleon's and a knight of the Legion of Honor. His name was François Vidal. My father drove to Washington once in his carriage to remonstrate with President Jackson about the Government's treatment of his people, sending on ahead a wagon of provender and the fresh horses, in charge of the Man, the native overseer, who was a full-blood Choctaw and my father's cousin. In the old days 'The Man' was the hereditary title of the head of our clan; but after we became Europeanized like the white people, we lost the title to the branch which did not permit itself to be polluted. The Man now lives in a house a little larger than the cabins of the Negroes—an upper servant. It was in Washington that my father met and married my mother. He was killed in the Mexican War. My mother died two years ago in '63, of a complication of pneumonia, acquired while superintending the burying of some silver on a wet night when the Federal troops entered the town, and of unsuitable food; though my boy refuses to believe that she is dead. He refuses to believe that the country would have permitted the North to deprive her of the imported Martinique coffee and the beaten biscuit which he had each Sunday morning and Wednesday night. He believes that the country would have risen in arms first. But then, he is only a Negro, member of an oppressed race burdened with freedom. He has a daily list of my misdoings, which he is going to tell her on me when we reach home. I went to school in France, but I didn't go very hard. Until two weeks ago I was a major in the——the Mississippi infantry, in the corps of a man named Longstreet, of whom you may have heard."

"So you were a major," Vatch said.

"That appears to have been my misfortune; yes."

"I have seen a rebel major before," Vatch said. "Shall I tell you where I saw him?"

"Yes," Weddel said. "Tell me."

"He was lying by a tree. We had to stop there and lie down, and he was lying by the tree, asking for water. 'Have you got any water, friend?' he said. 'Yes, I have water,' I said. 'I have plenty of water.' I had to crawl; I couldn't stand up. I crawled over to him and I lifted him so that his head would be propped against the tree, turning his face a little with my hands."

"Didn't you have a bayonet?" Weddel said. "But I forgot: you couldn't stand up."

"I had to crawl back. I had to crawl back a hundred yards, where——"

"Back?"

"It was too close. Who can get a decent shot that close? I had to crawl, and then that damn musket——"

"Damn musket?" Weddel sat a little turned in his chair, his hand on the table, his face quizzical and sardonic.

"I missed the first time. I had his head propped up and turned, and his eyes open, watching me, and then I missed. I hit him in the throat and I had to shoot again."

"Vatch," the father said.

Vatch's hands were on the table. His head, his face, were like the

123

father's, though without the father's deliberation. Vatch's face was furious, still unpredictable. His voice was level. "It was that damn musket. I had to shoot twice. Then he had three eyes, in a row across his face propped against the tree, all of them open, like he was watching me with three eyes. I gave him another eye, to see the better with."

"You, Vatch," the father said. The father stood, his hands on the table, propping his heavy body. "Don't you mind Vatch," he said. "The war is over now."

"I don't mind him," Weddel said. His hand went to his bosom while he looked at Vatch, the fingers disappearing among the foam of the linen. "I have seen too many of him for too long a time to mind one of him anymore."

"Take some whisky," Vatch said.

"Are you just making a point?" Weddel said.

"Damn the pistol," Vatch said. "Take some whisky."

Weddel laid his hand on the table. Instead of pouring, Vatch held the jug poised. He was looking past Weddel's shoulder. Weddel turned. The girl stood in the room. In the doorway beside her the mother stood. The mother said, as though she were speaking to the floor at her feet:

"I tried to keep her back, like you said. I tried to. But she is strong as a man; hardheaded like a man."

"You go back," the father said.

"Me to go back?" the mother said to the floor.

The father spoke a name: "——you go back."

The girl moved. She was not looking at any of them. She went to the chair on which lay Weddel's weathered and mended cloak. She opened the cloak, revealing on the inside a jagged seam where the beaver lining had been cut with a knife and removed. She was looking at the seam when Vatch caught her by the shoulder. Then the father grasped Vatch, who released the girl, who fell back, still holding the cloak. Weddel had not moved, his face turned over his shoulder, sitting, and beyond him the boy upraised out of his chair by his arms, his young, slacked face leaned forward into the lamp.

"I am stouter than you are, still," the father said. "I am a better man still, or as good."

They stood, lock-armed, eye to eye. "You won't be always," Vatch said.

The father looked over his shoulder at the girl. "Go back," he said. The girl went on across the room toward the door into the hall, her feet silent as rubber feet. "You——" the father said, calling the name again. The girl did not look back. She went out the door. The father looked at Weddel, sitting negligent yet alert in his chair, his single hand hidden again in his bosom. They looked at each other—the cold, Nordic face and the half Gallic, half Mongol face—the face thin and worn and yet like a bronze casting, the eyes like those of the dead, in which only the vision has ceased, and not the sight. "Take your horses and go," the father said.

VI

Outside the door, in the dark hall, it was cold, with the black chill of the mountain April coming up through the floor about her bare legs and her body in the single coarse garment.

"He taken and cut the lining outen his cloak to wrap that nigra's feet in," she said. "He did that for a nigra."

The door opened. Against the dim lamp a man loomed. The door shut behind him. "Is it Vatch or paw?" she said. Then something struck her across the back—a leather strap. "I was afeared it would be Vatch," she said. The blow fell again.

"Go to bed," the father said.

"You can whip me, but you can't whip him," she said.

The blow fell—a thick, flat, soft sound upon her immediate flesh beneath the coarse sacking.

VII

In the deserted kitchen the Negro sat for a moment longer on the upturned block beside the stove, looking at the door. Then he rose carefully, one hand on the wall, and stood so.

"Whuf!" he said. "Wish us had a spring on the Domain what run that. The stock would get trompled to death, sho mon." He looked at the door, listening, then he moved, letting himself carefully along the wall, stopping now and then to look toward the door and listen, his air cunning, unsteady and alert. He reached the corner and lifted the floor board, stooping carefully, bracing himself against the wall. He lifted the jug out, whereupon he lost his balance and sprawled on his face, his face ludicrous and earnest with astonishment. He got up and sat flat on the floor carefully, the jug between his knees, and lifted the jug and drank. He drank a long time.

"Whuf!" he said. "On the Domain we'd give this here stuff to hawgs. But these here ign'ant mountain trash——"

He drank again; then with the jug poised, there came into his face an expression of concern and then consternation. He set the jug down and tried to rise to his feet, sprawling above the jug, gaining his feet at last, stooped, swaying, with that expression of outraged consternation on his face. Then he fell headlong on the floor, overturning the jug.

VIII

They stooped above the Negro, talking quietly to one another—Weddel in his frothed shirt, the father and the boy.

"We'll have to tote him," the father said.

They lifted the Negro. With his single hand Weddel jerked the Negro's head up, shaking him. "Jubal," he said.

The Negro struck out, clumsily, with one arm. "Le'm' be," he said. "Le'm' go."

"You, Jubal," Weddel said.

The Negro thrashed, sudden and violent. "You le'm' be," he said. "I ghy tell the Man. I ghy tell um." He ceased, muttering. "Field hands. Field niggers."

"We'll have to tote him," the father said.

"Yes," Weddel said. "I'm sorry of this. I should have warned you." He stooped, getting his single hand under the Negro's head.

"Get away," the father said. "Me and Hule can do it." He and the boy picked the Negro up. Weddel opened the door. They emerged into the high, black cold. Below them the barn loomed. They carried the Negro to the barn. "Get them horses out, Hule," the father said.

"He can't ride," Weddel said. "He can't stay on a horse."

"You won't go now?" the father said.

"I'll have to stay until daylight. I will get him up then. We'll go then."

"Leave him here," the father said. "Leave him one horse, and you ride on."

"No. Not after four years. I've worried with him this far; I reckon I'll get him on home."

"I've told you," the father said.

"I'm obliged," Weddel said. "We'll move at daylight. If you and Hule will just help me get him into the loft."

"Leave him down here."

"It's too cold. He can't stand much cold. I'll get him into the loft." While the others held the Negro up, Weddel slapped him awake. They lifted him, setting his feet one by one on the steps of the ladder to the loft, pushing him up. Halfway up he stopped; again he flung out at them with his lax arms.

"I ghy tell um. I ghy tell the Man. I ghy tell Mistis. Field hands. Field niggers."

IX

Weddel and the Negro lay side by side in the loft, beneath the cloak and the overcoat and the two saddle blankets. The Negro

126

snored, his breath reeking, thick and harsh. Below, in its stall, the Thoroughbred stamped now and then. Weddel lay on his back, his arm across his chest, the hand clutching the stub of the other arm. Overhead, through the cracks in the roof, the sky showed—the thick, chill, black sky, which would rain again tomorrow and on every day until they left the mountains.

"If I leave the mountains," Weddel said, motionless on his back beside the snoring Negro, staring upward. "I was concerned. I had thought that it was exhausted; that I had lost the privilege of being afraid. But now I am happy—quite happy." He lay rigid on his back in the cold darkness, thinking of home. "Contalmaison. Our lives are summed up in sounds and made significant. That's why we must do so much to invent meanings for the sounds—so damned much. If you are unfortunate enough to be victorious—so damned much. It's nice to be whipped—quiet to be whipped. To be whipped and to lie under a broken roof, thinking of home." He let the words shape quietly in the dark. The Negro snored. "So damned much. What would happen, say, a man in the lobby of the Gayoso, in Memphis, laughing suddenly aloud? But I am quite happy."

His arm lay across his breast upon the torn shirt. The frilled linen shirt, with the mended shoes, had been replaced in the rucksack, though the thick butt of the cavalry pistol lay warm and heavy beneath his right armpit. He lay hugging himself with his good arm and with the stump of the one which he had lost while a company commander in Jackson's Army of the Valley, talking quietly to himself and then lying quietly without talking beside the snoring Negro, until he heard the sound. The loft was reached by a wooden ladder. The sound was somewhere about the ladder, mounting it toward the trap into the loft. He lay quite still then, the pistol butt in his hand, until he saw the dim orifice of the trap blotted out.

"Stop where you are," he said.

"It's me," the voice said—the voice of the boy. He came crawling on hands and knees across the dry, sibilant, meager fodder. "Go ahead and shoot." On hands and knees he loomed above Weddel, who had half risen on his elbow. "I wish I was dead," the boy said. "I so wish it." Weddel could hear him breathing, fast and hard. "I wish we was both dead. I could wish like Vatch wishes."

"Why does Vatch wish I was dead?"

"Because he hears them yelling still. He wakes up at night in a cold sweat, hearing them yelling still, and them without nothing except unloaded guns, yelling, Vatch said, like scarecrows across a corn patch, running."

"Yes," Weddel said. "I've heard them. But why do you wish you were dead?"

"She was trying to come herself. She had to——"

"Who? Your sister?"

"——had to go through the room to get out. Paw was awake. He said, 'If you go out that door, don't you never come back.' 'I don't aim to,' she said. 'Then make him marry you quick,' Vatch said. 'Because you are going to be a widow at daylight.' And she come back and told me about it. But I was awake. She told me to tell you."

"Tell me what?"

" 'I wouldn't care if you was a nigra. I wouldn't care.' "

"I'm obliged," Weddel said. "Was that what your sister wanted you to tell me?"

"I told her if you was a nigra, and if she did that—I told her that I—how I—" He breathed hard, harsh.

"What was it she said? What did she want you to tell me?"

"About that window into the attic where her and me sleep. There is a foot ladder up to it from outside, when I come back a night from hunting. I told her that if you was a nigra and she did that——"

Weddel could hear the boy breathe, fast and hard. "I never saw your sister but one time."

"But you saw her then. And she saw you."

"No," Weddel said.

"No what?"

"I won't do it. I won't climb that ladder."

"I could kill you easy," the boy said. "Even if you haven't got but one arm." Weddel heard the dry hay rustle, then he felt the boy's hard, big hands learn his position and take him by the throat. Weddel did not move. "I could kill you easy. And wouldn't none mind."

"Sh-h-h-h," Weddel said. "Not so loud."

"Wouldn't none care." He held Weddel's throat with hard and clumsy restraint. Weddel could feel the choking and the shaking moving up the boy's arms, inverted, spending itself. "Wouldn't none care. Except Vatch would be mad."

"I have a pistol," Weddel said.

"Then shoot me with it. Go on."

"No."

"No what?"

"I told you before."

"You swear you won't do it? Do you swear?"

"I have got to go home," Weddel said. "I haven't been home in four years. I want to go home and see what I have left there."

"What do you do there?" the boy said. His hands were loose and hard about Weddel's throat, his arms still, rigid. "Do you hunt all day, and night, too, if you want, with a horse to ride and nigras to wait on you—to shine your boots and saddle the horse—and you setting on the gallery, eating, until time to go hunting again?"

"I hope so. I haven't been home in four years, you see. So I don't know anymore."

"Take me with you."

"I don't know what's there. There may not be anything. The Yankees were there, and my mother died right after. I don't know what is there."

"I'll work. We'll both work. You can get married in Mayesfield. It's not far."

"How do you know I haven't got a wife already?" The boy's hands shut on this throat, shaking him. "Stop it," Weddel said.

"If you say you have got a wife I'll kill you." The boy's hands became rigid. Weddel could hear him breathe.

"No," Weddel said, "I am not married."

"And you don't want to climb that foot ladder?"

"No. I never saw her but once. I might not even know her if I saw her again."

"She says different. I don't believe you. You are lying."

"No," Weddel said.

"Is it because you are afraid to?"

"Yes."

"Of Vatch?"

"Not Vatch. I'm just afraid. I think that my luck has given out. I know that it has lasted too long; I'm afraid that I will find that I have forgot how to be afraid. So I can't risk it. I can't risk finding that I have lost touch with truth. Not like Jubal here. He believes that I still belong to him; he will not believe that I have been freed. He won't even let me tell him so. He does not need to bother about the truth, you see."

"We would work. She might not look like the Mis'sippi women that wear shoes. But we would work. We would not shame you before them."

"No," Weddel said.

"Then you go away. Now."

"How can I? He can't ride now. He can't stay on a horse." The sound of his voice faded into the chill silence out of which, a moment later, came the faint, abrupt whisper of the hay as the boy moved and stopped, tense, though Weddel had heard no sound. "Which one is it?" Weddel whispered.

"It's paw," the boy whispered.

"I'll go down. You stay here. You keep my pistol for me."

X

The dark air was high, chill, cold. In the vast invisible darkness the valley lay slumbrous, the opposite cold and invisible range black on the black sky. Weddel, clutching the stub of his missing arm across his chest, shivered slowly and steadily. They stood in the stable door.

"Go," the father said.

"The war is over," Weddel said. "Vatch's victory is not my trouble."

"Take your horses and nigra, and ride on."

"If you mean your daughter, I never saw her but once, and I don't expect to see her again."

"Ride on," the father said. "Take what is yours and ride on."

"No," Weddel said. They faced each other in the darkness. "After four years I have bought immunity from running."

"You have till daylight," the father said.

"I have had less than that in Virginia for four years," Weddel said. "And this is just Tennessee."

The father turned; his figure dissolved and vanished into the bulk of the hill. Weddel entered the stable and mounted the ladder. Motionless, invisible above the snoring Negro, the boy squatted.

"Leave him here," the boy said. "He ain't nothing but a nigra."

"No," Weddel said.

"I can show you a short cut down to the valley. You can get down to the valley road and be in Mayesfield by daybreak."

"No. He wants to go home too. I've got to get him home." Weddel did not lie down. He squatted in the hay beside the Negro. He fumbled the cloak about him, squatting, and spread the other garments about the Negro. After a time the boy crept away; Weddel watched him fill and empty the vague orifice of the trapdoor. After a while Weddel shook the Negro. "Jubal," he said. The Negro groaned; he turned heavily, sleeping again. Weddel squatted. "I thought that I had lost it for good," he said to himself—"the peace and the quiet; the power to be afraid again."

XI

In the thick cold daylight the cabin stood gaunt and bleak on the rocky slope. The two horses stood in the churned road before the sagging gate, the Negro on the Thoroughbred and Weddel on the sorrel. The Negro was shivering. He sat hunched and high, with updrawn knees, his face almost invisible in the oilcloth hood.

"I told you they was fixing to pizen us with that stuff," he said. "I told you. Them hillbilly red-necks. And you not only let um pizen me, you fotch me the pizen in your own hand. O Lawd, O Lawd! If we ever does get home——"

Weddel was looking at the cabin. "She has a young man, I suppose—a beau." He spoke aloud, in a musing tone, in his brushed, faded, clean cloak, the reins in his single hand. "He said to come in sight of a laurel copse where the road disappears, and take a path to the left. That was what he said, wasn't it?"

"Who was what?" the Negro said. "I ain't going nowhere," he said. "I going back and lay down in that loft."

"All right," Weddel said. "Get down."

"Get down?"

"I'll need both horses. You can walk on when you are rested."

"I ghy tell your maw," the Negro said. "I ghy tell um. Ghy tell um how, after four years, you ain't got no more sense than to not know a Yankee when you see um. To stay the night with Yankees and let um pizen one of Mistis' niggers. I ghy tell um."

"I thought you were going to stay here," Weddel said. He was shivering too. "Yet I am not cold," he said to himself. "I am not cold."

"How in the world you ever get home without me?" the Negro said. "What I tell Mistis when I come in without you and she ask me where you is?"

"Come along," Weddel said. He lifted the sorrel into motion. Behind him the Negro rode, hunched, invisible in his coat and hood, muttering to himself in woebegone singsong, interminable and meaningless. The road, which had ascended to the house on the previous day, began now to descend. It was still muddy, though it had not rained during the night, scarred in dark, thick red across the bleak land beneath the dissolving sky. It crossed a barren and rocky pasture, jolting in short pitches downward toward where the pines and laurel began. After a while the cabin disappeared beyond a shoulder.

"And so I am running away," Weddel said to himself. "When I get home I will not be very proud of this. Yes, I will. It means that I am still alive. Still alive, since I know fear and desire. Since life is an affirmation of the past and a promise to the future. So I am still alive. . . . He said, 'Come in sight of a laurel copse where the road disappears, and turn out to the left, into a path.' "

The copse came into sight, three hundred yards ahead. Weddel drew up, the Negro overriding him, hunched; the Thoroughbred stopped of its own accord, looking back at Weddel.

"But I don't see any path," Weddel said; then he saw a man emerge from the copse and begin to run toward him up the road. Weddel thrust the reins beneath his groin and withdrew his hand inside the cloak. Then he saw that it was the boy. The boy came up, trotting. His face was white and strained, quite pale in the thick, lowering daylight.

"It's right here," the boy said.

"Yes," Weddel said. "I couldn't find it."

The boy took the sorrel's bridle. "It's on the other side of the bushes," he said. "You can't see it until you are in it."

"In what?" the Negro said. "I ghy tell um. After four years you ain't got sense enough to know a Yankee when you see um."

The boy held the sorrel's bridle. "They know the path too," he said.

"We guess once and they guess once," Weddel said. "Is that it?" The boy held the bridle. He was looking down the road to where the road disappeared. "You go back home," Weddel said.

"They know the path too," the boy said. "I am sick of it."

"Well," Weddel said. He looked about, quizzical, sardonic, with his gaunt, wasted face. "I can't stay here. I couldn't even build a house and be contented here. I have to choose between three things. That's what throws a man off—that extra alternative. Just when he has come to realize that living consists in choosing wrongly between two alternatives, to have to choose between three."

"We'd work," the boy said. "We could go back to the house. And then we could ride back down the mountain, two on one horse and two on the other. We could get down to the valley and get to Mayesfield by dark and get married. We would not shame you."

"Has she a young man?" Weddel said. "Somebody that waits for her at church and walks home with her and has Sunday dinner, and maybe fights the other young men?"

"We'd work. We wouldn't shame you."

"You go back," Weddel said.

"I'll go a piece with you."

"This here Caesar horse won't let no stranger ride him," the Negro said.

"I ain't going to make nobody walk," the boy said. He drew the sorrel toward the roadside.

"You go back home," Weddel said. "The war is over now."

The boy did not answer. He led the sorrel into the underbrush. The Thoroughbred hung back. "Whoa, you Caesar," the Negro said. "Wait, Marse Soshay. I ain't going to ride down no——"

The boy looked over his shoulder; he went on, leading the sorrel. "You stay back there," he said. "You keep where you are."

"You go back home," Weddel said. "I see the path now."

"I'll go a piece," the boy said.

The path was a faint scar, doubling back upon itself, dropping downward. The horses moved gingerly, jolting downward on stiffened legs. It descended for a while in short pitches, then it flattened and broadened, curving away around a shoulder of rock matted with still unbloomed laurel and rhododendron. It was wide enough now for two horses abreast. The Thoroughbred came up; the boy walked now between the two horses. He looked back.

"You keep back there," he said. He stopped, pulling the sorrel up. He looked at Weddel. "We'd work," he said. "We could go back, and go back down the mountain. We'd work."

Weddel looked at the boy. "Do you think we guessed wrong?" The boy looked at him, holding the sorrel back. "We had to guess. We had to guess one out of three."

"I don't want you to think it was me," the boy said.

"I won't think so. What do you think we ought to do?"

"Turn back," the boy said. "We would——" He drew back on the bridle; again the Thoroughbred came abreast and forged ahead. Weddel spurred the sorrel, lifting the boy onward.

"Let go," he said. The boy held to the bridle, lifted onward until the two horses were abreast. On the Thoroughbred the Negro perched, high-kneed, his mouth still talking, flobbed down with ready speech, easy and worn with talk like an old shoe with walking.

"I done told him and told him," the Negro said.

"Let go," Weddel said. He spurred the sorrel, forcing its shoulder into the boy.

"You won't turn back?" the boy said. "You won't?"

"Let go," Weddel said. His teeth showed a little under his lip; he lifted the sorrel with the spurs. The boy let go the bridle of the sorrel and ducked under the Thoroughbred's neck. Weddel, spurring the sorrel forward, saw, across the Negro's hunched shape, the boy surge upward and on to the Thoroughbred's back, thrusting the Negro backward along the horse's spine. The Thoroughbred leaped forward; the Negro's single cry came back as, gripping the boy, he hung for a precarious instant between clinging and falling.

"They think you will be riding the good horse," the boy said; "I told them you would be riding——" Weddel spurred the sorrel; almost abreast again and running, the two horses reached the final bend where the path coiled back upon the rocky and laurel-matted shoulder. "Keep back!" the boy said, turning his face over his shoulder, the Negro clinging to him, still falling and still shouting.

Weddel roweled the sorrel. On his face was a thin grimace of exasperation and anger almost like smiling. It was still on his face when he struck the earth, his foot still fast in the off stirrup. The sorrel leaped and swerved and dragged Weddel to the path side, where it halted and whirled and snorted once, and began to graze. The Thoroughbred rushed on past the bend and whirled and rushed back, the blanket twisted under its belly and its eyes rolling. The boy lay face down in the path, his face wrenched sideways against a stone, his arms back-sprawled, open-palmed; above him the Negro crouched, looking at the copse where the path vanished. The Thoroughbred circled them and went to where Weddel lay beneath the grazing sorrel, and stood above Weddel's body, whinnying, watching the copse also, and a fading gout of black powder smoke not less reluctant than the sluggish twin reverberations dying recapitulant between wet rocks and the damp twilight of laurel and rhododendron and pines.

The Negro was on his hands and knees when the father and Vatch emerged from the copse. The father was running, carrying a musket. "That durn fool! That durn fool!" he said.

He stopped and dropped the musket; he became stone-still in the path, above the fallen musket, looking at the group in the road with an expression of shock and amazement, like a man awaking from a dream. Vatch carried a rifle. He did not pause; in the act of stopping, he swung the rifle up and began to reload it, watching the Negro. On his hands and knees above the body of the boy, the Negro looked back at the two white men, his irises rushing and wild in the bloodshot whites. Then he turned, and, still on hands and knees, he scuttled back to where Weddel lay on his back, his foot fast in the stirrup of the grazing sorrel, and crouched over Weddel and turned and looked at the father, standing motionless, his jaw slacked and his hands still open, palm out, at his sides, as when he had dropped the musket, and watched Vatch backing slowly away up the path, loading the rifle. He watched Vatch stop; he did not close his eyes or look away. He watched the rifle elongate and then diminish to a round spot upon the white shape of Vatch's face like a period on a page. Crouching, the Negro's eyes rushed wild and steady and red, like those of a cornered animal.

OUTLAW IN TOWN

MICHAEL FESSIER

A howling blizzard had all but extinguished the sun above Buffalo Bend and, although it was only a quarter past third-drink time, the lamps were lighted in the China-man's Chance Saloon. A dozen or so of us were lined up at the bar, gloomily discussing the chances of our cattle's surviving the blow, when a sound from outside caused us all to turn. It was a cheerful, trilling sound—as if somewhere out in the storm a meadowlark were singing a song of spring. It came closer, and then the doors flew open and, accompanied by a flurry of snow, a tall red-haired young man strode into the saloon, points of light flashing from his silver spurs and belt buckle. A handsome fellow with a small scar on his right cheek, he paused, his eyes searching the room as if for signs of danger; then, reassured, he came on to the bar. "Howdy, boys," he said cheerfully, "how do you like the weather?"

Big Bart McCormack looked unbelievingly at him, then turned to the rest of us. "Outside it's snowing and blowing," he orated. "Thousands of our cattle are liable to freeze to death, and if they don't freeze to death the range will be ruined; there won't be no grass for 'em to eat and they'll starve to death. In the face of all that, this red-crested bobolink has the unmitigated gall to come awhistling in here and ask us how we like the weather." He faced the stranger. "How," he demanded, "would you like a good, solid smack on the bugle?"

"I don't think I'd care for it, thanks just the same," said the

135

stranger, grinning amiably at Bart. He tossed a silver dollar onto the mahogany. "A dash of forty rod, if you please, barkeep."

"Out here," said Bud Conyears, a stickler for protocol, "we call our poison 'redeye.' The only ones that refer to it as 'forty rod' are Texans and other foreigners of that ilk. Where you from, mister?"

"I," said the stranger, "just rode in over the North Trail."

"Which, if you did, you sure enough accomplished a feat unparalleled in the history of Buffalo Bend," observed Bart McCormack. "To the north of here lies Buffalo Mountain, and not even a bighorn sheep could come down its sheer cliffs, especially in a blizzard."

"Does it really," asked the stranger, "make any difference how I reached your miserable little metropolis?"

"No, it don't," said Bart, "but it's been my experience that any man that lies about a simple thing such as the direction he come from must have an urgent reason for leaving wherever he was. I don't care where you been or what you did while there; it all boils down to the fact that I can't stand a liar."

Then, not intending to shoot the young man, but merely to intimidate him, he made a move for his gun.

The stranger's hand was a blur as it flashed down, jerked Bart's silver-handled revolver from its holster and then presented it to Bart, butt first. "Was this what you were fumbling for, mister?" he asked politely.

Bart stared at the stranger with dawning awe and admiration. "That," he said, "is a wrinkle in gun fighting I never even heard of. Whereabouts did you pick up that knack of handling other people's personal firearms, mister?" Then he turned to the rest of us. "I hereby announce that this here stranger in our midst has just recently accomplished a feat unparalleled in the history of Buffalo Bend—which he come down the sheer face of Buffalo Mountain in a blizzard; and anyone holding a contrary opinion will kindly step forward and have his face busted." He extended a huge paw to the stranger. "My name's Bart McCormack," he said. "What's yourn?"

"Name of Walt," said the other.

Billy Feeney, a small, troublesome man, had been staring intently at Walt. "Walt what?" he asked, thus violating an unwritten law of the West to the effect that one positively never asks a stranger his last name. There was a glint of cold steel in Walt's eyes as he looked down at Billy. "Do you really want to know?"

"Not specially," gulped Billy and cautiously drew away from Walt. "But," he declared when he'd reached a safe distance, "I bet I've seen your mug somewheres before." Then he made a hasty exit from the saloon.

In the meanwhile Shasta Cooney, a raven-haired bar girl who made the Chinaman's Chance her base of operations, had also been staring at Walt, and there was an avaricious gleam in her lovely eyes as she took in his expensive silver spurs and belt buckle. Finally he turned from the bar, and their glances met. She smiled and made a small, beckoning gesture, and he went over and sat at her table. "Is there anything I can do for you?" he asked casually, but not failing to note the bountiful manner in which her figure filled out her dress.

Shasta studied his good-natured, boyish face and, in her mind's eye, she saw the silver spurs and belt buckle added to the growing hoard of treasure she kept in a secret repository at home. "I wonder," she said demurely, "if you'd care to buy a lady a drink."

"I sure enough would," said Walt eagerly and turned to survey the room. "Where is she?"

"I," said Shasta, a slight edge to her voice, "was referring to myself."

"Are you," asked Walt, "a sure-enough lady? Well, I'll be dog-goned, here I been bumping into ladies in bars and such all over the West, and in my simple ignorance I didn't recognize 'em. All the time I thought a lady was something special and wouldn't be caught dead cadging drinks in a place like this." He regarded her with cynical amusement, whistling tunelessly through his teeth.

She glared murderously at him, and there was fire in her dark eyes; but finally she managed to control her anger for the sake of possible profit. "Out here," she said, "a lady has to earn her living the best way she can, especially if she's a widow lady." She searched his face for a sign of sympathy. "My husband," she explained, "was killed by a bandit only last year, down in Texas."

"I have been dealt that hand before," said Walt, "by a girl whose husband was killed by a sheriff. She had eyes like you and hair like you and she looked like you; and me being young and un-sophisticated, she had me lassoed and hog-tied in no time at all." There was the pain of an old hurt in his eyes as he went on, "One day I woke up minus my money, my silver spurs and belt buckle. I had to walk out of town, she having also relieved me of my horse."

Mentally Shasta reshuffled the cards and decided on a new deal. She gave Walt a disarmingly frank smile and said, "Inasmuch as I never accept anything from a man that I can't put in a suitcase, I wasn't making a play for your horse—only the silver spurs, belt buckle and whatever you've got in your poke." Then her voice was tantalizingly provocative, her eyes filled with invitation and promise as she went on, "Now that all the cards are on the table, would you care to try your luck, mister?"

"I think I'd like to buy you a drink at that," said Walt. "But unfortunately I just spent my last bean at the bar, and I'm broke. What's more, the spurs and belt buckle once belonged to a deceased relative of mine, and I wouldn't part with them even for the pleasure of your continued company." Again he grinned at her and whistled tunelessly between his teeth. "Would you," he asked, "care to play out that hand?"

Shasta Cooney saved every penny she made to pay off the mortgage on a ranch left her by her late husband and, for all of her abundant beauty and generous proportions, she had the miserly soul of a Scrooge. She had never been known to extend credit to any client; but this was a special occasion, and she decided to make a small investment toward Walt's humiliation. She rose and called to Minnie Redwing, the plump Indian woman who served as waitress in the Chinaman's Chance.

"Minnie," she said, "this poor man's broke and thirsty. Bring him a small beer and put it on my tab. And—oh, Minnie—I think he's hungry too. Throw in a pretzel." Then she sat down to enjoy Walt's discomfiture.

Minnie waddled over and placed a small beer on the table. Walt toyed with the glass, then rose and, with an almost tender look in his eyes, he poured the brew down the back of Shasta's neck. Shasta screamed, first at the shock of the icy liquid, then in rage; she slapped at Walt, then ran for the back room with derisive laughter ringing in her ears.

Minnie Redwing stood staring adoringly at Walt.

"I don't blame you, duck," she said. "The least that tightwad could of done was buy you a whole bottle of redeye. Well, anyway, your credit's good with me. You just name it and you got it."

"No, thanks, Minnie," said Walt. "I'm not thirsty."

"Well, if you happen to wish a drink, even for the purpose of pouring it down Shasta Cooney's neck when she comes back," said Bart McCormack generously, "it's on me."

"I," said Walt, "don't accept drinks I can't pay back. But," he went on, "I would like to play a little poker."

"How you gonna get money, duck?" asked Minnie Redwing.

"With this," said Walt; and then his hand was a white blur, and Minnie Redwing was looking down the barrel of a revolver.

"If this is a stickup, I ain't gonna resist you," said Minnie Redwing. "You can have anything on the premises. And that," she added, looking him in the eye, "includes me. I'll go peaceful."

"It isn't a stickup," laughed Walt. "I'm going to put up my gun for a stake in the game." Then he walked over to the card table.

Fifteen minutes later, Walt had lost the revolver, plus the cartridges, gunbelt and holster. Billy Feeney, who had just come in from the outside, watched until the winner had pocketed Walt's weapon. "And now," exclaimed Billy in a gloating voice, "I'm gonna tell you why this here jasper was so reticent about where he'd come from and why. He's from Texas, and his name's Walt Durkim, alias the Whistling Kid."

Walt leaped up from the table and lashed out at him, but Billy retreated to the safety of Bart McCormack's rear. He reached out from behind Bart and extended a yellowed square of paper. "And if you don't believe me, read this reward poster I found in the post office."

"Which this sure enough is a picture of you, Walt," said Bart, studying the poster. "And it sure enough describes you, including the silver spurs, belt buckle and habit of whistling at all times, especially when aroused or in the mood to kill."

Walt was whistling now, a sad little tune.

Bart perused the poster some more. "Wanted," he read aloud, "for mail robbery, bank robbery, stage robbery, payroll robbery, murder, manslaughter, desertion, treason, arson and kidnaping." Bart wagged his shaggy head in wonder. "Not to mention," he went on, "horse stealing, cattle rustling and the theft of two hundred mules belonging to the United States Army. My goodness, boy, it seems the only thing you ain't never purloined, stolen from or killed is a sheep."

"I," said Walt, tense and alert, "deny everything."

Shasta Cooney came in from the back room. "What's going on?" she asked Billy, and Billy pointed.

"This is the Whistling Kid," he said, "which his real moniker's Walt Durkim."

"Why, Walt Durkim is the man the Texas sheriff wrote me about," she said. Then she faced Walt. "You killed my husband," she declared.

"If I did, you have my commiserations," said Walt, "but not my apologies. I never killed a man in all my life who wasn't trying to turn me in for the reward money."

His eyes seemed to be boring into those of every individual present, and we all backed cautiously away. "Don't look at me," said Billy Feeney, "I wouldn't think of running to the telegraph office and notifying the nearest United States marshal, which it says to do in the poster. Even," he gulped, "if the reward is five thousand dollars."

"Well spoken, Billy," said Judge Gorman unctuously. "Never let

139

it be said that we of Buffalo Bend would betray a stranger who came among us seeking sanctuary." With that he began drifting toward the door. Several others started angling in the same direction, and then Billy Feeney averted what looked like an impending stampede. "You're wasting your time," he declared. "The telegraph line is down, and the office is closed." The move toward the door stopped, and there was a long silence in the room. "Well, isn't anybody going to do anything?" demanded Shasta Cooney. "He's unarmed, isn't he? Why don't you take him into custody?"

"In which case, someone's likely to get his teeth shot out with his own gun," said Bart. "In addition to which, I don't need five thousand dollars that much."

"Well, I do," said Shasta, "and the reward's rightfully mine. He killed my husband, didn't he?"

"Which your husband never was worth no five thousand dollars the best day of his life," said Billy Feeney. "Besides you forget that it was me that found the reward poster in the post office."

"By rights," said a voice from the rear, "he oughtta be community property for all of us to participate in like a public water hole, share and share alike."

"Does that poster say he's gotta be on the hoof?" asked another voice from the rear.

"It says dead or alive," replied Bart. "And if that gives any low-living bushwhacker any ideas of shooting the Whistling Kid in the back, I'll personally guarantee he won't live to enjoy his next breath, let alone the reward money." Then he turned to Walt. "You'd better hit the trail, mister," he said. "Sooner or later one of these coyotes is sure to try his luck when I ain't around."

"Where's he gonna go?" demanded a man who had just recently entered the saloon. "Both mountain passes leading outta town are blocked with snow. He'll freeze to death and, when it thaws, the coyotes'll eat him."

"In which case," said Billy Feeney, "there won't be any means of identifying him as the Whistling Kid, and he'll be a total loss to all of us."

"Well," Bart said to Walt, "it looks like you'll have to remain in our midst for a while longer. In the meanwhile I hereby offer to finance your creature comforts and whatever luxuries the town affords. And don't bother to thank me. I gotta hunch you ain't long for this world, and it won't cost me much to speak of."

"I never accept money I don't earn or steal," said Walt and then he laughed ruefully. "Here am I—practically a capitalist," he declared, "worth five thousand dollars in gold, and I haven't got the price of a short beer or a pot of beans. I'm a certified check which I can't cash."

"But one of us could cash you," said Shasta Cooney, her eyes shining with greed and inspiration. "What if one of us should advance all the money you'll need while in town—will you agree to go with him or her to the nearest United States marshal and let him or her turn you in for the reward when the roads are open?"

"Why, that's the most immoral proposition I ever heard of in all my days," said Walt in an outraged voice. "It's like asking me to sell my own life."

"It's either that or giving it away," declared Shasta. "Like Bart McCormack said, somebody's sure to kill you sooner or later. If you agree to my terms, at least you'll get to spend some of your reward money on yourself. Of course," she added, "you'll have to include your horse in the deal."

Walt glanced thirstily at the bar, and his whistle bubbled and gurgled like the soothing sound of redeye pouring out of a bottle. "Well," he said, "there's always a chance of a good lawyer getting me off. What's your offer?"

"One hundred dollars," said Shasta.

"I would rather be shot in the back," said Walt.

Zack Martin, a cattle buyer, stepped forward. "I'll make it two hundred dollars," he said.

"Personal I only got four bits in cash," said Minnie Redwing, "but I own a flock of merinos. I bid two hunnert sheep."

"Three hundred dollars," said Shasta.

"Three hunnert sheep," said Minnie Redwing.

"Four hundred dollars," said Zack.

"Five hundred dollars," said Shasta.

"Aw, heck, you only live once," said Minnie Redwing. "I bid six hunnert sheep." Then she turned to Walt. "Come with me, duck," she said. "I got a nice new wickiup near here all fixed up for light housekeeping."

"I think there's something you should understand, Minnie," Judge Gorman told her. "The highest bidder doesn't get Walt in person, only the right to turn him in for the reward, after which he'll be hanged by a rope until dead."

"I withdraw my bid," said Minnie Redwing. "Any time I squander six hunnert sheep on a man, he's gotta be alive, functional and available."

Others in the room, however, didn't care how unfunctional Walt might be in the near future. They saw in him five thousand dollars' worth of negotiable security, and they bid his price higher and higher. Shasta Cooney stayed with the bidding until it reached nine hundred dollars; then, at the end of her resources, she stepped aside. Finally Zack Martin won out at an even thousand dollars. "And now," said Walt, "let's see the color of your money."

"I haven't got it on me," said Zack. "It's in the bank at O'Leary's Lapse; but I'll establish a thousand dollars' worth of credit for you here in town, and you can spend it the same as cash." Walt agreed to the terms, and Zack went out to take possession of Walt's horse.

The first thing Walt did was to send to the general store for supplies, after which he proceeded to lay out a feast of canned lobster, turkey, ham, pickled pigs' feet and other rare and exotic viands the like of which were served in Buffalo Bend only on state occasions such as Christmas, weddings, funerals, hangings and other such related social events. For the rest of the night he presided over a Lucullan orgy, buying drinks for one and all, including a sextet of dance-hall girls recruited from down the street. Shasta Cooney watched as two of the girls sat on Walt's knees and stuffed food into his mouth, and her thrifty soul was revolted at the waste of it all.

"Well," Bud Conyears told her, "there ain't no sense in him saving up his money for his old age, is there?" The thought of Walt's dangling from a gibbet seemed to cheer Shasta up a little.

The next day Walt continued his rake's progress through the other saloons and dance halls in town, buying drinks and goodies for a small army of female admirers. Never had the young ladies encountered a more prodigal spender; and Shasta Cooney, who had no share in the bonanza, grew even more bitter. Walt encountered her in the Chinaman's Chance. "And now," he said, "I'll buy that drink you were hankering for yesterday."

"Do you," asked Shasta, "think I'd drink with the man who killed my husband?" With that she slapped him—hard.

"Put this on my tab," said Walt. Then he took her in his arms and kissed her at great length.

"Considering that they're enemies, and still he kisses her like that," gasped Billy Feeney, "I wonder what he'd do to her if they were friends."

Finally Walt released Shasta, leaving her reeling against the bar and gasping for breath. He started away, turned to give her a surprised look, then departed, whistling thoughtfully. "Somebody," said Bart McCormack, "bring Shasta a hooker of redeye; she's done fainted."

Later on in the day Bud Conyears entered the Chinaman's Chance and announced that he now owned sole rights to Walt and the reward money. "Which I exchanged twelve hundred dollars' worth of hay for him," he explained. An hour later Bud had paid off a fifteen-hundred dollar bill at Pott Barr's General Store with Walt. Pott Barr turned around and used him as down payment on a small ranch, the former owner of which soon thereafter bartered Walt for mining stock valued at seventeen hundred dollars. That night Bo Keester put up two thousand dollars against him and won Walt in a poker game.

What with low cattle prices and the blizzard, trade had been stagnant in Buffalo Bend, but two days after Walt's arrival there was a growing business boom, created partly by the lavish manner in which Walt spent his credit and partly by the profits the others made by dealing in him. In the latest transaction, Walt had gone for three thousand dollars. "Which he bolsters our economy considerable," said Bart McCormack, "and I foresee no end to our new era of prosperity."

Judge Gorman, however, took a pessimistic view of things and warned us of spiraling inflation. "Walt's a highly speculative commodity," he pointed out.

"What do you mean, 'speculative'?" demanded Bart McCormack. "He's backed by five thousand dollars in Federal currency, and he's as gilt-edged as a Government bond." Others shared Bart's optimism, and the trade in Walt continued to be brisk. Although there were occasional fluctuations, the trend was bullish. On the first day that the roads were open to travel, a group of businessmen from O'Leary's Lapse arrived in town. They caught the fever, formed a syndicate and acquired Walt on a bid of forty-five hundred dollars. The new asking price on him, they announced, would be six thousand, five hundred dollars.

"Why, that's fifteen hundred above par, and it's sheer insanity," declared Judge Gorman. "The Government's only offering five thousand for him."

"If the Government wants any part of the Whistling Kid," said the syndicate leader, "they'll have to pay our price. We got a corner on the market, ain't we?"

"You," said Judge Gorman, "have invested in a Mississippi Bubble. What if Walt breaks his word and escapes? When you try to deliver him to the United States marshal, how do you know his gang won't waylay you and confiscate him? Maybe that's what he's been planning all along."

When news of the judge's dire prophecy spread, panic set in, and the bottom fell out of the market. The O'Leary's Lapse men were all for shooting up Buffalo Bend on the grounds that we'd hornswoggled them, but their leader restrained them. "This town's full of suckers, and they'll come in on any deal if they can get in cheap enough," he told them. "Come on, we're gonna go after the small investors."

That night, when Walt emerged from the Chinaman's Chance, Shasta Cooney accosted him and, at pistol point, forced him into her buggy and drove away with him toward her mortgaged ranch. "This," said Walt, "is kidnaping and it's highly illegal—you know that, don't you?"

"I just won you in a raffle," said Shasta.

"I see," said Walt; "and now you're going to make sure I hang for killing your husband, is that it?"

"I forgot to tell you," said Shasta, "that before you killed my husband, he had deserted me and run off with a female faro dealer from Gila Bend."

The moon limned Shasta's dark beauty, and a pervasive perfume in the frosty air caused Walt to speak without considering the implication of his words. "Any man who could tear himself away from you for the sake of a female faro dealer," he said, "is out of his mind and better off dead."

"I," said Shasta, drawing closer to him for warmth and letting the pistol fall to her lap, "would hate to have anyone hanged for killing him."

"You aren't forgetting," said Walt, unable to believe his ears, "that I'm worth five thousand dollars at the end of a rope, are you?"

"The Mexican border isn't far off," said Shasta. Then she sighed. "The other night," she said, "you kissed me. You did it for spite, but it rocked me to my very foundation and changed my whole outlook on life. I felt a crazy, overwhelming impulse to give you everything I've got in my suitcase. No man has ever made me feel that way before, not even my husband." She looked sideways at him. "How did it make you feel?" she asked.

"Come to think of it," said Walt, "there does seem to be some sort of haunting memory attached to the episode, but I can't put it into words." Then he gazed at her out of new eyes and in a different light. "Maybe," he said, "I ought to refresh my memory."

The next day a group of us stood in the Chinaman's Chance and watched a United States Marshal as he studied the yellowed poster Billy Feeney had found in the post office. "This is indubitably Walt Durkim," the marshal finally conceded. "But, if he's here, he sure enough must be in a remarkable state of decomposition, considering that he's been dead eighteen months."

"Then who was the other guy?" asked Billy Feeney.

"Oh, that must have been Walt's brother, Dan," said the marshal. "He looks like Walt and he shares the family fondness for unearned

144

increment, but he doesn't go in for crimes of violence. He's more of a con man—makes his living by planting his brother's old wanted posters in towns like this and then waiting for human greed to take its course. He's been eating high off the hog for months, but so far as I know he hasn't done anything he can be arrested for."

"He swindled Zack Martin out of a thousand dollars. Ain't that illegal?" demanded Billy.

"How do you figure Zack was swindled," inquired Bart McCormack, "considering that he got his thousand back and made a profit on the deal?"

"And so did a lot of other people," said Bud Conyears, "including the O'Leary's Lapse syndicate, which they come out considerably more than even on the raffle."

"I don't get it," said Billy. "Somebody must of lost." Then he saw the light. "Sure, that's it!" he exclaimed. "Shasta Cooney. What'd she get for her money?"

"Shasta," said Bart, "only invested the price of a raffle ticket."

"In addition to which," said Judge Gorman, who had been standing by the window, "Shasta got Dan Durkim." Then, from outside came the rattle of wagon wheels and a merry, trilling whistle, as if a meadowlark were singing a song of spring. We all ran to the window and watched while Dan Durkim and Shasta rode by in a buggy, holding hands. It seemed that Shasta had finally succumbed to that overwhelming impulse, for in the back of the buggy was a suitcase. "I," said Judge Gorman, "married them last night."

PLAINSWOMAN

WILLIAMS FORREST

The cold of the fall was sweeping over the plains, and Nora's husband, Rolf, and his men had ridden off on the roundup. She was left on the ranch with Pleny, a handyman, who was to do the chores and lessen her fears.

Her pregnancy told her that she should hurry back East before the solemn grip of winter fell on the land. She was afraid to have the child touch her within, acknowledge its presence, when the long deep world below the mountains closed in and no exit was available—for the body and for the spirit.

Her baby had not yet wakened, but soon it would. But gusts of wind and a forbidding iron shadow on the hills told her that the greatest brutality of this ranch world was about to start. And then one morning Pleny came in for his breakfast, holding the long finger of his left hand in the fingers of his right. For some time he had concealed his left hand from her, holding it down or in his pocket; and from the way he had held himself, she had thought it was a part of his chivalry, his wish to have table manners, use his right hand and sit up straight with a lady. But now he held it before him like a trophy, and one he did not wish to present.

Nora had been thinking of New England when Pleny came in—of the piano and the gentle darkness of her mother's eyes, of frost on the small windowpanes, and the hearth fires, of holidays and the swish of sleighs, of men with businesslike faces and women who drank tea and read poetry, of deep substantial beds and the way the hills and the sea prescribed an area, making it intimate, and the way the towns folded into the hills. She was thinking of home and comfort, and then Pleny walked in; the dust trailed around his ankles, and the smell of cattle seemed to cling to his boots. A thousand miles of cattle and plains and work and hurt were clung like webs in his face.

Nora had made eggs, ham, bread and coffee for the breakfast, but Pleny made them objects of disgust as he extended his hand, as shyly but as definitely as a New England lad asking for a dance, and said, "I got the mortification, ma'am. I have to let you see it."

She looked at his index finger and saw the mortification of the flesh, the gangrene. He held the finger pointed forward, his other fingers closed. He pressed the finger with his other hand, and the darkened skin made a crackling sound like that of ancient paper or dangerous ice over a pond. And above the finger some yellow streaks were like arrows pointing to the hairs and veins above his wrist.

Nora smelled the food, gulped, stood up and turned away.

"I got to come to you, ma'am," said Pleny. "I finally got to come to you."

He spoke firmly but shyly, but she did not hear his tone; she heard only his demand. And her emotion rejected it and any part of it. Her emotion said that he should not have come to her and that she had nothing to do with it, and would not and could not. She walked toward the fireplace, staring into the low flames. She heard the wind coax the sides of the house. She said, pretending nothing else had been mentioned, "Pleny, there's your breakfast." She itemized it, as if the words could barricade her against him. "Eggs . . . ham . . . bread . . . hot coffee—hot coffee."

But after she had spoken she heard nothing but his steady, waiting breathing behind her. And she understood that she would have to turn and face it. She knew he was not going away and would not happily sit down to eat and would not release her.

The fire spoke and had no answer, even though it was soft. She turned and saw the weather on Pleny's face, the diamonds of raised flesh, the scars. And she knew that death was in his finger and was moving up his arm and would take all of him finally, as fully as a bullet or freezing or drowning.

"What do you expect of me, Pleny?" she said.

He moved with a crinkling hard sound of stained dungarees, hardened boots and his dried reluctant nature. "Ma'am," he said, "I don't want you to think I'm a coward. I just wouldn't want you to get that notion. I'll take my bumps, burns and cuts, just like I did with this finger on the lamp in the bunkhouse and then on the gate before it could heal. I'll take it without complaining, but I sure don't like to doctor myself." His lake-blue eyes were narrowed with thought, and the erosion in his face was drawn together, as if wind and sun were drawing his face closer together the way they did the land in the drought. "I just can't bear to cut on myself," he said, lowering his head with a dry shame. He lifted his head suddenly and said, "I suppose I'd do it out on the plain, in the mountains, alone. But I can't do it here."

His Adam's apple wobbled as he sought in his throat for words. His lips were cracked and did not easily use explanations. "It just seems sinful, ma'am," he said, "for a man to hack on himself." Suddenly his eyes were filled with burning knowledge. He spoke reasonably, without pleading, but an authority was in his voice. "Ma'am, you never saw a man do that, did you, when somebody else was around to doctor him?"

She had watched and listened to his explanation without a stirring in her; she had done so as if she were mesmerized, like a chicken before a snake. Gradually his meaning penetrated her and told her what he meant.

"Ma'am," he said, "would you do me the kindness to take off this here finger?"

She ran senselessly, as if she were attempting to run long, far back to New England. The best she could do was run through the rooms of the haphazardly laid-out house and get to her room and close the door and lean against it. She was panting, and her eyes were closed, and her heart was beating so hard that it hurt her chest. Slowly she began to feel the hurts on her shoulders, where she had struck herself against the walls and doors. Rolf had started this house with one room and had made rooms and halls leading off from it as time went on. She had careered through the halls to her room, as if fighting obstacles.

She went to her bed, but did not allow herself to fall down on it. That would be too much weakness. She sat on the edge of the bed, with her hands in her lap. Her wish to escape from this place was more intense than ever within her. And her reasons for it ran through her brain like a cattle stampede, raising acrid dust and death and injury—and fear, most of all.

Her fear had begun in the first frontier hotel in which she had spent a night. Rolf had been bringing her West from New England to his ranch in the springtime. The first part of the ride on the railroad had been a pure delight. Rolf's hand was big, brown, with stiff red hairs on the back, a fierce, comforting hand; and her own had lain within it as softly as a trusting bird. The railroad car had had deep seats and decor that would have done credit to a fine home. As those parts of the world she had never seen went past, mountain, stream and hamlet, she had felt serene; and the sense of adventure touched her heart like the wings of a butterfly. She was ready to laugh at each little thing and she had a persistent wish to kiss Rolf on the cheek, although she resisted such an unseemly act in front of other people.

"I know I'll be happy," she said. And his big quiet hand around hers gave her the feeling of a fine, strong, loving, secure world.

But the world changed. After a time they were on a rough train that ran among hills and plains, and after a while there was nothing to see but an endless space with spring lying flat on it in small colorful flowers and with small bleak towns in erratic spaces, and the men on the train laughed roughly and smelled of whisky. Some men rode on the roof of the car and kicked their heels, fired guns and sang to a wild accordion.

Rolf's hand seemed smaller. His tight, strong burned face that she had so much admired seemed remote; he was becoming a stranger, and she was becoming alone with herself. She, her love for him, her wish for adventure were so small, it seemed, in comparison to the spaces and the crudity.

One night the train stopped at a wayside station, and the passengers poured out as if Indians were attacking. They assailed the dining room of the canvas-and-board hotel as if frenzied with starvation. In the dining room Rolf abruptly became a kind of man she had never known. He grabbed and speared at plates like any of the others and smiled gently at her after he had secured a plateload of food for her that made her stomach turn. After affectionately touching her hand, he fought heartily with the others to get an immense plateload for himself. Then he winked at her and started to eat, in the same ferocious way as the others. His manners in New England had seemed earthy, interesting and powerful—a tender animal. But here, here he was one more animal.

That night they shared a bedroom with five other people, one a woman who carried a pistol. Rolf had bought sleeping boards and blankets, so that they would not have to share beds with anyone. The gun-carrying woman coughed and then said, "Good night, all you no-good rascals."

Rolf laughed.

The spring air flipped the canvas walls. The building groaned with flimsiness and people. Nora had never before heard the sounds of a lot of sleeping people. She put her face against Rolf's chest and pulled his arm over her other ear.

Late at night she woke crying. Or was she crying? There was crying within her, and there were tears on her face. But when she opened her eyes, the night was around her, without roof or walls, but there was the water of rain on her cheeks. Rolf bent over her. "We're outside," he said. "You were suffering. Exhausted, suffering, and you spoke out loud in your sleep."

"Why did you bring me out here?" The blankets were wet, but she felt cozy. He was strong against her. The night was wet but sweet after the flapping, moaning hotel.

Some water fell from his face to hers. Was Rolf crying? No, not Rolf, no. But when he spoke, his voice was sad. "I told you how it would be, didn't I?"

"I didn't know," she said. "I didn't know how awful it could be."

He spoke powerfully, but troubledly. "I can't always take you outside, away from things. I can't do that. There'll be times when I can't do for you, when only you can do it yourself."

"Don't be disturbed," she said, holding him closer. "Don't be disturbed." The smell of the wet air was sweet, and it was spring, and they were alone and small again in an enclosed world, made of them both, and she was unafraid again. "I'll be all right," she promised. "Rolf, I will be all right."

She slept with that promise, but it did not last through the next day. The train stopped after noontime in the midst of the plain. Cattle ran from the train. A lone horseman rode toward them out of curiosity. The sky was burning. Some flowers beside the tracks lifted a faint gossamer odor. Men were drinking and making tea on the stove of the car. Then they all were told that a woman two cars ahead was going to have a child, now. Nora was asked to go forward to attend her.

The impressions of the next few hours had smitten her ever since. The car in which the woman lay on a board suspended between seats across the aisle was empty except for herself and the third woman on the train. The cars before and after this one had also been emptied. The woman helping her said that the men were not even supposed to hear the cries of the woman in labor. It would not be proper. But were the men proper anyway? From the sounds in the distance, Nora could tell they were shouting, singing and shooting, and maybe fighting and certainly drinking.

She had seen labor before, when the doctor was unavailable, blocked away by snow, so she was good enough here, and there were no complications. But there was no bedroom with comforters, a fire and gentle women about. The woman helping her was the one who wore a pistol, and she cussed.

When the child, a boy, was born, the gun-toting woman shouted the word out the window, and the air was rent with shouts and shooting. The woman on the board lifted her wet head, holding her blanketed baby. "A boy to be a man," she said. "A boy to be a man." She laughed, tears streaming from her eyes.

The woman with the gun said softly, "God rest Himself. A child of the plains been born right here and now."

The train started up. Nora sat limply beside the mother and child. Men walked into the car, looked down and smiled.

"Now, that's a sight of a boy."

"Thank you kindly," said the woman.

"Now, ma'am, that boy going to be a cattleman?" said another.

"Nothing else."

"Hope we wasn't hoorawing too much, ma'am," said a tall man.

"Jus' like my son was born Fourth of July. Thank you kindly."

"Just made this tea, but it ain't strong's should be," said a man carrying a big cup.

"Thank you kindly."

Another man came up timidly—strange for him; he was huge. It turned out he was the husband. He did not even touch his wife. He looked grimly at his son. The woman looked up at him. "All these folks been right interested," he said.

The woman smiled. The train jerked and pulled. Her face paled. The man put his hand on her forehead. "Now just don't fret," he said. "Just don't fret."

"Thank you kindly," she said.

In her own seat, next to Rolf, Nora was pale. She flinched when the train racketed over the road. Rolf gripped her hand.

"Rolf?"

"Yes, honey?"

"She's all right. The woman with the baby—she's all right."

"I know."

"Then be quiet, don't be disturbed. I can tell from your hand. You're disturbed."

He looked out the window at the plains, at the spring. "The trip took longer than I thought," he said. "It's time for spring roundup. I ought to be at the ranch."

She was shocked. This great, terrible, beautiful thing had happened, and he was thinking of the roundup. Her hand did not feel small and preserved in his; it felt crushed, even though his fingers were not tightly closed.

"Rolf?" Her shock was low and hurt and it told in her voice. "Rolf. That woman had a baby on the train. It could have been awful. And all you can think of now is the roundup."

He looked around at the others in the car. Then he lowered decorum a little and put his arm around her.

He whispered, "Honey, I tried to tell you—I tried. Didn't you listen? On the plains we do what has to be done. Why, honey, that woman's all right, and now we've got to get to roundup."

"But can't we—can't we be human beings?" she said.

He held her. "We are, honey," he said. "We are. We're the kind of human beings that can live here."

She remembered all that and she remembered also that within two days after they had got to the ranch, Rolf had gone out with the men on spring roundup. That time, too, Pleny had been left with her to take care of the home ranch. She had been sad, and he had spoken to her about it in a roundabout fashion at supper one night. Pleny ate with her in the big kitchen when the others were gone, instead of in the bunkhouse. And he was shy about it, but carried a dignity on his shyness.

"Don't suppose you know that the cattle're more important than anything out here?" he said.

"It seems I have to know it," said Nora.

Pleny was eating peas with a knife. She heard about it, but had never been sure it was possible.

"Couldn't live here without the cattle," he said.

"It seems to me that living here would be a lot better if people thought more about people."

"Do. That's why cattle's more important."

"I fail to understand you."

Pleny worked on steak meat. "Ma'am, cattle's money, and money's bread. Not jus' steak, but bread, living. Why, ma'am, if a man out here wants a wife, he has to have cattle first. Can't make out well enough to have a wife and kids without you have cattle."

"I don't think it's right," she had said then in the springtime. "I don't think it's right that it should be that way."

And Pleny had replied, "Don't suppose you're wrong, ma'am. I really don't." He wiped his mouth on his sleeve. "Only trouble is, that's the way it is here, if you want to stay."

She hadn't wanted to stay. As soon as she was sure she was pregnant, she wanted to go home. The spring had passed, and the summer hung heavy over the plains. The earth, the sky, the cattle, the people had dry mouths, and dogs panted with tongues gone gray. The wind touched the edges of the windmills, and water came from the deep parts of the earth, but you could not bathe in it. The water was golden and rationed, and coffee sometimes became a luxury—not because you didn't have the coffee, but because the cool watery heart of the earth did not wish to serve you.

The fall roundup time came; and just before the outfit moved out, a cowboy, barely seventeen years old, had broken his leg. Rolf had pulled the leg straight, strapped a board to it and put the boy on a horse with a bag of provisions. "Tie an extra horse to him," Rolf had commanded Pleny, "in case something happens."

Pleny had done so. Rolf had asked the boy, "Got your money?"

"Got it right here."

"Now, you get to that doctor."

"Sure enough try."

"Now, when you're fixed up," said Rolf, "you come back."

"Sure enough will."

Nora knew that it would take eight to ten days for the boy to get to the nearest doctor. She ran toward the boy and the horses. She held the reins and turned on Rolf. "How can you let him go alone? How? How?"

Rolf's face had been genial as he talked to the boy, but now it hardened. But the boy, through a dead-white pain in his face, laughed. "Ma'am," he said, "now who's going to do my work and that other man's?"

"Rolf?" she turned.

Rolf turned to her, took her hands. "Nora, there isn't anybody that can go with him. He knows that."

The boy laughed. "Mr. Rolf," he said, "when I get my own spread, I'm going to go out East there to get a tender woman. I swear." He spurred with his good leg and, still laughing, flashed off into dust with his two horses.

"Rolf? He might die."

Rolf bowed his head, then fiercely lifted it. "Give him more credit."

"But you can't——" she began.

"We can!" he said. Then he softened. "Nora, I don't know what to say. Here—here there's famine, drought, blizzard, locusts. Here—here we have to know what we must do if we want to stay."

"I don't like it," she said.

A wind lifted and moved around them, stirring grass and dust. In the wind was the herald of the fall—and therefore the primary messenger of the bitter winter. In the wind was the dusty harbinger of work, of the fall roundup.

"Soon I'll have to go," he said, "for the roundup."

"I know."

"The plains are mean," he said. "I know. I came here and found it. But I—I don't hate it. I feel—I feel a—a bigness. I see—I see rough prettiness." He bowed his head. "That isn't all I mean." He looked at her. "Soon I have to go. You'll be all right. Pleny will take care of you."

She hadn't told him that she was sure she had a child within her. She felt that she must keep her secret from this wild place, because even if it were only spoken, the elements might ride like a stampede against her, hurting her and her child, even as they did in the dark when she was alone and the wind yelled against the walls beside her bed and told her how savage was the place of the world in which she lived.

There was a knock on her door. She looked up. Her hands, folded in her lap, gripped each other. She did not answer.

"Ma'am?"

She said nothing.

"It's Pleny. I just can't sit down and eat, ma'am, worrying about this mortification of the flesh I got. I just can't sit down to anything like that. I just have to do something."

She made her hands relax in her lap.

"I have it wrapped up in my kerchief, ma'am," said Pleny, "but that ain't going to do it no good."

She closed her eyes, but opened them at once, staring at the door.

Pleny said, "I ain't going to leave you and the ranch, ma'am. Couldn't do that. I have my chores to do."

A small unbidden tear touched the edge of her eye and slipped down.

There was a silence, and then he said quietly, "The doc's so far away, don't 'spect I could get there before that mortification took more of my flesh. Sure would hate that. Sure would hate that."

A second tear burned silver on the edge of her eye and dropped and burned golden down her cheek and became acid on her line of chin, and her wrist came up and brushed it away.

She heard the wind and many messages and she imagined Pleny waiting. She felt a sense of response, of obligation, of angry maternal love, as if all the wistful hope and female passion of her nature had been fused, struck into life, made able because she was woman and was here, and birth, survival, help, lay potent, sweet, powerful in her heart and in her hands.

She stood up. "Pleny?"

"Yes, ma'am?"

"What must I do?"

He was silent, and she opened the door. Angrily, then firmly, she said, "Let's go outside, Pleny."

"Yes, ma'am."

She held the kindling ax. Pleny had his finger on the block. He closed his eyes. The wind pulled her skirts. She looked up for a moment at the whirling light. Then, in necessity and tenderness, she swiftly did what must be done.

They were coming, the men were coming home from the round-up. The screen of dust was on the plain. She had been working on the meal and now it was the bread she was kneading. Working on the bread, she felt a kick against her abdomen.

She stopped, startled a moment, her hands deep, gripping in the dough—the kick again, strong.

Suddenly, in a way that would have shocked her mother, in a way that would have shocked herself not so long ago, she threw back her head and laughed, a fierce song of love and expectancy. She made bread and was kicked; she expected her man and she laughed, fiercely and tenderly. She was kicked, and a child of the plains had awakened within her.

THE MARRIAGE OF MOON WIND

BILL GULICK

It was their last night on the trail. Off to the northeast the jagged, snowcapped peaks of the Wind River Mountains loomed tall against the darkening sky and the chill, thin air of the uplands was spiced with the pungent smell of sage and pine. But Tad Marshall was not interested in sights or smells at the moment. A rangy, well-put-together young man of twenty with curly golden hair and sharp blue eyes, he leaned forward and spoke to the grizzled ex-trapper sitting on the far side of the fire.

"You'll fix it for me?"

"I'll try," Buck Owens said grudgingly. "But don't hold me to blame for nothin' that happens. Like I told you before, Slewfoot Samuels eats greenhorns raw."

"He takes a bit out of me, he'll come down with the worst case of colic he ever had."

"You're cocky enough, I will say that."

"Don't mean to be. It's just that I come west to be a beaver trapper, not a mule tender."

"With the knack you got fer handlin' mules, Captain Sublette won't want to lose you. He hears about this scheme you got to partner up with Slewfoot, he'll have a foamin' fit."

Tad shook his head. He liked Sublette and was real grateful for his chance to come west, but he wanted to see a chunk of the world with no dust-raising pack train clouding his view.

156

"Sublette can just have his fit. Me, I don't intend to go back to Missouri for a long spell."

"What're you runnin' away from—a mean pa?"

"Why, no. Pa treated me good."

"The law, maybe? You killed somebody back home?"

"Nothin' like that."

"Jest leaves one thing, then. Did you have woman trouble?"

Tad ran embarrassed fingers through his hair. "Guess you could call it that. There was three gals got the notion I was engaged to marry 'em. They all had brothers with itchy trigger fingers."

"Three gals wanted to marry you all to oncet?" Buck said in open admiration. "How'd that happen?"

"Darned if I know. Women have always pestered me, seems like. Now tell me some more about Slewfoot. You trapped with him for five years, you say?"

"Yeah. That's all I could stand him. Got a right queer sense of humor, Slewfoot has."

"A bit of joshin' never hurt nobody. I'll take the worst he can dish out, grin and come back for more."

"An' if you can't take it," Buck said, a gleam coming into his faded old eyes, "you'll stay with the mules like me 'n' the captain wants you to do?"

"Sure."

"Fine! I'll introduce you to Slewfoot tomorrow."

The word got around. During the half day it took the fur brigade to reach rendezvous grounds in the lush, grass-rich valley of the Green River, the men gossiped and grinned amongst themselves, and their attitude riled Tad.

Greenhorn though he was, Tad had learned considerable during the trip out from St. Louis. There were several kinds of trappers, he'd discovered. Some worked for wages and some for commissions, but the elite of the trade were the free trappers—men who roamed where they pleased, sold their furs to the highest bidder and were beholden to nobody.

Usually such men worked in pairs, but Slewfoot, who'd been queer to begin with, and was getting queerer every year, did his trapping with no other company than a Shoshone squaw he'd bought some years back. Campfire talk had it that Indian war parties rode miles out of their way to avoid him; she grizzly bears scared their cubs into behaving by mentioning his name; and beavers, when they heard he was in the neighborhood, simply crawled up on the creek banks and died.

None of which scared Tad. But it did make him look forward with considerable interest to meeting the man whose partner he hoped to be.

Shortly before noon they hit Green River and made camp. Already the valley was full of company men, free trappers and Indians from many tribes, come in from every corner of the West for a two-week carnival of trading, gambling, drinking, horse racing and fighting. Tad took it all in with keen, uncritical eyes. But other eyes in the party looked on with far less tolerance.

Traveling with the brigade that year was a minister named Thomas Rumford, a tall, hollow-cheeked, solemn-visaged man who was returning to a mission he had established some years earlier among the Nez Perce Indians, out Oregon way. Parson Rumford had made no bones of the fact that he disapproved of the language and personal habits of the mule tenders, and he liked even less the behavior of the celebrating trappers. While Tad was helping unload the mules, Parson Rumford came up, a reproachful look on his face.

"My boy, what's this I hear about your becoming a trapper?"

"Well, I was sort of figuring on it."

"Do you know what kind of man Slewfoot Samuels is?"

"Tell me he's some ornery. But I reckon I can put up with him."

Parson Rumford shook his head and stalked away. Feeling a shade uncomfortable, Tad finished unloading the mules. Then he saw Captain Sublette approaching, and the amused twinkle in Sublette's dark eyes made him forget the minister.

"Met your trapping partner yet?"

"No. Buck's takin' me over soon as we get through here."

"Well, the least I can do is wish you luck."

"Thank you kindly, captain."

"And remind you that your mule-tending job will be waiting, in case things don't work out."

Feeling more and more edgy, Tad joined Buck and they threaded their way toward the Shoshone section of camp.

"Lived with that squaw so long he's more Injun than white," Buck explained. "Even thinks like an Injun."

"I'd as soon you hadn't told everybody in camp what I was figuring to do. They're layin' bets, just like it was a dog fight."

"Well, you got my sympathy. Slewfoot's got a knack fer figgerin' out the one thing best calculated to rile a man. Goes fer a fella's weak spot, you might say. What's yourn?"

"Don't know that I got one."

"Mine's rattlesnakes. Slewfoot shore made my life miserable, once he found that out." Buck shivered. "Kind of gives a man a turn wakin' up from a peaceable nap to find a five-foot rattler lyin' on his chest—even if it is dead."

"Slewfoot done that to you?"

"Yeah, an' then near laughed himself to death."

They stopped in front of a tepee where a squat, red-headed trapper in greasy buckskins sat dozing in the shade, and Buck nodded his head. "Thar he is. Ain't he a specimen?"

Before Tad could make much of a visual appraisal, Slewfoot Samuels opened his eyes. Tad got something of a shock. One eye was green, the other black, and they were as badly crossed as a pair of eyes could be. Slewfoot glared up in Buck's general direction, took a swig out of the jug of whisky sheltered between his crossed legs and spat.

"Howdy, Buck. This is the greenhorn you're figgerin' on palmin' off on me?"

"This is him. Name's Tad Marshall."

"Sit," Slewfoot grunted.

They sat and Buck reached for the jug. Slewfoot extended his right hand to Tad. "Shake."

Tad gave Slewfoot his hand, which Slewfoot promptly tried to crush into jelly. Half expecting such a stunt and having a muscle or two of his own, Tad gave just about as good as he got, and they let go with the first engagement pretty much a draw. Slewfoot took the jug away from Buck.

"Drink, Tad? Or have you been weaned from milk yet?"

Tad raised the jug to his lips, held it there while his Adam's apple bobbed six times, then passed it back. "Been watered some, ain't it?"

"Have to cut it a mite, else it eats the bottom out'n the jug."

Slewfoot's squaw, a clean, sturdy-looking woman, came out and got an armload of firewood from the pile beside the tepee, and Slewfoot grunted something to her in the Shoshone tongue. She stared curiously at Tad, grunted a reply and disappeared inside.

Several dogs lay dozing in the shade. A half-grown, smooth-haired white pup wandered into the tepee, let out a pained yip and came scooting out with its tail tucked between its legs, followed by the squaw's angry scolding. The pup came over to Slewfoot for sympathy, got it in the form of a friendly pat or two, then trotted to Tad, climbed up into his lap and went to sleep.

Slewfoot grinned. "Seems to like you."

"Yeah. Dogs usually take to me."

"Mighty fine pup. I got plans for him."

A dark-eyed, attractive young Indian girl appeared, started to go into the tepee; then, at a word from Slewfoot, stopped and stared in open-mouthed amazement at Tad. He colored in spite of all he could do. Suddenly she giggled, murmured something in Shoshone, then quickly ducked into the tepee.

"Who's that?" Buck asked.

"My squaw's sister. Name's Moon Wind."

"Tad is quite a man with the ladies," Buck said, gazing innocently off into space. "They was three gals at oncet after him, back home. Caused him some trouble."

"A woman can pester a man," Slewfoot said, "less'n he knows how to handle her. Have to lodgepole mine ever' once in a while."

"Lodgepole?" Tad said.

"Beat her."

"Can't say I hold with beating women."

Slewfoot grinned. "Well, you may have to beat Moon Wind to make her leave you alone. She sure admired that yaller hair of yourn." Slewfoot yawned. "I'm hungry. I'll git the women to stir up some vittles."

The squaw came to the tepee entrance. They talked for a spell, then Slewfoot looked ruefully at Tad. "She says we're plumb out of meat. Kind of hate to do this, but when a man's hungry he's got to eat. I'd be obliged, Tad, if you'd pass me that pup."

"This pup?"

"Shore. It's the fattest one we got."

"I ain't really hungry yet. Ate a big breakfast."

Slewfoot grabbed the pup by the scruff of the neck, handed it to his squaw and waved her inside, then turned to Buck and began a long-winded tale. Tad's mind wasn't on the story, but with Buck sliding a look his way every now and then, there was nothing for him to do but sit there and pretend to be enjoying the company. Would the squaw skin the thing, he wondered, or just toss it into the pot with the hair on? For the first time in his life, he felt a little sick to his stomach.

After a while the squaw brought out three wooden bowls of greasy, rank-smelling stew, and Tad, hoping his face didn't look as green as it felt, accepted his with a weak smile.

"Hungry now?" Slewfoot asked.

Glassy-eyed, Tad stared down at the mess in the bowl. If he didn't eat dog he'd have to eat crow, and, of the two, he reckoned tame meat was the easier to swallow. Grimly he dug in with his spoon.

"Why, yeah I am. Hungry enough to eat a horse. Shame you didn't have a fat one to spare."

When they headed back to their own part of camp a while later, Buck asked, "How'd you like that stew?" '

"Fine, 'cept for its being a shade greasy."

"Bear meat usually is."

"Bear? I thought it was dog."

"Shoshones ain't dog eaters. Slewfoot could of lodgepoled his woman till Doomsday an' she still wouldn't of cooked that pup for us. That was just his idea of a joke."

"Didn't think it was very funny myself."

"You said you could take his worst, grin an' come back for more."

"I can."

"Well, I'll hang around and watch the fun."

There were times during the next week or so when it wasn't easy for Tad to grin. The day Slewfoot near drowned him while pretending to teach him how to build a trout trap was one. The night Slewfoot put the physic in the whisky was another. But he came closest to losing his good nature the evening he got scalped by Moon Wind in sight of the whole camp.

Slewfoot arranged the thing, no doubt about that, even though it was rigged to look plumb accidental. The boys had got to finger wrestling around the campfire. Two trappers would pair off, face each other and interlace the fingers of both hands. At the word "go," they'd have at it, each one trying to force the other to his knees or break his back, according to how stubborn the fellow wanted to be.

Slewfoot threw all comers. Looking around for fresh meat, he allowed as how a certain young fellow from Missouri would chew good, so there was nothing for Tad to do but climb to his feet and give it a try.

Captain Sublette was watching. So were Buck Owens, Parson Rumford, the pack-train mule tenders and a whole mess of Indians. The bets flew thick and fast as Tad and Slewfoot squared off. Staring over Slewfoot's shoulder, Tad found himself looking right at Moon Wind, who was sitting on the ground with her deep black eyes glittering in the firelight and her soft red lips parted in excited anticipation. Kind of a purty little thing, Tad was thinking. A sight purtier than the girls back home. If only she wouldn't keep staring at him that way.

"Go!" Captain Sublette said.

Slewfoot grunted, heaved, and the next thing Tad knew, he was lying flat on his back on the ground. Dimly he heard the yelling of the crowd as he got to his feet.

Slewfoot gave him a cockeyed grin. "Want to try it again, partner?"

"Sure."

This time Tad kept his mind on the chore at hand. For some minutes they rocked this way and that, then Tad made his move. Slewfoot's knees buckled and he went down with a thud. The crowd roared even louder than before.

"Hurt you?" Tad asked solicitously.

"Once more," Slewfoot grunted, getting up.

They locked hands. Judging from the look on his face, Slewfoot really meant business this time. So did Tad. But the kind of business Slewfoot had in mind was a shade different from what Tad expected. Because they'd no more than got started good when Slewfoot dropped to his knees, heaved and threw Tad clean over his shoulders.

Tad did a complete somersault in the air, landing with his feet in the crowd and his head on the ground right close to Moon Wind's lap. Foolishly he grinned up at her. She gave him a shy smile. Then she whipped out a scalping knife, grabbed a handful of hair and lopped it off.

The crowd went crazy. So did Tad. He jumped up and made for Moon Wind, but she fled into the crowd. He whirled and went for Slewfoot, who was laughing fit to kill. Sublette, Buck Owens and half a dozen other men grabbed him and held him back.

"Easy, son; easy!" Sublette said between chuckles. "There aren't many men who get scalped and live to brag about it!"

After a moment Tad quit struggling and they let him go. His face burning, he stalked off into the darkness.

Morosely Tad finished his breakfast and accepted the cup of coffee Buck poured for him. *Yellow-Hair-Scalped-By-a-Woman.* That was the name the Indians had given him. Buck eyed him sympathetically.

"I told you he was ornery. But you were so cocky——"

"He caught me off guard. It won't happen again."

"He's too cunning for you, boy. Why, I'll bet you right now he's windin' himself to prank you again."

"He gets wound up tight enough," Tad said grimly, "I'll give him one more twist and bust his mainspring."

"Better get ready to twist, then. Yonder he comes."

Uneasy despite his brag, Tad ran absent fingers over his cropped head as Slewfoot came shuffling up, looking as pleased with the world as a fresh-fed bear.

"Mornin', gents. Any coffee left in that pot?"

Buck poured him a cup. Slewfoot hunkered on his heels, his black eye studying Tad while his green one gazed at the mountains off in the distance. "That was a dirty trick we played on you last night,

Tad. It's sort of laid heavy on my conscience. So I've decided to make it up to you."

"I can hear him tickin'," Buck muttered.

"Just how are you going to make it up to me?"

"I know you don't like yore new Injun name. So I had a talk with a Shoshone chief that happens to be a friend of mine. He says he'll fix it."

"How?"

"Why, he'll just adopt you into his tribe an' give you a new name. That'll cancel out the old one. It'll cost me a mite, but I figger I owe you somethin'."

"Adopt me?"

"Yeah. Injuns do that now an' then."

Buck eyed Slewfoot suspiciously. "Who is this chief?"

"Seven Bears."

"Why, ain't he the——"

"Yes, sir, he's top man of the whole tribe. No Injun'll dare laugh at an adopted son of hisn."

Tad thought it over. If there was a catch to it, he sure couldn't see it. He looked at Buck. "What do you think?"

"I ain't sayin' a word."

"Well," Tad said, "in that case——"

The ceremony in Chief Seven Bears' tepee took a couple of hours. A dozen or so of the most important men in the tribe were there, and one look at their solemn faces told Tad this was serious business with them. Slewfoot must have been dead serious, too, because before the palaver began he gave Seven Bears a couple of horses, half a dozen red blankets, a used musket, several pounds of powder and lead, and a lot of other trinkets in exchange for his services.

When the ceremony was finally over, they left the tepee and Slewfoot walked to the edge of the Shoshone section of camp with him. His grin seemed genuine.

"How does it feel to be an Injun?"

"Fine. What was that new name he gave me?"

"White Mule. It's a good name."

"Reckon I'm obliged to you."

"Don't mention it. Well, I'll see you later."

Buck was taking a nap when Tad got back to his tent, but at the sound of his step the old trapper's eyes jerked open. "What'd they do to you?"

"It was all real friendly. Name's White Mule now."

"So he did do it! What'd it cost him?"

"Well, he gave Seven Bears some blankets, a couple of horses——"

"Hosses? Fer two hosses he could of bought you a——" Buck suddenly broke off and stared at something behind Tad. He shook his head. "He did too. Look around, boy."

Tad turned around. Moon Wind was standing there, smiling shyly. Behind her were four horses, two of which he recognized as the ones Slewfoot had given Seven Bears a while ago, and all four were laden down with Indian housekeeping gear. As Tad stared at her with stricken eyes, Moon Wind gestured at him and at herself, then made a circling motion with both hands.

"She wants to know where she'd ought to pitch your tepee."

"My tepee?"

"Yourn and hern."

"She's—she's mine now?"

"Reckon she is. Slewfoot bought her for you."

"But Seven Bears——"

"Is her pa. Also happens to be Slewfoot's squaw's pa."

"Tell her I don't want her! Tell her to go home!"

Buck laid a restraining hand on Tad's forearm. "This may be just a prank where you an' Slewfoot're concerned, but I don't reckon it's one Moon Wind and her pa would laugh at much. She must have liked you. An' Seven Bears must have thought a lot of her, else he wouldn't of outfitted her so fancy an' given you back them two hosses of Slewfoot's as a special weddin' present."

"Well, I sure can't keep her!"

"Easy. They's a way out of this, maybe, but it'll take some tall thinkin'. Let her set up her tepee. You an' me are goin' to have a talk with Captain Sublette."

Captain Sublette was not in the habit of losing his temper, but when they told him what had happened he was fit to be tied. So was Parson Rumford. When Tad declared that what he had a mind to do was grab a club and beat Slewfoot half to death, then make him take Moon Wind back to her father and explain the whole thing, the parson gave the idea his hearty approval. But Sublette shook his head.

"You can't send her back. No matter how much explaining Slewfoot did—assuming we could make him do any—the whole Shoshone tribe would be so angry they'd be down on our necks in a minute. You've got to accept her and pretend to live with her until rendezvous breaks up."

"I won't hear to such a thing!" Parson Rumford exclaimed.

"I said 'pretend,' sir. . . . When the brigade goes back to St. Louis, you'll go with it, Tad. I'll tell Moon Wind that you're coming back next summer to stay. That will save her pride and our necks."

"But I won't come back? Is that the idea?"

"Yes."

Tad gazed off at the mountain peaks rimming the valley. "Seems kind of a dirty trick to play on her. Lettin' her wait for a man that won't never be comin' back to her. It's downright deceitful."

"Better a little deceit than a full-scale Indian war. She won't wait for you long, I'll wager. Next year I'll cook up some story about your having died of smallpox or something, and she'll be free to pick herself another man."

Reluctantly Tad nodded, but the deceit of it still weighed on his mind. "She's an innocent little thing and not to blame for this. I'd kind of like to give her something to remember me by—for a while, anyhow. Could I draw some of my wages and buy her a trinket or two?"

Sublette smiled understandingly. "Of course."

Pausing with the clerk in charge of the trade goods to pick out a few items he thought might appeal to her, Tad walked back to the spot where his tent had been pitched. But the tent was gone. In its place stood a roomy, comfortable skin tepee around which a dozen or two Shoshone women bustled, chattering happily as they helped Moon Wind set her household in order.

Seeing Tad, the women smiled, exchanged knowing looks amongst themselves, then quickly wound up their tasks and drifted away. When the last one had gone, he went to Moon Wind, who was on her knees building a fire.

"Moon Wind, I got something for you."

Her eyes lifted. Black eyes, they were, black and soft and deep. He got the sudden notion that she didn't know whether he was going to beat her for what she had done to him last night or caress her because she was now his woman. He took her hand and pulled her to her feet.

"These here trinkets are for you."

He dumped them into her hands. One by one, she examined them. First the glittering silver-backed mirror. Then the long double strand of imitation pearls. Then the small gold ring, which by some accident just managed to fit the third finger of her left hand. For a long moment she stared down at them. Then without a word she whirled away from him and ran toward the Shoshone section of camp.

She was gone so long that Tad, weary of trying to figure out what had got into her, went into the tepee and took himself a nap. Except for an unpleasant dream or two about Slewfoot, he slept fine. Presently he was awakened by angry voices arguing violently in the Shoshone tongue outside the tepee. He got up and went out to see what the ruckus was all about.

There, toe to toe, stood Slewfoot Samuels and his woman, jawing at each other like a pair of magpies. Off to one side and admiring her new trinkets stood Moon Wind.

Suddenly Slewfoot saw Tad and spun around. "What in the name of all unholy tarnation do you think you're doin'?"

"Me?" Tad said. "Why, I was just takin' a nap."

"That ain't what I'm talkin' about!"

"What are you talking about?"

"Them things!" Slewfoot roared, pointing a trembling hand at the ornaments Moon Wind was admiring. "That foofaraw she's wearin'! You got any idea how much that stuff costs?"

"Sure. I bought it. What business is that of yours?"

"My squaw wants the same fool trinkets!"

"Well, buy 'em." "Waste a big chunk of my year's wages for junk like that?"

"Then don't buy 'em."

"If I don't, she'll pester the life out of me."

"Lodgepole her. That'll make her quit."

Slewfoot shot his woman a sidelong glance and shook his head. "Don't hardly dare to right now. She'd raise such a racket I'd have all her relatives on my neck." Slewfoot sidled closer, a pleading look in his eyes. "Look, boy, the joke's gone far enough. Now you take that foofaraw away from Moon Wind an' cuff her a time or two. Then my woman won't be jealous of her no more."

Tad looked at Slewfoot's squaw, who had gone over to Moon Wind and was gabbling with her over the beads, mirror and ring. Sure was queer how some men would spend any amount for their own pleasure, but wouldn't put out a dime for their women. He grinned and shook his head.

"Why, I don't have to cuff 'em to make 'em behave. Treat 'em kind, I say, if you want the best out of 'em. Buy 'em presents, help 'em with the chores, give 'em the respect they're due and crave— that's the way I treat my women."

Slewfoot stared at him. "You're goin' to keep her?"

"Sure am. Going to marry her, in fact, soon as I can get Parson Rumford to tie the knot. Come to think about it, I'll make a real shindig of it. Invite her pa and ma and all her relatives. Invite the whole camp. After the wedding I'll throw a big feed with food and drinks for all."

"That'll cost you a year's wages!"

"What if it does? Man like me only gets married once."

"But when my woman sees it," Slewfoot said hoarsely, "she'll squawl to high heaven fer the same treatment. First thing you know,

I won't dare lay a hand on her. She'll keep me broke buyin' her foofaraw. She'll have me totin' wood an' takin' care of the hosses an' wipin' my feet 'fore I come into the tepee—why, she'll have me actin' jest like a regular husband!''

"I wouldn't be at all surprised," Tad said, and strolled off in search of Parson Rumford.

It was quite an affair, that double wedding, and the party afterward was real good fun for all concerned. Except for Slewfoot Samuels, who didn't seem to enjoy it much. He'd lost his sense of humor, somehow. Maybe he'd get it back after they'd spent a few months in the mountains trapping beaver. Tad sure hoped so, anyhow. Worst thing you could have as a partner was a man that couldn't take a joke, grin and come back for more.

DEAD-MAN TRAIL

ERNEST HAYCOX

Johnny Potter had only squatted himself in the cabin's doorway for a smoke when he heard Plez Neal's footsteps rattling along the stony trail in a rapid return from town. Plez came across the sooty shadows of the yard and made a mysterious motion at Johnny. He said, "Come inside."

Johnny followed Plez into the cabin and closed the door. A third partner, Thad Jessup, lay on a bunk, stripped to socks, trousers and iron-stained undershirt. He had been half asleep, but his eyes opened and were instantly alert.

"Buck Miller's in town again," said Plez Neal. "He's huddled up with that saddle-faced barkeep in the Blue Bucket. They were talking about me—I could tell." He went over to a soapbox to fill his pipe from a red tobacco can.

"Add those three other fellows that drifted in yesterday," said Thad. "There's your crowd. They smell honey."

"They smell us," said Plez. "Now we're sittin' ducks, not knowin' which way we'll be flushed."

"How'd you suppose they know we're worth a holdup?" asked Thad.

"Talk of the camp. I wish we hadn't let that damned dust pile up so long."

Johnny Potter sat hunched over on the edge of a box, arms across his knees. He spread out his fingers and stared at them while he listened to the talk of his partners. Both Plez and Thad were middle-aged men from the Willamette who had left their families behind them to come here and grub out gold enough to go back and buy valley farms. He was the youngster who had a good many more years to throw away than they had; he didn't dread the loss of the dust as they did, but he understood how they felt about it. He riffled his fingers through his hair, and once he looked toward the fireplace, beneath whose stones lay twenty thousand dollars in lard cans. His eyes were a flashing blue against the mahogany burn of his skin; he was a slender young man and his face had a listening silence on it. In the little crevices around his features, boyishness and rough knowledge lay uneasily together.

"We've made our stake," said Thad. "We could pack and pull out."

"Won't do. We've got some protection in camp. On the trail we'd be easy marks."

"But," said Thad, "if we stay here we'll get knocked over. It's a Mexican standoff. If they want us they'll get us. Just a question of how and when."

There was a silence, during which time Johnny Potter decided that his partners had no answer to the problem. He straightened on the box and made a small flat gesture with both hands against his legs.

"The three of us would travel too slow, but one of us could travel light and fast," he said. "I'll take my horse and your horse, Plez. Tonight. With a head start, I can outrun that crowd and get into The Dalles with the dust in four days or less."

"Why two horses?" asked Plez.

Johnny nodded toward the fireplace. "That stuff weighs around ninety pounds. I'll change horses as I go."

Plez said, "We'll cook up some bacon and you can take bread. You can make cold camps."

"I got to have coffee," said Johnny. "Pack the dust in the two sets of saddlebags."

Thad said, "If they're watchin' us, they'll notice you're gone in the morning."

"While you're packing," said Johnny, "I'll drop in at the Blue Bucket and play sick. Tomorrow you tack a smallpox sign on the cabin. They'll think I'm in bed."

Plez thought about it, sucking at his pipe. "Johnny, it's a long way to The Dalles. If they pick up your tracks you're a gone chicken."

"Fall of the dice," said Johnny, and opened the door and stepped into a full mountain darkness. Cabin lights and campfires glimmered through the trees and along the gulch below him, and men's voices drifted in the windless air. He took the trail to the creek bottom, threaded his way past tents and gravel piles thrown back from bedrock, and came upon Canyon City's shanties wedged at the bottom of the ravine. The sound of the saloons reached out to him. He turned into the Blue Bucket, stumbling slightly; he saw a few friends at the poker tables and nodded to them in a drawn and gloomy manner, and he made a place for himself at the bar beside Pete Hewitt. The saddle-faced barkeep was at the far end of the counter, talking to a man whose face Johnny couldn't see at the moment. The barkeep broke off the talk long enough to bring Johnny a bottle and glass, and went back to his talk. Johnny took his cheer straight and poured another. The saddle-faced barkeep was at the edge of his vision; he noted the man's eyes roll toward him.

Pete Hewitt said, "What's the matter with you, Johnny?"

"I ache. I'm hot, I'm cold, I feel terrible."

"Ague. Get good and drunk."

Johnny eased his weight on the footrail, swinging to have a look at the man with the barkeep. It was Buck Miller, no question—big nose, face the color of an old gray boulder, a set of rough and raking eyes.

Johnny called the barkeep back to pay for his drinks. He said to Hewitt, "I'm goin' to bed, and I'm not getting up for a week."

As he left the bar, he felt Buck Miller's eyes upon him. Outside, he remembered a chore and dropped into the Mercantile to buy caps for his revolver; when he came from the store he again noticed Buck Miller in the doorway of the Blue Bucket, staring directly at him. Short gusts of sensation wavered up and down the back of Johnny's neck as he traveled the stony gulch back to the cabin. *No question about it*, he thought. *He's got his mind made up for that dust.*

Plez met him in the yard's darkness and murmured restlessly, "Come on."

He followed Plez along the creek to a corral which boxed in a bit of the hillside, and found the horses packed to go. He tried his cinches and patted the saddlebags. There were two sets of bags, one behind his saddle and one hooked to a light rig thrown over the spare horse. Plez said, "Bacon and bread's in your blanket roll. Coffee, too, but get along without it, Johnny. A fire means trouble."

"Got to have coffee, trouble or no trouble."

"Tobacco and matches there. It's Thad's rifle in the boot. Shoots better than yours."

Johnny Potter stepped to his saddle, taking hold of the lead rope. Thad whispered, "Listen," and the three of them were stone-still, dredging the night with their sense. A few stray sounds drifted up the slope; a shape passed across the beam of a campfire. "Somebody around the cabin," whispered Thad. "Get out of here, Johnny."

Plez said in his kind and troubled voice, "Don't hold no foolish notions. If you get in a vise, dump the damned dust and run."

Johnny turned up the ravine, reached the first bench of the hill, and paralleled the gulch as it ran northward toward the wider meadows of the John Day, two miles distant. He was tight with the first strain of this affair; he listened for the sound of a gun behind him; he made quick searches of himself for things done right or done wrong, and presently he fell down the hill into the John Day and saw the dull glittering of the creek's ford ahead of him.

He held back a moment. There were lights along the valley, from other diggings and other cabins, and the trail was well traveled by men going to and coming from Canyon City. At this moment he neither saw nor heard anybody, and left the shadows of the hill and soon crossed the creek. The racket of his horses in the water was a signal soon answered, for, looking behind him, Johnny saw a shape slide out of the canyon shadows and come to the ford. Johnny swung from the trail at once and put himself into the willows beside the river.

He waited, hearing the rider cross the water and pass down the trail perhaps two hundred feet and there stop and remain motionless for a full three minutes. Suddenly Johnny understood he had made a mistake; he had tipped his hand when he had gone into the store to buy the caps. It wasn't a thing a sick man would do.

The rider wheeled and walked his horse toward the ford. His shadow came abreast of Johnny and faded, but at the creek he swung again and came back, clearly hunting and clearly dissatisfied. It was time, Johnny guessed, to use a little pressure; drawing his gun, he cocked the hammer and sent that lean dry little sound plainly into the night. The rider whipped about immediately, racing over the ford and running full tilt toward Canyon City. He would be going back for the rest of Miller's bunch.

Johnny came out of the brush and went down the trail at a hard run, passing cabins and campfires, and sometimes hearing men hail him. He followed the windings of this rough-beaten highway as it matched the windings of the river; he watched the shadows before him; he listened for the rumor of running horses behind him, and once—the better to catch the tomtoms of pursuit—he stopped to give the horses a blow and to check the saddlebags. The lights of the diggings at last faded, and near midnight he reached another cluster of cabins, all dark and sleeping, and turned from the valley into the hills. Before him lay something less than two hundred miles of country—timber, rough mountain creases, open grass plains and rivers lying deep in straight-walled canyons.

He slowed the horses to a walk and wound through the black alleys of these hills while the night wore on and the silence deepened. In the first paling dawn he stopped at a creek for a drink and a smoke, and went on steadily thereafter until noon found him on the edge of timber overlooking a meadowed corridor through these hills. Out there lay the main trail, which he watched for a few minutes; then he staked the horses, cooked his coffee and curled on the needle-spongy soil to rest.

It was less than real sleep. He heard the horses moving; he came wide awake at a woodpecker's drumming, and drifted away again, and moved back and forth across the border of consciousness, straining into the silence, mistrusting the silence.

He woke before sunset, tired. He threw on the gear and moved the horses to the creek and let them browse in the bottom grasses while he boiled up another pot of coffee. Afterward, he returned to the edge of the timber and, as long as light lasted, he watched the trail, which was a wriggling pale line across the tawny meadows below. He had to take that trail for the speed it offered him, but when he took it he also exposed himself. Thus far, he had been pretty secure in the breadth of country behind him—a pinpoint lost within a thousand square miles of hills and crisscross gullies. Ahead of him, though, the trail squeezed itself narrowly through a bottleneck of very rough land. Buck Miller knew about that, and might be waiting there.

Under darkness he moved over the flats to the trail and ran its miles down. He stopped to water at a creek, and later, well beyond the creek, he paused to listen, and thought he heard the scudding of other horses, though the sounds were so abraded by distance that he could not locate them. Riding west, he saw the ragged rising of hills through the silver gloom. The trail went downgrade, struck the graveled bottom of a dry wash and fell gradually into a pocket at the base of the hills. His horse, seeing some odd thing, whipped aside, going entirely off the trail. A moment later it plunged both forefeet into a washout, dropped to its knees and flung Johnny Potter from the saddle.

He turned in the air, he struck, he felt pain slice him through; the odor of blood was in his nostrils and his senses ran out like a fast tide, leaving him dumb on the ground. His left leg burned from hip to ankle and he kicked it out straight with a rough wish to know the worst. Nothing wrong there. He tried his right leg, he moved his arms, he stood up. He was all right.

He crouched in the washout and ran his hands along the down horse's front legs and discovered the break. He wanted a smoke, risk or no risk, and he filled his pipe and lighted it close to the ground. Then he brought in the lead horse, which had strayed out toward grass, and transferred the gear to it from the down horse.

When he was ready to travel again, he put a bullet into the head of the down horse, that report shouting and rumbling and rocketing away in all directions. It appeared to follow him and point him out when he rode forward.

In the first streaky moments of dawn he found himself in the bottom grasses and the willow clumps of Bridge Creek near its junction with the John Day. The ridges rose to either side of him, and he sat a moment motionless in the saddle and felt naked under such exposure; it would be a better thing to get out of this meadow land and to lose himself in the rough and treeless stringers of earth which made a hundred hidden pockets as they marched higher and higher over the mountains toward Central Oregon. But that was the slow way, and he had not enough knowledge of the country to leave the trail, and thus, his restless nerves pricking him into action, he went down the creek bottom at the best gallop he could kick out of his horse and reached the still more open bottoms of the John Day.

It was a wonderful thing at last to see the trail rise up from the river through a notch and go directly into the broken land. As soon as the ridge permitted him, he went up its side and got into another draw; he pressed on, climbing and turning and searching the land until he felt his horse lag. Thereupon he changed his course until he reached a ridge from which he saw the trail visible in the ravine below. He fed the horse and put it on picket in a gully and lay down to rest.

Through his curtain of sleep, broken as it was by strain and weariness, he heard the clear running sound of horses below. He reached for his rifle, rolled and crawled to the rim of the ridge all in a motion, and saw four men swinging along the trail below him; the lead man's head was bent, carefully reading signs, and in a moment this man signaled for a halt and swung his horse around, bringing his face into view—that dark skin and big-boned nose sharp in the sunlight. The four made a close group on the trail while they talked. Their words lifted toward Johnny.

"No," said Buck Miller, "we've gone too far this way. The kid left the trail back there where the ridge began. He went the other side. We'll go back and pick up his tracks."

"He's tryin' to fool us," said another man. "He may be settin' behind a rock waitin' for us to walk right into his shot."

"He's just a kid," said Buck Miller. "He'll run; he won't stand and fight. All he wants to do is keep ahead of us and get to The Dalles."

The other man wasn't convinced. He said, "You go back and pick up his tracks while I ride this way a couple miles. If I don't see anything, I'll cut over the ridge and find you."

"No," said Buck Miller. "If I see anything moving ahead of me, I'll shoot it, and it might turn out to be you. We'll stick together. When we locate the kid we can box him in. He ain't far ahead. He's got two horses, and the dust weighs enough to slow him down."

The other man said, "He's got the advantage and I don't like it much. He can watch us come and he's above us."

Miller shook his head. "If it was a hard customer we were trailin', I'd say you were right. But he's never shot a man. That makes a difference, Jeff. It's a hard thing to pull the trigger if you ain't done it before—and while he's makin' up his mind about it, we'll get around him. I figure we can bring him to a stop. Then one of us can slip behind and get above him. I can hit him with the first bullet, anywhere up to four hundred yards."

Johnny Potter drew his rifle forward and laid its stock against his cheek. He had Buck Miller framed in the sights, with no doubt left in his mind; it was a matter of kill or be killed—it was that plain. Yet he was astonished that Buck Miller knew him so well; for he had trouble making his finger squeeze the slack from the trigger. It was a hard thing to kill, and that was something he hadn't known. *Well,* h thought, *I've got to do it,* and had persuaded himself to fire when th group whirled suddenly and ran back along the trail. He had missed his chance.

It would take them a couple hours, he guessed. With Miller behind him, he had a chance for a clear run on the trail, and maybe he could set a trap. He figured it out in his mind as he rode directly down the ridge's side into the trail and galloped westward. They were careless in the way they boomed along; they had no particular fear of him—which made the trap possible, maybe.

He came to a creek and turned the horse into it; he dismounted and dropped belly-flat in the water at the feet of the horse, and drank in great, strangling, greedy gusts. Somewhere ahead of him the canyon would run out and the trail would then move directly up the face of the hills. When he took that, he was an open target. Meanwhile the creek, coming closer to its source, fed a thicker and thicker stand of willows, and presently he left the trail and put the horse well back into the willows. He walked a few yards away from the horse, parted the willows and made himself a covert. He took a few trial sights with the rifle down the trail, and sat back to wait. He closed his eyes, gently groaning. Canyon City was maybe a hundred miles behind him, and The Dalles a like distance ahead.

It was well into the afternoon when he heard the small vibrations of their coming. He turned on his stomach and brought the gun through the willows and took another trial sight, and had the muzzle swung against the bend when they came around it, riding single file and riding carelessly. They had convinced themselves he wouldn't stop to fight. They came on, loosely scattered, the lead man watching the trail and Buck Miller bringing up the rear.

Miller was the man he wanted, and he had terrible moments of indecision, swinging and lifting the gun to bring it on Miller, but the others made a screen for Miller, and at last Johnny took a sure aim on the lead man, now fifty feet away, and killed him with a shot through the chest.

He dropped the rifle and brought up his revolver as he watched the lead man fall and the riderless horse charge directly up the trail. The others wheeled and ran for the shelter of the bend. Two of them made it, but Johnny's snap shot caught the third man's horse, and it dropped and threw its rider into the gravel. The man cried as he struck, and his arm swung behind him in an unnatural way; he got to his knees and turned his face—bleeding and staring and shocked— toward Johnny. He tried to get to his feet, he shouted, he fell on his chest and began to crawl for the bend on one arm.

Johnny retreated into the willows, got his horse and came into the trail at a charging run. The fallen man made no move; the two others were sheltered behind the point of the ravine. Rushing along the trail, away from them, Johnny overtook the riderless horse, seized its reins as he passed by, and towed it on. He was, presently, around another turn of the trail and thus for a moment well sheltered, but in the course of a half mile the trail reached a dead end, with the bald rough hills rising in a long hard slant, and up this stiff-tilted way the trail climbed by one short switchback upon another.

He took to the switchbacks, coming immediately out of the canyon. Within five minutes he was exposed to them against the hillside, and waited for a long-reaching rifle bullet to strike. He looked into the canyon, not yet seeing them. He shoved his horse on with a steady heel gouging. He rode tense, the sharp cold sensations rippling through him; he jumped when the first shot broke the windless, heated air. The bullet, falling short, made its small "thut" in the ground below him. He kept climbing, exposed and at their mercy, and having no shelter anywhere.

He kept climbing, his horse grinding wind heavily in and out. He tried a chance shot with his revolver and watched both men jump aside, though he knew the bullet came nowhere near. They were both aiming, and they fired together. It was the foreshortened distance of the hillside which deceived them and left their bullets below him again. By that time he had reached a short bench and ran across it, temporarily out of their sight; then the hill began again and the trail once more began its climbing turns, exposing him. At this higher level he was beyond decent shooting, and he noted that the two had abandoned their rifles and were bending over the man lying on the trail. An hour later he reached the top of the hill and faced a broken country before him, bald sagebrush slopes folding one into another and hollow rocky ravines searching through them.

He dismounted and gave the horses a rest while he sat down on the edge of the hill and kept watch on the two dark shapes now far below. They hadn't come on. From his position he now had them on his hip unless they backtracked through this slashed-up country and took another ridge to ride around him. As long as he stood here they couldn't climb the open slope. He stretched out, supporting his head with a hand. He closed his lids and felt gritty particles scraping across his eyeballs, and suddenly he felt a sharp stinging on his cheek and jumped to his feet. He put a hand to his cheek and drew a short bit of sagebrush from his skin. He had fallen asleep and had rolled against the sagebrush.

The two men were at the creek, resting in the shade of the willows, no doubt waiting night. He rose to the saddle of the borrowed horse and started along the ravine which circled around a bald butte. Near sundown the ravine came out to the breakoff of this string of hills, and he saw the slope roll far down into a basin about a mile wide, on the far side of which lay a dark rim. Beyond the rim the high desert ran away to the west and the north; through the haze, far to the west, he saw the vaguest silhouette of snow peaks in the Cascades. He descended the slope as sunset came on in flame and violence.

Darkness found him beside a seepage of water in a pocket of the high rolling sagebrush land. He fed the horses half the remaining oats, ate his bacon and bread and built a fire to cook his coffee. He killed the fire and made himself a little spell of comfort with his pipe. Haze covered the sky, creating a solid blackness; the horses stirred around the scanty grasses. He rose and retreated twenty yards from where his fire had been and sat against a juniper. He got to thinking of the two men; they knew he was somewhere in this area, and they no doubt guessed he'd camp near water. If he were in their boots, he decided, he wouldn't try to find a man in this lonesomeness of rolling earth; he'd lie out on some ridge and wait for the man to come into view. The trail—the main trail to The Dalles—was a couple miles west of him.

He seemed to be strangling in water; he flung out a hand, striking his knuckles on the coarse-pebbled soil, and then he sprang up and rammed his head against the juniper. He had been sleeping again. He walked to the seepage and flattened on his stomach, alternately drinking and dousing his head until coldness cleared his mind; then he led the horses to water and let them fill, and resumed his ride, following little creases he could scarcely see, toward a shallow summit. An hour later he came upon the main trail and turned north with it. Having been once over this route, he knew the deep canyon of the Deschutes was in front of him, with a wooden toll bridge, but of its exact distance from his present location he had no idea. Around midnight he identified the blurred outline of a house ahead of him—a single wayside station sitting out in the emptiness—and he left the trail to circle the station at a good distance. By daylight he found himself in a rutty little defile passing up through a flinty ridge, and here, at a summit strewn with fractured rocks, he camped his horses in a pit and crawled back to the edge of the trail, making himself a trench in the loose rubble. The defile was visible all the way to its foot; the plain beyond was in full view. Two riders were coming on across the plain toward the ridge.

He settled his gun on the rocks and, while he waited, he slowly squirmed his body against the flinty soil, like an animal gathering tension for a leap. They were still beyond his reach when they came to the foot of the defile and stopped; and then, in tremendous disappointment, he saw that they would not walk into the same trap twice. They talked a moment, with Buck Miller making his gestures around the ridge. Afterward Miller left the trail and traveled eastward along the foot of the ridge, away from Johnny, for a half mile or so before he turned into the slope and began to climb. The other man also left the trail, passing along the foot of the ridge below Johnny.

Johnny crawled back into the rocks and scrambled in and out of the rough pits and boulder chunks, paralleling the man below him. He went a quarter mile before he flattened and put his head over the rim, and saw the rider angling upward. Johnny retreated and ran another short distance, gauging where he'd meet the man head on, and returned to the rim. He squeezed himself between two rocks, with the aperture giving him a view of the rider so slowly winding his way forward. He looked to his left to keep Buck Miller in sight, and saw Miller slanting still farther away as he climbed. He returned his attention to the man below him, and pulled his rifle into position; he watched the man grow wider and taller as he got nearer, he saw the man's eyes sweep the rim. Suddenly, with a fair shot open to him, Johnny stood up from the rocks—not knowing why he gave the man that much grace—and aimed on a shape suddenly in violent motion. The man discovered him and tried to turn the horse as he drew. Johnny's bullet tore its hole through the man's chest, from side to side.

The pitching horse threw the man from the saddle and plunged away. Johnny gave him no more thought, immediately running back toward his own horses. Miller, having reached the crest of the ridge half a mile distant, paused a moment there to hear the shot, to orient it, and to see Johnny. Then Miller ran down the slope, toward the toll bridge, toward The Dalles. Johnny reached his animals and filled his pipe and smoked it while he watched Miller fade out of sight in the swells of land to the north. Now he had trouble in front of him instead of behind him, for there was no way to reach The Dalles except by the toll bridge. But the odds were better—it was one and one now. When he had finished his pipe he started forward, plodding a dusty five miles an hour along a downhill land under a sky filling with sunlight. The trail reached a breakoff, the river running through a lava gorge far below. He took the narrow trail, winding from point to point.

Rounding a last bend and dropping down a last bench, he found the bridge before him—a row of planks nailed on two logs thrown over waters boiling violently between narrow walls. There was a pack string on the far side and four men sitting in the dust. Coming to the bridge, he had a look at the men over the way, and the shed beyond the house, and the crooked grade reaching up the hill behind the bridge. He went across and met the tollkeeper as the latter came out of the house.

"Two dollars," said the tollkeeper.

"Can you fill that nose bag with oats?"

"All right."

Johnny Potter pushed the horses toward a trough and let them drink. He waited for the man to furnish the oats and went to a water barrel with a cup hanging to it. He drank five cups of water straight down. When the man brought the oats, Johnny scattered a good feed on the ground for the horses. He paid his bill, watching the packers, watching the shed, watching all the blind corners of this place.

"Man pass here little while ago?"

The tollkeeper nodded and pointed toward the north. Johnny looked at the hill before him, the long gray folds tumbled together and the trail looping from point to point and disappearing and reappearing again. The sight of it thickened the weariness in his bones. "How long into The Dalles?"

"Ten, twelve hours."

Johnny said, "You know that fellow ahead?"

The tollkeeper said most briefly, "I know him." Then he added, "And he knows me." But this was still not enough, for he again spoke, "You know him?"

"Yes."

"Well, then," said the tollkeeper, and felt he had said everything necessary.

That made it clear, Johnny thought. Since Miller knew that the tollkeeper knew him, he probably wouldn't risk a murder so near witnesses. It was his guess he could climb the canyon without too much risk of ambush; it was only a guess, but he had to go ahead on it.

A hopeful thought occurred to him. "That pack outfit going my way?"

"No. South."

Johnny mounted and turned to the trail. Half an hour of steady riding brought him to a series of blind, short turns above which the gray parapets of land rose one after another, and the sense of nakedness was upon him once more. His muscles ached with the tension of waiting for trouble, and his nerves were jumpy. When he reached the summit, long afterward, he faced a country broken into ridges with deep canyons between.

In the middle of the burning afternoon he reached the beginnings of a great hollow which worked its way downward between rising ridge walls. The road went this way, threading the bottom of the hollow and curving out of sight as the hollow turned obediently to the crookedness of the ridges. He followed the road with his growing doubt, meanwhile watching the ridges lift above him, and studying the rocks and the occasional clusters of brush. Three miles of such traveling took him around half a dozen sharp bends and dropped him five hundred feet. He thought, *This is a hell of a place to be in*, and thought of backing out of the hollow. But his caution could not overcome his weariness; the notion of extra riding was too much, and so he continued forward, half listening for the crack of a gun to roll out of some hidden niche in the hills above him. The road curved again, and the curve brought him against a gray log hut a hundred yards onward, its roof shakes broken through in places, its door closed and its window staring at him—not a window with its sash, but an open space where a window once had been.

He halted. He drew his gun and he felt the wrongness of the place at once. Why, with the cabin showing the wear and tear of passing travelers, should the door be closed? He kept his eyes on the window square, realizing he could not turn and put his back to it; a rifle bullet would knock him out of the saddle long before he reached the protection of the curve. Neither could he climb the steep ridge and circle the cabin, for on that slope he would be a frozen target.

He got down from the horse and walked forward, the gun lifted and loosely sighted on the window square. The chinking between the logs, he noticed, had begun to fall away, but the logs, from this distance, didn't appear to have spaces between them large enough to shoot through. At two hundred feet he began to listen, knowing that if Miller was in the place he'd have his horse with him. He heard nothing. He pushed his feet forward and began to fight the entire weight of that cabin. It shoved him back, it made him use up his strength, it was like walking against a heavy wind.

The sun had dropped behind the western ridge and quick shadows were collecting in the hollow; he felt smaller and smaller underneath the high rims of the ridges, and the empty window square got to be like an eye staring directly at him. His stomach fluttered and grew hollow. He called out, "Hello! Anybody in there?"

His voice rolled around the emptiness. He stooped, never taking his eyes from the window square, and seized a handful of gravel from the road—walnut-sized chunks ground out of the roadbed by the passing freight teams. A hundred feet from the cabin he heaved the rocks at the window square. He missed the opening, but he heard the rocks slap the log wall, and suddenly he heard something else—the quick dancing of a disturbed horse inside the cabin. He jumped aside at once, and he straightened his aim on the squared window. A shadow moved inside the cabin and disappeared. Johnny broke into a run, rushing forward and springing aside again. He had thought there could be no moisture left within him after this brutal day, but he began to sweat, and his heart slugged him in the ribs. Energy rushed up from somewhere to jolt his muscles into quickness. A gun's report smashed around the inside of the cabin and its bullet scutted on the road behind Johnny. He saw the shadow moving forward toward the window. He saw Buck Miller stand there, Miller's face half concealed by his risen arm and his slowly aiming gun.

Johnny whipped his shot at the window, jumped and dodged, and fired again. Buck Miller's chest and shoulders swayed; the man's gun pulled off and the bullet went wide. Johnny stopped in his tracks. He laid two shots on that swinging torso and saw his target wheel aside. He ran on again and got to the corner of the house, hearing Miller's horse threshing about the cramped enclosure. Johnny got to the door, lifted the latch and flung it open; he was still in quick motion and ducked back from the door to wait out the shot. None came.

He held himself still for ten or fifteen seconds, or until a great fright made him back away from this side of the house and whirl about, half expecting to find that Buck Miller had got through the window and had come around behind him. He kept backing until he caught the two sides of the cabin. He stepped to the right to get a broader view of the cabin through the doorway, and presently he saw a shape, crouched or fallen, in the far corner. He walked toward the doorway, too exhausted to be cautious. The figure didn't move, and when he reached the doorway he found Buck Miller on his knees, head and shoulders jammed into the corner. He looked dead.

Johnny caught the horse's cheek strap as it got near the doorway; he pulled it outside and give it a slap on the rump, then stepped into the cabin and went over to Miller. He moved Miller around by the shoulders and watched him fall over. Miller's hat fell off, and he rolled until he lay on his side. This was the fellow who figured that he, Johnny Potter, would run rather than stand up and kill a man. He thought, *How'd he know that much about me? He was right, but how'd he know?* He was sick and he was exhausted; he turned back through the doorway and leaned against the casing a moment to run a hand over his face and to rub away the dry salt and caked dust. His horses were three hundred feet up the road. His knees shook as he walked the distance, his wind gave out on him and he stopped a little while; then he went on and pulled himself into the saddle and started on through the growing twilight.

Even now, knowing he was safe, he found himself watching the shadows and the road with the same tension. It wouldn't break; it had been with him too long; and he reached the hill and rode down a last grade into The Dalles near ten o'clock at night with his ordeal behind him and the watchfulness screwing him tight. Wells Fargo was closed. He had to get the agent's address and go find him and bring him down to the office; he leaned against the desk while the dust was weighed out, and took his receipt. He found a stable for the horses, and from there went to the Umatilla House and got a room. He walked into the bar, went over to the steam table and ate a meal. Then he went to his room, took off his boots and laid his gun under the pillow. He flattened on the bed with nothing over him.

He thought, *Well, it's done, and they can buy their damned ranches.* He lay still, and felt stiffness crawl along his muscles like paralysis, and his eyelids, when he closed them, tortured him with their fiery stinging. The racket of the town came through the window, and a small wind shifted the curtain at the window. He opened his eyes, alert to a foreign thing somewhere in the room and searching for it. Finally, he saw what troubled him—a small glow of street light passing through the window and touching the room's wall. The curtain, moved by the wind, shifted its shadow back and forth on the wall. Saddle motion still rocked him and, soothed by this rocking, he fell asleep. It was not a good sleep; it was still the tense and fitful sleep of the trail, with his senses struggling to stay on guard, and quite suddenly the strongest warning struck him and he flung himself out of bed, straight out of his sleep, seized the revolver from beneath the pillow, and fired at the wall.

The roar of the gun woke him completely, and he discovered he had put a bullet through the curtain's shadow which wavered along the wall. He stared at it a moment, reasoning out his action, and he listened for somebody to come up the stairway on the heels of the shot. But nobody came; apparently this hotel was accustomed to the strange actions of people out of the wild country. He put the gun on the dresser and rolled back under the quilt and fell so deeply and peacefully asleep that a clap of thunder could not have stirred him.

GUNSHOT AT NOON

ARTHUR LAWSON

The Government had sent surveyors into the Cherokee Outlet to cut up its six million acres into quarter-section homestead tracts, and the Army to see that the cattlemen pulled stakes and took their herds off this rich land that they had leased from the Indians. In the Winding Creek country, the TTT boys were drifting beef into temporary corrals preparatory to trailing them back to Texas. Down by the big bend where the North Fork comes in, Ty Dixon was whacking brush for strays.

He shouted in surprise when a rifle shot sounded close by, and his startled horse bucked him into a wild-plum thicket. Ty hollered again. Since he had no enemies, he figured that the gunner had mistaken him for a maverick or deer that he wanted to cut down for meat. But Ty's shouting only placed the target for the hunter, who angled around for another shot. Ty dragged the pistol from the waistband of his pants and cocked it over a live shell.

Then the cowboy sighted the enemy. Both men fired at once and both, in their haste, missed. For a moment, Ty had the advantage. You can trigger a double-action Colt six-shooter quicker than you can work the lever on a Winchester. Though Ty had intended only to wound this man, the bullet ranged to the right, killing him instantly. Ty was sorry about that, especially sorry when he got a good look at the man who had been stalking him. His face was that of an honest, even a pious man. It was not the face of a killer.

Ty Dixon had a pint of whisky in his saddlebag. This pint was strictly a snake-bite kit. Ty did not have the habit of drinking on the range or around the bunkhouses. But this was a snake-bite occasion. Ty had killed a man, a man he did not know, a complete stranger. Ty needed more than a drink.

He caught his horse and picketed him upwind from the dead man. The liquor settled the sickness in Ty's stomach and gave him the courage to go through the dead man's pockets. There was a jackknife with a dull blade that showed the owner had not been a whittler. There were a couple of tally books and a Bible. That Bible made the killing seem even more wrong to Ty Dixon—even though the stranger had taken the first shot at him.

Ty looked into the tally books. The first was headed: *New Boston Company*. There were names under this heading, sums of money listed, property in wagons and cattle. There was "Hiram Needam, daughter Sarah (18 yr maiden)—four draft horses—1 Studebaker waggon in gd cond—1 chest drawers—sundry household articals— $200 in hand." There were others: "Horace (Fiddlin Horace) George & childrn." He, apparently, had neither horses nor money, and the "childrn" were too numerous to be named. There were a couple of dozen more in that book—a blacksmith, a schoolteacher, an entire little village listed as the New Boston Company. Ty began to feel as if he knew them.

"Didn't mean to shoot this feller," he felt himself explaining to Sarah Needam or Fiddlin' Horace or to Sarah most likely. "But he was sure set on cutting me down, and I had to do something."

He looked in the second book. This was a sort of diary. "The Lord has led me to the site of New Boston. Confluence of two streams. Wooded. Water power for our Mill." Another entry said: "The cattlemen have set a young man to following us." Ty wondered if the man had a partner. He read on, uncomfortably feeling that he was being watched. "I had the spy in my sights today, but the rifle jammed." That was yesterday. Ty felt crowded. "Today sent Sam back to Kansas with data and maps. This spy is intent on blocking our Utopia on Earth. I shall stay and eliminate him."

Ty Dixon took another drink before gathering the rest of the man's belongings. Lacking a shovel, he buried the body in a tree, Indian fashion, setting it on a platform. He kept the tally books, but left the Bible. Maybe this man would need the Book, wherever he was going.

"Take care of this hombre, God," Ty made a short prayer. "Maybe he's better off where he's at. He needs lookin' after. Amen."

Ty finished his snake-bite kit and rode away. Mechanically, he hazed a few steers toward the TTT corrals.

At roundup camp Ty told the foreman what he had done. "He was a sooner, I reckon. Got worried. Thought I was going to jump his claim. He was crazy. Look at these books."

The foreman glanced through the diary. They learned that the dead man was Sim Leslie, president of the New Boston Company, and certainly a sooner—a man who had come to the Outlet sooner than the date set for staking claims.

"Forget it," the foreman said. "That gent had no business being in the strip, anyway. Probably was scouting along the creek for this townsite. Don't let it worry you."

But Ty could not forget. He hung around camp a couple of days thinking about the New Boston Company and the opening of Indian lands. The more he thought about it the more he pictured the little dream valley where the Winding and the North Fork come together. You could make a home there. You could quit pounding yourself to bits on the backs of horses that were one half rawhide and the rest dynamite. And with those grangers coming in, you would not be so lonesome all the time.

Ty left the lamplit bunkhouse to walk around in the dark. It was midsummer. The night was soft and the stars brilliant. Ty looked up the foreman.

"Been thinking of claiming one of those quarter sections," he told the boss. "Got a little money saved. Maybe I can run some Herefords."

The boss laughed at him. "Now, you didn't happen to cross over into Kansas on company time, did you?" He picked a name at random—one he had remembered from the tally book. "You didn't happen to look up that Sarah Needam?"

Ty blushed. He had sort of been thinking of her. Four horses, a wagon, a chest of drawers. He had forgotten the two hundred dollars in hand. Money was not a thing that counted in a dream like this. Likely it was her old man's, anyhow. She was eighteen and unmarried.

"I ain't seen a girl since we was in Coffeeville," he said. "But there's no harm in hoping."

"You get mixed up with those grangers," the boss warned, "and you'll be plenty sorry." Then he shrugged. He saw how it was. "You can come back to the TTT any time. We're opening up a ranch in New Mexico. We'll need a foreman over there."

Ty and the boss shook hands.

Ty rode over to Kansas and got the dope from a land agent. On the sixteenth of September a gun would be fired at high noon, signal that you could cross into the territory and drive your stake into any claim that happened to take your fancy—provided you got there first. You could take up one hundred sixty acres for nothing.

The cowboy hung around the Kansas border a while, keeping his ears open, but hearing nothing about the New Boston Company. The countryside was full of soldiers now who were trying to keep the sooners from crossing into the Outlet. Every day more people crowded up on the starting line. It soon became evident to Ty Dixon that getting his hundred sixty acres would not be so simple as it had seemed. There were going to be a great many more people here than there were quarter sections.

I'm not going to let those grangers jump my claim, Ty told himself.

So he crossed the border one night, managing to avoid the Army, and rode in to Winding Creek. He rode over "his" land once more. He walked on it. He drank water from a spring. Here, he said, he would build his house, just one room at first, but designed to grow. There would be a cool breeze up from the creek in summer, and shelter from blizzards in winter. You would have a view of blue water behind willows, and you could go fishing with the kids.

This beautiful picture unbalanced Ty Dixon. He rode east to the Ponca Indian Agency, where he stole six horses. He stationed these in tiny corrals along the way from the site he had chosen to the nearest point on the border. Then, the night before the run, he crossed into Kansas. A soldier challenged him and took a shot at him when Ty put spurs to his tired horse. In town, another guard stopped him.

"Where you from, mister?" he asked. "That horse is plenty sweated up."

"From Mizzouri," Ty said. "I been riding hard, to get here."

"Seems like I seen you around here a couple of weeks ago," the guard said.

He was going to run Ty in. Now that the cowboy had located his house on that land and dreamed of fishing with the kids, nobody could take it from him. He was just about to hang his fist on the soldier's chin when a girl spoke up from nearby.

"Why, hello!" she said. "When did you arrive?"

Ty stuttered, "Just a couple of seconds ago."

"You know him?" the guard asked.

"Of course," the girl said. "We've been waiting for him. Didn't he tell you he was from Missouri? He's one of our party."

The guard saluted the girl. "Sorry we bothered him, miss. There's all sorts of gents fooling around the Outlet. This feller looked familiar. And he don't look like he came from Missouri. . . . Sorry, mister."

"Think nothing of it," Ty said generously. "I like to see a man who takes his job seriously."

The soldier said, "Next run I'm going to be in on it. . . . Evenin', miss . . . mister."

He went on, watchful. Ty heard some shooting down the line—another man like himself trying to sneak in over the border. That man screamed. Ty glanced at the girl. Her face was pinched a little, worried.

"Why'd you do that?" he asked.

"You were going to punch him," she said. "You might have been hurt."

"What's it to you if I get hurt?" Ty asked.

"It's everything," she said. "And it's nothing. It's not you. For anyone else I would have done the same. Too many foolish people are always getting themselves into unnecessary trouble."

That only made Ty angry. He tipped his hat and bowed deeply to the girl. "This foolish person," he said, "thanks you."

He walked off into the darkness, leading his horse, stiff of back and feeling a bigger fool than ever.

Ty Dixon found a whisky tent. An enterprising citizen had set up a tent over some kegs of whisky. This stuff sold at five bucks for a tin cup. Well, why not? Tomorrow they would all be landowners, they would all be rich. So five dollars went for a dipper of rotgut.

The cowboy looked across the border into that fabulous land that he had once thought so commonplace while he punched cows for the TTT. It is odd how another man's ground is just dirt. When it is yours it becomes a part of you.

You put a corral on it and a house. You get yourself some good stock and grow your own feed. You get a woman. Ty Dixon came back for a second cup of bad whisky.

Now he could see the woman who was going to live with him there on Winding Creek. She had eyes as black as his were blue; black eyes and black hair, a full-breasted, slim-waisted girl who came, most likely, from Missouri.

Ty threw the whisky on the grass and tossed the tin mug into the tent. He wandered on, looking for her now, along the border, along the line of fires and the wagons lined up to go. There was a train, loaded to the roof. Folks were singing hymns. In a wagon, two men were bickering. A youngster, hardly old enough to file a claim, was standing beside a high-wheeled bicycle.

"With her," he boasted, "I can beat any train in the country. And you can't find a horse that can keep up with me. What I'm going to do is file on the best city lot in the townsite of Cross. The bicycle is going to put horses out of business, except for plowing. I'm going to start me a bicycle shop in that city block."

Ty drifted on. A baby was crying. A woman sitting by a fire nursing the child was talking to a man who squatted there with a pipe and a jug.

"I'm so nervous, Ed," she said, "it gets to the baby."

"Have a snort," Ed suggested.

"That'll hit the baby, too," the woman said.

Ty had unconsciously stopped to listen. The man gestured to him.

"Jine me in a little drink," he invited. "The old lady's off the jug these days. I could stand some drinkin' company."

Ty said, "I'll set a minute, if you don't mind, but I'm off the jug too."

The man poured his own. He was talking. "This'll be a new beginning for us," he said quietly. "We didn't do so good in Kansas. Always running out of water. Figger on picking a place by a creek——" Ty stared at him. "What's the matter?" the man asked.

"Nothin'," Ty said. He got up and bowed to the woman. "Got to be looking after things. Glad to of met you. Maybe we'll be neighbors."

The woman looked suddenly hopeful. For a moment Ty had hated the man. He had felt that the stranger was stealing his claim. Ty was sweating coldly. What if those stolen Ponca horses had broken down their corrals and gone home? What if his own horse stepped into a hole and never did get there? Ty felt the weight of those two tally books in his breast pocket. Maybe Sim Leslie, president of the New Boston Company, had not been so crazy, after all.

Ty Dixon made sure that the land agent saw him next morning, and he took care to be seen by others—Army officers, soldiers, plain people. He talked to everyone. He wanted to be sure that nobody would later accuse him of being a sooner. He studied the various outfits as he killed the endless morning. Some would break down before they fairly crossed the border. Others were rich, and you would have thought that the folks who owned them could have bought land somewhere else and left this territory for the landless. There was one group of settlers with well-kept rigs. They seemed to be together—and with them was the girl from Missouri. She was sitting on the seat of a fine Studebaker wagon. Four horses were hitched to it, waiting patiently.

Ty drifted over to her. He touched his hat and smiled. Her eyes were on a level with his. They were hostile, not welcoming.

"Want to beg your pardon, miss," he said. "Thanks for helping me last night. I'm sorry I got sore."

Her generous mouth lifted at the ends.

"Oh, that's all right," she said. "I was only doing what I could. I wish you success today."

"Thank you," the cowboy said. These people who apparently were traveling with her were a cold, harsh lot, like the man Ty had killed. He bet that the first building they would put up would be a church, then a school. If they wanted it that way, who was he to object? As for Ty Dixon, he wanted his corral first, then a house. The church could wait. You could pray in the kitchen. Ty added, "Well, I hope you find a good home."

He had been looking straight into the girl's black eyes while these thoughts went through his mind.

"That was a nice thing to say," she said. "A good home. Nobody ever said anything like that to me. It's funny you should say it. You look like a cowboy. Cowboys don't have homes."

An acutely uncomfortable suspicion was working through Ty's head. He waved his hand toward the south. "I used to work down there, for the TTT. I know that country. Follow me and I'll show you the best site in the Outlet. With those horses, you should be able to keep up with me."

She shook her head. Two black, tight curls danced under the wide flare of her sunbonnet. "I'm with the company," she said. He had been afraid of that. One Studebaker wagon, he remembered, four horses, daughter Sarah, eighteen.

A man much like the others swung up onto the seat beside her. He had a watch in his hand.

"Father, this young man——" the girl started.

Gunfire sounded through the dusty, hot sky. It was the signal. In an instant the whole mass of men and vehicles, of animals and trains, rushed south with a great thunderous roar.

Early in the run Ty passed the boy on the bicycle who was going to stake the best claim in the townsite of Cross. That lad was sweating valiantly, but was making poor time on the rough grass.

"Get a horse!" Ty suggested.

"Get a wagon!" Sarah Needam added over the racket of her teams and great wagon.

Yonder a locomotive whistle screamed and passengers began to pile off to stake claims closest to Kansas, willing to let others find better land if there was such in the interior.

Ty was in the lead now. Spurring his horse relentlessly, he was approaching the first corral, where he was to swap saddle with one of his stolen horses. He had worried so about those animals that he was surprised to find the first one waiting as he had planned. He had shifted his saddle and was stepping aboard when the big Needam wagon roared by.

It was then that the cowboy learned that he was not the only one who had made careful plans.

Four of the New Boston Company's wagons were leading the race. The canvas cover of Sarah's had ripped, somehow.

Inside, instead of a chest of drawers and sundry household articles, were two saddled horses getting a free ride. There were men to ride them, and they were better mounts than those Ty had stolen from the Ponca Agency.

But Ty regained the lead. He found a remount in his second corral, and another in the third. When he reached Winding Creek he was so far ahead he could stake his claim leisurely, roll a cigarette and lie on his back to blow smoke into the sky. Then he stirred restlessly, hoisted himself on an elbow and looked down the valley. The first of the riders were coming, stern-faced men, weary to exhaustion. One fell from his horse only a few yards from Ty Dixon and drove a stake into the ground. He knelt there a moment, praying. When he stood up and shouted, "Eure-eka!" Ty stood too. The cowboy had his carbine in the crook of his arm.

"Beat it, mister," Ty ordered.

The man turned dull eyes on him. With his rifle, Ty gestured to the stake he had driven himself.

"It's impossible," the man said. "There was no one ahead of us."

"I was ahead," Ty said.

A second rider had come up. His eyes were like ice.

"He was there at noon, talking with my daughter," this one said. "This claim is his."

The first man wordlessly pulled his stake and climbed back onto his horse. More men came out of the haze. All afternoon they passed Ty's quarter section. None bothered him after the first. Each seemed to know exactly where he was going. After the men came the women driving the teams, hauling the household goods and children. At the tail end of all were the four wagons that had led the race, those that had been sacrificed for the good of the company.

The claims were all gone when they arrived, so they halted just below Ty Dixon's boundary line, where a fire had been built and canvas wagon covers had been stretched for shelter. Here, as night fell, big pots of food were put on to cook. Ty built a fire, too, but was too uneasy to sit by it. He prowled his quarter section, looking for claim jumpers.

From the highest point of his land he could see lights flickering all over the prairie, men and women on their homesteads, just as he was on his, folks who had won the day's race.

He came back to squat by the glowing embers of his fire. Below him, the New Boston Company had gathered to sing a hymn. It was cold and lugubrious. A shadow moved toward Ty in the gloom. By the graceful curve of her hips, Ty recognized the girl from Missouri at a distance. She stopped near his embers, leaning against a cottonwood tree. Her face was white, her mouth a dark line.

"They found him," she said.

Ty Dixon sat more tightly against the ground. This was his land. They could not booger him off it. He had proof right here in his pocket that Sim Leslie had been gunning for him, proof in the man's own writing.

"You certainly made a beeline for this place," the girl said bitterly. "You certainly had a fast horse. He even had time to change his color." She turned away. Over her shoulder she said, "A good home."

She went back down the slope to the fires where the company was holding a funeral for its late leader.

Ty slept with his rifle, but was not bothered, nor did any of the company come onto his land the next day. They left him strictly alone while they went about their business of organizing their community. That night they gathered to sing some more doleful songs.

The cowboy had not done anything all day except brood over his cocked rifle, waiting for them to come for him. When it seemed that they never would try to run him in for shooting Sim Leslie, he swung into the saddle and drifted down there. They treated him with courtesy.

Ty stepped down from his mount, wondering if he had stuck his neck into a hang noose.

"I got a book here that I took off Sim Leslie," Ty said slowly. He hesitated. They were watching him warily. The women were back in the shadows, holding silent children. The men had come forward to judge him. "I want to read a piece."

Hiram Needam nodded gravely. "We'll listen, son."

Ty's voice choked as he read. "I had the spy in my sights today. . . . This spy is intent on blocking our utopia on Earth. I shall stay and eliminate him."

Ty handed the book to Hiram Needam. "It's the leader's hand,"

Needham said. He passed it on to a man who held a violin and was surrounded by small children. Fiddlin' Horace nodded.

"Folks," Ty said tensely, "I don't even know what a utopia is. I was working for the Triple T, trying to get our beef out before the deadline. I never even saw this feller until he took a shot at me. I hollered, in case he was making a mistake." Ty's voice drifted off. He added, "I've known this country for years. I always figured if I ever settled, I'd settle here."

Fiddlin' Horace had been watching the stars. "There is no such thing as a utopia," he said. "It's a dream, a chimera. Your dream is your own personal utopia. The leader's was ours—to live together in a community, to share equally, to work together. But utopias do not actually exist. You may come and go, my boy, and move in peace amongst us. Thou shalt not kill. But it was the leader who broke the law. You were only the instrument."

The other men agreed, nodding gravely. They were not going to hang the cowboy; they were not even going to cuss him out, and he knew, as if it were a revelation, why Sim Leslie had acted with such blind violence. Ty, who was not the sort of man to go gunning for anybody, had been about to do the same that afternoon, waiting up there on the slope with a cocked rifle.

There was more to it. Ty said, "Sim Leslie died for that claim, so I'm giving it to one of his people, to a girl who got here too late to get a claim of her own. Maybe she'll build her home up there where I staked out the corners for my shanty. I'm looking for my utopia somewhere else."

He heard Sarah Needam cry out as he threw a leg over the cantle and spurred up the hill. For a second he stopped there on the peak to look down to the stream where he had planned on fishing with the kids. The company was singing again. Fiddlin' Horace's violin was sending out its tune. There was no dirge in this song that was a song of praise.

In two weeks Ty Dixon had found only four of the six horses he had stolen from the Ponca Indian Agency. He spent a few more days inquiring for the strays before giving up and riding to the agency. He refused the award that was offered him, a little suspicious that he was being rawhided.

"Why—uh—when I found these horses on my hands," Ty explained, "I sort of used them. There were a couple more. I guess it's my fault they're lost. So——"

The agent understood. "The others came home the day of the run," he said. "Stake a good claim?"

192

"Heck, no!" Ty said. "None at all. I'm heading for New Mexico. I'm a cattleman, not a farmer."

He rode west, a free man again, forking a horse whose color would not change on the way. He rode to Texas to the home ranch of the TTT. When he arrived, he had his story organized.

"Grangers all around me," he said to the boss. "You were right about them. Millions of grangers. Made me feel crowded. That New Mexico job still——"

"It's waitin' for you," the boss nodded. "Been expectin' you the last three-four days."

"Three-four days?"

"The lady said you'd be along as soon as you took back some horses you'd borrowed," the boss said with a straight face.

Ty was panicked. A door had opened and the Missouri girl had come into the room. That pinched look was gone. Her expression was radiant, and Ty thought she was the most beautiful thing in the world.

"Why—gosh!" he said.

"You told me to follow you," the girl said simply. "Remember?" He remembered, all right. "So I gave that claim to the company to build their town on, if Hoke Smith approves." Hoke Smith was the Secretary of the Interior, and responsible for such things. "I made a trade with pa to bring me down here. He's gone back. They're going to call the town Utopia."

Ty's panic was passing. "The place that don't exist," he mused, and he knew that his utopia had never been on that claim, nor was the girl's with the company. She would have gone crazy living with those people.

"Remember, in Kansas," she said. "You told me you would show me where I could make a good home. Remember?"

"Why—sure." Ty's grin warmed up. He thought of New Mexico and the foreman's job. She had said cowboys don't have homes, but he reckoned that even a cowboy could make out on a foreman's pay. "I'll show you," he said.

THE HASTY HANGING

MORGAN LEWIS

The coffeepot spouted steam from its snout, finally forcing its way through Chris Holden's painful musing. He set it back to draw and was again still, standing hip-shot beside the stove, a tall and rangy youngster just past twenty with a shock of wild black hair. His wide-spaced gray eyes wandered over the room with all its closely familiar things: the battered old dresser, the table and chairs made in slack winters, the magazine pictures tacked to the wall and, in the next room, his stripped bunk, the bedding rolled for travel.

He had been on his own since he was fourteen, and the fight to survive and amount to something had stamped its marks in the tough angles of his brown young face. He had schooled himself to be hard and efficient, like big Jim Dunkle, who owned the vast Box D ranch down on the flats, but a glint of misery showed in his eyes; getting this last meal on his ranch was a sad thing. The arctic cold and obliterating snows of the winter had wiped him out. Now, in the springtime, the bodies of his cattle rotted where they had died. And there was no chance for a fresh start; panic had the country by the throat, prices were below costs and money was scarce as water in the desert.

A hail from outside startled him and took him out onto the shallow porch.

Jim Dunkle sat his bay horse five feet from the house, a solidly built man with a face flat as a spade, his coat buttoned against the fresh spring breeze. Behind him the broken foothills fell away to the lush, level plateau that was his.

He slapped his hard thigh with a gloved hand. "Grab your horse, Chris, and come along! We've got the buzzards that've been stealin' stock! Ed Fuller and Stumpy are holdin' 'em over on Pawnee Flats." Anger was a vibration in his voice.

From habit Chris nodded and turned away. Dunkle had employed him for three years, had helped him to get a start, and he felt a certain obligation. He took two steps, turned back.

"I don't reckon I'll go along, Mr. Dunkle." The big rancher liked to have a handle put to his name. "I'm finished here. I was aimin' to pull out."

Thick tufts of reddish hair above Dunkle's ears and a trick of widening his amber eyes gave him an owlish look. "Last winter was a snorter, but I didn't know it cleaned you." His voice was grave. "I don't like to see you leave—I like to have one man around here I can depend on." There was a touch of the feudal overlord in his manner. "Maybe we can work out a way to get you started again." Impatience came into his voice. "Anyway, get your horse and come along. We'll talk about it later."

Chris felt a tremendous admiration for this successful rancher. Jim Dunkle had drive and force, a single-track mind and a relentless determination to get what he wanted, qualities which had carried him to the top. And Chris wanted to be at the top.

"All right, Mr. Dunkle," he said, and ducked back into the house for his gun belt. Jim Dunkle never went back on his word; if he said he would help a man, he would do it.

Dunkle was already moving out when Chris joined him. He said, "These gents are the ones killed Sam Helfinger over to Sentinel the other day."

"Did they own up to it?"

"Hardly! But they've got his stock, no bill-of-sale, and Sam is dead. That draws a picture."

Chris nodded. It would seem so. "How many of 'em?"

Dunkle hesitated for the flicker of an eyelash. "Three." He turned in the saddle and put his heavy-lidded gaze upon Chris. "A lynchin' always raises a stink when just one outfit does it." His voice was utterly calm. "That's why I want you along. You can see things are done fair and square." A glint of humor showed in his eyes.

Chris scrubbed the flat side of his jaw. "You're not takin' them into Sentinel for trial?"

"It don't pay. We tried it with a couple last year and they went scot-free. Townspeople don't feel the way we do—they ain't bein' hit."

"They'd swing for killin' Sam Helfinger."

"If we could prove it. But no one saw them do it." He shook his heavy head. "We'll take care of this ourselves and then we'll know it's done."

They came down the timbered flank of a ridge and onto Pawnee Flats. The line shack was centered in a pine clearing and, as they rode in, Ed Fuller hoisted himself from the doorstep, a lanky man, black of hair and of eyes.

Dunkle swung down, letting fall the reins to ground-hitch his horse. "Any trouble?"

"Nope. They ain't been out." Fuller gave Chris a careless nod. "Come along for the fun?"

Chris tilted an eyebrow. "Is that what you call it?"

Fuller grunted and dug the makings from his shirt pocket, a man who never smiled or showed any emotion at all.

As Chris stepped from the saddle, Stumpy came into the clearing, lugging a pail of water. Dunkle crooked a finger and Stumpy set the pail before him, a short, bowlegged puncher with a freckled red face that was never done peeling. He gave Chris a brief grin, and Dunkle lifted the dipper, drank deeply and dropped it back into the pail.

"Nothin' like water when a man's dry." Dunkle wiped his lips on his sleeve.

Stumpy looked at the shack, and quickly looked away. "Whisky is better for some jobs."

"All you need is a little sand," Dunkle said brusquely.

No air stirred in this clearing ringed with virgin pine, and sun's heat fell straight down with full force. Chris tied his horse off in shade and tramped back.

"Where's the stock?"

Ed Fuller put his black-eyed stare upon him. "Over yonder in a pocket. You got to see everything?"

"Why not?" Chris's voice was sharp.

And then Dunkle interrupted. "Take him over, Stumpy. I want him to see."

They went down a moderate slope and Stumpy pointed upward. "Plenty of straight limbs around here." His voice was wry. It was plain the coming hanging weighed on the little puncher's mind.

The cattle were bunched in a pocket through which a stream swiftly ran. They were mostly she stuff, wearing different brands. In addition, each had been recently branded with a Lazy S. Mixed in with them were some ten head of Dunkle's Box D stock, the only animals without the Lazy S brand.

As they started back Chris said, "I reckon that Lazy S is a road brand. Looks like part of a trail herd, except for Dunkle's stuff."

"That wasn't smart." Stumpy waggled his head. "They might've got by if they hadn't grabbed his stock. The rest of the brands ain't from around here."

Dunkle swung around as they came back into the clearing. "Satisfied?"

Chris nodded. "Looks like a trail herd. How does Sam Helfinger figure in this?"

"The gent trailin' this herd was about broke when he reached Sentinel. Sam bought some of his stuff dirt cheap. These gents in here"—Dunkle jerked his thumb at the shack—"killed him and ran off his stock."

"How do you know this?"

"I was in Sentinel yesterday." Dunkle turned to Ed Fuller. "Bring 'em out."

Fuller kicked open the door. "Come on!"

They filed out: a tall, gaunt old man with white hair; a considerably younger man with a strained, starved look on his lean face, and taffy-colored hair that straggled over his eyes and hung low on the collar of his blue shirt; and—Chris felt a deep shock run through him—the third was a girl.

She came out into the sunlight to stand beside the two men and he saw that she was almost as tall as the younger man. And she was young, about eighteen, he judged. Her hair rippled back in waves the dark gold of wild honey, and was held by a ribbon at her neck. Her eyes were a startling blue, but with a wildly troubled look.

Now her eyes flashed terribly at Dunkle. "You have no right to hold us! We have done nothing wrong!" Her voice was hot and wild, and the younger man put his hand on her arm, saying, "Hush, Lissa," in a low voice.

Chris drew Dunkle aside. "You didn't tell me there was a girl mixed up in this. Hadn't we best take them into Sentinel?"

"That's the main reason I won't." Dunkle's tone was forceful. "A woman can always swing a jury." He tapped Chris on the chest. "I'm not askin' you for advice. You're here to witness that things are done fair an' square."

He walked back to confront the three, and Chris shrugged and followed. She was probably the younger man's wife and Dunkle was right in believing a jury would think twice before handing in a conviction. Anyway, this was Dunkle's show.

The big rancher planted himself before them. "We'll give you a chance to clear yourselves. Now, who are you?"

"Randolph Fickett." The younger man pointed to the tall old man. "My uncle, Jake Fickett, and this is my sister, Melissa."

"All right, Fickett." Dunkle nodded. "We find you with cattle wearin' five or six different brands—what have you got to say?"

"I told your foreman. They're from a trail herd that was headin' for market. The owner was short of cash. We're lookin' for summer range. I hear there's some up in the Owls."

Dunkle pulled his sharp, curving nose. "How about the ten head of my stock over there with them?"

The man spread wide his hands. "I reckon this is your range with your stock runnin' it. They must've drifted in during the night."

"And they'd drift out again—with you!" Dunkle snapped. "But we'll let that slide. Where's your bill of sale?"

Some of the certainty went out of Randolph Fickett. He turned troubled blue eyes to the old man, who stared vacantly at the surrounding pines. "I don't know. Uncle Jake took it, but he can't recollect what he did with it."

Chris knew now that the man was lying. Here was the old pattern, the familiar cry of thieves caught with stolen goods: They had lost their receipt—it had mysteriously disappeared.

Dunkle looked at the blank-faced old man. "What's the matter with him? Is he half-witted?"

"He is not!" The girl Lissa came forward. "It's just"—she lowered her voice—"he was kicked by a horse. Look at his forehead. When he gets excited his mind turns—well, sort of cloudy. He doesn't know——"

"You expect me to believe a tale like that?" Dunkle interrupted. "Who'd let an idiot handle their business?"

Color came into the girl's thin face. "He was all right when he got the receipt."

Dunkle stretched wide his eyes. "So? Who signed it?"

She hesitated, and turned back to her brother. "What was his name, Randy?"

"I——" He paused and his brown forehead furrowed. "I just can't seem to speak it."

"Was it by any chance Sam Helfinger?"

Randolph Fickett's eyes conferred with his sister. "I believe it was. I believe it was him gave it to us. But Uncle Jake handled——"

And now Dunkle's voice became silky smooth. "Was it before or after you shot him?"

They stared numbly, then it hit the girl and she went back a step, hands trembling to her throat while the blue eyes became too large for her face. "Is—is he d-dead?"

For a moment Chris's hard skepticism was shaken; it was possible she did not know what her brother had done. Then he dismissed the thought; they were too closely tied.

Randolph Fickett shoved back his tangle of taffy-colored hair with a hand that would not hold steady. He licked his lips. "When was he shot?"

"The night you stole his cattle," Dunkle said grimly.

"We didn't! I tell you we didn't!" Fickett's voice rose high, shrill with desperation. "We bought them. He was all right when we left."

"You can't even keep your story straight." There was open contempt in Dunkle's face. "First you said you got them from a trail herd; now you admit it was from Helfinger." He swung around to Ed Fuller. "No sense in stringin' this out. Get your rope!"

The girl's face whitened with fear as Fuller started for his horse, and her eyes darkened to purple. "Wait! You can't do this! These cattle were part of a trail herd, but Mr. Hel—Helfinger bought them and sold them to us. I—I guess he made a little money." She turned to her brother and put her hands on his arms. "Can't you think where Uncle Jake put the paper?"

He stared at her, a wildness in his eyes. "I don't know. Helfinger gave him the paper; then he was talkin' to me; we were lookin' at the stock. I didn't see what Uncle Jake did with it." He raised his eyes to Dunkle. "But I know he got it. I saw him take it right in his hand."

"Did you try his pockets?" Dunkle spoke with the godlike patience of a man whose mind is made up.

"We have, but I'll try again." He went up to the old man and took him by the shoulders. He shook him. "Where's the paper, Uncle Jake? What did you do with it?"

Something shadowy moved in the depths of those gray eyes. The old man put his hands to his hat and settled it more firmly on his head, and now Chris saw the white crescent in the brown forehead just above the eyebrows, the horns pointing at the hairline.

"He can't remember!" Fickett shook his head in a helpless way and began a swift rummaging of pockets, emptying out their contents, turning the pockets inside out until the old man was a white-patched scarecrow. He ran his fingers inside the waistband, he ripped the coat lining and felt inside.

"Try his boots," Dunkle suggested in the voice of last justice.

"I never thought of that!"

Fickett made the old man sit down, and with nervous, eager fingers, pulled off the boots. He held them up and he shook them. He rammed his hand deep into them. He pulled off the socks and turned them inside out while Uncle Jake stared at his bare toes.

Fickett slowly dropped the last sock and shook his head. "It might have been in his pocket and come out when he pulled out his tobacco and he not noticed." Despair was in his voice.

"Sure he didn't give it to you?" Dunkle's voice was properly grave, but it came to Chris that he was playing with Fickett, sure that there was no paper and never had been.

Fickett shook his head. "No-o-o-o, I'm sure." But he started through his own pockets. He dropped to his knees and made a little pile of his belongings; a pocket knife, a bandanna, some loose change, the odds and ends that a man collects. He looked up at Dunkle. "It's no use. We haven't got it!"

"How about your boots?"

Fickett stared. A flush came into his face and his lips tightened. "So, you're havin' your fun!" He swept up the things and stood up.

Chris put a hand to his face and, surprisingly, found it damp. It was one thing to hang a man and quite another to string it out like this. And the girl being here made it tough.

Dunkle turned to Fuller, who was standing by, the rope coiled on his arm. "We'll take the old one first."

Fuller pulled Uncle Jake to his feet and Lissa gave a queer, muffled cry and flung herself upon the gaunt old form.

"You can't! He hasn't done anything! He——" Her voice broke on a sob.

Fickett came up to Dunkle. "At least give us a jury trial." His voice was hoarse, as though he had been shouting. "Give us a chance." Sweat ran in bright worms down his face. "If you kill us, what'll my sister do? Where will she go? If you'll just give us a chance——"

For the first time, Dunkle showed anger. He put the rough edge of his stare upon the man. "There's nothin' on God's green earth I hate like a killer; a man that will murder another for no good reason. Sam Helfinger was found with two bullets in his back. We'll give you the same chance you gave him!" He slapped his thigh with his rolled gloves. "I've seen your kind before; sneaking through the country, stealin' everything they could lay hands on. You're just no damn good!"

He brushed past him, put his hands on the girl's shoulders and tore her loose from the old man. "Take him away, Ed!"

The girl screamed. She twisted in his grasp, and Fickett gave a low moaning cry and went for him. Dunkle lashed out with his fist, caught him alongside the head and knocked him off his feet. "Stumpy!" His voice was harsh. "Put your gun on him! If he moves, shoot!"

Fickett got up unsteadily, his face red where the fist had landed, and Stumpy pulled his gun and stepped behind him. Dunkle released the girl and went over to where Fuller was getting the old man onto a horse from which the saddle had been stripped.

Lissa took her brother's face between her hands, holding it so for a moment. Then she came straight to Chris.

"Please——" Her voice shook. She closed her eyes, face inches from his, and bright drops squeezed from beneath the lids and lay upon her cheeks. "Please, can't you—won't you—stop this?" Her voice broke and her hands writhed together. "Have you no pity?"

Her voice plucked nerves deep in his body. Heat flowed through him, flooding into his neck and causing its pressure. He flicked a glance across the clearing and met Dunkle's skeptical gaze. Chris looked back to the girl, his face hardening. "As much pity as they showed Sam Helfinger."

"They didn't do it!" Her eyes opened wide, showing their inward fire. "They didn't do it! Won't you believe me?"

This beating she was giving his emotions stirred anger within him. "There's nothing can be done," he said roughly. "You'd best go inside; this ain't somethin' you want to see."

"I won't go in!" Her voice rose, husky, panting, as though torn from her throat. "I'll watch! I'll remember! And then I'll see that Dunkle is hanged!"

Her blue eyes seared him with their fierce burning. She whirled and marched back to her brother, shoulders stiff. But then they started to shake and she threw herself forward upon his chest with a sob that was half groan. Randolph Fickett gazed over her at Chris with a terrible violence in his eyes.

Chris turned and moved to the side of the clearing where Fuller and Dunkle were working. Most of his life had been spent on the rough edge of things; he had seen men swing, he had witnessed various forms of violent death, and he had hardened himself and fought his way up in a bitter world. Dunkle's way was the successful way, but his palms grew damp, and for a moment he had his black doubts. Then he encountered the calm certainty of Dunkle's glance and felt assurance come back to him.

Uncle Jake was on the horse, the noose about his neck, his bare feet stuck out stiffly at either side, with the toes turned up instead of hanging, Indian fashion. Fuller led the horse beneath a sweeping limb, threw the rope over it and snubbed the free end, while the old man gazed stupidly ahead, untouched by these portents.

The only sound now, in the heated air of this bright clearing, was Lissa's dry sobbing. It grated on Chris; it filled him with a hurrying, an urgency to get this over and done with. He threw a glance backward and saw that her face was still buried in Fickett's chest. Behind them was Stumpy with drawn gun, his eyes immovably fixed upon the old man beneath the tree. He kept licking his lips.

A pulse pounded in Chris's head as Fuller cut a withy branch and methodically began to strip it for a whip.

As Dunkle watched a muscle began to jump in his cheek and, with a grunt of impatience, he grabbed the branch from Fuller. "Stand back!" He whirled it above his head, and momentarily it poised high in air. Dunkle's lips pinched together; with full-arm swing he slashed down across the horse's rump.

The startled brute bolted forward, the rope jerked the old man backwards, his legs flew up as he went off the horse, and he fell straight down. There was a jerk and the rope twanged. He kicked twice, his hands clawed upward and dropped. He was still, slowly spinning, his shadow stretching out long and black.

The breath went out of Chris with a sighing sound. He dully noticed that the sobbing had stopped and he made a half-turn.

Lissa was on her knees, hands balled beneath her chin and her lips were silently moving while Fickett stood awkwardly stiff behind her, staring as though inward pressure would force his blue eyes from their sockets. There was no sign of Stumpy, and then there came a retching sound from behind the shack.

Chris tramped after the horse, which had stopped just beyond the edge of trees. The sun was losing its brightness, and looking up he saw it beginning its nightly descent behind the Owls. Day was short here under their high-flung pinnacles, and the chill, advancing breath of night brought the feeling that he had seen his last day of full brightness. But having started they must go on. They could no more turn back than they could halt the black flow of shadow from the peaks.

He returned with the horse as Fuller released the rope, letting the old man slump to the ground.

Dunkle bent and removed the noose. "All right, let's get this finished." His voice was brisk.

Uncle Jake's hat had rolled off, and his white head lay upon the brown, dead pine needles. It seemed indecent to leave him there, bare toes pointing starkly at the sky. Chris picked up the hat, mechanically straightening it, putting his hand into the crown and pushing out the dents. It was warm from the old man's head, and the sweatband was damp under his fingers.

He looked over at the man and girl in front of the shack. Lissa was standing now and the horror, the fierce loathing in her eyes, came across the fifty feet of space and hit him a blow.

Stumpy came uncertainly from the shack, his freckles black against the sickly hue of his face, and took his place behind them. It was strange Fickett had not run while unguarded, Chris dully thought, and then he knew; Lissa held him more effectively than any armed guard, and by that he sensed the greater fear that must be in the man's mind.

His jaw muscles clamped and his fingers strongly gripped the hat. Then a tightness froze his muscles. He stared into the crown at this paper that had not been there before. It had slipped from under the sweatband. Slowly he put out his hand and as he took it an awareness of tragedy seeped into him through his fingertips. He let fall the hat and in the act of opening this paper knew what it would be. He raised his eyes to Dunkle.

The big rancher had paused and was watching with a sudden strained attention. Now he came to Chris and read over his arm.

Chris held open the paper for a full minute, aware of the change in Dunkle's breathing, before slowly refolding it. And this paper seemed to have grown insupportably heavy, so that its weight ran into his arms and numbed them.

He said, heavily, "We've made a bad mistake."

His eyes went around the edge of the clearing, saw the horse standing under the big limb, the old man lying so still in the sunlight, and Fuller, with the rope coiled in his hand, watching, as though he suspected, and was amused at, this turn of events. And now Stumpy, sensing trouble, came over to Fuller with his rolling walk.

Chris saw Dunkle's face lose its assurance. "We've made a bad mistake," he said again.

Dunkle turned his big body, he stared at Lissa and Fickett, he turned back again, looked at the body of Uncle Jake, raised his eyes to Chris; doing all this slowly, giving himself time to think. When he spoke it was with the deliberation of a man who has done his reckoning and come to his answer.

"Maybe we're wrong—and maybe we ain't. Sam Helfinger is dead. It's my bet these are the men did it; nothin' to prove they ain't. And they've got ten head of my stock."

There was a confused heaviness in Chris's head. "Maybe you're right, Mr. Dunkle," he said uncertainly. "But maybe somebody killed him for the purchase money. We'll just have to wait and see. And if you're wrong, we—we'll have to face the music."

"Wait?" Some of the color left Dunkle's heavy face. "Do you

know what will happen if they get loose? They'll ride straight for the sheriff!"

Chris nodded. "I reckon they will. Wouldn't you?"

A fine beading of sweat appeared on Dunkle's forehead. He put his face close to Chris. "If you hadn't found that paper we'd have strung up the second man and that would've ended the business." His eyes opened wide. "What's to stop you touchin' a match to it?"

Shock, like a cold blade, hit Chris in the belly. He stared at the rancher. "And then what?"

Dunkle's eyes were hot, dogged. "We go on like we hadn't found it. The girl's got no proof. She can't make trouble. We'll ship her out of the country."

Cold spread through Chris from his stomach, deadening his muscles, freezing him in its icy grip. He licked his lips. "Do you know what you're sayin', Mr. Dunkle? A while back you told how you hated a murderer."

Red came into the rancher's big face. He took out his bandanna and wiped his forehead. "Chris," he said solemnly, "I'm talkin' as much for you as for me. That bill-of-sale don't prove they didn't kill Sam. We've got to look out for ourselves. You just leave things to me and we'll come out all right."

He put his hand on Chris's shoulder. "I said I'd help you and I will. What would you say if I gave you enough stock for a fresh start? And how'd you like a chunk of that level land next to yours?"

Chris had seen men die for far less than this bribe that was being offered him. And maybe Dunkle was right. He shoved his hand into his pocket and the fingers clamped hard on the paper. Here was the big ranch he had always wanted, and some of Dunkle's fine heavy stock. Dunkle had got to be big and powerful by driving straight for what he wanted without thought or care for anyone else. That was the pattern to follow. He would not have to leave his ranch and go back to the weary grind of punching other men's cattle.

His eyes fell upon the body of Uncle Jake lying beneath the big limb, and an invisible something stirred in the shadowed air and took him by the throat. He could have his big ranch, but it would be darkened by the shadows of two hanged men. And the memory of the girl would be a torture that would shrivel his soul until it became a dead thing like—like Dunkle's.

He looked at him with a new appraisal, seeing the essential ruthlessness, the blind selfishness that would sacrifice anyone to its own ends; and he knew he could not force himself into Dunkle's mold. He said slowly, "I don't want it that bad, Mr. Dunkle."

The friendliness, the persuasiveness faded from Dunkle's face, leaving it strained. He went back a step, studying, gauging, and Chris saw fear start in his mind, saw it grow and spread, saw it crowd into his eyes; and he saw the signs of breakage as the man's inner fiber went to pieces under the force of its hammering. In these still moments he witnessed the death of much that had been fine and good in the man. And now Dunkle threw a swift glance at Ed Fuller and went back, step by step.

Chris saw the sudden alertness on Fuller's dark face and beside him, Stumpy, gun in hand, his face still green—and danger sharpened him and turned the air cold in his nose.

"Chris!" Dunkle's voice was harsh. He stopped moving and his eyes strained wickedly wide. "I will not let you turn them loose. Give me that paper!" His lips drew back, giving him the look of a fighting stallion, the flesh sucked tight to the skull.

Seeing that look, Chris got a full, dismal awareness of what was coming. Nothing could change Dunkle; nothing could stop him. There could be but one end to this. His face went bone-hard. He said, "I will not give it up!" and waited, muscles bowstring-tight.

For a moment there was a wild hope that Dunkle would back down, and then that hope died as Dunkle's hand started for his hip. Chris whipped up his gun and fired.

The bullet shook Dunkle and rocked him back on his heels. He teetered while red stained his shirt front and the blazing light in his eyes dulled. The gun slid from his hand and he pitched forward to strike on his face. Off to the side, Fuller was frozen in the act of drawing; Stumpy's gun was rammed into his ribs, and Stumpy said in a voice that was a miserable croak, "There's been enough killin'. Let go your gun, Ed!"

The stench of burned powder was strong in the air. Chris said, "Thanks, Stumpy. You still want to use that gun, Ed?"

Fuller's hand left his gun. He stared down at Dunkle and he shook his head. "I work for money. Who'd pay me now if I shot you?" He was still for a long minute staring down at the body. Then he shrugged, tramped to his horse and stepped into the saddle. He gathered the reins and looked over at Stumpy. "I'm pullin' out. If you've got good sense you'll do the same."

"Can't be too fast for me," Stumpy said fervently. "I'm right with you." He hustled to his horse, flung himself up, lifted his hand to Chris and followed Fuller into the pines.

As the muffled beat of hoofs died away, a barren loneliness came to Chris, and a sense of loss. He had just had to kill the man upon whom his life had been patterned, and with him all his old standards. He was shaken and adrift.

In the shadows filling the clearing the still face of old Jake Fickett mutely accused him and he saw with a fearful clarity how far he had gone along Dunkle's path.

He started as a hand gripped his arm. "I was watchin'. You found it?" Randolph Fickett's blue eyes were blazing. He flopped back the taffy-colored hair.

Chris handed over the bill of sale. "In his sweatband."

Fickett's eyes raised to Lissa as she came beside him. They dropped back to the paper and his face tightened, showing his thought; it had come just too late for Uncle Jake.

"Dunkle still wanted to hang Randy, even after he knew?"

Chris felt the horror in Lissa's voice. He saw the fairness and honesty in her, the good human feeling, and now he knew a black disgust at himself. Had he not been blinded by his own chance to gain he would have seen that these people could not have shot Sam Helfinger.

Without waiting for an answer she turned and walked slowly to Uncle Jake. She knelt and in silence looked down upon the still face. Her fingers closed the gray eyes and smoothed back the white hair, lingering on it. She arose and got the socks and returned to pull them on the bare feet.

As he watched, a sense of guilt grew in Chris and became an oppressive torment. He went over and hunkered down across from her. "I'm sorry——" He stopped, his voice rough in his throat. Nothing he could say would change things. The deed was done; that was the hard and bitter truth.

Melissa's head came up, showing damp blue eyes. "I know." Her voice was softly brooding. "I know how you feel. This is a rough, wild country without much law. Sometimes men have to take things into their own hands; but if it had not been for you, Randy would have died." A gentle expression came into her face. "You must not blame yourself; we owe you too much."

Chris had expected hate and he found forgiveness. It stirred him, it made him feel worse. He had an overwhelming desire to help her. "Look," he said in a strained voice, "you don't have to go lookin' for grass. I've got a place over the ridge a piece. You move your stock there." The words rushed out, without thought or heed.

Her eyes opened wide, startled. Warmth lighted them and she reached out and put her hand on his arm. "You are generous, but we couldn't use your range, we couldn't crowd you."

"You don't owe us a thing," Fickett said beside him. "You wiped the slate clean when you threw down on Dunkle."

The girl's hand fell away as they stood up, but Chris could still feel its warm, disturbing pressure on his arm.

His eyes came upon Dunkle's body, shadowy in the glassy twilight. He said, "I'll have to pack him in to Sentinel and report to the sheriff."

"We'll go with you," Randolph Fickett said in a firm voice, "and see you don't run into trouble. You had to shoot in self-defense, but it won't do any harm to have witnesses along."

"We certainly will!" Melissa said quickly. "And you have no guilt about Uncle Jake. It was Dunkle! Why, when you found there'd been a mistake you risked your life to save Randy! No jury would convict you!"

Chris stared off into the darkening pines. They were generous, even in their grief. They would help him from their overflow of human compassion, their fairness. It made him feel humble; it roughed him up inside.

He swung around to Fickett. "I meant what I said about usin' my place. You won't crowd me. Last winter killed off my stock. I was leavin' anyway."

Fickett shook his head, his face pinching with the understanding of a man who has endured his own share of troubles. He turned to his sister and for a long moment they wordlessly conferred.

"We're in a bad way," he said at length. "Short-handed, no grass and no place to stay." He hesitated. "If you're shy of stock we might work a deal. It would sure help us, and you wouldn't have to leave. It might work out well for all of us."

Seeing the sudden hope in the girl's face, a warm tide moved in Chris. He had never known people like this. Theirs was a different pattern from the one he had followed, but he knew deeply and with certainty that it was the better one. It made him feel warm, it made him feel fine. Out of evil would come something good. Otherwise they might have met and passed, each unaware and heedless of the other's need.

He put out his hand to Randy Fickett. "I reckon it will work out. I reckon it will work out fine."

EARLY AMERICANA

CONRAD RICHTER

It has slipped almost out of reality now, into the golden haze that covers adobe walls and the Alamo, so that today, behind speeding headlights or in the carpeted Pullman, it seems as if it might never have really been.

But if you are ever on the back of a horse at night far out on the windswept loneliness of the Staked Plains, with no light but the ancient horns of the Comanche moon and that milky band of stardust stirred up by the passing of some celestial herd, a cloud may darken the face of the untamed earth, the wind in your face will suddenly bring you the smell of cattle, and there beyond you for a moment on the dim, unfenced, roadless prairie you can make out a fabulous dark herd rolling, stretching, reaching majestically farther than the eye can see, grazing on the wild, unplanted mats of the buffalo grass.

And now with sudden emotion you know that the faint, twinkling light you see on the horizon is a distant window of that rude, vanished, half-mystical buffalo settlement, Carnuel, as it stood that night sixty years ago, the only fixed human habitation on a thousand square miles of unfriendly prairie, with great ricks of buffalo hides looming up like bales of swarthy cotton on a Mississippi levee, and with John Minor standing silently on the gallery of his buffalo post, looking with unreadable eyes on the rude rutted trail running out of sight in the moonlight on its four hundred miles to the railroad, and thinking how many days it had been that no one, East or West, North or South, had come to Carnuel but the rugged old Kansas circuit rider for the settlement's first wedding.

As a rule, there were hide buyers in hired buggies rattling in the protection of a wagon train coming back from Dodge; and across the prairie, hunters fresh from the big herds yelling wildly as they rode up to Seery's saloon, the only place of refreshment in a dozen future counties; and clattering in from every direction, small freighters, their wagons piled high and lapped over the wheels to the ground with hides, so that they looked like huge hayricks bumping over the plain, swaying at every grass clump and threatening to crack the boom pole and spill the wagon. And at night the settlement would be full of bearded men stumbling over wagon tongues, roaring out lusty songs from Seery's bar and in the smoky light of the post hefting the new rifles and buying cartridges and coffee.

But tonight the only sound from the gallery was the monotonous wind of the Staked Plains blowing soft and treacherous from the south, flapping the loose ends of five thousand buffalo hides, and bringing in from the prairie, now faint, now strong, the yelping of wolves from where cheery campfires of buffalo chips usually glowed.

In the adobe saloon, marked on the walls with notorious names and ribald verses, Dan Seery and a single customer played euchre, the whisky-stained cards rattling on the drumlike hardness of a flint-dry buffalo-hide table.

In his little adobe house, the bridegroom, Jack Shelby, took a last look at the room Nellie Hedd had put firmly in place for their wedding tomorrow, from the stove ready to be lighted by the bride's hand to the starched pillow shams on the bed, and then carefully stretched his own bedroll on the kitchen floor.

And in the living quarters behind John Minor's buffalo post, Chatherine Minor, aged sixteen, tried not to listen to the voices of her father and the circuit rider coming low and grave from the storeroom as she brushed her black hair for bed by the light of a square buffalo-tallow candle, and thought of Laban Oldham, who had seldom spoken to her and never even looked at her, and wondered whether he might ask her for a square dance tomorrow night when they celebrated the wedding.

But ten miles out at Oldham Springs, in his father's dugout high and dry in the *cañada* bank, Laban Oldham wasn't thinking of Chatherine Minor. Straight and untalkative, for all his boyish cheeks, his eyes a deep crockery blue, the long rawhide-colored hair spilling violently over his linsey collar, he sat with his true love across his knees, polishing the octagon barrel, swabbing out the gleaming bore with bear oil and rubbing the stock with tallow until it threw back a golden reflection of the candle.

For nearly four years he had done a man's work in the saddle. Tomorrow he would really be a man and his own boss at eighteen, and could go riding out of Carnuel, a buffalo hunter on the Staked Plains at last, leaving chores and drudgery forever behind him, his Sharps rifle hard in its scabbard under his legs and his voice joining Frankie Murphy's in a kind of shouted and unrhymed singing:

> *I left my old wife in the country of Tyron.*
> *I'll never go back till they take me in irons.*
> *While I live, let me ride where the buffalo graze.*
> *When I die, set a bottle to the head of my grave.*

His mother, a small dark woman, bent her face over her needle as if to blot the rifle from her eyes. His father, with a full, tawny mustache and a back like a bull, sat almost invisible in the shadows, silently smoking his pipe. And all evening there was no mention of missing freighters or buffalo hunters, or that it was the boy's last night in the dugout, only that the rotting tow sacks over the ceiling poles were letting the dirt sift through and that what they should do was go away for a night and leave the door open, so a polecat could come in and rid the place of mice.

"The wind's kind of bad from the south tonight," Jesse Oldham once remarked.

The others listened, but you couldn't hear the wind in a dugout.

"I stopped at the Hedds' today," Jesse Oldham spoke again. "Nellie sure looks pretty for her weddin'."

Another ten minutes passed while Jesse Oldham used the cotton-wood bootjack and made himself ready for bed.

"You're staying in the settlement till after the wedding, Laban?" his mother begged him.

He nodded, but to himself he said that it was nothing to his liking. With his young eyes hard and pitying on Jack Shelby for giving in so weak to a woman, he would stand with the other men at the kitchen door and never go near the dancing. And at daybreak, when the celebration would be over and Jack Shelby would find himself tied for life to a house and a woman's corset strings, he and Frankie Murphy would be riding free as air out of Carnuel toward the Little Comanche, where the prairie was alive and moving with a dark tide, and where for ten miles you could hear the endless bellowing of fighting bulls, a dull, unceasing thunder that rose to an unforgettable roar by dawn.

Something came into his blood at the thought, so that he could scarcely sit still. He could see himself and Frankie riding all spring and fall in the backwash of that shaggy tidal wave as it swept, eddied and scattered over the far northern plains. They would sell their hides at Dodge and Hays City, and perhaps Cheyenne. He would see strange tribes and people, the Arkansas River and the Platte, and the northern mountains that looked like blue clouds floating over the plain. It was a free life, a king's life, with always a new camp and a new country just over the rise. And at night, rolled snug with his companions in their blankets, with the moon sailing high or the snow falling softly, with roast buffalo hump keeping him warm and tomorrow another adventure, he knew he should never come back to sleep again in a house at Carnuel.

Long after the dugout was in darkness, he lay awake in his homemade pole bed, with the familiar scent of earthen walls and rye straw in his nostrils, feeling the warmth of his young brother under the blue quilt beside him and listening to his father and mother breathing in the red-cherry bed that had come in the wagons from Kentucky. His mother's breath was the faster. Rapidly it caught up to his father's deeper breathing, chimed with it, passed it, for all the world like the hoofbeats of Ben and Fanny, his father's and mother's saddle horses, on their way to Nellie Hedd's wedding tomorrow.

On his own speckled pony, Calico, he rode away in the morning, with no more fuss than Cass, his young brother, running admiringly beside him in the other wheel track, as if they were not going to see each other in a few hours at Carnuel. Perched on the bleached skull of a buffalo, the young boy waited until horse and rider were high on the rise against the sky.

"Good-bye, Laban!" he shrilled.

Laban lifted his hand and rode down into his new world. If it hadn't been for Cass, he would have liked to turn his head for a last look at the place to carry with him into the country of the Cheyennes and the Sioux—the smoke lifting from his father's dugout almost invisible within the bank; his mother's great black kettle for which he had gathered wagonloads of buffalo chips; and swinging their long horns as they came in single file down over the cap rock, his father's red Texas cattle that had grazed the night with antelope and stray buffalo.

Down in the deep prairie crack along the Carnuel River, he passed the Hedd place, busy with preparation for the wedding, the bride-groom's saddled horse already tied to the cottonwood, the bride drying her dark red hair in the sunshine and her father's pole buckboard waiting for horses by the door. And when he was up on the cap rock again, he could see rising behind the south ridge a cloud of dust that was surely a crowd of buffalo hunters riding in for Jack Shelby's wedding.

With his long, rawhide-colored hair leaping at every jump, he turned his pony southeast to meet them, but when he reached the top of the long grassy ridge, the dust had disappeared. And though he stayed there for hours, the wide plain below him stayed empty of the crawling ants that would have numbered Frankie Murphy in his deerskin vest and Sam Thompson and Captain Jim Bailey bringing their wives home from their buffalo camps along the Little Comanche.

He had the strangest feeling when at last he turned his pony and rode slowly back to Carnuel. The tiny remote settlement lay in the westering sun like a handful of children's blocks thrown and forgotten on the immensity of the prairie. Still several miles away, he could see a small cluster of persons standing on the gallery of the post, but neither his parents' horses nor the Hedd buckboard had come up from the river.

When he reached the settlement, the spare form of the storekeeper moved out in the rutted trail to meet him.

"Nellie and Jack didn't get them a new day for their weddin'?" he asked in a low voice, but his gaze was sharp and piercing.

"Not when I passed there this mornin'." Out of the corner of one eye, the boy glimpsed Chatherine Minor in a new maroon cashmere dress moving quietly to the side of her father. His hand tightened on his bridle rein. "I'll ride down and see what's keepin' them," he said briefly.

John Minor opened his leathery lips as if to say something, and closed them again, but the girl had stiffened.

"Don't go, Laban!" she cried after him.

He made as if he hadn't heard, sitting very straight in the saddle and not looking back, riding away at a steady lope on the familiar trail for the Hedd house and his father's dugout. He would have gone now if a norther had been blowing, white and blinding, across the prairie, but he had never seen the Staked Plains more gentle and mild. The wind had gone down and the late-afternoon sunlight slanting across the motionless grass was soft and golden as the candle burning in the little shrine on the wall of Mrs. Gonzales' house in Carnuel when her man, Florencio, was somewhere out in this desolate land.

Like a long shadow felled across his path, he reached the edge of the canyon and saw below him that his morning's trail of bright sunshine now lay in twilight and gloom. He pulled up his pony and listened. The rocky depths with their untamed fertile bottoms tangled with shanghai grass and willows, and even the river itself, were utterly silent. For a little he sat there looking back at Carnuel, that had somehow become a distant and golden speck on the sunlit prairie. Then he urged his pony down the trail that the indefatigable pick of Sebastian Hedd had cut wide enough for his buckboard in the sloping canyon wall.

It wasn't so bad, once he was down and accustomed to the heavy shadows, with Calico splashing cheerfully through the shallow river and the echo of iron shoes thrown back from the rocky walls. A little farther on, the canyon would be homelike, with Sebastian Hedd's fields green in this wild place with winter wheat, and beyond them the peeled logs of the Hedd cabin, with the buckboard drawn up to the door and Jack Shelby's horse tied under the cottonwood. Even Calico freshened and stepped briskly around the bend in the canyon wall.

It was there, as he expected—the house and the fields Sebastian Hedd had wrested from the wilds, and the old slatted buckboard standing in front of the house. And yet there was something wrong with the familiar scene, something that caused him slowly to stiffen and his pony to halt and snort in the gloomy trail. Jack Shelby's horse was curiously missing and the pole of the buckboard had been propped up on a boulder, and over it had been bent some peculiar and unfamiliar object, pale and glistening in the shadows, and utterly still.

With a fine, inexplicable sweat breaking out of his pores, the boy watched it, little by little edging his pony nearer and leaning over the saddle horn that he could better see. Then, as if struck by a rattlesnake, he stopped. He had made out a feathered shaft like a long, thin, uplifted finger warning him grimly not to come on. And now for the first time he knew the naked and mutilated object on the buckboard tongue for what it was.

A hundred times, night and day, sun and shadow, Laban had traveled this trail, but never had the walls of the canyon pushed in and choked him as they did today. He could feel the dark, open door of the wronged little house watching him. And far above him, the layers of cap rock still brilliant in the sun, were the bright walls of the holy city that he could never hope to reach again.

For endless minutes he sat there on Calico, his knees wedged against the pony's shoulders, rigid, waiting, twitching, listening. All he could hear was an unseen horned lark winging its way back to the cap rock from the river, uttering its nameless cry that never betrayed the direction from which it came or whether it was bird or spirit. And all he could see were the contents of a bride's leather trunk, starched muslin underwear and petticoats, feather-stitched and trimmed with ruffles, and nightgowns high on the throat and tatted on the wrists, one of them given by his own mother, and all carefully folded away for the bridal journey, now torn and scattered like bits of white rubbish along the trail.

And now, examining again the loaded chamber of his old Sharps with the octagon barrel, he forced his rearing and plunging pony by the tragic little house, his eyes mechanically counting the three pitiable things lying motionless on buckboard tongue and ground.

Everywhere as he rode on rigidly through the canyon dusk, through the clumps of tangled willows that took on the shapes of bows and rifle barrels, and through the tall rank grass that twisted like snaky braids and eagle feathers, he could see his father more clearly than he had ever seen him in the life—splashing his face in the wash tin before supper, wetting his hair, combing his long, tawny, imperturbable mustache, sitting without expression as he smoked in his chair after supper. And he could see his mother, her black hair combed tightly back from her forehead, tilting the huge coffeepot, carving a slice from the loaf, or riding sidewise on her man's saddle, her right knee hooked over the horn, and behind her, his young brother holding on with both hands to the cantle and scratching his itching cheek against the rough homespun back of her basque.

Every fresh turn in the murky trail, boulders lying on the ground twisted the hand on his woolly rawhide reins, and up on the home side of the cap rock in the last searching rays of the sun, distant white specks in the grass flattened his cheeks until he knew them to be forgotten piles of bleaching buffalo bones. And when at last he reached the rise from where he had lifted a hand to Cass that morning, he could see below him in the grassy *cañada* the silent bank that was his father's dugout and the door standing idly open on its wooden hinges.

Minute by minute he put off the grim duty, and when slowly he pushed his way into the doorway, he found the place as if a shell had struck it—the ticks ripped open, the floor littered with staves of his mother's sourdough keg and broken pieces of the beautifully polished red-cherry bed that had come all the way from Kentucky in the wagons, and flour and savage filth over everything. The buffalo robe where Cass used to lie of an evening on the floor before the earthen fireplace was gone without a trace, and so were Cass and his father and mother, the hoofprints of the unshod Ben and Fanny lost among the endless trample of unshod ponies.

Long after darkness had fallen, the boy half ran beside his grunting pony climbing out of the deep silent canyon. Up here on the cap rock he could breathe again. The stars seemed only half as far away. And far across the blackness of the plains he could see that reassuring small spark of yellow light, steady, alive and more beautiful than all the stars in the sky.

He told himself that his father, who knew the country better than an almanac, might have left his mother in the soft radiance of that light at this moment. And when he rode up in front of the lighted post, the first thing he did was to peer from the saddle toward the dusty panes. But all he could see was the candlelight shining on brand-new cinches and cartridge belts and skillets strung along the rafters and on the full skirts of three women, none of whom was his small mother with her black hair combed tightly back from her forehead.

"That you, Labe?" the voice of the storekeeper came from the dimness.

The boy moved his pony back deeper into the shadows.

"Could you come out here, Mr. Minor?" he said in a low tone. "The women, I reckon, better stay where they're at."

At the peculiar quality in his voice, four men, two with rifles, moved with silent stiffness from where they had been standing unseen on the dark side of the gallery—the storekeeper and the saloonkeeper, the gaunt circuit rider and Seth Falk, a buffalo hunter from Indian territory, thick, bearded, in a buckskin shirt and an old pied brown-and-white-calfskin vest.

"What's the matter, boy?" the circuit rider demanded.

Laban only looked at him, his eyes burning like coals in the darkness.

"I reckon," after a moment he told them, "there won't be a weddin' in the settlement now."

Silence followed, except for the short, rapid puffs of Dan Seery's pipe and the circuit rider's hard breathing. Only Seth Falk changed no more than an Indian.

Laban could see him standing there in the dim light, leaning on his rifle, taciturn, inscrutable, his heavy forehead bent characteristically forward, so that his unreadable black eyes watched the boy from under the edge of his twisted hatbrim.

"They get Jack and the girl both?" he questioned without emotion.

"They got them all," the boy said thickly.

"How about your folks?" John Minor wanted to know.

Laban told him. And when he spoke again, it was very low, so the girl, who, he knew, was standing at the open door of the post, couldn't hear him.

"I got Nellie here on Calico now. She's wrapped up in my sugan." He made every effort to keep his voice from breaking. "You better tell the women not to open it. They did her up mighty bad."

The circuit rider, who was standing nearest the dim shadow of the pony, stiffened as if touched by a grisly hand, and Dan Seery's eyes rolled white in his beard. But Seth Falk and John Minor never moved.

For a time the four of them stood staring at him and out into the night and at each other and through the open door of the post to the untold women, while a stark awareness grew on the boy that not a wolf or coyote howled on the cap rock this evening.

"We better get Jack and Bass tonight—if we want to bury them," he said bleakly.

"I'll ride down with the boy," Seth Falk spat, and moved off toward the rock corral with his rifle, for all his size as light on his feet as a mountain cat in the darkness.

The Comanche moon hung low in the west as the two horses came slowly and heavily back across the plain from the canyon. In the shadow of the post, John Minor and the circuit rider stood waist deep in a wide, sandy trench. There were no boards to waste on a coffin. The three women came slowly out of the post, and the circuit rider put on his long dark coat to read the burial service. A tall, gaunt, unforgettable figure in rusty black, towering there in front of a pile of shaggy buffalo hides, his voice rang out into the night as if to reach and sear the red infidels where he pictured them lying on the ground like wolves and harlots with their sinful and bloody scalps.

Laban had bared his long sandy hair at a burial before, but never one that constricted him like this—the late hour, the small handful of people, the rising and falling of a real preacher's voice making the hair on the back of his neck to stir, and all the time the grated tin lantern with its tiny pane of glass and scattered air holes throwing grotesque shadows on the men with rifles, on the full skirts of the women still dressed for the wedding, and on the house of Jack Shelby, empty and silent yonder in the darkness.

Even here, when she stood only a few feet from him, the boy did not glance at the tight-lipped face of Chatherine Minor. A blur of maroon dress was all he saw or cared to see. White women didn't belong out here. Their place was back in a gentler land where farmers never heard of turning a furrow with a rifle lashed to the plow handles and where, on a Sunday morning, his mother used to say, she could still remember the peaceful sound of church bells drifting across the blue-grass. And tonight, if they had stayed there, no girl with luxuriant dark-red hair would be lying out here to be buried

216

without it in an old mended sugan for a coffin, and his mother might be surely alive and rocking on a board floor in a Kentucky town with a lighted lamppost on the corner.

"The Lord giveth," the circuit rider declared, "and the Lord taketh away. And no man knoweth the hour at which the Son of Man cometh."

As if in pagan challenge to the Christian words, a sign appeared slowly out in the darkness, then another. And presently, as they stood there watching, with the lips of Mrs. Gonzales moving in Spanish and her hand convulsively crossing the black shawl folded on her breast, three fires far out on the plain burned red holes into the night, a scarlet triangle around the little settlement, fading and flaring in some savage code.

" 'And I stood upon the sand of the sea,' " the circuit rider said, with abomination in his voice. " 'and saw a beast rise up out of the sea, having seven heads and ten horns.' "

Sternly, when the rude service was done, John Minor ordered the women into the post, and for a time there was only the whisper of falling sand.

"What are they sayin', Falky?" Dan Seery asked.

"I ain't sartain I savvy," the buffalo hunter muttered. But Laban observed that he gave John Minor a meaning look, and then stood with his head thrown forward grimly, watching the fires wax and wane.

For long minutes while they burned to smoldering red sparks on the prairie, John Minor mechanically mounded the wide grave with his shovel, his face bleak and marked, as if what he thought lay too deep in his mind to fetch up without herculean effort.

"There's something I want to say to you, men," he said at last unsparingly.

The boy had been watching his face. He wasn't sure what the storekeeper was about to say, but whatever it was, he was with him. Only the buffalo hunter seemed to know. He swung around slowly. All evening he had said little, and he said nothing now, but his eyes were like burning black fragments as they threw a deep, unutterable look around the little circle, not as if searching their faces but from some powerful, unspoken feeling.

"I've no notion," John Minor went on harshly, "of letting our women go through what Nellie Hedd went through before those devils scalped her."

Laban felt a sharp, prophetic stab of coldness, as if slivers of blood had congealed in his veins. But John Minor had picked up an old buffalo horn and was bent over his shovel, scraping off the blade with all the deliberation of a man who expected to use it for a long time to come.

"What's this you're talking about, man?" the circuit rider demanded sharply.

"The women." John Minor didn't look up at him. "Three of us got to keep extra guns loaded. We'll hold out as long as we can. Then, if it has to be, it's an act of mercy."

He said no more, but Laban felt strangely weak in the knees. Dan Seery's eyes were white and glistening in his beard, and for a moment even the rugged face of the circuit rider lost some of its color. Only Seth Falk stood there stony and unchanged. And presently he brought out a deck of worn Mexican cards that fetched the quick censure into the circuit rider's cheeks.

"I've throwed out the queen of clubs," he told John Minor.

"I reckon that's good as any other way," the storekeeper said. "Who must we say for the queen of spades? Mrs. Gonzales. And Sadie Harrison for the queen of diamonds. And the queen of hearts"—for a moment his face was like leather strained over a drum—"will have to be the other one." He turned and started to pull down a hide that had worked loose from the pile.

"You all savvy?" Seth Falk's gaze swept the men.

With its grotesque legs and clotted ruff, the hide lay on the ground like some dark misshapen omen, scarred and bloodstained, its swarthy wool matted with ticks and sandburs, bearing the tin lantern and the pack of cards face downward beside it.

"You draw fust, Dan," the buffalo hunter said briefly.

The saloonkeeper made no movement—just stood there looking down at the deck as if paralyzed. John Minor knelt and lifted a card. When Laban saw them glance expectantly at him, he stiffened his back and drew the second. It was the four of spades. The buffalo hunter followed. Relentlessly now, the drawing went on. With strong disapproval on his face, the circuit rider moved away, and came back again in his long black coat to watch like a gigantic dark moth drawn to the flame.

It seemed to the rigid boy that, except for the slight hiss of the slipping cards, the Staked Plains had never been so hushed. The horned moon had set. The fresh grave slept peacefully. Not a sound came from the post. Their little circle of light lay on the ground like a golden coin in all this illimitable darkness which somewhere held his father and mother and little Cass.

He was dimly aware of turning up a card with a broken corner which suddenly froze in his hands. It was a woman riding a horse, as the queen does in the Mexican deck, her colored raiment stained and blemished, her face almost obliterated, and above the horse's head the small, curious-shaped Mexican heart. And as soon as he laid it down on the swarthy hide, it turned into the slender body of Chatherine Minor lying silent on the dark adobe floor of the post in the full skirts of the maroon cashmere dress she had made for Nellie Hedd's wedding.

He remembered afterward John Minor's granite face, and Seth Falk tossing down the queen of yellow diamonds with no more expression than a card in a poker hand, and the latter's little black buffalo eyes watching him as if his face bore some unbecoming color.

"Come in and John'll give you a drink," he said gruffly.

Laban stood there, rude and unhearing. When the others had gone with the lantern into the post, he kept walking with his rifle between the dark piles of hides.

The strong reek of the skins gave him something that he needed, like a powerful medicine brewed from the Staked Plains themselves. It reached where no whisky could. Kiowas or Comanches were nothing. After what he had seen in the canyon this afternoon, he could mow the painted devils down all day and stay icy cold with hate and clear of regret. But a white person, a woman, and only a girl! For more than an hour he kept walking up and down between the dark piles, and all the while, in the tightened sinews of his arms and legs and in the growing flatness of his cheeks, he seemed to be curing, hardening, drying, almost like one of the buffalo hides itself.

It was very quiet in the post when he came in. Over in a corner, so deep in shadows it seemed impossible to distinguish the faces of the cards, Seth Falk was playing a stolid game of solitaire on a boot box, a pair of rifles lying beside him on the floor. Sitting under a candle, his Bible open on his knees, was the circuit rider, his rugged face alight as if the sun were shining into some rocky canyon. Dan Seery had just poured himself a stiff drink in a tumbler from a jug beneath the counter. And John Minor, with two guns leaning against the wall, sat writing slowly and methodically at his littered table.

He glanced up as Laban came in and silently indicated an extra rifle lying across a sugar barrel, with several boxes of cartridges on the floor. Something unutterable passed through the boy as he saw it, but he walked over, lifted and sighted it in his cold hands, the newest in buffalo guns, with a coil-spring lever and a long round barrel. His stiff fingers tried a cartridge into the chamber, then they filled the magazine.

And now he knew that nothing could keep him from looking at the women. They had refused to go to bed, and there they sat in the two high-backed chimney seats. The Mexican woman, Mrs. Gonzales, was asleep, her chin forward on her breasts, breathing into her tightly drawn rebosa. Beside her, the elderly Sadie Harrison's eyes were tightly closed in their bony sockets, her gray hair awry, her long face a picture of aged and bitter resignment.

Only the girl Chatherine was erect and awake, sitting alone on the other bench, her back toward him, hidden behind a post, except for one shoulder and for her full red skirts flowing over the side of the bench to the floor. Once he felt that she was about to turn her head and glance back at him, and he dropped his eyes and began pushing cartridges from the new boxes into the empty loops of his belt.

The clock struck, and the long silence that followed rang louder than the gong. It was this waiting, waiting, Laban told himself, that was going to tell on him. He saw that the circuit rider had closed his Bible and was holding it tightly, like some golden talisman that would warm his cold hands. Seth Falk had shoved up the rows of his unfinished game and was stacking the cards on the box. Leaving one of his rifles against the door jamb, he stepped outside, and Laban could hear his boots clicking no more loudly than a cat's claws up and down the adobe floor of the dark side of the gallery.

John Minor picked up one of his own rifles and started toward the kitchen.

"I'll watch it out there, Mr. Minor," Laban said quickly.

He was glad to get out of this place, where, no matter which way he turned his head, he could feel a red woolen dress burning into his eyes. He stepped through the darkened kitchen and out of the kitchen door. Not a star shone in the blackness. No sound rose but the faint stamping of horses around to the front, where they had been tied for the night to the gallery posts.

Once he heard the clock strike the half hour and afterward the rumbling of a moved bench in the post, and then the circuit rider's unmistakable ecclesiastical voice. It seemed to go on and on, and when Laban pushed in the kitchen door, it rang suddenly louder. Curiously he made his way in the dimness to the other door. The candles in the post had burned out and only a pale rosy glow from the dying embers in the fireplace faintly illumined the long spectral room. In a little circle of shadows, everyone seemed to be standing, the gaunt shadow that was the circuit rider towering above them all, something upheld in one hand, the other dipping into it like the mysterious hand of God. And his voice rang out with powerful solemnity in this unaccustomed place:

"I baptize thee . . . Chatherine Lydia Minor . . . in the name of the Father . . . and the Son . . . and the Holy Ghost."

Slowly the import of the thing came over the boy, and with his fingers biting deeply into his rifle, he slipped back to a kitchen bench. But all the time he rigidly sat there he had the feeling that even in that faintest of fantastic light Chatherine Minor had marked his tall form standing and watching at the kitchen door. And when it was all over, he heard her step coming toward him in the kitchen and then her fingers lighting the stub of a candle on the table.

"Can I make some coffee for you, Laban?" she asked.

And now he knew that nothing on earth could keep him from raising his eyes and letting them fall rigidly and for the first time directly on this girl whom, before the sun was an hour high, he might have to turn suddenly and bleakly upon.

There she stood, her dark eyes calmly facing him, taller than he imagined, but already, at sixteen, a woman, her body sturdy as a young cedar in the river brakes. The strong cheekbones in her face turned abruptly inward, giving a resolute cast to the mouth. But what held his eyes most was her long black hair, parted in a clear white streak, lustrous hair that, he knew, a Kiowa or Comanche would sell his life for.

He shook his head. She did not go away abashed; only stood there looking at him.

"You look thin, Laban," she reproved him. "You haven't had anything to eat since this morning."

He could see now that her eyes were not black and brazen, as he had thought. They were steady and slaty gray. But what made him steel himself, sitting there with a rifle across his lap, was where her left breast, swelling gently in the folds of her tight red basque, marked the target of her heart.

"I'm not hungry," he said harshly.

She turned quietly away, and he thought she would go, but he could hear her hand on stove and water bucket and kitchen utensils, and the heel of her firm foot on the adobe floor, and finally there was the fragrance of coffee through the kitchen, almost choking him, and he tried not to look at the picture she made, straight and with a disturbing womanly serenity, handing him a heavy, steaming, white cup and saucer, and then bearing one in each hand into the post.

She set a plate of cold roast buffalo hump on the bench beside him and quietly washed the cups and saucers in the wash tin and put them away on the calico-hung shelves as if she would surely find them there in the morning. Then her competent hands filled the stove, and with a dour mouth he watched her throw her skirts forward to seat herself, sturdy and erect, on the other kitchen bench.

"Papa wants me to stay out here," she said quietly, as if it were the most common thing in the world.

He said nothing. His face, framed in his long, rawhide-colored hair, was deaf and wintry. He waited grimly for her woman's chitchat, but she sat composed and silent as a man while the stub of a candle flickered out behind them, leaving the scent of burned wicking floating through the dark room.

For a long time they sat in utter silence while the clock struck and a faint gray began to drift like some thin, ghostly semblance of light through the dark window.

"It's starting to get morning, Laban," she whispered. "Are you awake?"

"I'm awake," he told her.

"I think I hear something," she said quietly.

His hands made sure of his rifles. Rising, he felt his way along the cool wall to where an iron bar, fashioned from an old wagon tire, bolted the door. Minutes passed while he stood there listening, and the black eastern sky grew into a long, lonely stretch of gray, unbroken except for a single well of green that lay like a pool reflecting the evening on a dark lava plain. He had never heard it more preternaturally still. The post at their backs was like the grave. Even the stamping horses were still. He could fancy them in his mind, standing out there in the early light, curving their necks to snuff and listen.

"It isn't anything," he told her. "Just the blood in your ears."

But now that he would deny it, he could hear it for the first time himself, very far away, like the wind in the grass, or the distant Carnuel River rushing down its canyon after a rain, nearer, always faintly nearer, and then evaporating into nothing more than the vast sweep of dark gray sky torn with ragged fissures like the chaos of creation morning.

"It wasn't anything," the girl agreed, whispering. "Just the blood in my ears."

But Laban's fingers were tightening again on the eight-sided barrel of his old Sharps. Something was surely out there, hidden from the post in the mists, like the abandoned hide wagons bleaching their bones on the Staked Plains. And now, far out on the prairie he could see them breaking out of the fog rolling in from the river, a thin line of loping riders, the long-awaited crawling ants his eyes had strained for from the ridge that day so long ago that was only yesterday afternoon.

A bench was suddenly overturned in the post. Seth Falk's iron gray nickered. And now they could hear the pleasantest sound in more than a week—the distant hallooing of rough, stentorian voices. And presently the post was filled with bearded men twenty-four hours overdue for Nellie Hedd's wedding, men who had ridden all night in wet checkered-linsey shirts and soaked blue flannel shirts and steaming buckskin shirts that smelled of countless hides and buffalo-chip campfires and black powder and Staked Plains rain. And all morning the thick tobacco smoke in the post drifted to the grave talk over Jack Shelby and the Hedds and the uprising of the Kiowas, who meant to sweep every white hunter from the buffalo country, and the lost hides, wagons and hair of the men who had waited too long before raising dust for the big outfits corralled together on the Little Comanche.

For two days and nights Laban Oldham sat cross-legged or lay in his blankets beside the campfire of Frankie Murphy's men. But all the time while he heard how his mother had ridden into a buffalo camp with her black hair streaming into little Cass' face, and while he listened for the long train of freighters coming with the women and hides, Laban couldn't feel anything half so clearly as Chatherine Minor's snug, warm kitchen, and Chatherine Minor handing him a cup of coffee with the steam curling over her raven hair, and Chatherine Minor sitting up with him most of the night in the darkened kitchen and whispering to him in the morning if he were awake.

Tall and stiff, the third evening, his long rawhide-colored hair gravely swinging, he walked through the post into the now-familiar kitchen doorway and beyond, where a girl with her sleeves rolled high stood stirring sourdough leaven into flour that was not so white as her arms. She did not look around at his step, but her bare upper arms brushed, with quick womanly gestures, stray hairs from her face.

"It's a warm evenin'," he greeted.

"Good evening, Laban." She bent over her work, and her hands made the mixing pan sing on the table.

"Did you hear the freighters are campin' tonight at Antelope Water?" he went on awkwardly. "Bob Hollister just rode in."

"I reckon you'll be glad to see your folks," she answered, but he thought her deft white hands kneaded more slowly after that.

He sat on the familiar bench and waited unhurriedly for her to be through. The kitchen felt snug and pleasant as the dugout at home—the blur of the red-checkered cloth folded back from the table and the sputter of river cottonwood in the stove and the homely scent of the sourdough crock. He could close his eyes and know that either his mother or Chatherine Minor must be here. And when the tins were set to rise on the lid of the red flour bin, she washed her hands and seated herself on the other bench, throwing her full skirts skillfully forward, as she had that sterner evening a day or two ago, until they rustled into their rightful place.

For a long time they sat there looking at the wall that held no rifles now, and at the harmless black window, and at each other. And he told himself that he had never thought she would be a woman like this, with her flesh white as snow where it came out of the homespun at her throat, and the soft strength of her young mouth and the deep old mystery in her young eyes.

"I'm followin' the herd north when it moves, Chatherine," he stammered at length. "But I'm comin' back."

She answered nothing to that.

"I reckoned," he went on rigidly, "maybe you'd wait for me till I got back?"

She looked at him now, and her glance was firm and steady as the prairie itself. "I couldn't promise to wait for a single man, Laban," she said. "Where you're going is a long ways off. And a buffalo hunter can easy forget the way back."

The warm color stung his cheeks at that, and he stood on his feet very tall, and stepped across the floor and sat down on the bench, and laid his linsey-clad arm rudely around her shoulders.

"The circuit rider isn't gone back to Dodge with the freighters yet," he told her sternly. "You can make it that he didn't come to Carnuel for nothin', if you want to, Chatherine. Then you won't have to do your waitin' for a single man."

She didn't say anything, but neither did she shake him off, and they sat quiet again while the talk in the post receded to a mere faraway drone and the kitchen candle burned out again, leaving its fragrance and all the room in darkness, except where a dim rectangle of post light fell across the floor. And suddenly he noticed that her breath caught up to his, chimed with it and passed it, for all the world like the breathing of his father and mother in the beautiful red-cherry bed that had come from Kentucky in the wagons.

And everything, he thought, was well when of a sudden she buried her face in his shirt and cried, and what she said after that, he thought, was very strange.

"Oh, Laban," her voice came brokenly, "she had such beautiful hair!"

Before the week was out, the circuit rider scratched out the names of John McAllister Shelby and Nellie Hedd from an official paper and firmly wrote "Laban Oldham and Chatherine Lydia Minor." And the settlement had its wedding with four women on the pole-backed chimney seats, and with Mrs. Oldham, her dark hair combed back tightly from her forehead, sitting on the chair of honor, and with Jesse Oldham, his back like a bull and his imperturbable mustache, standing with John Minor, and with buffalo hunters along the counter and the freighters in a reticent knot by the door.

The circuit rider's voice rang in the pans and skillets hanging on the smoke-stained rafters. And when it was over, a huge shaggy hunter rode his horse halfway into the post's open doorway and bellowed for Dan Seery to unlock the saloon. And when he saw the silent couple and the black book of the circuit rider, he stood in his stirrups and roared, shaking his long gray mane and the blood-stained, weatherbeaten fringe of his buckskins till he looked like an old buffalo bull coming out of the wallow:

> "I left my old wife in the county of Tyron.
> I'll never go back till they take me in irons.
> While I live, let me ride where the buffalo graze.
> When I die, set a bottle to the head of my grave."

HIS NAME
WAS NOT FORGOTTEN

JOEL TOWNSLEY ROGERS

The old sorrel horse had come to the end of another furrow, down at the far corner of the cleared land. The gaunt man in deerskin leggings and bearskin moccasins heeled his bar-spear plow with an easy grip on the smooth-worn handles, as the old horse plodded around.

"Ho!" he said.

The flash of something streaked black and white, like a woodpecker, had caught the hinder edge of his vision for an instant, flitting between trees of the young woods beside him. He turned his mild wrinkled gaze as the old horse stopped, though too late to see what it had been.

For the moment he paused, relaxing, stretching his backbone, scratching his naked ribs, savoring all the good smells of the virgin soil turned up black by his moldboard, and of the May woods and the south wind blowing.

Only one more furrow to plow, up along the thin woods' edge, and then back to his new-built cabin in the field's far corner. He would have time to finish setting in the puncheon floor this afternoon or perhaps to do a little fishing before returning at sundown to Bersheba and the young ones, at the station a mile away.

He had stripped off his linsey shirt a while back, and left it draped on the old oak stump which stood over toward the middle of the plowed land, with his ax resting against it. His flat-chested torso, pale as buttermilk after the long winter of store-tending and crowded indoor living at the little backwoods station, was oiled with a pleasant sweat beneath the noon sun. The life-giving rays tingled through his skin. He felt the light wind stirring the roots of his gray-streaked hair and beard.

Pink and yellow flowering shrubs spotted the woods beside him. Through the sapling trunks and dappled undergrowth he could glimpse the sparkling waters of Long Run, where it went between its grassy banks a hundred yards away. Birds sang and twittered, flitting about, building their nests. The gaunt man fumbled his lips, stirred with an impulse to try imitating their exultant notes. But he was of an inarticulate nature, and even though there was no one to hear him, his lips felt dry and his throat constricted.

Purty, he thought. *Durned purty*.

He was forty-two years old, and his life had been meager and toilsome. He had never learned to express himself in any way. Even as a boy, there had never been any time for him of carefree joy. The weight of poverty and responsibility had always lain heavily on him. A hewer of wood for other men, a plower of others' fields, a wandering trapper and a landless squatter, a small storekeeper at impoverished backwoods settlements doling out needles and pins, with no great love for business, and the shillings few, and losing repeatedly, through bad judgment and lack of trading sharpness, what small gains he made, the barren years stretched back of him. Hunger and want, and defeat and grief—all the things which a man has learned to know when his eyes have become wrinkled and there is gray in his beard—had been his in full measure. Yet for the moment now he felt all the ecstasy of the spring as much as the singing birds.

Like them, he had his own nest this spring—the new cabin which he and his two big boys, Mort and Josh, had built during the past winter, on the Government land grant for his war service which had come through for him at last. He liked to pause down here at the end of the field to admire it in perspective, where it stood at the upper corner of the plowed land, catercorner across the deep furrows from him, at the edge of the pine woods, close to the entrance of the trail that came down from the station.

It was no mere half-face hunter's shelter, built of felled sapling trunks and beaver skins, with only a hearth of piled stones at the open end to huddle over against the winter's cold, such as he and his strong-limbed, competent Mary had known during those hard years of his young manhood when Mort and Josh had been small, and the little girl who had died. No floorless, unchinked field hand's shack, either, too poor even to quarter black slaves in any more, like the one which he had had to take his young Anne to, in that time of youth

227

and brief first love, back in Virginia so long ago. It was a complete four-wall cabin, solidly laid, of spacious dimensions, fourteen by eighteen feet, with a stone fireplace at one end, with a split-slab roof tightly weather-lapped, and with a puncheon floor soon to be installed—a home such as any man might be proud to own.

This was an end to the meager years, the homeless years, the years of insecurity and grief. Mary Shipley lay dead somewhere beside the yellow Ohio, in an unmarked grave, and his young love Anne back across the mountains, in a land that he would never see again. There were times when he almost forgot her.

He had not done too well by either of them. He had not done too well by Bersheba, either, poor young thing, in the six years they had been married. Crowded quarters behind a calico curtain in shared cabins, with the dogs and crying children underfoot, and the drunken quarreling and laughter, and the snoring and the steaming of snow-wet bodies, and no privacy and dignity to it all. Why, at Hughes Station this past winter there had been nineteen families in the eight cabins, a total of more than a hundred souls, including the nine babies which had been born, and not counting the itinerant trappers and Indian traders who might be bunking for a week or two at a time in the blockhouses. That was too crowded living for anyone who liked to breathe. A man couldn't feel that he belonged to himself. And a woman like Bersheba, with her poetry reading and her dainty airs and her feckless dreaming—always areading books and adreaming, when she should be putting the dinner in the pot and getting the washing done—must find it even harder than he did, though she had never complained.

Nothing like that anymore. His own land and his own cabin. A faint curl of smoke rose from the chimney, from the banked wood coals on the hearth keeping warm his dinner of johnnycake and beans. His rifle leaned beside the door. The pelt of the bobcat which he had shot last week was pegged upon the slabs. A seven-foot length of split log, thirty inches wide, lay on the ground near the door, needing only auger holes to be bored in its round underside for legs to make a dining table. With a few last items completed and with a crop in, he would soon be able to move the family out, and they would all live here in freedom and security on the good earth for the rest of their days, his two big boys, Mort and Josh, and Bersheba with her baby girls and little Tom.

It was almost as if his life were just beginning, with all the happiness of untasted springs stored up for him, to be enjoyed from this time forth. He was not an old man yet. He was just at the beginning of his prime. Already, with a dream in his faded eyes, he saw the bare earth green and yellow with tall standing corn. Already he saw windows of clear glass set in the blank cabin walls. Already a barn for cows and horses, and more fields and meadows cleared away, down to the edge of Long Run and beyond, where the deep woods stood on the other side. Already apple trees white in the spring, and chickens pecking in the dooryard, and himself standing in his doorway in a plum coat with brass buttons on Sundays, looking out over his rich acres. Perhaps someday he would even be elected to the territorial legislature and they would call him squire.

The house that he had built, on the land that God had given him. With his hands upon the handles of his bar-spear plow, the gaunt man lifted up his face.

He was an inarticulate man. He had never been able to stand up to give testimony in meeting. He had never prayed aloud, even to himself alone. Yet there was such a pressure of almost unendurable happiness about his heart that he must give utterance to it, as the birds were doing. His bearded lips fumbled and he swallowed.

"I thank Thee, Lord," he said.

And suddenly the locked gates seemed to open. The flood of words came surging forth. He was blessed with the gift of tongues.

"I thank Thee, Lord," he said, his face upturned, while the patient horse waited. "I thank Thee for this here rich land of Kaintucky which Thou hast given to Thy people. I thank Thee that Thou tookest me, a poor man, and led me over the mountains with Dan'el Boone beneath the shadder of Thy wing. I thank Thee for the worldly riches which Thou hast showered upon me; for my good old sorrel hoss, Brandywine, here, worth eight pounds; for my bar-spear plow and tackling, worth two pounds, five shillings; for my brindle cow and calf back at the station, worth four pounds ten; for my dozen pewter plates, worth a pound and a shilling; for my ax, worth nine shillings; for my three weeding hoes, worth seven pounds; for my Dutch oven and cule, worth fifteen shillings at a shilling to the pound weight; for my handsaw and my bucksaw, my adze and auger, my drawing knife and currying knife, my three bedsteads with turkey feathers, my two good rifle guns, worth fifty-five shillings and three pounds ten, and my old smooth bore, worth ten shillings, all a total of nigh on seventy pounds.

"I thank Thee for the increasing riches and civilization which Thou has caused in Thy bounty to be brought upon this here land, for the newspaper that they are atalking of starting up next year in Lexington, and for the academy that they are agoing to have in Louisville, to learn reading and writing to the young ones, and ciphering through the rule of three. I thank Thee for the tailor and the dancing master that are already there. I thank Thee for the good five hundred acres I have here beside Long Run, seven of them already cleared, and for the fine substantial cabin which Thou hast helped me to build.

"I thank Thee for my two able boys, Mordecai and Josiah, that Mary Shipley bore me sixteen and fourteen year ago, that will be a prop and support to me in my old age, and a credit to me after I am gone. I thank Thee for my good wife, Bersheba, who, although kind of dreamy and not very up and gitting, is still a good woman and strives to walk well in Thy sight. I thank Thee for my two purty gals, Mary and Nancy, that she bore me last year and the year before, that will grow up to be fine women and the mothers of men and the solaces of their helpmeets, because of Mary Shipley that they were named after and Anne Boone, my first wife, that Thou gavest me, that I laid away beneath the sod in old Virginny so long ago, with her yaller curls and the blue ribbon in her hair, and her little baby in her arms, when she was no more'n sixteen. I thank Thee also for my little Tom, that Bersheba bore me five year ago; though he is a dreamer like her and will never amount to much in the world, like Mort and Josh.

"I thank Thee for the United States of America and for its divine freedom, which Thou hast given it, and I ask that Thy peace may be upon it from this time forth. I thank Thee for all the blessings which Thou hast bestowed upon me, a poor and humble man, and for the tribulations too. I ask Thee, Lord, to watch over my little Tom in the hard life that he must lead, and be kind to him also, as Thou hast been kind to me. And, O Lord, I don't ask nothing more, only that I may stay upon this land here for the rest of the days which it shall please Thee in Thy wisdom to bestow upon me, and that my name shall be honorable in this great country after I am gone. For Thy Son's sake, amen."

It seemed to him that a hand was laid upon his shoulder in that moment; that he heard a voice speak in his ear while all the world was still. *Thy seed shall be a star in the heavens. Thy name shall be known to the generations.*

He stood there with face uplifted while a shiver ran through him. It was only the soft wind blowing. It was only the quiet rippling of Long Run beyond the trees. It was only the glorious sun shining down on him, tingling all his blood with its strength of life immortal.

He wiped his forearm across his face. He pulled out a brown tobacco leaf from the waistband of his leggings and tore off a fragment of it, methodically folding it and inserting it into his cheek, with a half grin at himself, a little ashamed of his outburst of emotion, and glad that there was no one to know about it. He gripped the handles of his plow again, setting his blade to rip up the last furrow. And in that moment he realized that all the world was still.

The waters of Long Run still sparkled beyond the dappled trees with that rippling over stones. The south wind still blew, lazy and warm. But in the woods the birds no longer sang. And suddenly, in that instant, the gaunt man felt cold. There seemed a shadow on the bright day. The marrow of his bones felt cold.

From the corner of his eye he had glimpsed again within the woods a flash of black and white, like a woodpecker. Behind a sloping sycamore bole it had been, a hundred or a hundred and twenty feet within the woods, darting into sight and out again, at about the height of a man's head from the ground.

He did not turn to look this time. He spoke to his old sorrel horse easily. "Giddy-ap, Brandywine!" But his eyes slanted in their sockets, measuring the distance catercornered across the plowed ground to his cabin, where his rifle leaned beside the door, and to the entrance of the dark trail nearby. And he felt the long sinews of his thighs and calves flex and tighten, and his throat, as he chewed his tobacco leaf, was tight.

Again, from the edges of his eyes, he caught another black-and-white flash in the woods farther up, closer to the field's edge than the big sycamore. And there was still no song of thrush or oriole. But there was a catbird's cry. The catbird's cry. It had been years since he had heard it, but he knew it. There was the flash of a third black-and-white-painted face with a feathered topknot.

In a time of peace like this. In the bright spring day. Wabashes, from up north of the Ohio. A whole war party of them. He had thought all that was done. A civilized country, schools and newspapers. Great towns of hundreds and thousands of people, like Louisville and Lexington. It was all a freezing nightmare. It was all unreal. But now, now! Creeping on him from Long Run's deep banks, through the woods, with their painted faces and shaved heads, adorned for death and war.

He did not turn his head. He moved a step still onward, and another step, behind the plodding sorrel. But his hands were light upon the handles of his plow, and he eased his knees to spring and run. Not for nothing had he run with Dan'el Boone. Not for nothing had they called him Deerlegs and Long Slim up on the Ohio fifteen and twenty years ago. He was forty-two years old, and maybe he was a mite less spry than he had been once, and the rheumatism of wet clothes and bitter winters had got into his bones, but he was still about as fast as any in Kaintucky.

For his life. For his life within the instant he must run, as in those days with Mary up on the Ohio. Within a time of twenty seconds the speed within his legs must save his desperate life or lose it. Across the plowed land, in long leaps, flying like the wind. He should be half across the field before they could break from the woods and unleash their whanging arrows. Zigzagging, dodging, with speed he could reach his rifle or the packed-earth trail back to the station before the whooping hostiles could overtake him, before the whanging arrows caught him and brought him down.

He balanced on the balls of his feet, with lean leg sinews flexing, estimating the distances in a glance, noting each furrow that he must leap, and where to dodge and turn. He seeped a soft breath in his flattened lungs. His old sorrel, feeling the plow drag light, had stopped. Now——

He saw, within that split second as he started to break, a flash of white emerging from the entrance of the forest trail near his cabin across the field, five hundred feet away. He heard the carefree young voices. O God, Mordecai and Josiah had come down from the station. O God, that white was little Tommy's shirt. They had brought little Tommy with them, five years old.

"Hi, pappy!" shouted Mordecai. "Sheba took over the store for us'ns! Come to help you finish that table and set the floor! Brung your auger that you forgot!"

He swallowed in his tight throat. Just for a moment still he had the terrible impulse instantly to run, shouting to them to turn around themselves and fly. With their head start, the two big boys, though not so long-limbed as he, could get away, with him pounding on their heels, back up the hard-packed path toward the station. Mary's boys, his two big fine stalwart boys, the pride of his manhood, the hope of his posterity. The two of them and he. Within this instant, if he started now. But, O God, there was little Tom.

He eased down flat-footed on his heels again, with his hands still on the plow.

"Take Tom into the cabin out of the sun, Mort, and give him a drink out of the hard-cider jug!" he called without a qua- ver. . . . "Josh, you trot back to the station and fetch my gold watch for me! I done forgot the time!"

They stood staring at him across the sunlit field from the edge of the forest shadows, the two big boys, with golden-haired Tommy between them. Their faces were wan. They stood like wooden toys.

For endless seconds they seemed motionless, while in the thin woods beside him the catbird screamed and the painted faces came flitting on.

They knew that he had no gold watch. They knew that he had no jug of cider in the cabin, and if he had, that it would not be for little Tommy to drink. He was afraid that they might shout back and ask him what the joke was.

But they understood. Oh, thank God, they understood. Suddenly, little Tom had begun to cry. Big Mordecai had him by the hand, and was dragging him, whimpering and wailing with an unknown fear, toward the cabin door. Josiah had turned and vanished back up the trail, running.

A matter of ten seconds lost. Or twenty. Those flitting shapes within the woods were so near now, they were so near he dared not look to see. Yet if he could only start off now toward the cabin at an easy pace, with apparent unconcern, they might wait for Josh to return with the gold watch. They might—at least, for a few seconds more—hesitate and delay. If he could only gain half the field or at least a quarter——

But Josh's gesture of flight had been too spasmodic and abrupt, or the little fellow's frightened wails too revealing. He had taken one long easy step away from his plow, and a second, and a third. There was the whooping scream behind him.

He broke and ran, bent from the waist. He leaped aside, with long legs sprawling, his knuckles touching earth, as the whanging arrows shot above. He was on his feet again instantly, with a lunging stagger. He ran with sprawling headlong strides, leaping the cloddy furrows with a sobbing breath, feeling his twisted ankle shot with fire and buckling underneath him, while those howling whoops came at his heels like a dozen wildcats' screams.

Mordecai, across the field, had snatched the rifle at the cabin door. He had got little Tom inside. But for himself, he was a man with a leaden leg, and those seconds of lost time while he shouted to the boys and stood waiting for them to move had let those painted faces get too near.

He was still a leap from the stump in middle field when the whanging, flint-tipped shaft got him between the shoulders. He staggered forward with a great sobbing groan. He fell upon his knees, reaching for his ax where it leaned against the stump, sprawling half around. Up the field's edge his old horse was running, dragging the bumping plowshare, with an arrow in its flank. But he had it between the shoulder blades, close to his heart, and all the world was dim.

Two of the whooping black-and-white-painted faces were rushing at him with lifted tomahawks. From his knees, from the ground, he swung the heavy ax. It went crashing into the side of one of those devil shapes beneath a lifted arm, and the savage screamed. He tried to get to his feet from his sagging knees, to swing again. But the strength of him was like spilled water, and the sun had faded.

He lay upon his face. He heard the quiet waters of the Rappahannock in old Virginia, and in the twilight he was lying on its honeysuckle banks again with his young love, with the ribbon in her yellow hair.

"Anne," he whispered. But in another world than this.

From the door of the cabin a hundred yards away a puff of smoke rose, and the painted savage who was bending over with scalping knife threw up his arms with a yell.

The rifle cracked again. The painted shapes with their catbird screams were dodging among the furrows. The gaunt man lay on his face by the stump in middle field. Close by him lay two of the painted shapes, and another back toward the thin woods' edge.

Behind the cabin door the boy Mordecai loaded the long rifle coolly again, with dead black eyes. The little boy Tom whimpered and sobbed in a corner against the wall, with sniffling nose and dirt-streaked face.

"Shut up, you little sniveler!" said Mordecai. "You're worse of a woman nor your ma Sheba. They hain't agoing to get his scalp. What are you crying fur?"

He thrust his rifle forth and fired again, with a catamountain screech.

Up the trail through the pine woods the boy Josiah ran. He heard the whooping screams, the rifle cracks. He ran with sobbing breath. Still there was a tingling excitement in him, mingled with his fright. It was like the times which he had heard his father tell of before he could well remember, of days with Simon Kenton and Dan'el Boone. He had been afraid that such exciting days would never come again, with the country all so civilized.

"Injuns!" he shouted. "Injuns! the Injuns are out!"

The alarm bell at the station was ringing before he got there, and men with rifles were running down the trail toward him. He turned and ran back with them to the cabin, from which Mordecai's rifle still coolly cracked. On the field's far side, in the thin woods by Long Run's edge and in the deep woods beyond the stream, the painted shapes fled and the catbird screaming died away.

The men with rifles gathered about that gaunt figure with the gray-streaked hair, lying beside the stump in middle field.

"Poor feller," said one of them. "One of the old-timers. Come over the mountains with Dan'el Boone, I've often heard him say. What was his name? Old Ike, old Abe, or so'thing like that. Been trading with him all winter from my place up the crik, and never could remember his name from one time to the next. Well, it don't make no difference what it was, I don't reckon. They ain't going to name no counties after him. He left a widdy, didn't he? Somebody had better go ahead and tell her we're bringing him."

It was night, and the woman Bersheba sat at the little writing table in the cabin at the station.

The women had been kind. They had taken care of her boy and the baby girls for her, giving them their supper and putting them to bed. One of them had lent her a black cashmere shawl to throw over her butternut gown for widow's weeds. They had given her their condolences, and now, in greater kindness, for a little while they had left her alone.

Her dark hair was parted in the middle and smoothly brushed. In the pine-knot firelight her delicate face had an elfin quality. An intaglio brooch with a gold rope band which her Grandmother heed had brought over from Scotland was pinned beneath the white collar at her throat. The women sometimes commented behind her back, she was half aware, over the time she spent in the brushing of her long hair and over the little touches which she gave her dress, as if she thought she was too fine for them and could not forget that her people had been gentry back in Carolina. Yet she could not help that. All her life she had lived half in a dream of beautiful splendid things, of gracious worlds beyond this world, of what she did not know.

She had laid upon the little writing table the big Bible, printed in London, which had come from Philadelphia and over the mountains from Virginia. A horn of elderberry ink stood on the table, and a goose-quill pen. She opened the ponderous book to the pages in the center, of glossy heavy paper, with their border adornments of cupids and broken marble columns for the recording of marriages and of births and deaths.

A sadness too deep for tears lay in her. He had been such a kind man, and life had given him so little. A poor man in a hard young land, and himself not quite assertive and shrewd enough to make his way in it. He also had had his little dreams, she knew. Little dreams of being respected and esteemed, a man of some importance, a man to stand out. Yet he had lacked the forcefulness or luck. Humble and obscure, he had gone through life without significance; and now the end of it must be written in the book, and hereafter it would be as though he had never been.

He was the only man who had ever been in her life or who would ever be. She had been an old maid, twenty-six years old, when he had married her. No other man or boy had ever courted her. She was not strong and robustly built, she was inept with her hands, and all the details of practical living did not have sufficient reality for her. A boy or man choosing a helpmeet didn't want to be burdened with a wife who couldn't milk, make soap, render lard, help harvest a crop or even keep a fire going beneath a pot without getting lost in a far-off dream. She didn't know why he had married her, except that there had been such a dearth of other women, and he had needed one to mother his two boys.

He had not been the dashing cavalier that she had dreamed of, but she had learned that life is never like the dreams. He had been kind to her, and she had come to love him dearly. She had tried to do the best she could. Still she had given him so little. Only a shadow in his life. His eyes, though gentle, had always passed her by. His thoughts had always been with his competent Mary Shipley, his young manhood's mate. His heart and secret dream had always been with his first love, in the springtime of his life so long ago.

She had given him so little. Her boy had meant nothing to him beside Mary Shipley's boys. He had not even wanted the boy named after him, when she had suggested it; saying it was a kind of comical name, he guessed, and why inflict it on the little fellow. The little girls had meant something more to him, she thought, because of Mary Shipley's little girl, who had died in infancy, and Anne Boone's, who had been buried with her child mother. But that was all she had given him—two baby girls to name after his dead loves.

The boy, only a few minutes ago, had been quietly sobbing to himself where he had been put to bed behind the curtain, but the baby girls had gone at once to sleep. They would have no memory of this day and night, no memory of the gaunt man, laborious and humble and obscure, who had been their father. They would go on into life and marry, and their children would not know where their grandfather had been born, nor where he had died and been buried, not even perhaps his name. Her little Tom would remember longer. Yet even to him it would be no more than a dark dream.

Next door to the cabin, in the adjacent corner blockhouse, there were the sounds of sawing and hammering as they made the pine coffin. Mordecai and Josiah were helping with it. The two boys had been up and down the little station street all afternoon and evening, bursting with excitement and a feeling of triumphant manhood, telling the story over and over to fresh groups of incoming settlers of how Mort had held those tarnation varmints off, and how Josh had run for help. It was like the old exciting days. Once their mother, their own real mother, not Sheba, had held off a whole swarm of them danged Wabashes in the camp on the Ohio. They had been only little fellows then, but Mort remembered him and Josh hiding in a hollow log as quiet as chipmunks, and Josh hadn't been more than a year old, but he hadn't let out a squeak. Not like that danged howling little Tom. If Mort had only been able to move toward the rifle at the cabin a mite faster, without having to drag Tom along, or if the old man had been able to start running a quarter minute sooner, without having to wait to see that little Tom was safe—

She felt a pang of futile but agonizing responsibility. It had been at her suggestion that they had taken little Tom along. She had given him nothing. She had even robbed him of his last desperate chance of life.

She had found the page of births and deaths in the Bible where his name was entered, beneath his father John's: "Born in Redstone, Pennsylvania, August 17, 1744." She dipped the goose-quill pen. By the red firelight she wrote the final word: "Died Hughes Station, Jefferson County, Territory of Kaintucky, May 13, 1786."

And that was all. An obscure and humble man he had lived and died, and his name would be soon forgotten by those few who had ever known it.

There was a knock upon the door. She put down the pen. She arose and stood against the fireplace.

"Come in," she said.

A young man in a white buckskin jacket of rare and elegant design, jackboots and doeskin riding breeches which fitted his strong thighs like gloves, came in the door. He doffed his three-cornered hat, which had a military cockade on it. He was a stocky young man, with blue eyes and yellow hair that came down on his shoulders.

"The Widdy Linkern?" he said.

"Yes," she said. She was a widow now.

He came toward her with his bold buccaneering eyes fixed on her in male admiration, though she was not aware of it. She made a picture by the fireplace, with her smooth dark hair and crimson mouth, and her great eyes in her pale face.

"Captain George Pomeroy, of General George Rogers Clark's command, from Louisville," he said. "I just rode in. I'm sorry to hear about your trouble, ma'am. He was a good man, I hear."

"Yes," she said. "He was a good man."

"I'm sorry to bother you in your time of grief," he said. "Yet it is a business about which you would not want me to wait. General Clark has been organizing an army, ma'am, to go against the Wabash nation. They have been doing this same thing up north of the Ohio, and it has got to stop. I have been detailed to make up a subscription list for the equipping and provisioning of the expedition, from the various towns and stations. I would like to put you down on the list for what in the way of guns or provender you are able to contribute."

"He had two rifle guns," she said, "and one old smoothbore. You are welcome to them, sir."

He drew a sheet of paper from the bosom of his buckskin jacket, with his hat pressed beneath his arm.

"I'll set the two rifle guns down, ma'am, if you have pen and ink handy," he said with satisfaction. "On the table with your Bible here, I see. They'll be appraised at a fair price, and compensation made if not returned. I reckon those two big boys of yours will be wanting to come along to use them. I was talking to them in the blockhouse. They aim to get a scalp or two. A pair of fine boys, of whom any mother should be proud."

"I am, indeed," she said.

She bit her trembling lip. She was, of course, proud of them. Yet it was always Mary Shipley's boys. Mary Shipley's boys to bury and avenge him. Even if her little Tom were old enough, perhaps he would be afraid. He had her helpless blood in him, and she had spoiled him too much, in her yearning for something to which to cling. "Is there anything else you would want?" she said.

"No," said the young captain. "The guns will be enough for your fair share, I reckon. Don't want to strip you, ma'am. I'll put it down, two rifle guns from the Widdy Linkern."

"That's not the way to spell it," she said.

Her lip was still trembling. He had been a poor man, he had been an obscure and unimportant man. None of his ancestors had ever attained to any fame. There would be no towns named after him, like Colonel Boone. He would not even have a tombstone. The place where he should be buried would be forgotten. Yet he might as well have his name spelled right. He had always been a mite particular about it.

"There," she said. "Like that."

She pointed to the Bible on the table, where the ink was not yet dry on the last entry which she had made.

Abraham Lincoln, born Redstone, Pennsylvania, August 17, 1744. Died Hughes Station, Jefferson County, Territory of Kaintucky, May 13, 1786.

And that was all. The record of his life. But she wanted the name spelled right.

"Lincoln," she said. "Like that."

The young captain copied the name on his list dutifully. "The Widdy Lincoln, two rifle guns," he said. "Don't worry, ma'am; I've got it right."

Perhaps he was amused that she should bother with the precise spelling of the name of an obscure man like that. Did she think it was a name to go down in history, like Jefferson or Washington?

Bersheba Lincoln stirred from a dream. She went across the room. Her little Tommy had got out of bed. In his long nightgown sweeping the rough planked floor, he was stumbling toward her from behind the curtain, sobbing.

"Oh, mammy, I had a dream!" he sobbed. "He was lying dead and the whole world was crying!"

Bersheba picked up the weeping boy in her arms. She held him tight against her breast. So close was he to her, blood of her blood and spirit of her spirit, that she could see the vision which he saw of that gaunt, humble man lying dead beneath the assassin's stroke. She stood rocking the boy with her eyes rapt. And for the moment there was the sound of martial music playing in her ears, with muffled drums, and there were draped flags and the cry of a nation mourning.

"Perhaps someday you will have a son, my little Tom," she said, "and name him Abraham."

TRAIL TO ABILENE

JACK SCHAEFER

A boy and a horse. A thin, knobby boy, coming sixteen, all long bones and stringy muscle, not yet grown up to knuckly hands and oversize feet, and a big, gaunt, old draft horse. They stood by the rickety fence of a half-acre enclosure, the boy leaning against a big foreshoulder, the horse waiting, patient, big haltered head sagging against a short lead rope tied to a fence rail. Off near the center of the enclosure the frame shack that served for a schoolhouse quivered on flimsy foundation as about fifteen children of assorted ages and sizes scattered from the doorway.

The boy leaned against the old horse and watched a stout, soft-stomached man appear in the doorway and walk toward the road running past the enclosure gate and take a small bottle from a pocket and raise it to his lips while he walked. Activity died away, and the boy watched the stout man dwindling toward the cluster of ugly false-fronted buildings a half mile down the road.

"Shucks," said the boy. "I've had about all I can take of that. He don't know no more'n me, which sure ain't much." He untied the lead rope and stepped back along the gaunt body, holding the rope, and in one easy movement was astride the bare back, and the old horse raised its head and swung to start toward the gate. Through and around a corner of the enclosure and the boy and the horse moved into the distance, sliding into distance of Colorado plain.

"You ain't much either," said the boy. "But let's see what you can do." Obedient, the old horse leaned forward into a clumsy trot.

"Trying to wear out my backbone, aren't you?" said the boy.

The old horse swiveled an ear, feeling the current along the rope, the tingle in the thin legs down its sides, and leaned forward more into a lumbering caricature of a lope. The big old back swayed and bounced, and the boy sat flat to it, body moving in unthinking rhythm with it, a part of the horse beneath him. Now another horse. Solid and compact, power plain in muscles bulging under the sleek hide, pride in lift of the tail and arch of the thick neck, it stood by high end rails of a small corral beside a small barn. Fifteen feet away the boy leaned against side rails, chin resting on the top rail, looking over. "Montelius! You, Monteeelius!"

The boy turned on too-big old work shoes toward the leaning two-room frame house fifty yards away. The woman in the open doorway had been tall once, and well figured, but was now stooped and becoming shapeless in a dragging, overall tiredness.

"You, Montelius! Can't you hear me?"

The boy moved toward the house and stopped by the stone doorstep. She held out an earthen crock half full of potato peelings. "Chickens," she said. The boy took the crock and turned. "You finished plowing that garden patch? Know what your father said."

The boy swung back. "Yeah. And you know how it is. I'll plant it, and I'll take care of it, and he never does a thing around here. Except holler at me."

"He pays for the food you eat," she said.

"Yeah," said the boy. "And I earn every crumb doing all that ever gets done. What's he ever do but hang around town and talk big?" The boy turned away again.

"Please, Monte. I saw you. Don't you go near that stud. You know how your father feels about——"

"He ain't my father!" The boy turned back, scuffing dust. "My father's dead." He looked up. "What'd you ever have to go take up with this one for?"

"We been fed," she said softly. She brushed a hand across her face. "A woman's got to do something."

He saw the warning flush creeping up her cheeks, the mistiness forming in her eyes. "Aw, shucks, quit it, ma." He moved away fast toward the little lean-to chicken house by the barn.

He stood by the netted chicken yard watching the hens and one scraggly rooster peck in frantic busyness at the peelings, seeing but not seeing, ears attuned to the soft thuddings as the stallion moved in the corral on the other side of the barn. He became aware of the crock in his hands and set this down. Slowly he moved past the front of the barn to the corral and leaned against rails.

The stallion and the boy looked at each other, and the stallion raised its head higher and swung away, indifferent, looking into the distance of Colorado plain.

"Shucks," said the boy. "It's a horse, ain't it?" He looked toward the house. The door was closed. He moved into the barn and came out with a flattish pan partly filled with coarse grain. He crouched by the near side of the corral and slid the pan under the bottom rail.

The stallion's ears twitched, and it turned its head. The boy pushed the pan farther in and withdrew his hand, and the horse moved forward, as if accepting tribute, and dropped its head to the pan. The boy picked up a small stick. Carefully he reached in and nudged the pan farther along. The stallion's head followed, and the compact body turned some until it was roughly parallel to the rails of the corral.

Slowly the boy stood up and began to climb the rails. The horse, intent on the grain, ignored him. Slowly he eased one leg over the top rail, then the other, and was sitting there, feet inside on the next rail down. The horse swung its head a bit, rolling an eye, fixing him there. It dropped the head back, ignoring him.

Suddenly the boy was out from the rails, long thin legs straddling the powerful back, hands fastening into the mane. The horse reared, breath whistling through nostrils. It plunged and bucked in furious action, and the boy clung, eyes alight, hair flying, thin legs locked to the twisting, wrenching body. The horse reared again, tottering on hind legs close by the far-side rails, and dropped down, crashing into them. The shock shook the boy loose, and he pushed out and fell scrambling to regain his feet and ran for the near side of the corral and threw himself flat and squirmed under the bottom rail as forehoofs pounded into the ground behind him. He stood up and a small, wry grin showed on his lips, and he looked at the horse inside the rails and saw the smudged bruising on the one foreshoulder.

He turned toward the woman running, white-faced, from the house. "I'm all right, ma," he said. "And that thing's just scraped some is all."

She stared at him, frightened. "What will your—what will he say?"

The boy said, "He maybe won't even notice. He don't need to know."

In the slow dusk of the plains a sturdy buckboard rested in front of the small barn. The thin, half-starved mustang that had drawn it was with the old draft horse in the skimpy pasture beyond the chicken house. Inside the barn, in the darkening dimness, the boy hung the harness on a high peg, the bridle on another.

He moved out of the barn toward the house, shivering in the

dropping night chill. Lamplight shone through the one front window, and he stepped into the patch of light to peer in. The woman was busy by the cookstove. The man relaxed in a chair by the table was big and bulky and florid-faced. He wore dark, oiled boots and striped trousers tucked in and a white shirt with black string tie. His soft, dark hat and frock coat hung on the wall behind the chair. His voice reached through the flimsy wall of the house.

"Tilman's bringing a mare out tomorrow. Seven dollars' stud fee. He squawked on that, but I got the only horse with Morgan blood in him anywheres around. A gold mine, that's what that horse'll be."

"Morgan blood," muttered the boy. "In a pig's eye." He moved on into the house and eased onto another chair well around the table from the man.

"You take care of that pony?"

"Yeah," said the boy. "Why'n't you let me give him a good feed sometime?"

"He gets enough," said the man. "You finish that plowing?"

"Yeah," said the boy.

"You feed that stud?"

"Yeah."

"Is he all right?"

"Aw, shucks," said the boy. "He got jumpy and scraped himself on the fence, but that won't slow him none."

The man stared steadily at the boy. He rose from the chair, reaching back to take the frock coat and shrug it on. He strode to the door, took a lantern from the wall beside it, lighted this with a match from a coat pocket and went out.

Silence in the dingy front room of the flimsy frame house. The woman had turned and was looking at the boy.

"You going to tell him?" said the boy.

The man came back in and closed the door. He blew out the lantern and hung it on its nail, stepped across the room and took off the coat and hung it on its hook. "Limping," he said. He turned to the boy. "You been monkeying with that horse?"

The boy sat on the edge of his chair, body tense. "What would I do that for?"

"Because——" said the man, anger breaking in his voice and being caught and controlled again. "Because you're a damn fool about anything on four legs." He turned to the woman. "Has he?"

She said nothing. Silence in the dingy room except for the small, sobbing catch of breath in the boy's throat.

Suddenly the man moved, leaping to get around the table, but the boy was quicker, whirling up and around and heaving his chair into the man's path, diving headlong for the doorway. He yanked the door open and was out.

He ran toward the outbuildings, the man pounding after. He started along the corral and reversed, dodging back, along the front of the barn. The buckboard was in the way, pocketing him in the angle it made out from the barn. He turned and dashed through the open wide doorway into the dark interior.

The man stood in the doorway. "All right," he said. "Come on out of there."

"I ain't coming!" The boy's voice snapped out of the blackness. "You ain't agoing to lick me ever again."

"No?" said the man. He turned sideways in the doorway and pulled at the old sliding door to narrow the opening. He staggered, caught off balance, and went down as the lean weight of the boy hurtled into him out of the blackness. He caught one foot in its heavy old work shoe as the boy jumped over his fallen body. He grunted, letting go, as the other heavy old shoe stomped down hard on his arm. He heard footsteps fade away along by the pasture beyond the chicken yard.

He pushed up and moved slowly toward the house, brushing dust from his clothes. The woman in the doorway backed on in as he approached. "He'll come in," he said. "When he gets hungry and cold."

The house and the barn were dark, hunched shapes on the face of the big land in the dim suggestion of light of the new moon dropping down the western sky. Close by the barn the boy sat on the ground, a ragged saddle blanket up around his shoulders. He sat still, watching the house, the two patches of light that were the one front and the one side window of the front room.

Time passed and a new patch of light appeared, the window of the back room.

Time passed and the front-room patches of light faded, and there was only the patch of light of the back room.

Time passed and this too faded and was gone, and far off a coyote howled and another answered, and the boy shifted restlessly and was quiet again.

Time passed and the boy rose and laid the saddle blanket aside. Shivering in the night chill, he moved toward the house. He stood on the doorstep, listening. Faintly he could hear the slow rhythm of heavy snoring and breathing. Gently he turned the doorknob and eased in, standing silent by the near wall.

In the faint light of the moon through the front window he could see on the table a plate heaped with a cold, congealed mass of beef stew. Quietly he moved past the table to the inner doorway. Inside, on the brass bedstead, he could make out the woman asleep under an old quilt and beside her the bulk of the man, lying on his side.

He backed away and moved to the far corner of the front room where a straw mattress lay on the floor with a blanket over it. He took a ragged denim jacket from a hook on the wall and picked up the blanket. With these under one arm, he moved to the table and picked up the plate. He eased through the outer doorway and closed the door softly behind him.

Thirty minutes and three miles later he stood by the wagon ruts of a stage road snaking ghostlike in the last light of the moon through the endless miles of sagebrush. He walked off into the darkness of the lonely road.

The sun was well up, aiming at noontime. Its welcome warmth lay over the big land, over the four mules plodding along, pulling a freight wagon loaded with well-filled grain bags. The man on the driving seat was short-legged, short and round of body, with huge shoulders and thick arms. Under his wide-brimmed hat his face was broad and sun- and wind-tanned. Behind him, sprawled on the grain bags, lay the boy, mouth open, sound asleep.

The road dropped to cross a dry arroyo, and the wheels jolted on stones, and the boy stirred and sat up.

"Come on up here," said the man. "You ain't much company back there."

The boy scrambled forward and sat on the seat. The man turned his head, and a slow smile creased his broad face. He said, "When you stumbled into my camp about sunup, you was plenty beat."

The boy said, "Just tired was all."

The man gave his attention to the mules. "Where'd you come from?" he said.

The boy edged farther away on the seat. He reached back and took his blanket and set this on his knees. "Nowhere much," he said. "Back the road a piece."

The man looked straight ahead, watching the mules. "Got any folks?"

"No," he said. "Not now."

"Dead?" said the man.

The boy hesitated. "No," he said. His muscles tightened toward the leap out and away, and the man's right hand jumped across him and grasped the side rail, the thick arm pinning him to the seat. The man looked straight ahead.

The boy struggled against the arm, felt the strength in it, and sat still. "I ain't agoing back!" he said.

"Of course you ain't," said the man. "And you ain't doing any jumping. I knew a man broke a leg that way."

The mules plodded on. "Maybe you've shook that notion," said the man.

"Maybe I have," said the boy.

"Maybe won't do," said the man.

The boy looked at the tanned face sideways to him, watching the road ahead. "All right," he said. "I ain't agoing to."

"Of course not," said the man. He let go of the side rail, and his right hand rested on his right knee. "Running away's the thing sometimes. I did it myself." He slapped the reins down on the mules' rumps, and they paid no attention and plodded on. "It was a cow. A crazy old milk cow. That silly damn cow had to keep breaking into my ma's garden. I chased her out and I fixed that fence so many times I got me a mite mad. Took my pa's shotgun and pried the buckshot out of a shell and put some beans in. Figured to pepper her good. Sure enough, next day she was back in, and I grabbed that gun and blazed away. Plenty surprised to see her drop like somebody'd poleaxed her. How was I to know when I was off somewhere my pa'd seen a hawk and used that gun and maybe cussed like he could when nothing much happened and put a new shell in? I grabbed a few things and took out fast."

The boy looked at the man beside him, and a small grin showed on his lips.

The mules plodded on. "Where you going?" said the man.

"Anywhere there's a job," said the boy.

"A job's nothing," said the man. "Only something to do. It's the kind of a job that counts."

"A cow outfit," said the boy. "That's what I want. A cow outfit."

"Not milk cows?" said the man.

"No," said the boy. "Not milk cows."

"Of course not," said the man. "Only there ain't any cow outfits around here. Not yet anyway." The mules plodded on. The man sat up straighter. "Station's not far now. We ought to come in looking good." He slapped with the reins, and the mules paid no attention. "Forgot my whip," he said, "or I'd make 'em hop."

"Let me get on that lead mule," said the boy, "and I'll make 'em move."

The man asked, "Think you can?"

"Sure. Sure thing."

"Try it," said the man, beginning to pull in on the reins.

"Shucks," said the boy. "You don't need to stop." He climbed over the front of the wagon and stood on the long, swaying tongue.

He moved out, past the wheelers, to the lead team. He hopped astride the left leader. It grunted and tried to buck, bumping heels against the front doubletree. The boy sat tight to it and drummed heels against its sides. It plodded on, ignoring him.

He reached and took hold of a long ear and twisted. The mule grunted again and, as the twist tightened more, lunged into a trot, yanking the others into this with it. The wagon moved forward at a fair clip.

Ahead the road swerved around jutting rock to the two log buildings of the stage relay station. The mules swerved with it and came to a stop by the first building. The agent appeared in the doorway of the other building, watching. The boy jumped off the mule, and the man climbed down out of the wagon.

"Lucky these things know where to stop," said the man. "I couldn't do much, not with you sitting on the reins. You help me unload these bags, which the agent here won't do, and I'll speak to the driver when the stage comes along. He'll give you a lift to the next stop."

With the ease of long practice the man swung a grain bag up to one huge shoulder. The boy heaved and struggled with another, getting it to one thin shoulder.

"Name," said the man.

"Monte," said the boy.

"Rest of it," said the man.

The boy hesitated. He looked at the man, at the broad, solid face. He straightened some under the bag. "Walsh," he said. "Monte Walsh."

They were back by the wagon, other bags on shoulders. "Monte," said the man, "I got a cousin over in the Indian nation's got a road ranch. North of Darlington some on the Chisholm Trail. Name's Martin. Redheaded he is. Trail herds stopping there. You manage to get there and hang around, maybe he'd feed you and maybe somebody'd take you on. Think you could make it?"

Monte Walsh stood straight under his load. "I'll get there," he said.

"Of course you will," said the man.

The shadow of the unfinished homestead cabin was long in late-afternoon sun as Monte Walsh unloaded stones for the fireplace from a makeshift stoneboat. He rolled the last rock off and unhitched the meager Indian pony and hung the harness on a knob of the cabin wall.

"Well, now," said the gray-mustached man in worn overalls standing in the doorless cabin doorway, "you sure got more out of that horse in an afternoon'n I ever could. Come on. Food's ready."

Monte sat inside on a small keg by the wooden box that served as a table and contemplated the empty plate in front of him that had been filled three times.

"Well," said the man. "You sure you can't hold more? I ain't got any cash, not right now, but I got plenty to eat."

"Shucks," said Monte.

"Always like to see a young one eat," said the man. "Always wonder where they put it all. Well, now, why'n't you stay around a few days. I got plenty grub."

"No," said Monte. "Thanks. I got to get where I'm going."

"Not tonight," said the man. "I got blankets. In the morning I'll fix you up with some breakfast and something to take along." He was looking at Monte's old work shoes, at what remained of them and the bare toes poking through. He looked away and back. He began to take off his hard-worn but still stout boots.

"Try these," he said. "I got another pair I been saving some."

Rolling country this, rolling into distance everywhere, broken only by far, scattered low thickets of scrub oak. The road, despite a few wheel tracks, was little more than a horse trail. The sun, slanting into afternoon, sent down a steady glare. In the small shade of an oak thicket some thirty feet from the trail Monte Walsh sat. He was seventeen days and some three hundred miles on his way, a day and a half from his last meal. The blisters inside his boots were rubbed raw.

He sat motionless. Nothing seemed to move anywhere. He caught the sound of hoofs and turned his head to look along the trail to the left. Over the last rise came an old Indian, the years long since lost in the many wrinkles of the stern old face, riding bareback on a squat, bunch-muscled pinto. He was naked from the waist up, wearing only some kind of faded canvas trousers and moccasins. He was leading on a twenty-foot length of rope a heavy-shouldered dark-gray mustang.

He came along the trail at a steady dog-trot and looked to neither side, yet when he was opposite Monte he stopped, and the mustang stopped behind him, and he swung his head to look steadily at Monte in the shadow of his thicket.

There was no discernible expression on the old face. He raised an arm in an arc, pointing on ahead along the trail.

Monte nodded his head vigorously. "Martin's ranch," he said.

The old Indian might not have heard. No flicker of expression showed. He raised the arm again and pointed at the mustang.

"You bet!" said Monte, jumping up. He hobbled forward and around the pinto and approached the mustang. It stood motionless, head turned slightly, watching him with one rolled eye. He put a hand on its withers. It stood, motionless. He leaped to throw a leg over, and as he leaped it hunched its back and he hit off balance, and it bucked, head going down, hindquarters rising in sudden surge, and he pitched forward and hit the ground.

Monte flipped over and away and sat up. He stared at the old Indian. The old body was rocking on the pinto, shaking in tremendous silent mirth.

"Like that, is it?" said Monte, mad. He stood up. The blisters were forgotten. He leaped and was astride the mustang before it could hunch. It reared, angry in turn, and pounded down and forward, bucking, and the rope was yanked out of the old Indian's hand and Monte clung, long legs gripping the heaving sides.

The old Indian sat still, watching.

The mustang was scattering dust like a small whirlwind. Monte was leaning down, upper body tight along the neck, arms around. He caught hold of the dangling rope and whipped a coil around the mustang's nose. He sat up, pulling hard, and the coil tightened, and the mustang squealed, fighting for breath, and slowed. It stopped, legs braced, resigned to the day's fate. Monte pulled its head around, going back toward the pinto.

The old Indian regarded him, impassive, expressionless. The old Indian raised a hand, palm outward, in what could have been a kind of salute. He nudged the pinto into its dogtrot along the trail and beckoned to Monte to follow.

The scrub thickets cast long shadows over the big land. Two other long shadows moved among them, cast by an old Indian on a squat pinto and a knobby boy on a dark gray mustang.

They came to a sharp fork in the trail. The old Indian stopped, and the boy pulled up beside him. The old Indian raised an arm and tapped himself and pointed out along the south prong. He pointed at the boy and out along the north prong.

"Shucks," said Monte Walsh. "I guess this is where I get off." He slid from the mustang's back. He handed the rope end to the old Indian. "Thanks," he said. "I hope you know what that means."

The old Indian raised the arm again and pointed at Monte, then at the mustang. He shook again in silent mirth. He swung the pinto to start along the south prong of the trail, and the rope tightened and the mustang followed.

Monte Walsh watched them go. They dropped from sight into a hollow, and he turned to start along the north prong.

The blisters broke into pain, and he hobbled slowly. Time passed, and he hobbled on and there was nothing but the trail leading on, rising as the land sloped upward. "Shucks," he murmured. "Wonder if that old buck thought it'd be funny to lose me out in the middle of nowhere."

The shadows were stretching to merge together as he topped out on the rising land, and the ground fell away before him in long, slow slope, and in the last light of the sun he saw it, several miles away still, out on the level, the long, thin ribbon, only a ribbon from here, there narrowing and widening and narrowing again and rods wide at the narrowest, the great trail cut deep through brush and sod by thousands of hoofs moving north.

His head turned as his eyes followed it swinging northward. There it crossed the Cimarron, the "Red Fork of the Arkansas." There it snaked on through a natural clearing in the black jack forest of stunted oaks that came down to the river and stopped. There, where the clearing widened in huge sweep, was the big cattle corral, big enough to hold twenty-five hundred head, and some distance away the smaller horse corral and the two stockade-style log buildings.

"What do you know," murmured Monte. "I guess I've got there."

Monte Walsh swept the plank floor of the bar-store-trading post with an Indian brush-broom with conscientiously daily regularity. He carried assorted items from the other building, storehouse and cookhouse, and put them on shelves as needed and as directed by a gruffly genial redheaded man. He slapped an ancient cavalry saddle on an always mean-tempered Indian pony and rode out with a coiled rope over one shoulder and rode back dragging firewood for the querulous but competent bent-legged man who ruled the cookhouse. He ate enormous meals to the amused amazement of the redheaded man and the never-expressed satisfaction of the bent-legged man, and his thinness tightened toward the rawhide leanness of a young animal.

And every day or two dust rose to the southward and drifted over the great trail and came on and was a herd of Texas cattle and these were bedded for the night and men lean and hard and squint-eyed from wind and sun, wearing high-heeled boots and huge spurs and low-slung cartridge belts with holstered Colt .45's, long-barreled and wooden-handled, jingled in for supplies and something to rake the dust from their throats. And each time Monte looked for the one quieter than the others with responsibility on him and edged close and asked his question—and was shushed and pushed aside.

And one afternoon when Monte was sweeping and the redheaded man was checking antelope hides left by an old Indian who always pointed at Monte and sketched in the air with his hands an imaginary mustang and shook with silent mirth, hoofs sounded outside and a well-lathered cow pony slid to a stop and a man entered. He was young, as most of them always were, but big-framed, with wide, sloping shoulders, and a hard-worn dusty competence came from him.

The redheaded man looked up and set a bottle and small glass on the counter. He said. "Hat Henderson! Wondered if you'd be coming up this year."

"Certain I'm coming," said the man. "And all hell's coming with me." He poured a drink and downed it. "I get shoved up to trail boss. And what happens? Nothing but trouble. Spookiest bunch of cows ever rattled horns. Running most every night. Then I lost a man crossing the Washita. Now another one has to go bust a cinch and break a leg."

"Rough," said the redheaded man.

"But we ain't shy any cows," said the man. "You got a bed upstairs for Petey—it was Petey broke that leg."

"Of course," said the redheaded man.

"Supposing we put them damned cows in that big corral for tonight?"

"Go right ahead," said the redhead.

The other started for the door. Monte stepped forward. "Hey, mister——"

"Quit it, kid," said the man. "I ain't got time for you."

Twenty-two hundred longhorn steers were in the big stock corral. Seventy-three cow ponies were in the horse corral. In the upper room of the two-story building a lean, whipcord man, maybe all of twenty, lay on a cot with barrel-stave splints along one leg. Downstairs, apart from the seven men around a big table, the redheaded man leaned on the inside of the high counter he used for a bar. Hat Henderson leaned on the outer side, cradling a drink on one big hand. Monte Walsh sat on a box nearby, listening.

"Hey, kid," shouted someone at the table. "Bring us another bottle."

The redheaded man handed a bottle to Monte and made another mark on a piece of paper. Monte took the bottle to the table and came back to his box.

"—shift young Jenkins to regular riding," Hat Henderson was saying. "But then who will wrangle the cavy?"

"Damn it," said Monte. "I'm here."

"So you are. What there is of you. Think you can handle horses and ride?"

"I can ride anything you've got."

"You don't say," murmured Hat. He swung toward the redheaded man. "Mighty big talk," he said.

The redheaded man chuckled, shrugging his shoulders. He sobered. He nodded his head just a bit.

"All right, kid," said Hat. "We'll try it anyways. Be around in the morning."

And later, when the others had left and were rolling into blankets outside and the redheaded man and Monte had finished cleaning the place some, the redheaded man pointed to the three new saddles on their racks by the rear wall. "Maybe you could use one of those," he said.

"I can't pay for it."

"Don't I know that," said the redheaded man, gruff, seeming angry. "I ain't dumb. You trying to do me out of a sale? Pay me when you come back through or send it by somebody."

And in the morning when the chuck wagon had taken on supplies and was moving on and the men were swinging loops in the horse corral and one of them, grinning, led out a rangy dark bay, Hat Henderson said, "Might be fun. He sure talked big. But we ain't got time for games. Bring us that little dun."

And when the dun was brought, Monte Walsh slapped his new saddle on it and swung up, and the dun broke in two mildly, getting the kinks out of its backbone, and Monte rode out the little storm and Hat said, "All right, kid, likely you'll do. That one and the little black over there and that pinto will be your string. Come on, we'll get the bunch moving. They're pretty well trail-broke."

And while the others loped for the big stock corral, Hat and Monte hazed the rest of the cavy out of the horse corral and started it following the chuck wagon. "Stop when cooky stops," said Hat, "and keep 'em bunched handy," and left.

Like a great sprawled snake, weaving and changing shape, but always re-forming into the long, wide line of crackling hoofs and rattling horns, twenty-two hundred steers moved north along the great trail. Off to the left, drawing ever more in advance, the chuck wagon bumped along, and behind it trailed the cavy and behind this rode Monte Walsh.

Another young one was riding north with a trail herd, with the lean, hard, squint-eyed men and the lean, hard, rawhide horses taking the Texas longhorn to the farthest shores of the American sea of grass, uncaring, unknowing that he and his kind, compound of ignorance and gristle and guts and something of the deep, hidden decency of the race, would in time ride straight into the folklore of a weary old world.

TOP HAND

LUKE SHORT

Gus Irby was out on the board-
walk in front of the Elite, giving his swamper hell for staving in an
empty beer barrel, when the kid passed on his way to the feed stable.
His horse was a good one and it was tired, Gus saw, and the kid had a
little hump in his back from the cold of a mountain October
morning. In spite of the ample layer of flesh that Gus wore carefully
like an uncomfortable shroud, he shivered in his shirt sleeves and
turned into the saloon, thinking without much interest *Another
fiddle-footed dry-country kid that's been paid off after roundup.*

Later, while he was taking out the cash for the day and opening up
some fresh cigars, Gus saw the kid go into the Pride Cafe for
breakfast, and afterward come out, toothpick in mouth, and cruise
both sides of Wagon Mound's main street in aimless curiosity.

After that, Gus wasn't surprised when he looked around at the
sound of the door opening, and saw the kid coming toward the bar.
He was in a clean and faded shirt and looked as if he'd been cold for a
good many hours. Gus said good morning and took down his best
whisky and a glass and put them in front of the kid.

"First customer in the morning gets a drink on the house," Gus
announced.

"Now I know why I rode all night," the kid said, and he grinned at
Gus. He was a pleasant-faced kid with pale eyes that weren't shy or
sullen or bold, and maybe because of this he didn't fit readily into
any of Gus's handy character pigeonholes. Gus had seen them young

and fiddle-footed before, but they were the tough kids, and for a man with no truculence in him, like Gus, talking with them was like trying to pet a tiger.

Gus leaned against the back bar and watched the kid take his whisky and wipe his mouth on his sleeve, and Gus found himself getting curious. Half a lifetime of asking skillful questions that didn't seem like questions at all prompted Gus to observe now, "If you're goin' on through you better pick up a coat. This high country's cold now."

"I figure this is far enough," the kid said.

"Oh, well, if somebody sent for you, that's different." Gus reached around lazily for a cigar.

The kid pulled out a silver dollar from his pocket and put it on the bar top, and then poured himself another whisky, which Gus was sure he didn't want, but which courtesy dictated he should buy. "Nobody sent for me, either," the kid observed. "I ain't got any money."

Gus picked up the dollar and got change from the cash drawer and put it in front of the kid, afterward lighting his cigar. This was when the announcement came.

"I'm a top hand," the kid said quietly, looking levelly at Gus. "Who's lookin' for one?"

Gus was glad he was still lighting his cigar, else he might have smiled. If there had been a third man here, Gus would have winked at him surreptitiously; but since there wasn't, Gus kept his face expressionless, drew on his cigar a moment, and then observed gently, "You look pretty young for a top hand."

"The best cow pony I ever saw was four years old," the kid answered pointedly.

Gus smiled faintly and shook his head. "You picked a bad time. Roundup's over."

The kid nodded, and drank down his second whisky quickly, waited for his breath to come normally. Then he said, "Much obliged. I'll see you again," and turned toward the door.

A mild cussedness stirred within Gus, and after a moment's hesitation he called out, "Wait a minute."

The kid hauled up and came back to the bar. He moved with an easy grace that suggested quickness and work-hardened muscle, and for a moment Gus, a careful man, was undecided. But the kid's face, so young and without caution, reassured him, and he folded his heavy arms on the bar top and pulled his nose thoughtfully. "You figure to hit all the outfits, one by one, don't you?"

The kid nodded, and Gus frowned and was silent a moment, and then he murmured, almost to himself, "I had a notion—oh, hell, I don't know."

"Go ahead," the kid said, and then his swift grin came again. "I'll try anything once."

"Look," Gus said, as if his mind were made up. "We got a newspaper here—the *Wickford County Free Press.* Comes out every Thursday, that's today." He looked soberly at the kid. "Whyn't you put a piece in there and say 'Top hand wants a job at forty dollars a month'? Tell 'em what you can do and tell 'em to come see you here if they want a hand. They'll all get it in a couple days. That way you'll save yourself a hundred miles of ridin'. Won't cost much either."

The kid thought awhile and then asked, without smiling, "Where's this newspaper at?"

Gus told him and the kid went out. Gus put the bottle away and doused the glass in water, and he was smiling slyly at his thoughts. Wait till the boys read that in the *Free Press.* They were going to have some fun with that kid, Gus reflected.

Johnny McSorley stepped out into the chill thin sunshine. The last silver dollar in his pants pocket was a solid weight against his leg, and he was aware that he'd probably spend it in the next few minutes on the newspaper piece. He wondered about that, and figured shrewdly it had an off chance of working.

Four riders dismounted at a tie rail ahead and paused a moment, talking. Johnny looked them over and picked out their leader, a tall, heavy, scowling man in his middle thirties who was wearing a mackinaw unbuttoned.

Johnny stopped and said, "You know anybody lookin' for a top hand?" and grinned pleasantly at the big man.

For a second Johnny thought he was going to smile. He didn't think he'd have liked the smile, once he saw it, but the man's face settled into the scowl again. "I never saw a top hand that couldn't vote," he said.

Johnny looked at him carefully, not smiling, and said, "Look at one now, then," and went on, and by the time he'd taken two steps he thought, *Voted, huh? A man must grow pretty slow in this high country.*

He crossed the street and paused before a window marked *Wickford County Free Press. Job Printing. D. Melaven, Ed. and Prop.* He went inside, then. A girl was seated at a cluttered desk, staring at the street, tapping a pencil against her teeth. Johnny tramped over to her, noting the infernal racket made by one of two men at a small press under the lamp behind the railed-off office space.

Johnny said "Hello," and the girl turned tiredly and said, "Hello, bub." She had on a plain blue dress with a high bodice and a narrow lace collar, and she was a very pretty girl, but tired, Johnny noticed. Her long yellow hair was worn in braids that crossed almost atop her head, and she looked, Johnny thought, like a small kid who has pinned her hair up out of the way for her Saturday night bath. He thought all this and then remembered her greeting, and he reflected without rancor, *Damn, that's twice,* and he said, "I got a piece for the paper, sis."

"Don't call me sis," the girl said. "Anybody's name I don't know, I call him bub. No offense. I got that from pa, I guess."

That's likely, Johnny thought, and he said amiably, "Any girl's name I don't know, I call her sis. I got that from ma."

The cheerful effrontery of the remark widened the girl's eyes. She held out her hand now and said with dignity, "Give it to me. I'll see it gets in next week."

"That's too late," Johnny said. "I got to get it in this week."

"Why?"

"I ain't got money enough to hang around another week."

The girl stared carefully at him. "What is it?"

"I want to put a piece in about myself. I'm a top hand, and I'm lookin' for work. The fella over there at the saloon says why don't I put a piece in the paper about wantin' work, instead of ridin' out lookin' for it."

The girl was silent a full five seconds and then said, "You don't look that simple. Gus was having fun with you."

"I figured that," Johnny agreed. "Still, it might work. If you're caught short-handed, you take anything."

The girl shook her head. "It's too late. The paper's made up." Her voice was meant to hold a note of finality, but Johnny regarded her curiously, with a maddening placidity.

"You D. Melaven?" he asked.

"No. That's pa."

"Where's he?"

"Back there. Busy."

Johnny saw the gate in the rail that separated the office from the shop and he headed toward it. He heard the girl's chair scrape on the floor and her command, "Don't go back there. It's not allowed."

Johnny looked over his shoulder and grinned and said, "I'll try anything once," and went on through the gate, hearing the girl's swift steps behind him. He halted alongside a square-built and solid man with a thatch of stiff hair more gray than black, and said, "You D. Melaven?"

"Dan Melaven, bub. What can I do for you?"

That's three times, Johnny thought, and he regarded Melaven's square face without anger. He liked the face; it was homely and stubborn and intelligent, and the eyes were both sharp and kindly. Hearing the girl stop beside him, Johnny said, "I got a piece for the paper today."

The girl put in quickly, "I told him it was too late, pa. Now you tell him, and maybe he'll get out."

"Cassie," Melaven said in surprised protest.

"I don't care. We can't unlock the forms for every out-at-the-pants puncher that asks us. Besides, I think he's one of Alec Barr's bunch." She spoke vehemently, angrily, and Johnny listened to her with growing amazement.

"Alec who?" he asked.

"I saw you talking to him, and then you came straight over here from him," Cassie said hotly.

"I hit him for work."

"I don't believe it."

"Cassie," Melaven said grimly, "come back here a minute." He took her by the arm and led her toward the back of the shop, where they halted and engaged in quiet, earnest conversation.

Johnny shook his head in bewilderment, and then looked around him. The biggest press, he observed, was idle. And on a stone-topped table where Melaven had been working was a metal form almost filled with lines of type and gray metal pieces of assorted sizes and shapes. Now, Johnny McSorley did not know any more than the average person about the workings of a newspaper, but his common sense told him that Cassie had lied to him when she said it was too late to accept his advertisement. Why, there was space and to spare in that form for the few lines of type his message would need. Turning this over in his mind, he wondered what was behind her refusal.

The argument settled, Melaven and Cassie came back to him, and Johnny observed that Cassie, while chastened, was still mad.

"All right, what do you want printed, bub?" Melaven asked.

Johnny told him and Melaven nodded when he was finished, said, "Pay her," and went over to the type case.

Cassie went back to the desk and Johnny followed her, and when she was seated he said, "What do I owe you?"

Cassie looked speculatively at him, her face still flushed with anger. "How much money have you got?"

"A dollar some."

"It'll be two dollars," Cassie said.

Johnny pulled out his lone silver dollar and put it on the desk. "You print it just the same; I'll be back with the rest later."

Cassie said with open malice, "You'd have it now, bub, if you hadn't been drinking before ten o'clock."

Johnny didn't do anything for a moment, and then he put both hands on the desk and leaned close to her. "How old are you?" he asked quietly.

"Seventeen."

"I'm older'n you," Johnny murmured. "So the next time you call me 'bub' I'm goin' to take down your pigtails and pull 'em. I'll try anything once."

Once he was in the sunlight, crossing toward the Elite, he felt better. He smiled—partly at himself but mostly at Cassie. She was a real spitfire, kind of pretty and kind of nice, and he wished he knew what her father said to her that made her so mad, and why she'd been mad in the first place.

Gus was breaking out a new case of whisky and stacking bottles against the back mirror as Johnny came in and went up to the bar. Neither of them spoke while Gus finished, and Johnny gazed absently at the poker game at one of the tables and now yawned sleepily.

Gus said finally, "You get it in all right?"

Johnny nodded thoughtfully and said, "She mad like that at everybody?"

"Who? Cassie?"

"First she didn't want to take the piece, but her old man made her. Then she charges me more for it than I got in my pocket. Then she combs me over like I got my head stuck in the cookie crock for drinkin' in the morning. She calls me bub, to boot."

"She calls everybody bub."

"Not me no more," Johnny said firmly, and yawned again.

Gus grinned and sauntered over to the cash box. When he came back he put ten silver dollars on the bar top and said, "Pay me back when you get your job. And I got rooms upstairs if you want to sleep."

Johnny grinned. "Sleep, hunh? I'll try anything once." He took the money, said, "Much obliged," and started away fron the bar and then paused. "Say, who's this Alec Barr?"

Johnny saw Gus's eyes shift swiftly to the poker game and then shuttle back to him. Gus didn't say anything.

"See you later," Johnny said.

He climbed the stairs whose entrance was at the end of the bar, wondering why Gus was so careful about Alec Barr.

A gunshot somewhere out in the street woke him. The sun was

gone from the room, so it must be afternoon, he thought. He pulled on his boots, slopped some water into the washbowl and washed up, pulled hand across his cheek and decided he should shave, and went downstairs. There wasn't anybody in the saloon, not even behind the bar. On the tables and on the bar top, however, were several newspapers, all fresh. He was reminded at once that he was in debt to the Wickford Country Free Press for the sum of one dollar. He pulled one of the newspapers toward him and turned to the page where all the advertisements were.

When, after some minutes, he finished, he saw that his advertisement was not there. A slow wrath grew in him as he thought of the girl and her father taking his money, and when it had come to full flower, he went out of the Elite and cut across toward the newspaper office. He saw, without really noticing it, the group of men clustered in front of the store across from the newspaper office. He swung under the tie rail and reached the opposite boardwalk just this side of the newspaper office and a man who was lounging against the building. He was a puncher and when he saw Johnny heading up the walk he said, "Don't go across there."

Johnny said grimly, "You stop me," and went on, and he heard the puncher say, "All right, getcher head blown off."

His boots crunched broken glass in front of the office and he came to a gingerly halt, looking down at his feet. His glance raised to the window, and he saw where there was a big jag of glass out of the window, neatly wiping out the Wickford except for the *W* on the sign and ribboning cracks to all four corners of the frame. His surprise held him motionless for a moment, and then he heard a voice calling from across the street, "Clear out of there, son."

That makes four times, Johnny thought resignedly, and he glanced across the street and saw Alec Barr, several men clotted around him, looking his way.

Johnny went on and turned into the newspaper office and it was like walking into a dark cave. The lamp was extinguished.

And then he saw the dim forms of Cassie Melaven and her father back of the railing beside the job press, and the reason for his errand came back to him with a rush. Walking through the gate, he began firmly, "I got a dollar owed——" and ceased talking and halted abruptly. There was a six-shooter in Dan Melaven's hand hanging at his side. Johnny looked at it, and then raised his glance to Melaven's face and found the man watching him with a bitter amusement in his eyes. His glance shuttled to Cassie, and she was looking at him as if she didn't see him, and her face seemed very pale in that gloom. He half gestured toward the gun and said, "What's that for?"

"A little trouble, bub," Melaven said mildly. "Come back for your money?"

"Yeah," Johnny said slowly.

Suddenly it came to him, and he wheeled and looked out through the broken window and saw Alec Barr across the street in conversation with two men, his own hands, Johnny supposed. That explained the shot that wakened him. A little trouble.

He looked back at Melaven now in time to hear him say to Cassie, "Give him his money."

Cassie came past him to the desk and pulled open a drawer and opened the cash box. While she was doing it, Johnny strolled soberly over to the desk. She gave him the dollar and he took it, and their glances met. *She's been crying*, he thought, with a strange distress.

"That's what I tried to tell you," Cassie said. "We didn't want to take your money, but you wouldn't have it."

"What's it all about?" Johnny asked soberly.

"Didn't you read the paper?"

Johnny shook his head in negation, and Cassie said dully, "It's right there on page one. There's a big chunk of Government land out on Artillery Creek coming up for sale. Alec Barr wanted it, but he didn't want anybody bidding against him. He knew pa would have to publish a notice of sale. He tried to get pa to hold off publication of the date of sale until it would be too late for other bidders to make it. Pa was to get a piece of the land in return for the favor, or money. I guess we needed it all right, but pa told him no."

Johnny looked over at Melaven, who had come up to the rail now and was listening. Melaven said, "I knew Barr'd be in today with his bunch, and they'd want a look at a pull sheet before the press got busy, just to make sure the notice wasn't there. Well, Cassie and Dad Hopper worked with me all last night to turn out the real paper, with the notice of sale and a front-page editorial about Barr's proposition to me, to boot."

"We got it printed and hid it out in the shed early this morning," Cassie explained.

Melaven grinned faintly at Cassie, and there was a kind of open admiration for the job in the way he smiled. He said to Johnny now, "So what you saw in the forms this mornin' was a fake, bub. That's why Cassie didn't want your money. The paper was already printed." He smiled again, that rather proud smile. "After you'd gone, Barr came in. He wanted a pull sheet and we gave it to him, and he had a man out front watching us most of the morning. But he pulled him off later. We got the real paper out of the shed onto the

Willow Valley stage, and we got it delivered all over town before Barr saw it."

Johnny was silent a moment, thinking this over. Then he nodded toward the window. "Barr do that?"

"I did," Melaven said quietly. "I reckon I can keep him out until someone in this town gets the guts to run him off."

Johnny looked down at the dollar in his hand and stared at it a moment and put it in his pocket. When he looked up at Cassie, he surprised her watching him, and she smiled a little, as if to ask forgiveness.

Johnny said, "Want any help?" to Melaven, and the man looked at him thoughtfully and then nodded. "Yes. You can take Cassie home."

"Oh, no," Cassie said. She backed away from the desk and put her back against the wall, looking from one to the other. "I don't go. As long as I'm here, he'll stay there."

"Sooner or later, he'll come in," Melaven said grimly. "I don't want you hurt."

"Let him come," Cassie said stubbornly. "I can swing a wrench better than some of his crew can shoot."

"Please go with him."

Cassie shook her head. "No, pa. There's some men left in this town. They'll turn up."

Melaven said "Hell," quietly, angrily, and went back into the shop. Johnny and the girl looked at each other for a long moment, and Johnny saw the fear in her eyes. She was fighting it, but she didn't have it licked, and he couldn't blame her. He said, "If I'd had a gun on me, I don't reckon they'd of let me in here, would they?"

"Don't try it again," Cassie said. "Don't try the back either. They're out there."

Johnny said, "Sure you won't come with me?"

"I'm sure."

"Good," Johnny said quietly. He stepped outside and turned up-street, glancing over at Barr and the three men with him, who were watching him wordlessly. The man leaning against the building straightened up and asked, "She comin' out?"

"She's thinkin' it over," Johnny said.

The man called across the street to Barr, "She's thinkin' it over," and Johnny headed obliquely across the wide street toward the Elite. *What kind of a town is this, where they'd let this happen?* he thought angrily, and then he caught sight of Gus Irby standing under the wooden awning in front of the Elite, watching the show. Everybody else was doing the same thing. A man behind Johnny yelled,

"Send her out, Melaven," and Johnny vaulted up onto the boardwalk and halted in front of Gus.

"What do you aim to do?" he asked Gus.

"Mind my own business, same as you," Gus growled, but he couldn't hold Johnny's gaze.

There was shame in his face, and when Johnny saw it his mind was made up. He shouldered past him and went into the Elite and saw it was empty. He stepped behind the bar now and, bent over so he could look under it, slowly traveled down it. Right beside the beer taps he found what he was looking for. It was a sawed-off shotgun and he lifted it up and broke it and saw that both barrels were loaded. Standing motionless, he thought about this now, and presently he moved on toward the back and went out the rear door. It opened onto an alley, and he turned left and went up it, thinking, *It was brick, and the one next to it was painted brown, at least in front.* And then he saw it up ahead, a low brick store with a big loading platform running across its rear.

He went up to it, and looked down the narrow passageway he'd remembered was between this building and the brown one beside it. There was a small areaway here, this end cluttered with weeds and bottles and tin cans. Looking through it he could see a man's elbow and segment of leg at the boardwalk, and he stepped as noiselessly as he could over the trash and worked forward to the boardwalk.

At the end of the areaway, he hauled up and looked out and saw Alec Barr some ten feet to his right and teetering on the edge of the high boardwalk, gun in hand. He was engaged in low conversation with three other men on either side of him. There was a supreme insolence in the way he exposed himself, as if he knew Melaven would not shoot at him and could not hit him if he did.

Johnny raised the shotgun hip high and stepped out and said quietly, "Barr, you goin' to throw away that gun and get on your horse or am I goin' to burn you down?"

The four men turned slowly, not moving anything except their heads. It was Barr whom Johnny watched, and he saw the man's bold baleful eyes gauge his chance and decline the risk, and Johnny smiled. The three other men were watching Barr for a clue to their moves.

Johnny said "Now," and on the heel of it he heard the faint clatter of a kicked tin can in the areaway behind him. He lunged out of the areaway just as a pistol shot erupted with a savage roar between the two buildings.

Barr half turned now with the swiftness with which he lifted his gun across his front, and Johnny, watching him, didn't even raise the shotgun in his haste; he let go from the hip. He saw Barr rammed off the high boardwalk into the tie rail, and heard it crack and splinter and break with the big man's weight, and then Barr fell in the street out of sight.

The three other men scattered into the street, running blindly for the opposite sidewalk. And at the same time, the men who had been standing in front of the buildings watching this now ran toward Barr, and Gus Irby was in the van. Johnny poked the shotgun into the areaway and without even taking sight he pulled the trigger and listened to the bellow of the explosion and the rattling raking of the buckshot as it caromed between the two buildings. Afterward, he turned down street and let Gus and the others run past him, and he went into the Elite.

It was empty, and he put the shotgun on the bar and got himself a glass of water and stood there drinking it, thinking, *I feel some different, but not much.*

He was still drinking water when Gus came in later. Gus looked at him long and hard, as he poured himself a stout glass of whisky and downed it. Finally, Gus said, "There ain't a right thing about it, but they won't pay you a bounty for him. They should."

Johnny didn't say anything, only rinsed out his glass.

"Melaven wants to see you," Gus said then.

"All right." Johnny walked past him and Gus let him get past him ten feet, and then said, "Kid, look."

Johnny halted and turned around and Gus, looking sheepish, said, "About that there newspaper piece. That was meant to be a rawhide, but damned if it didn't backfire on me."

Johnny just waited, and Gus went on. "You remember the man that was standing this side of Barr? He works for me, runs some cows for me. Did, I mean, because he stood there all afternoon sickin' Barr on Melaven. You want his job? Forty a month, top hand."

"Sure," Johnny said promptly.

Gus smiled expansively and said, "Let's have a drink on it."

"Tomorrow," Johnny said. "I don't aim to get a reputation for drinkin' all day long."

Gus looked puzzled, and then laughed. "Reputation? Who with? Who knows——" His talk faded off, and then he said quietly, "Oh."

Johnny waited long enough to see if Gus would smile, and when Gus didn't, he went out. Gus didn't smile after he'd gone either.

RIDE A GOLDEN HORSE

STEWART TOLAND

In the lonely places of lonely men, where beast and element and life and death are the only kin and neighbor, man sees how small he is against this earth. It takes more for him to live—and less for him to die—than for most creatures. He has not the free gifts of wisdom and strength and clothing and acceptance as the beasts have. He is supreme only in hands and tongue—and conceit.

And this was a lonely place, this Texas, and not too long from its taming. Men still looked at men hard, and they measured in this way—man was the prey of the elements, and beasts were the prey of men, and men were the prey of men. For this was the hunters' day when nothing belonged to itself, but only to the strong. The weak, the coward, the fool, the innocent would all find death a quick and kinder place.

Perhaps that explained Ollie Yalden and his son Chess, why they thought of death. Only this time the prey wanted to choose the hunter.

That was the West. And strangely, the East had a similar thinking about the world belonging to the strong. But the strong was gold. Five thousand dollars in gold would buy anything. And so a man came out of the East with a bag of gold to buy a legend.

He got off the train with the gold in his hands, a leather round bag with a drawstring and a golden dollar sign painted big on its belly. To his left there was a guard with a rifle, and to his right a guard with a shotgun, and in front of him there was an artist come to kneel and sketch his picture so the periodicals back East could print just how it was. And he was a fine sketch of a man, with a black beaver hat and a gold watch chain and a smile from here to there. And after the artist made the picture of the train and the smoke and him standing beside it, he walked to the depot and nailed up a poster.

And everyone who had come to watch the train go by went to read the poster. They gathered round, and the artist drew that—the boots, the slouch hats, the bandannas, the gun belts, the flat, horse-sitting bottoms with the sweat line plain on their legs. It was sure enough a picture of the West squinting in the sun and reading.

Reward! 5000 Dollars Gold!
Wanted Alive

The wild horse known as Gateado.

Or sometimes The Ghost. Or sometimes The North Wind. The horse they say is faster than the wind and stronger than the mountains and clever as God and fierce as hell. The gold-colored horse with a tail that drags four inches along the ground and a mane to his knees, and a stripe down his back as thin and dark as hate.

Five thousand in gold will be paid by the undersigned for this horse unharmed, or not harmed beyond healing and with a rope on his neck and a rope on each leg—horse and ropes all stoutly secured in my freight wagon.

Phineas T. Barnum

And then a team of eight horses came down the street. This great red-and-yellow freight wagon with iron bars came to stop beside the bag of gold. And the guards put the gold in the chest bolted to the wagon bed and they climbed to the wagon top. The artist sat beside them, and the man in the beaver hat sat with the driver, and he turned to the crowd and said, "Which way is it to the wild-horse range?"

But there wasn't anyone left to answer. There was just a cloud of dust blowing from the south, and he sat there and smiled on it like he'd known it all along.

And the driver said, "Gateado's range is some three hundred miles to the south. It's lonely country of thorn and rock and shadows. That's why the horse hasn't been caught before. It's been tried, you know. Some say he isn't a horse, but only another shadow in the shadows he hides in. For five years men have hunted him."

"For five thousand dollars?"

And the driver said, "No," and headed the team south.

It was sunset and the time of the wild horses. The games and fights and flights of the day were forgotten for just this while as the wild horses turned to the west and watched the changing of the hours. It was strange. They stood so still, so intent, so knowing. They didn't say what it meant to them, this good-bye of the sun that was their friend. But if they had, no one would have heard but a boy.

He stood there alone in this place of loneliness where the sky was like a sea—shoreless and unknown. And the land was like a second sea—brown waves washed against isles of thorn and the reefs of stone where the horses stood. The boy watched the dark shadows of them. He watched the one standing apart, the stallion with the tail that lay along the ground, and he said, "Are you the one?"

And he waited for the answer that never came. He had been a boy-sized boy when first he'd asked that, and now he was almost man-sized and knew he wouldn't ever know—not for sure. He tried to remember if there was some other mark besides the length of tail and the look in the eyes and the stripe down the back. But it had been seven years ago, and he had only been a child. He had been hiding in the rocks of the wild-horse range from the whipping he was going to get when he got home and he came upon a mare and her colt, and they were dead. And he started to run away—because he was afraid of dead things—when the colt opened its eyes and looked at him. It wasn't dead; it was a little horse-child alone in this loneliness. And Chess remembered how it was when his mother died and he stopped and knelt and fell under a spell of magic. It was in the colt's eyes, like a fire burning there.

And the winds came to see and play with the colt's mane and tail that were longer than ever he'd seen, and the little horse struggled to meet the wind, to smell of its secrets and to snap at it as though the wind was his to tame. But he knew he was too young to tame it now, and he lay down again and watched the boy to see what it was that men were made to do.

And Chess said, "I found you, and that makes you mine. I have no brother and no friend and I would like to have you for my friend." He held out his hands. "See how delicate they are; I cannot make them strong. So, people say I'm weak. I've ridden a donkey since I was five, but I cannot ride a horse. It's not that I'm afraid of the horse; it's the ground going by so fast and far away and hard, and I am afraid of it. So, people call me a coward. I'm slow. I don't think of things right off. Like today—pa sent me to errand for him, and I had to go horseback. I know I'm always to have a drag rope to catch him by when I'm thrown, but I forgot. So when the horse threw me, I couldn't catch him. And I will be whipped when I get home; because if I'm whipped enough, maybe it will make me remember. You can see I am not much and not strong enough to keep you for my friend. I will give you to the wind."

And because he knew that a colt that isn't petted and fondled in its first night and day will be wild, Chess didn't lay a hand on it. He wanted to; he wanted to feel how warm and soft and strong it was. But he didn't touch it. He took his knife and cut the mare's mane and her lovely tail and he basket-wove them into a little hair blanket. It was very slippery and falling apart even before it was done, but it was enough to wrap around the colt's belly and keep the man-smell from laying on him as Chess picked him up and ran. The colt was surprisingly heavy and it kicked; it was almost too heavy, and Chess was running deeper into the wild-horse range and away from home, which would mean two whippings instead of one. But the magic of the colt was strong enough for both. And he ran and ran.

He ran until he sighted the wild-horse herd. He ran into the night, through the squealing and the neighing of the stallions, to the hour when even horses sleep. And he tiptoed until he heard the lazy swishing of a tail and a pawing at the ground and the soft insistence of a colt butting its mother. He had come to where the harem stood. And he laid the colt on the ground and he said without saying it at all, "Please God, let it find a kind mother who will give it milk."

And the prayer must have been answered, for when the morning came, there was no little orphan left behind, but only a black hair mat trampled in the dirt. And Chess ran to get it and keep it, so he couldn't ever forget that he had a friend.

And when the men of his pa's cow outfit found him, he was whipped—once for losing his mount and once for losing himself. For that was what he said he had done with the night, as there weren't words to tell how he could give a fine horse to the winds. Horses were worth twenty dollars, and who but a fool would throw twenty dollars to the wind?

That was seven years ago. And six years ago men began talking of a young horse on the wild-horse range that ran faster than the wind. He had eyes of fire and a coat that shone like the sun and the longest tail anyone had ever seen. And Chess heard and he ran to the wild-horse range, until he saw them standing there against the sun, and he cried, "Are you the one? Are you my friend? Did you live, and grow to be as fine as this?" The horses only turned and ran, for they knew no good of man. But the yearling waited longer than the rest. For just a moment he stood puzzling over the boy and then he snapped at the wind as though it were his. And he was gone.

That was six years ago. Five years ago men began hunting the horse. They named him and loved him and cursed him. And a legend was born. For this was the hunters' day, and anything that could be stronger than they became a legend and a challenge. And Chess watched in wonder and awe and no fear at all. For he believed in that gold-colored horse.

And he stood there now, smiling on it, not really needing the answer to his question, for the stallion always turned to look at him and bite the wind. And that was answer enough.

The sun had touched the earth and the shadows grew longer and darker still, like men creeping to find the night. Chess saw them, yet didn't see them. He thought how like men they were, yet didn't see the men they were. He didn't see the guns.

Perhaps a pebble rolled and told; perhaps the angel of the lost was flying low. Chess turned and saw and screamed. And the herd fled over the sea of shadows toward the other end of their range thirty miles away.

And the men dashed in fury for their mounts, for they had been the first. But one stopped long enough to lay his hate and his lariat on the boy. "If you were a year older, I'd kill you for that! But you're still young enough to be a fool and live!"

Chess said, "Does saving a fine horse make one a fool? There are other horses for you to kill if you are a leather man, or hungry. There's your own horse."

"Kill? We wasn't about to kill him, but only to crease him and lay him down till our ropes was on him. Where's your eyes, fool? Can't you read what's written on the trees? There's five thousand gold for that horse alive and tied in a show wagon. Someone's going to get that spending money, and I aimed it to be me!" And he laid that lariat like lightning over the boy. Chess crouched, weeping on the ground, because out of the shadows his father had come. That was why he wept—not for the blows of a rope, but the blow of eyes seeing him helpless beneath an old man's whip.

But then the man and his rope were gone, for he too had seen Ollie Yalden. And Ollie Yalden was a legend of his own—and a power. He had lived through the Indian wars, the States' war and the furies that were left behind. He had fought in all the wars with courage and honor. Until now, he had been strong enough for two. And so the stranger hadn't killed Chess. He'd only wanted to.

Ollie Yalden sighed. It was a sad sound. He said, "I carved a home-place out of the unknown and I loved it and I was proud. And now I hate it all. I hate what my wife died for. For I must leave this, everything I worked for, to the man who comes after me. And what I have done, it seems, my son will throw away."

He looked at Chess then. "I have whipped you as this country whipped me when first I came. I have saved you from too many deaths, because you were young and because you were my son. And I waited. You are almost a man in years and bone, but still you are tears and untamed fears and foolish things. Are these only childish things, Chess, to be thrown away? Or is your age telling it true, and you are not a child, and these things are not to be thrown away, for they are you!"

He waited, and there was no word. Ollie Yalden said, "I was wrong. And I am tired—and too weak to fight it any more, for what is a father but the shadow of the son!"

Chess said, "Pa, I tried to be the boy you used to be. All the braveries people tell of you, I've tried on one by one. And none of them are mine, so it must be true that I am a coward or a fool or both."

They looked at each other, and Ollie Yalden said, "You saw how the horse Gateado has its hunters. Even the strong are hunted. And you will be hunted. For you will be richer than five thousand dollars. This land I own is a small state, and the hunters won't wait. They will take you first because you are easy and because after you are gone I will be easy. Nothing will matter, not even land I bled to buy. So it is plain that neither of us will grow old. But perhaps still we have the choice of choosing our hunters. As to being the prey there is no doubt.

"What will your hunter be? Will you be whipped to death by old men? Or shot by a coward? For cowards can hold guns too; in fact, they most always do, and that has been one of my hopes, because you couldn't hold a gun. Will you choose that men will be your end or will it be the elements or a fool's way?

"Will you be thrown and lost in a waterless place—and not think to dig because no one is there to tell you to? Or will you sleep in the dry of a river bed because the silt is so soft and comfortable a place, and forget that water can come from the hills faster than man or horse can run the distance it takes to escape drowning? Or will you sit on a log before you remember to look on its other side for the rattlesnake asleep in its shade? What is your choice, Chess? For you must make a choice; you are almost a man, and I am tired, and this is not an easy land. Here only the dead can rest."

It was wicked. It was a man killing his son because he loved him too much. It was the same thing that wrapped Chess's fingers about a gun when the horse Gateado was tied down until the only part of him he could move was his ears and his eyes and his teeth biting at the wind. For he was caught. He had to be. He was only a horse, and not a miracle.

The horse had killed the first two to lay rope on him—one because he was old and not quick, and the other because he was young and not wise. And the artist painting his picture on the wagon exultantly laid two dead men under his hoofs. It made a wonderful picture.

But out of the dust of every dead man, fifty had risen to take his place. And they ran that horse. They ran him till he dropped in his foam. Any other horse would have been ruined, but not Gateado. He had been born to run. But the foam was choking him, and he had to rest, and they got ropes on him. And the man who got his rope on him first stood there shouting for the gold. Oh, he was a rich man as he tied a neck rope to a boulder here and a leg rope to a boulder there, and riders were sent off to bring the freight wagon and everyone else for a hundred miles—even Ollie and Chess Yalden. And Chess was sick to his stomach. And Ollie looked at that horse and the way he had been run for no more reason than gold. And he said to the man dancing round his ropes, "I'll give you six thousand dollars."

And the man stopped dancing and figured out how much more six was than five. And he liked the sound of it. But just then the red-and-yellow wagon pulled up, and the man in the beaver hat said, "Seven. Seven thousand gold." For who would not come to see a seven-thousand-dollar horse?

Ollie Yalden never turned his head. He said, "Eight."

And the man in the beaver hat said, "Ten."

And Ollie Yalden didn't say anything at all, for he didn't have eleven thousand to give away—not just right off like that.

So the artist began painting in his two bags of gold beside the two dead men. And folk sat their horses in a great silent circle as the dancing man began edging toward ten thousand dollars. It was a pretty sight, for he had a good working horse. He had two of them, and when they were almost to the wagon, he got off the one and left it holding Gateado while he took the extra neck rope and ran it through the wagon and out the bars at the other end, and he and his second horse began pulling on that. And Gateado was so near to being choked dead that just as easy as tallow he dragged him up the ramp and into the wagon, and the door was shut. And he ran around, tying ropes here and there, because there had to be five of them secure before he got those bags of gold. And folks were just a mite disappointed, for Gateado had been so brave a legend.

The man tied the neck rope first, and then the two front legs. That was his mistake, for a horse doesn't use his hind legs for sipping tea. They lashed out and tried the bars; and they seemed strong enough, so the stallion tried the wooden wall. He went right through, one hoof here, one there, like meteors brightening up a night. And all the time the man who was trying to get those ropes was jumping up and down, and the people shouted and laughed, for who is going to rush to save someone else's ten thousand dollars?

That was how Gateado got away. And men had thought about that—Ollie Yalden for one. He eased his horse out of the ring and got his rope so he could swing. And two brothers on the other side were doing the same and they were watching Ollie. And Gateado was looking over his shoulder and watching the hole he was carving, and he tore the tied ropes loose and jumped out and was free, except for the one more dead man he had to cross. For the dancing man who had almost touched a fortune couldn't let it go, not even if he had to hold it with his bare hands.

Ollie Yalden was the first after him. But the two brothers had thought of that. One roped Ollie right off his horse, while the other roped Gateado, and the both kept roping and tying. Before the horse could do anything but scream, they had eight ropes on him, and all he could move was his ears and his eyes and his teeth, biting for men. And the brothers said they'd be pleased to sell him for ten thousand dollars. Gold. They'd have the money or Gateado's leather. And to make sure that eight ropes were enough, and no one would have to take watch and watchabout, they got teams and moved boulders until there was a rock corral like a mountain around him. And they topped that with a few loads of cactus and horned skulls lying here and there. And the brothers said they'd give a thousand dollars to anyone who would go rip up a railroad spur, wherever there might be one, and bring a smith and let him bar up a cage that would be stronger than a train and could be pulled right over the horse as he stood. They were clever-thinking men. This time there wasn't any doubting about it being their gold.

And everyone wanted to be their friend and set them up for a drink or two, for the drinking parlors had brought out their barrels. And the Eating Palace had brought a kettle and beans and butchered a steer, and the tonsorial parlor brought its mugs and perfumes, and the gamblers some cards and tricks, and it was like fair time.

The fires burned all night and the night beyond, and the laughter was louder than it should be, for a beast that had been stronger than all wasn't anymore. And a man—he wasn't rich enough to buy the horse he wanted, wasn't strong enough to take it and he had been laid in the dirt, and the men who did it lived. People shrugged and looked at the son and said, "Blood will tell." And it was a good-tasting bitterness on their tongues, for it is a pleasant thing to watch the crumbling of a king.

And Ollie Yalden sat his horse and listened and watched his son, standing by the great iron cage that was almost done. Chess walked inside and tried it bar by bar. Then he went to the rock corral and climbed up on the jumble of horns.

It was sunset and the time of the wild horses. Only Gateado had been tied to the east, so even this had been stolen from him—the last sunset. And he was grieving for it. It was the loneliest look that Chess had ever seen.

And he ran to his father and he said, "Pa, is it true that things can die of no more than a broken heart?"

And his father said he thought it could be true. And he looked at his boy he didn't know, at the urgency that had made him forget he was shy. Ollie Yalden slid off his horse. He said, "The will to live is sometimes so strong that things will die for it—the wild, free things that are not born to be caged and cannot understand that all of us are caged. There are bars of iron about each of us. You are bound by everything people thought you ought to be because you are your father's son. And I am bound by everything people want to take from me because I have been strong too long." And he thought about that. "The horse Gateado has the easier cage. Come let us roll in our blankets and sleep."

They walked beyond the fires and rolled in their saddle blankets, and Chess said he was cold and asked to sleep close to his father—so close his hand lay on the gun in the gun belt under his father's head. And when Ollie was breathing slow enough to be asleep, Chess pulled out the gun and tiptoed into the night.

He went to the rock corral and crawled up and over and down into the blackness of it. And he said, "If your heart is too strong to die, I will set you free. I have a gun, and there are two bullets in it." And he thought about what two men would do if, instead of ten thousand dollars, all they had was leather. And he knew. The prey had chosen its hunters. And he was not afraid. And after a little he said, "But tonight we are alive and together and we will talk of what might have been."

And he told of the colt he had wanted for his friend. Only he'd been too poor and weak a thing to own and guard a friend. And he told about men, about their gold and their measures—about his father and how Chess had cried because he could not be like him.

And the horse blew softly in his nose, testing to see if there was breath enough. And he snapped his teeth to see if the taste of freedom was in them still.

And the boy and the night listened. Then, the boy began talking again, for it seemed easy to talk once you started. He said, "Do you know what men call you? They say you are an honest horse because you know what you are. You have counted out all your talents and you tell what they are and you are what you are."

He looked at his hands, as though he had never seen them before—as he never really had, for all his life he had measured only the talents he didn't own. He had never been honest with himself, but only tried to be a counterfeit. He looked at the horse and its talents, and he said, "I have a talent too. I have gentle hands." And he searched all inside himself to see if there might be another talent. And he found understanding for the lost and lonely. He had two talents, and that ought to be enough for any man.

And he crouched there looking at the horse, for he had talked the night away, and it was the time just before the morning, the time when ghosts can be seen and before you can know they are only mist. And he saw all the things that used to be when the horse was second only to God, when his name was the same as God. That was what the Indian called the horse, and how he loved him. One does not beat down gods. And so, for his horse, the fierce Indian had only held gentle hands—for his horse and his son. It was the way he tamed them. And Chess thought about that, but still he talked—little cooings and softlings of words that had nothing to tell but love, as the sound of the anvil thundered over the land, louder than a boy voice or the roaring of a gun if one should roar.

The cage was finished, even to ankle irons. And they dragged it to the rock corral and began tearing an opening. And they were so busy huffing and puffing they didn't notice Chess against the inside wall. He looked as though he slept. And the horse Gateado, tied rigid in his ropes, seemed to be sleeping too.

And the brothers yelled, "Ho!" so every shoulder would bend and push the cage through and over the house like a sock coming over a leg. And they got their knives to cut the ropes as the bars passed. But before the cage could move, there came the softest sound, like a hissing.

"No!" The leaning men leaned a little more. And it came again. "How can a man have a thing to sell if all he owns of it is the wrapping?"

The brothers cursed their way into the corral. A hundred men tore their clothes and hands crawling over the rocks and cactus and horns to see if what they'd heard was what they heard. And they saw the horse Gateado drowsing in his ropes and they saw the boy Chess drowsing against the wall and the brothers lifting him up by the coat on the point of their knives. He hung there between them like a long, thin sack of meal. And one of the brothers slapped him across the mouth, for slapped mouths usually say what you want them to say. And sure enough, this mouth said something.

It said, "The ropes are yours. But the horse Gateado is mine. And he is not for sale."

This time the slap was harder. It bloodied him and sent him into the dirt. And the horse Gateado opened his eyes to watch. And a hundred men turned to watch Ollie Yalden, and Ollie Yalden watched his son as he was laid in the dirt and drawn upon, for the brothers held guns. And Chess looked at them and went on sleeving off the blood, but he never moved his right hand that still stayed in his coat pocket.

He said, "I stole my pa's gun last night, for I thought I might have some killings to do. I don't know how I'll do, for I've never killed before. But I might have beginner's luck." And he smiled like he wasn't afraid at all—to kill or die, whichever it was to be. And he wasn't. For what the brothers couldn't see beneath the coat was that the gun was pointed at Gateado, there just between the fire of his eyes. And Chess said, because he had figured it all out before, "I wonder if the papers back East would like to know that Mr. Barnum bought a stolen horse for his two bags of gold."

Ah! The papers back East that thought all the world was their prey and that they were stronger than gold, or boys or even men with guns.

And the man in the beaver hat said, "I saw them rope him, and that is all one has to do to own a wild horse. Who says they do not own him?"

"The horse. And horses are honest, and men can lie. The brothers' ropes say he is theirs; my tongue says he is mine. Let us prove who lies. Let the horse have his say. Let him sit his master on his back."

A hundred tongues licked as many lips and said, "Let the horse have his say!" For if there was one thing the West liked better than living, it was seeing how fools died. So, they looked at the freight wagon with the remnants of three dead men painted on its splinters and they yelled, "Let the horse decide!"

And Ollie Yalden said not a word. He'd told enough when he told his son to choose his hunters. He'd heard enough when he pretended sleep to know what had wrapped his boy's hand about a gun; and he heard him talking a horse all the long of a night, doing what he didn't know he did—for horses like to be talked to most of all. It seems that words soothe the furies in them. So Ollie Yalden clung to the skull he crouched on, and people watched him watching that horse and they watched him watching his son, and an uneasiness crept round that throng, for there was something to see here that they didn't see.

The brothers looked to the mounds no one had bothered to put crosses on and they said no. "The ropes are ours—that is proof enough!"

Chess picked up one of the knives. "I'll give you back your ropes, and that will be a better proof."

They meant to, they could have shot him right then—only there is a fascination that holds one rigid watching a man walking to his death.

Chess cut the neck ropes from the boulders and he bundled them and walked along them, closer and closer still, not a stalking walking, but a strolling—like a man who has no place to go and all of a lifetime to go it in. He reached the end of the rope and laid a hand on the gold-colored horse that was still tied too tight to do any more than scream and tremble. All of him trembled as though a great illness had come upon him as the boy's hand smoothed over his body—slowly, gently.

And the throng held its breath and watched and knew what he was doing. For most had heard of how the Indians tamed their horses; for with the scalps of all his battles plain on his lance, an Indian didn't need to break his horse with fury. He didn't have to ride him down to prove his strength; he could gentle him and not be ashamed, as Chess wasn't ashamed. For he had two talents and he laid them on that horse, on every inch of him. He crawled under the belly, he laid his hands in the warmth of the thighs, he cut the ropes. One by one he dropped them in a little pile like dead snakes. And then he came to the ropes on the hind legs that had crushed three skulls. He leaned his cheek against one leg, and there were men later who said he cried. Surely he was trembling, as the horse trembled.

And when he found he wasn't dead, Chess stood and laid his arms across the horse's back, lifting himself a little, hardly more than tiptoe. He did it again and again, each time a mite higher, until he raised his leg and sat that horse. And the beast's eyes showed more white than dark as Chess closed his knees and wrapped his fingers in the thick of the mane. The ears were so far back that he did not seem to have ears, and he pawed the ground. Chess lay along his neck and said things men couldn't hear because of a shout from that throng— for if there's one thing the West liked better than most, it was a strong man being strong.

But the brothers yelled and cursed in fury—and poverty. "It's a trick! He's a horse thief!" And they triggered their guns, for anyone has the right to kill a horse thief.

One bullet went for the heart and one for the head, for the brothers always worked in a team like that.

But Chess had known he was the prey; he knew his hunters, and that the moment he sat that horse he would be dead—if he sat there longer than it took to trigger a gun. He didn't wait. Just as though he had practiced it most of his life, Chess fell off the horse and let the bullets find some place else to go. But as he landed, he grabbed hold of the mane like it was a drag rope and he yelled, "How do you want to be dead, from the front hoofs or the hind?" And he touched the horse, not with a firm gentleness, but with a tiny, hating tickling like the biting of a fly, and up went those front hoofs in a terrible climb. And away went the brothers, as if they just remembered they'd promised the smith a thousand dollars to make an iron cage out of any handy railroad track. And Chess stood there quiet and safe beneath those hoofs, for he had built a stronger cage.

And the man in the beaver hat looked on and puzzled over his bags of gold, and men crowded around Ollie Yalden so he could know they were his friends, and said what a wonderful son he had and how blood will tell. They didn't know how he'd done it, but he'd won again.

And he looked round this land he had carved out of the unknown of a wilderness. And he looked at the man his son had carved out of the unknown of a boy. And he said, "Chess, I only hope it can be true that a father can be the shadow of his son."

And Chess looked at the pride in his father's eyes, and for a moment he cried, and he climbed on the stallion and walked him out of the corral into the west. They went slowly, awkwardly, because he was lame from being tied too long—or maybe it was only that they would learn of this new world together just step by step.

THE ROAD THAT LED AFAR

LULA VOLLMER

Phoebe Durgin had taken up her watch in the yard an hour before midmorning. It was noon now, and her slender young body still leaned against the gate. Her unwavering brown eyes looked out from a child's face, but they held the first glint of a woman's knowing. Phoebe's gaze was fixed on the bend, half a mile away, where a jut of land turned the road and hid it from sight.

It was a makeshift road, rutted here, washed out there, and mounded with crusts of dry red mud. The road skirted the fence of the Durgin yard, hooped a mountain a little beyond, and stretched on—to town, Phoebe's father had told her, but where it came from Gil Durgin didn't know and never wondered.

Town, to Phoebe, was but a name, the place where unraised victuals and unmakable things, like shoes, came from. She had never traveled the five miles to that small point of civilization, but she had walked the road "a fer piece t'other way," and she knew it climbed higher into the hills, crossed one, maybe, and she vaguely pictured the road ending somewhere at "his" house.

"He" was the only regular traveler the road could boast, except for Gil Durgin, whose feet often staggered homeward, and an occasional rattling wagon from the Jenkins house a mile down below. From somewhere to town, and from town to somewhere, he, the rider, had passed every Saturday for three years until the Saturday that was day before yesterday.

277

Accustomed to being alone, Phoebe did most of her thinking aloud. Only dim, unconnected thoughts lay quiet in her mind.

"He didn't go a-tradin' on Saturday; looks like he'd be bound to buy provisions by Monday," she told herself, and she looked at the sun to measure the hour.

Her calico bonnet slipped off and hung limply at the back of her neck, giving the breeze a playing chance on a head of dark curly hair. Her skin showed fair beneath a touch of summer tan. Her face was small, oval; the soft line of her mouth and the delicate turn of her chin tempered its chiseled strength.

At the sight of the sun straight overhead Phoebe's hopes suddenly drooped. She remembered that the stranger had never passed as late as midday, but she pushed the thought aside with determined speech: "'Cause a thing ain't never bin is no reason hit cain't be."

To ease her weariness she shifted her position, and then, to get a better view of the bend, she climbed the fence. It was here, on the top board, beside this post, she had sat that day when he first spoke to her. Her face reddened a little under the sunburn and she lowered her head, half whispering: "Me barefooted, and a-straddle of the rail at that."

She consoled her shame with the thought that, ever since his first greeting, she had sat sidewise on the fence, her feet tucked under, as she waited to answer, "Howdy, mister," to the sandy-haired stranger's "Howdy, little girl," his only salute, until——

"Hit must be a good year now," she calculated aloud, and the same shyness crept over her that she had felt when she realized she could not speak from the fence anymore. That day she had dressed herself in her company dress, put on her Sunday shoes, and sat in a chair on the porch to wait for his passing. She remembered the jump of her heart when she thought he was going by without seeing her, and she felt again the stopping of her breath when he had touched his hat and said, "Howdy, ma'am."

That night Phoebe had let down the hem of her company dress, and since, with a greater nearness of knowing, from the greater distance of the porch, she had bowed and smiled to his new salutation.

Now he had failed to come. Hope and fear wrestled within her. Fear won. He might never come again.

Suddenly her ears caught a sound—thud, thud, like the jog trot of a mule's feet on hard ground. The road was still empty, but her heart bounded as she heard it again. She must get to her chair. Quickly she slipped from the fence, but, as her feet touched the ground, she caught sight of something moving on the dead hickory tree, and she stopped still. Anger brought back her breath, and as she shied her bonnet at the tree, she almost shouted, "Gittin' plumb flighty to let a woodpecker bird teetotally fool me."

The bird flew away and Phoebe stood again in her loneliness. "No use of waitin' life away," she reasoned, and reminded herself of the washing that ought to be on the line.

Reluctantly she turned her eyes from the road and faced the three-room cabin that leaned sidewise, as if standing on one foot to rest. Crossing the rickety porch she hesitated and looked down the road once more. She would wait for him, she decided, until the shade of the house began to fall in the front yard. She sat down, and hunching one of the rockers out of a crack, gave her restlessness some relief by swaying back and forth.

Finally, she argued against her disappointment: "He ain't nothin' but a stranger, nohow."

Phoebe wondered who he was. For the first time that tall figure with the smiling face assumed an individuality beyond the only identification she had ever given him—the traveler. She realized that he had a name, knew people he called by name, had folks of his own, while she had been only "little girl," and then "ma'am" to him. In a surge of jealousy she made a decision. When he passed again—if he rode by once more—she would speak her name and ask him his.

Shade came to the front yard, and moved on to the gate. Still, Phoebe sat on. Fragments of new thoughts met fragments of old, and bubbled together in her mind.

When the sun was gone and the shade was all shadow, she spoke again, "Paw'll come home hungry if he comes a-tall."

She arose and made her way through the dusk of the big room to the lean-to kitchen beyond.

When she awoke the next morning hope was in command. "He's bound to come today," she thought, and hurried out of bed. "But a watched pot never boils." She picked up a calico slip and put her shoes and Sunday dress aside.

As she bent over the tubs at the back door she tried not to listen for hoofbeats, but more than once the rub of the clothes against the board made the sound of a jog trot that ceased when she rested her arms and lifted her head to hear. The sun had quartered the sky when she hung the clothes on the line. Carrying the empty pails back to the house she laid life out for herself.

"If he don't pass by Saturday a-comin', I'll give him up fer good and gone."

In the kitchen she warmed up a hasty meal and was about to sit down at the table when a sound of knocking stopped her. She listened, unbelieving. It came again, a louder rap at the front door. A visitor could mean only one thing.

"Paw's found dead or drunk whar he oughten to be." She hurried to meet the news carrier.

In the middle of the big room, she stopped, confused. Her feet were bare, her old dress suds-drenched, and the caller who stood in the door, hat in hand, was her traveler. For a moment, neither spoke. Then Phoebe's trembling body moved forward and she stood within touch of him.

"Howdy, ma'am," he said.

"I wuzn't ever expectin' you to stop to howdy me," she apologized, with a glance at her feet and dress.

"I ain't exactly jest passin' today, ma'am."

He paused and stepped back from the door as if his errand were finished. Fear that he was going emboldened Phoebe and she slipped past him and stood on the porch.

"Take a chair and set a spell, mister."

"No'm," he thanked her. Silence followed. Struggling vainly for words, Phoebe sat down in the rocking chair. The man took a step toward her and spoke haltingly, "I take hit—you be single, ma'am?"

"I be single," she managed to whisper.

He studied the floor for a moment, and then his blue eyes sought her dark ones.

"I come a-courtin', if you air willin'."

She struggled for breath to carry the words, "I air willin'."

There was silence, and his eyes were again searching the ground. A fearful thought leaped to life in her mind—had she been too eager?

"You got a paw, or somebody I could ask?" He looked toward the door.

"Paw ain't a-keerin'," she told him simply.

"Ready then?" His face gentled with a smile.

He was her traveler again. Now she knew him. Now she could speak, and the woman in Phoebe was suddenly full grown. She laughed a little as she arose and stepped out of his reach, though his hand had not moved to touch her.

"In a powerful hurry, ain't you, mister?"

"Yes'um," he answered, with something more to say, but her words were quick now.

"Wonder you wouldn't 'a' stopped afore and gimme time to sewed a little."

"I ain't bin a widow man long," he said solemnly.

"Oh!" Pain nipped her happiness, but she put it aside, wanting for words to comfort him.

"Thar air a few young'uns," he told her honestly, "that be needin' you."

"I air a right good hand with baby pigs and biddy chickens." Her voice carried a promise.

"I'm a-hurryin' you 'cause I'm bound to go a few days' journey tomorrow, and they air little and helpless at home by tharselves."

"I'll ready myself."

The man was on his mule when Phoebe came out of the gate, carrying her possessions tied up in a shawl. He took the bundle from her, slipped one arm through the loop, and gave her his free hand to aid her mount. Settled safely behind him, she gave the word. The man clicked under his tongue and the mule started.

Phoebe gave one backward glance of farewell to the cabin with the closed door, and hoped paw would come home that night, so the pigs and the chickens wouldn't have to fend for themselves too long.

"Looks like frost is due soon," the man commented.

"Due soon," she agreed.

Then silence between them.

The jogging of the mule suddenly threw her toward him and she grabbed the bagging side of his coat for support. He put back a hand to steady her and reined in the mule. She was balanced, she assured him, but she held on to his coat, pleased with the rough texture of the cloth under her fingers. Now and then her knuckles bumped against the hard flesh over his ribs and an akinness with him swept her and pacified the aloneness of all her years. The odor of man was in her nostrils; breeze-washed sweat, the healthy damp of hair under a leather hatband, the tang of male flesh, combining a fragrance that was pleasing to her senses.

A mile down the road the Jenkins house slipped into sight, and a woman stopped sweeping the steps to watch them pass. As they trotted by, the man touched his hat, and Phoebe called: "Miss Jenny, when you see paw agin, tell him I've gone off a-marryin'.'"

The old woman nodded with little concern. The mule picked up a brisker clip, and the man spoke again:

"We'll have to go a fer-about way this time."

"I ain't a-mindin' ridin' bush-hittin' trails," she told him.

"We air bound to go by the county seat to git the marriage license."

"Yes, sir," and to cover her embarrassment over the forgotten details, she quickly added, "We shore have."

They sat in silence as the mule climbed higher into the hills. Atop, the deep woods showed their first rust of autumn color. Once, at the end of a steep pull, the mule halted for a rest. The road edged a deep cliff. Below them lay a valley. Beyond the valley rose hills, and behind the hills mountain ranges marked their smoky lines across the sky and seemed to end distance.

Watching the scene, Phoebe reflected that it was prettier than anything at home, and the awe of it brought forth her first speech not in answer to one of his.

"Mountains allus 'per to me to be God's embroidery work."

"Yes'um?" His eyes twinkled at her picture of God's femininity. "He shore has done a heap of fancy work round here," he acknowledged gracefully.

Then they went on.

All at once they were out of the woods and on a white hard road that reminded Phoebe of the marble-topped table in Miss Jenny Jenkins's company room; it seemed a pity for the mule to step on it. An automobile whizzed by and the saddle riders shied more than the beast under them.

All her life Phoebe had wondered about town, but she made no comment until the fairyland of houses, painted and pretty, caught her enthralled sight.

"Town houses grow up near'bout thick as corn, looks like," she stated.

Her companion answered, "'Pears to me like town folks 'ud plumb smother."

When they had passed the small residential section and struck the one main street crowded with stores and business houses, Phoebe clutched a little tighter at the man's coat and leaned a little nearer his body. Dizzy with watching and confused with hearing, she wanted to shut out the town and go on remembering it was her wedding day.

In the dingy office of the courthouse, when she gave her name to the indifferent clerk across the counter, the man beside her repeated, "Phoebe Durgin," as if making a mental note to remember. Her age, she told the clerk, was "Turned eighteen, this last month a-gone." She heard the traveler give his name. "Brad Lawson, twenty-nine—widow man."

"Brad Lawson." She tried the name in her mind. It suited him good, hard and strong, like his face, yet gentle to think on.

Phoebe did not question where the ceremony was to take place, but Brad told her when they reached the street and had mounted the mule once more. "The preacher is a-waitin' at home to marry us."

"He yo' kinfolks?" she inquired for something to say.

"No'm, he come a-Sunday, and he stayed over to take keer of the young-'uns today. He's good as any at marryin'."

Brad started the mule, then stopped him. He took a dollar bill from his pocket and indicating a doorway down the street asked shyly, "Wouldn't you like to step in a dry-goods store and git you some purty or 'nother?"

Phoebe answered, "No, thank you," a little afraid of the town bustle around her, and more eager to get on with their marriage.

Brad picked his way through the confusion of traffic and soon the rattle of the town was behind them.

In the middle of the afternoon, when they were high in the hills again, Brad spoke over his shoulder, regret in his voice, "Shucks, I aimed to git you some sardines and crackers in town, and I plumb fergot hit."

"I et hearty this mornin' and ain't hungry a speck," Phoebe lied.

The quiet between them went on unbroken for an hour. Then he told her casually, "Our nighest neighbor is ten miles off. You mought be sorter lonesome at first."

"I air used to aloneness," she said to him, but to herself there was an unspoken whisper: "I ain't never goin' to be lonesome agin."

Toward sunset Brad turned off the road and took a trail that led down the mountain.

"Nigh 'bout thar," Phoebe thought, but she asked no questions. Another half mile and she knew they were nearing valley ground. The chill of evening crept around them and she shivered.

"Home ain't much further," he said reassuringly.

Phoebe strained for the sight of a housetop, but she saw only woods. She kept her eyes lifted over his shoulder, for she knew the trick of a mountain path—a sudden turn, then a hidden world spread in full view.

Excitement seized her as she thought of her home—their home— not much farther. Vaguely it came to her that all she knew of this man was his face and his name. "Brad." She measured the word on her lips without sound, and then she reminded herself, "I must call him Mr. Lawson to his face, but when I recollect him he'll allus be Brad."

The sun had gone now and twilight sparred with the dark. Sudden- ly they were in a clearing; and then they were riding along a patch of whitewashed palings which encircled a treeless yard. At the far side of the yard a cabin squatted close to the ground, dark and lonely. It was much like her paw's house, Phoebe thought, though she believed it had an attic upstairs. A sense of foreboding sank into her heart. This place left her fancy of his home unsatisfied. She hoped it was an empty cabin and they would ride by, but Brad said "Whoa" at the gate, and she knew she was home. No sound, nor sign of life, greeted her; only a door, opening into deeper darkness, to welcome her.

"Whar air the young'uns?" she asked, as Brad helped her dismount.

"About somew'ers," he said, turning to lead the way.

Brad entered the cabin first. As he looked around for a place to put her bundle, Phoebe stood in the doorway, surveying the room. Shadows banked it all, except for the hearth, where the coals of a dying fire flared in spasms of light. In this glow she saw the figure of an old man sitting by the fireplace, asleep. His hands pinned a long white beard to his stomach, halting a head that tried to fall backward. For a moment she wanted to laugh, but a movement on the opposite side of the hearth drew her attention; she saw a huddle of children, their little white faces looking at her, waiting. She moved toward them, and Brad lighted a lamp. The smoky blaze revealed a little girl, about seven, sitting in a rocker, a tiny infant held in her arms like a doll. Crowded into the same chair was another little-girl figure, her three-year-old face scared, and haunting in its appeal. Two boys, twins, Phoebe thought, stood, one on each side of the chair, their five years seeming to weigh heavy on their gallused shoulders.

Brad named the children: Eloise, the eldest girl; Sally, the second; Trap and Hutch, nicknames for the boys.

"The baby we ain't got around to callin' nothin', yit," he concluded. Stepping to Phoebe's side, he said tenderly, "Children, this here lady is to be yo' new maw."

The four little named faces looked at Phoebe in wondering silence until Sally hid her face against her sister and sobbed loudly: "My mamma's dead." Tears slipped from Eloise's eyes, and the two boys hung their heads.

Phoebe, remembering that cry from her own child self when there was no one to hear, knelt by the chair, whispering, "I've come to help you bear hit the best I kin." She coaxed Sally to her and got up with the child in her arms.

The old man was awake and standing now, and Brad introduced him. "This here's Preacher Bailey, a-waitin' to marry us, Phoebe."

The minister shook her hand with a firm clasp. His ripened voice seemed to hold blessing as he told her, "I'm proud to meet you." Then, as if the ceremony needed hurry, he took a step backward and, with gentle authority, bade them: "Stand together within hand-tetchin' distance."

Her bonnet still on and the weight of the child, Sally, against her shoulder, Phoebe moved to the side of Brad Lawson. In her eyes, the comical white beard of the old man changed into a sacred vestment as she heard his voice strain into sanctity.

"We stand here gathered together in the sight of God——"

"In the sight of God." The thought filled her with a surge of reverence.

"——to join together this man and woman in holy wedlock——"

"Holy," and she had pictured it in a white dress, with dancing and fiddle playing.

"——an estate made by God and honored by the law."

The preacher paused for a moment and lifted his eyes beyond them.

A sudden fear touched her. Had he forgotten the words?

But his recommencement was heated with a new fervor as he charged: "If ary one of you know reason why you may not lawfully be joined together in marriage, do you now confess hit."

In the silent wait for such confession Phoebe heard the beating of Brad's heart and felt her own answer its racing. Could there be—but the preacher was speaking again, and his confidence quieted her.

"Brad Lawson, do you take this woman to be yo' wedded wife? Will you love her, comfort her, keep her in sickness and health, for her forsakin' all others so long as you both do live?"

"Forsaking all others," and a feeling of infinite security was hers when she heard his firm answer, "I will."

The preacher was saying her name.

"Phoebe, will you take this man——?"

Hadn't she taken him, and with him all of life, that day he first said, "Howdy, ma'am"?

"Will you obey him, serve him?"

"Yes, sir," she interrupted tremulously.

"Will you keep him in sickness and in health, for him forsakin' all others so long as you both do live?"

Hardly audible, but without falter, she answered, "So long as we both do live, I will."

"What God hath joined together let no man put asunder."

"No man, no thing," she took secret oath.

The preacher raised his hands in benediction and pronounced them man and wife.

Brad offered his hand to Phoebe, a little smile lighting his face. She wanted terribly to cry, but she managed to smile as they shook hands. Letting her hand go, he said kindly, "I reckon you kin take off yo' bonnet now and git supper."

He took Sally from her shoulder as he spoke to the boys, "Trap, you and Hutch fetch wood from the shed and git the fire a-goin'." The boys ran out of a side door, seemingly glad of the escape.

Adjusting Sally on one hip, Brad took the baby from Eloise and bade her show her maw around. While Phoebe prepared supper over the hearth, he sat by, holding the two children in his lap, miraculously rolling them both under one arm now and then as he rose to help her lift a heavy pot.

When they sat down to the table Brad told Phoebe the supper tasted right good, and she told herself, "I'm the gladdest I've ever bin."

When Phoebe had washed and put away the dishes she joined the family gathered around the fire. Timidly she set a chair in the empty place beside her husband. Brad did not look up. Apparently busy in thought, he kept his gaze steady on the flames while one arm reached back of him and slowly rocked the cradle where the infant lay. Next to him the preacher drowsed in a chair, his thin legs spraddled in relaxed contentment. At the far corner of the hearth the four children sat on a bench, pressed together as one, silent and watchful. Sitting down, Phoebe smiled at the four pairs of young eyes that were fastened upon her, but the fixity of their expression gave no recognition of her friendliness. In further effort she invited Sally to sit on her lap. The child squirmed around and looked toward the wall, while the three others stared on hungrily, yet distrustfully.

Phoebe had never felt so grown up and far away from children before, and she quickly searched back to her own first motherless days to find something to say. "You children got ary pet, sech as a kitten or a dog?" she finally asked.

A more concentrated observance of her was the only answer until Brad prompted them: "Say yes'um."

In unison four little voices took up the "Yes'um."

"Which un you got?" Phoebe wanted to know.

Again Brad cued them, "Kitten."

"Kitten," chorused the four.

"Wouldn't you like a puppy too?" Phoebe tried to tempt them. They waited for their father's lead. "Tell her yo' pap's got a ole hound dog."

"You've done told her yo'self," Sally flashed reproachfully.

Brad laughed a little as he explained, "They air skittish as possums, but they'll weary yo' ears a-talkin' when they git to knowin' you good."

The two men exchanged a casual prophecy regarding tomorrow's weather, and the conversation was over. Gradually the preacher's chin seemed to fold on his chest as he dozed. Eloise leaned her tangled head against the chimneypiece, and Sally put her face in her sister's lap, her active heels finally crowding the boys to the floor. One by one, the children gave up their stare to sleep. Phoebe, looking up, saw Brad nod and then struggle to wake. The bump, bump of the cradle rockers on the creaking floor slowed down, and then stopped, as Brad slept soundly.

The room was filled with breathing. Even the fire seemed to draw in and out as it sputtered rhythmically.

A greater loneliness than she had ever known before caught Phoebe for a moment, but she brushed it aside with plans. The first thing in the morning she would comb Eloise's hair, pretty. She would wash all the children and change their clothes. She would make them sugar cookies, even if she had to sweeten the dough with sorghum. Sugar was low, she had noticed. All children were scared of their stepmother at first. She looked at her husband, powerful and life-living even in his sleep. Pride entered her mind and eased her hurt. She had won their paw. With tending and tendering she would win his children too.

Sally turned and half slid from the bench. Clutching to right herself, she cried out in fright. At the cry of the child, Brad came out of his sleep with an anxious start, calling, "What is hit, Mary, what?" He looked blankly, unknowingly at Phoebe as she explained: "Little Sally thought she wuz a-fallin'." After a moment's pause, he said, "Oh, yes." Phoebe knew now that Mary was his first wife's name.

Brad leaned over and rubbed the sleep from his eyes, and then spoke back of a yawn: "Reckon I'd better put the young'uns to bed." Phoebe rose to help him. She saw a closed door at the back of the room and moved toward it, asking, "Do they sleep in here?" In an instant Brad was on his feet and at her side to stop her. "Not there," he said brusquely as he caught her arm. He saw the surprised hurt that came into her face, and he smiled down at her and spoke kindly: "I'll put 'em in the shed room tonight." When he picked up one of the boys, she bent over to lift the other little sprawling form. He stopped her. "No'm, they air all too heavy fer you to tote."

She watched him carry them, one by one, through a door at the side of the room. After he had gone out with the fourth child, he closed the door behind him. Phoebe wished that she had offered to undress the children, but she hesitated to follow him now. She bent over the crib and looked at the sleeping baby. Its littleness surprised and touched her. "Hit looks like hit ain't bin born good yit," she reflected. Then her eyes lifted to the closed door at the back, and she wondered why Brad had stopped her.

"Why, the back room is ourn," she thought, trembling a little.

She got up from the crib as Brad came in. He stood in thought for a moment before saying, "Better leave the little un whar he is, I reckon."

He went to the table and picked up the lamp. With the other hand he gathered up her shawl bundle.

"I'll show you whar to sleep."

Instead of going to the back room, he led her up the stairs, saying, "Me and the preacher will set up a spell."

In the empty attic room the lamplight made ghostly faces out of the cobwebs that hung in the corners and down from the low rafters.

"'Tain't as clean as hit ought to be," he apologized, setting the lamp on the head of an old barrel.

"I'll make out," Phoebe assured him.

Man and wife stood facing each other for the first time alone together. For several moments neither found words. Phoebe, lifting her downcast eyes for a fleeting instant, thought she saw unshed tears blurring his eyes, but when he spoke his voice was firm, hardened even with a little curtness.

"The preacher and me'll be making off afore good day. If you hear us a-stirrin', don't bother to git up and fix no breakfast."

"I'm used to early risin'," she protested.

There was the authority of a command in the words that came quickly, "You ain't to git up till good day to breakfast yo'self and the children."

"Yes, sir," she agreed quietly.

"I'll git back as soon as I kin," he spoke softly now. "I'll be gone two days and maybe three."

"I'll tend the young'uns good."

He looked at her, almost smiling, then turned and started away. Where the steps went down from the loft he stopped and, looking back, said simply, "I'm much obleeged to you, ma'am, fer marryin' me."

"You air more than welcome," she answered truthfully.

She listened to his quiet steps on the stairs, reflecting that he trod soft for a man.

Phoebe glanced around the room. There was no window, but the cracks in the walls were good air holes. Things were piled in the corners. Old bits of harness, rope and wire hung on the walls, molded in with dust as if they had been built there with the house. Only the bed had order. It was clean and freshly made. Phoebe felt the unusedness of the room and it came to her that here his first wife had never slept, and, in thoughtfulness, he had offered it to her, his bride.

She opened her bundle and undressed, grateful for this privacy. She put on the gown she had hand-worked and never worn. Then she blew out the lamp and crept into the rustling cornshuck mattressed bed. Her heart began to beat wildly as she lay and waited. She wondered if she ought to pretend to be asleep when he came. Suddenly fear seized her and she longed to be back at paw's house. She sat up in bed. If there were a way to get out—then she reminded herself that she was a married woman. All women married. Brad Lawson was her man, the man she had picked and held in her dreams. Life had made her for this night. This was the beginning of her womanhood. She put her head on the pillow again and thought of his other wife. She felt pity for the dead woman who had had to give him up.

She wished that she and Brad could have had a talking courtship. In that time he might have kissed her, armed her, and made her more at home with him. She remembered when her maw was living and her paw sober, they had kissed; she, a child, envying them. If Brad had just kissed her once before he left the room, or even called her Phoebe. But she was a married woman now, and as her husband thought, she must obey.

An hour passed, then two. She heard no returning step on the stairs.

Her wedding night. It wasn't as she had notioned it day after day when she thought of him, ashamed before herself for her fancied closeness in his arms. But life wasn't cut out by your mind's pattern. Hadn't she been bound to have a pair of shoes for the spring all-day singing and had to wait until Christmas following? Woman's will was bent to man's. Her maw had told her that.

Outside, a rooster crowed for midnight. That meant rain tomorrow. He'd be gone and she in a strange house with a dead woman's children. Three days before he'd be back. Waiting was a woman's portion. God had fashioned them so, that man's lot might be easier.

The darkness of the room seemed to grow heavier as another waiting hour tolled by. Weariness touched her body, clamped her mind until her thoughts flitted here and there, now holding nothing to be important.

She slept and dreamed that she was on the valley dip below the road at home. She was running and jumping glad for the aliveness of her body. She remembered it was Saturday and she must get to the road before her traveler passed. She was headed for the steep climb when a squall of distress stopped her. It sounded like a child crying, but it must be one of ole Mary Jenkins's lambs caught in a brier patch or lost from its mammy. She would rescue it as soon as the traveler had passed. She tried to scramble up the rocks, but the bleating seemed to push her back and weight her feet. Straining against the load of herself, she awoke with a start. A child was crying the hitching, agonizing wail of an infant. She sat up, listening, and remembered where she was. The cry rose higher and more urgent. She got up and slipped on her dress.

At the head of the steps she looked down into the room below. In the light of the fire she could see the wrenching movements of the baby's arms and feet as it cried hungrily. She made sure that Brad and Preacher Bailey were not in the room, and then hurried down to the cradle. As she picked up the baby she noticed that the back room door was slightly ajar and a low light burned in the room. The men must be asleep in there, she thought, and she joggled the baby gently against her shoulder to quiet it, while, with her free hand, she heated and bottled the milk. The child drank eagerly and was soon asleep in her arms.

She liked holding its littleness. She sat on, tendering it until she heard a wagon drive up in the yard. That told her that the men were outside, making ready for the journey, and reminded her of Brad's order that she was not to get up until he was gone. Quickly she laid the sleeping baby in the cradle and hurried up the dark stairs, but before she could step into the loft the two men entered the front door, leaving it open wide. She stopped and turned thinking to explain, if Brad had seen her, but without looking up, he went straight into the back room, the preacher following him.

They had not eaten, she thought, for the table was clear. Brad might let her cook his breakfast if he knew she was up. Balancing her fear of his displeasure against her desire to be useful, she waited. Should she go back in the loft and call down to him? Then she heard the sound of labored footsteps. Peering over the stair rail, she noticed that the lamp in the back room had been put out. In the half light from the fire she saw Brad back out of the room, his hands grasping the end of a wooden box. His strength seemed to sag under the load and she knew from the shape of the crate that the preacher buckled under its heaviness on the other side. Slowly Brad stepped backward and slowly the box lengthened. Longer and more narrow it slid into view. A cold fear shook her at the thought of the thing the chest suggested. Then the old man staggered into the doorway and the end of the burden was in sight. She knew the unpainted box was a homemade coffin.

Like lightning in the night, thoughts darted into her bewildered mind, and like lightning went out, leaving a light. In some untold way this was the reason for her uncourted marriage, and the strangeness of the night just spent. Secrecy was his wish, and she had oathed before God to obey. He must never know that she knew. She must raise strength to stand until he was outside.

The room's journey was almost ended when the door from the

shed opened and the flickering firelight shone on four tiny white faces, drawn and oldened.

With a scream Eloise ran forward, and in a moment four little sobbing creatures clung to the box, trying to hold it back.

A look passed between the two men, and gently they lowered the coffin to the floor. Brad gathered the children together and, stooping beside them, drew them all into his arms. Their cries rose higher as he tried to comfort them. He held them closer and, with a voice grief-torn from its control, spoke over their weeping, "She ain't in the box. Yo' mommy is gone whar hurtin' cain't tetch her."

Unsteadily, Phoebe crept into the loft. The sorrow in the room below stirred her pity and kept back, for a moment, the horror that was crowding her. But its realization came full as she turned into the darkness of the attic. While she was a-marryin', on the other side of that shut door the children's mother lay unburied. While she had waited through the night for some word of love, her husband's heart had watched in the back room. Deeper in her lashed the thought that Brad had married her to be handy.

Phoebe let the children stand at the gate until the wagon was out of sight and the sound of its wheels lost in the misty, daybreak air. Waiting in the doorway, a witness to their loneliness, she felt her own pain lessen. Their need had brought her here. That told her that should she die in giving birth to a son of Brad's, another woman would be ready to care for her child. Children had to go on. They couldn't wait for love a-grownin' between man and woman. All marriage, in time, led over some rocky life path. Hers had come quicker than most. She was Brad's wife. Through his children she would win his caring.

She went to the gate, and the tear-washed faces turned to her wonderingly. "Children," she said softly, "I'm a-cookin' yo' breakfast. Don't you want to ready yo'selves fer the table?"

"Yes'um," Eloise answered trustfully.

Hutch looked like his paw as he turned toward the wagon way, and then back at her. Confidence in her steadied his voice as he inquired, "A'ter breakfast, would hit be a sin if we played a little, like we used to?"

"When we've et," Phoebe told him, "I'll play with you-all, all day."

THE GRAMPUS
AND THE WEASEL

STEWART EDWARD WHITE

Two men stood atop the low cliffs on the seaward side of the Peninsula of Monterey. They were wholly unlike in every particular of dress, of equipment, of physical make-up, of age; yes, even of occupation, for while the one was gazing steadfastly across the sea, the eyes of the other were occupied as steadfastly with his companion.

The latter was indeed worthy of survey. He was long, lean, wiry and tanned. His head was bound with a kerchief. The upper part of his body was muffled in a voluminous garment without buttons; the front flaps overlapping deeply across the chest, held in place by a wide beaded belt. This garment was heavily thonged or fringed around the bottom of its skirt and along the seams of its sleeves, but many of the thongs were missing, having been cut away for use as occasion had required. The belt supported a pouch of considerable capacity, a knife in a sheath, and a narrow-bladed small ax. From a strap across the man's shoulder depended a stoppered buffalo horn that had been scraped so thin that the grains of gunpowder could be discerned through its substance. His lower extremities were incased in leggings which, startlingly, had no seat, and on his feet he wore ornamented moccasins. The material of the various garments was the same. It looked like some kind of soft and shiny black satin, but was in reality buckskin, worn by long use. At this moment he was resting his chin on the back of his hands, which were, in turn, clasped across the muzzle of a rifle so long of barrel that, though he was well over six feet in height, it furnished a comfortable support. He was clean-shaven and lean-faced, and might have been anywhere from thirty to fifty years of age.

He seemed totally oblivious of the other man's existence; though the latter was, in his way, quite as worthy of remark. This was a short, broad man. He wore thrust back on his head a flat-crowned, wide-brimmed black hat, probably of straw, though it had been so heavily glazed by varnish that it might have been of tin. The ends of its wide ribbon band hung in swallowtails alongside his ear. A knit jersey, striped horizontally in blue and white, defined every muscle in his powerful torso. His trousers fitted nearly as closely as far as the knees, when suddenly they flared into what might almost be described as miniature skirts. His feet were bare and brown. As for his age, that, too, was indeterminate, though something simple, almost childlike, in the expression of his face deprived it of the other's maturity, if not of his years. Indeed, at this moment that expression was of a rather awed small boy at a circus. He was staring at the other man, his mouth half open, in a species of admiring incredulity to which its object paid not the smallest attention. Several times he seemed about to speak. At length he cleared his throat with visible determination.

"What you lookin' at, mate?" he rumbled in a hoarse voice.

The other did not glance in his direction. Nevertheless, he replied.

"The sea," he answered.

The sailor squinted his eyes.

"I don't make out nothin'," he said after a moment. "There's nothin' out there."

The tall stranger raised his head, stretched as though awakening, turned toward his questioner.

"I've never seed it afore," said he.

"Never seed it afore! The sea?" echoed the sailor stupidly.

"I've seed the Big Salt Lake, back yander"—he waved a vague hand toward the east—"and that's a heap of water, looked like to me. But allus they been tellin' me of the sea. So I made up my mind I'd come look."

The sailor spat and shifted his quid to his other cheek.

"Well, what do you think of her?" he asked.

"She's awful flat," submitted the Mountain Man simply.

The sailor burst into a hoarse laugh.

"Say that off'n Cape Stiff!" said he.

"Anon?"

"Cape Stiff—Cape Horn."

"You been thar?"

"How'd you think I'd get here? Fly?"

"You a sailor?" asked the Mountain Man, with a sudden show of interest.

"What you think I was?"

"I couldn't figger. What for you wear yore pants like that? Foofaraw?"

"Pants? Like what?" the sailor was taken aback.

"Looks like it's mouty tanglin', walkin' in things like that. What for all the slack?"

"Tangling, my eye!" snorted the sailor indignantly. "I'd like to see you roll them things"—he glanced with scorn at the other's tight leggings—"when you go to sluice decks." He stooped rapidly and demonstrated.

The other laughed in a pleased fashion, but without making a sound. He laid the rifle on the ground, squatted on his heels. From his belt he drew the ax, and from the pouch produced a sack of tobacco. It now appeared that the handle of the ax was hollow, and that the nub on the butt of the narrow blade was also hollow, so that, held upside down, the ax became a pipe. The sailor contemplated this with admiration. But evidently the pants business still rankled.

"Look a here," he said suddenly, "whyn't you scrape your ax handle? She's so greasy and slippery now that a man couldn't hang onto her to save his neck."

The Mountain Man glanced up at him with surprise; then down on the implement in his hand.

"Why," said he presently, "in the first place, she ain't an ax; she's a tomahawk. And in the second place, so fur from scrapin' her, I just nat'rally grease her up good so she will slip."

He glanced about him, selected his mark in a dead cypress stub, drew back his arm and cast. The weapon flashed through the air to embed itself quivering deep in the wood. The Mountain Man arose slowly to retrieve it.

"She's got to slide easy from your hand or she won't turn right in the air," he observed. He filled the pipe side and lighted it with a quiet air of satisfaction, as though honors were now even in the pants business. He puffed it well alight and offered it to the sailor. The latter declined. "I'm chawing," said he, and could not understand the mistrust that flitted briefly across the other's face. He knew nothing of pipe etiquette and friendship smokes.

"Well," observed the Mountain Man presently, "I got to be gittin' back."

"Back where?" asked the sailor.

"To the mountains, whar I come from. I calc'late," said he, "it mout take me, this season of the year, risin' on three weeks, and I got rendezvoo with a pardner."

"Three weeks," marveled the sailor; "that's quite a voyage."

"Mebbe more eff'n the Injuns make trouble."

The sailor looked up quickly.

"You seen Injuns—back where you came from?" he asked with interest.

The Mountain Man stared a moment, to see if the question was serious. Then he shoved aside the kerchief on his head. A curious semicircular scar fitted across the top of his forehead like a cap, and disappeared in the long hair above his ears.

"Started to sculp me," he explained gravely, "but I got him afore he had a chance to yank."

"Gor a'mighty!" muttered the sailor. "Let's set us down and you tell me how come about."

"I got to be gittin' on now, I tell ye." The Mountain Man knocked the ashes from the tomahawk and thrust it in his belt.

But the sailor caught him by the arm. He persisted. It took some moments for him to realize that by "now" this strange being meant on that very instant. He was, furthermore, abysmally astonished to find out that the Mountain Man had only that day reached the coast; that between his arrival from those three-weeks-distant mountains and his return thereto only this short hour was to intervene. He could not understand any reason for such hurry.

"I'm in no hurry," disclaimed the Mountain Man, "but I've seed what I come for."

"Do you mean to tell me you come all that way and back just to take a squint at that?" The sailor waved his hand at the ocean.

"I never seed it afore," said the Mountain Man patiently.

"But now you're here"—the sailor's indignation was mounting—"ain't you going to look around any? Ain't you even goin' over to Monterey?"

"Monterey nigh yere?" asked the other with mild interest.

"Nigh here!" the sailor spat with disgust. "Nigh here! Don't you even know where you're at? How in tarnation did you get here?"

"The sea lay west," said the Mountain Man, "so I come west. As for Monterey, I got no use for these yeller-belly pueblos. I seen a plenty. Nor for yeller bellies. Nor they fer me." He laughed in his hearty but silent fashion.

"And you're going back—all that ways—without even lookin' around?"—the seaman was still incredulous.

"I seen what I come to see," replied the other.

"Well, I think you're crazy!"

"Mebbe so," agreed the trapper mildly.

Nevertheless, an hour or so later the two walked together down the hill and into the pueblo of Monterey. Bob Scarf, for so the Mountain Man named himself, strode along at a light, long, easy gait, leading his horse. Bill Carden, who was the sailor, rolled alongside, two steps to his one. The sailor was triumphant. His desire to show off this strange specimen to his mates at the *pulqueria* of Portugee Joe had seized upon him mightily. He had flung himself heart and soul into persuasion. None of his first baits had taken. *Muchachas*—leetle devils, and not so good as the Injun gals at that. Aggerdenty—Bob knew all about that stuff, and one drunk a year was enough for any man, and rendezvous was the place for that. And then a casual mention of Bill's ship——

"I never yet seen a ship," observed Bob wistfully. "Eff'n I thought you'd take me aboard a ship——"

"Sure I will!" said Bill, with a confidence he did not feel, for he could see neither Captain Jordan nor Bully Hawes, the mate, permitting a seaman such a privilege. "Sure, you'll get aboard," he repeated, with the confidence now so genuine that Scarf sensed the difference. The latter's look of inquiry was so compelling that Carden had to explain. "Just as you said that, a grampus blowed," said he, "and when that happens, it means you get your wish."

The walk across the peninsula is a long one. Bill plied his new friend with many questions. His interest in what the latter had to say was keen beyond mere curiosity.

"Gor a'mighty!" he sighed with envy. "I sure do wish I could see that country and fight Injuns!"

Scarf uttered an amused laugh, that checked suddenly. At the exact moment Carden had uttered his wish, a weasel had darted across their path from right to left.

"Yo're a-goin' to," said he, "eff'n the Injuns is right in what they believe!"

They entered the pueblo. Carden steered his friend toward Portugee Joe's. The trapper followed lingeringly and reluctantly. He had no eyes for the picturesque and scattered buildings of the pueblo itself, nor for the even more picturesque men and women lounging or loitering about, who surveyed him with curiosity, a little hostility and a little covert admiration. His attention was fixed on the brig, lying at anchor just off the customhouse. In his direct fashion, he wanted to go aboard at once. Bill Carden muttered uneasily to himself. It was belatedly borne in on him that explanations and excuses might not prove too easy to make to this fellow. The fact that he could point out the ship's shore boat on her painter astern of the brig sufficed as an excuse for present delay. And now that he was here, Scarf consented readily enough to sample Joe's aggerdenty. So far, so good.

But as the two rounded the corner of the building, Carden stopped for a moment and uttered a curse. Leaning indolently against the door lintel was the burly figure of the mate, Bully Hawes, and Bully Hawes was not one to pass over so obvious a subject for curiosity as this. Bully Hawes stuck his nose in everything, damn him! He had more questions in his system than a fish had eggs. And it suddenly came to Bill Carden that he himself should have gone aboard the brig in that longboat now dangling at her stern.

However, to his relief, and his vast surprise, Bully Hawes did no more than cast upon the two a look of speculation. The sailor hurried his companion past into the dim interior of the *pulqueria*, where they took seats at one of the three small tables, and Bill demanded loudly the attendance of Portugee Joe. After a moment that great fat man appeared. He served the *aguardiente*, gestured at wiping the table, wandered away. Bully Hawes summoned him to the door. He listened to Bully Hawes a moment, nodded, and trundled back to his lair in the darkness. After a few moments, he came back to the table. He bore a bottle. He placed this on the table. He clapped Bob Scarf on the shoulder.

"For you!" he said. "You *americano!* I like *americano!* Long time no have seen *americano!* No, no! No monee! I drink! You drink! No?" His moon face was wreathed in oily smiles. He whisked away the glasses and laid out three fresh ones, which he hastily filled from the bottle. "We drink!" he urged.

Bill Carden was staring in astonishment.

"You sure got a way with you, mate. I never see Portugee Joe give away a drink before."

The three lifted their glasses and drank. Bully Hawes stood in the doorway looking at them.

II

It was this same Bully Hawes who, some hours later, pulled Bob Scarf from a bunk to the floor of a dark forecastle and half lifted, half kicked him to a reeling deck. The Mountain Man was only confusedly aware of this. His head was swimming, his legs and arms had no strength, his eyes would not focus, and the motion of the ship had combined with the drug Portugee Joe had slipped into his glass to fill his whole being with nausea. One thing only was certain—he was on a ship; and Bob Scarf, even in his bewilderment and misery, grinned wryly at the prompt fulfillment of his wish. It was his only flash. He was only half conscious of the blows from the mate's boot, and did not identify them for what they were. But someone at his side thrust a rope in his hand.

"Pull on this," a voice whispered. The voice sounded friendly. "Anyways, pretend to. Slow and easy like."

Mechanically, Scarf obeyed. After a little, his head began to clear. He was able to see, and to take stock of his situation. This he did from beneath his brows, without changing his expression or his occupation. His eyes swept the deck but once; nevertheless, no detail, strange to him though it was, escaped his scrutiny and his appraisal. On a raised and railed platform at the back—as he would have phrased it—one man stood at a wheel with spokes and another paced slowly back and forth. On the same level as himself, another, whom he recognized as the man at Portugee Joe's, was standing, his legs apart, looking upward critically at a cross stick with a canvas attached that was rising slowly up the mast. The Mountain Man knew nothing of sails, but his quick eye caught at once the connection between this motion and the rope at which he was still mechanically pulling. He jerked his head to look, and discovered that behind him were five other men, also pulling on the rope. The one nearest was Bill Carden. Bill's eyes met his, wide and troubled. Full recollection returned. Bob Scarf dropped the rope.

"What in hell's all this?" he demanded with mounting anger.

"Grab a hold! Pull!" Carden's eyes showed panic, but his uneasy glance was toward the mate, still gazing aloft.

"Belay!" bellowed the latter.

Carden's face showed relief. He threw the bight of the halyard about its pin, muttering out of the corner of his mouth, "Obey orders, for cripe's sake!" Scarf seized him by the shoulder. "Lemme be. Later. Our watch off." Then, as the Mountain Man's grip tightened, "I did not, I tell ye!"

"Didn't what?"

"Crimp ye. I swear it! I'd no idee!"

Bully Hawes bellowed some order. Carden wrenched his shoulder free and hastened after the other men across the deck. Scarf remained where he was, staring after him. Hawes was shouting something at him; then, as he failed to comprehend, strode over to him.

"Lay to on that sheet!" he repeated, with a string of oaths. The Mountain Man simply stared. The mate kicked him with his heavy sea boot.

Now, Bob Scarf was most decidedly a rugged individualist. He was accustomed to the complete freedom of a wide and empty land. He had always been his own boss in all matters, great and small. He knew nothing of any discipline other than the self-imposed. He did not yet comprehend why he was here. So, when Bully Hawes kicked him, he at once started fighting.

This pleased Bully Hawes. It was what he had hoped, for it was the shortest way. Also the usual way and the easiest, for Hawes was a bucko whose seamanship was only a minor qualification. He had gained and held his job because he could rule the tough waterfront crews of that day with his fists, and could, and did, lick any man who stepped. He was proud of that ability, and he rejoiced at any excuse to exercise it. When he hit them, he liked to boast, they stayed hit. And his methods comprehended neither compunction nor mercy.

But in the first few seconds of the encounter it became evident that this strange new specimen had methods of his own. Apparently less powerful than the burly mate, Bob Scarf was, nevertheless, long, lean, wiry, and, after his own fashion, accustomed to battle. He had none of his usual weapons of hand-to-hand encounter, but the buckskins he still wore were wet from spray and as slippery as butter. Bully Hawes found his sledgehammer blows avoided and himself locked in close grips with a writhing eel on which his strength seemed able to get no purchase. The men stopped hauling and stood, the sheet in their hands. The man on the quarterdeck sauntered to the rail, against which he leaned on crossed elbows, a cheroot in the corner of his mouth, looking down.

Rough-and-tumble was old stuff to the mate. In a manner of speaking, he had made his living at it over all the seven seas. But it was also old stuff to Bob Scarf, and he had played it on plain and mountain for higher stakes. There was between the two the difference between livelihood and survival; between the need to dominate and the need to destroy. The Mountain Man had before now saved his scalp by one or another of these Indian tricks, and shortly Bully Hawes rolled in the scuppers with a broken arm.

Throughout the encounter the man on the quarterdeck had made no move to interfere, either in person or by command. He had continued to watch with an interest almost Olympian in its complete detachment. Now, however, he removed the cheroot from his mouth and laid it carefully to one side. He strolled slowly to the companionway just forward of the wheel.

"Mr. Tate!" he called. His voice was smooth and without emotion. After a moment, the head of the second mate appeared above the hatch, yawning as though just awakened. "Will you call Dan and the Swede?"

Tate glanced at the situation in the waist of the ship, and grinned. He disappeared, to return almost instantly, followed by the bos'n and the carpenter. All four then descended from the quarterdeck.

No pride of prowess attended them. Bully Hawes monopolized that. This was a job—a necessary job. There was even no animosity. Each plucked a belaying pin from the rack. Bob Scarf had not a chance. He fought like a panther, but the odds were too many. He held his own briefly, to the admiration of the fascinated crew, and was badly battered before he dropped unconscious. Bully Hawes, nursing his broken arm, staggered forward to aim a kick with his heavy sea boot, but was checked sharply.

"Attend me in my cabin and I will set your arm," ordered Captain Jordan.

The latter turned without a backward glance, clambered heavily up the companion ladder to the quarter-deck, picked up his cheroot, on which he puffed experimentally to see if it was still alight.

The second mate and Chips doused the Mountain Man with sea water and dumped him unceremoniously into the forecastle. Tate took charge of the deck. He summoned all hands to shift sail. The ship's business went forward.

After a little, Bill Carden sneaked down into the empty forecastle. He lifted Scarf into his bunk. Then, before returning to the deck, he raised the ticking on his own bunk and gazed gloatingly on what lay beneath it—the long rifle, the tomahawk, the throwing knife, which Bill Carden had secretly salvaged at the shanghaiing of the trapper. He'd need them when that weasel omen was fulfilled. The grampus had certainly made good!

Bob Scarf recovered consciousness only after a considerable interval. When barely able to stand, he was haled aft to the break of the quarterdeck. Captain Jordan leaned on the rail, looking down at him.

"Now, my man," said he crisply, "you are a sailor aboard this brig, and you will obey orders as such. If you refuse duty, you have had a taste of what you may expect."

"I'm no sailor," returned Bob Scarf, "and I ain't aboard this ship of my free will."

"That will do," Captain Jordan cut him short. "If you are no sailor, you soon will be. Mr. Tate will instruct you in your duties." He walked away.

The second mate approached his task warily, with a belaying pin handy and assistance within easy call. To his surprise, and, at first, to his distrust, he had no trouble. Furthermore, the Mountain Man proved astonishingly apt. He caught on quickly. Aloft, from the very start, he was surefooted and without fear. Bob Scarf had done plenty of climbing, and his life had given him control of his body balances.

His only mistakes were those of a good dog—when he did not understand. A man's comprehension, in those days, was customarily quickened by a blow or a kick, but Tate had tact enough—perhaps it was caution enough—to do a little explaining. Scarf had been assigned to Tate's watch. Bully Hawes held off for the time being, possibly because of his crippled arm, possibly warned by the gleam in the trapper's otherwise expressionless eye when the two came in contact.

The Mountain Man rarely spoke. His expression never changed. The crew at once feared and disliked him, for his contempt for them was evident. He could not understand why the many should submit to such treatment by the few. That they did so placed them, with Scarf, as no men at all; supine, unreliable creatures, without the spark of real manhood. He had no knowledge of the necessary basis of ship's discipline, nor of such legalities as barratry and mutiny. Bob's mind was simple and direct. With the exception of Bill Carden, he had no word for any of them. He kept himself to himself. And even Bill Carden did not get far with him. The sailor had insisted on setting himself right as to any connivance in the actual shanghaiing. He even managed to compel Scarf's reluctant admission that it was useless to think of bucking the ship's officers single-handed, and a dim comprehension that circumstances had so arranged a ship and its conduct that orders must be obeyed.

"You can't do a one-man mutiny," said Bill Carden.

"Then why be a sailor?" argued Bob contemptuously. "It's a life for slaves, not men."

To this, Carden, as a proper sailor, agreed heartily, for a proper sailor always imagines that he hates the sea, and will leave it, but never does. Fighting Injuns, he implied, was really his ambition; and at the first opportunity——Scarf grunted, but whether in approval or skeptically, it would be difficult to say. "Well, I notice you're taking orders!" cried Bill, stung. Rebuffed by the other's attitude, he repressed his impulse to tell of the long rifle and the other equipment beneath his mattress.

Captain Jordan congratulated Tate.

"That man's getting to be one of the best sailors aboard," said he. "Does he make any trouble?"

"None," said the second mate. "I've never even heard a growl out of him. He's all right if you give him a chance to be."

He glanced sidewise at Bully Hawes, whom he disliked.

The latter grinned wolfishly.

"He got his medicine plenty at the start. And it took," he pointed out. "If he hadn't caught me foul when I slipped——"

It was true that Scarf never uttered a word of objection or complaint. He had been in this situation before—when the Pawnees had held him as prisoner and used him as a slave. He had then performed, uncomplainingly and without objection, much more degrading tasks than tarring ropes or scrubbing decks, while he watched the situation and waited his chance. That was the way to do. When things are hopeless, lie low and watch. Had these men on the brig *Mary Scarlett* more experience of his kind, they would have known that from the cover of this apparently complete compliance he was noticing every disposition of the ship and its company. At the end of not many days, Bob Scarf knew the disposal of all things— where and when men slept or waked; where they went and what they did; what weapons there were and where they were kept. And he had weighed all possibilities and chances, and had come to his own slow and careful conclusions that finally had become convictions. Just as he had watched and weighed and estimated in the Pawnee village, under cover of submission, until the moment came. "You can't," Bill Carden had said, "do a one-man mutiny." "I can," Bob Scarf was able to tell himself at last, "if I can get hold of arms."

The *Mary Scarlett* beat her way southward in long tacks, against the prevailing trade winds. At the end of the second week, she ran into dirty weather. The summer gale was brief, but savage while it lasted, and sudden in its onslaught. All hands were summoned to shorten sail. This was at night and during Scarf's watch below. He tumbled out with the others, but was thrown by a heavy sea across the forecastle. He fetched up sprawled across Bill Carden's bunk. Regaining his feet, his eye caught a glint of metal beneath the mattress, which his fall had slightly displaced. Thus he came again into possession of his long rifle and his belt with the tomahawk, the shot pouch, the powder horn and the throwing knife.

He showed neither surprise, gratification nor hesitation. Methodically he loaded the piece, ascended to the deck, made his way up the companion ladder to the quarterdeck, managed in the darkness to elude the notice of Captain Jordan and the quartermaster at the wheel, and slipped the whole equipment beneath the canvas lashed over the small deckhouse to protect its hatchway from rain and spray. That is where he had long ago figured out that he wanted it. Then, still unobserved, he returned to his duties, for in his inexperience he conceived the ship to be in danger, which was not the case.

The gale abated after twelve hours, and was succeeded by thick weather and a gentle fair wind and mountainous seas. The *Mary Scarlett* wallowed along with all sails set to take advantage of the favorable breeze before the trades might again control. Captain

Jordan, having checked to his satisfaction his dead-reckoning calculations, glanced at the compass to assure himself that the brig was on the course he had designated, and went below.

Two hours later, the lookout shrieked frantically in warning, but almost instantly thereafter the *Mary Scarlett* struck, bumped thrice and came to rest at a steep cant, partly broadside to the seas, which fell upon her with the fury of long pursuit at last terminated.

Captain Jordan was instantly on deck. His first act was to rush to the binnacle. His face was red with anger, but as he read the compass card the anger gave place to bewildered incredulity. The needle indicated the ship's direction as S. by W. ½W., as he had ordered. There was no time for considering the sources of his blunder. The immediate situation was desperate. The breaks of the forecastlehead and the quarterdeck alone were above water when the great combers swept the reef. Nothing could stand against them. The boats were gone. The bulwarks were gone. The men on watch were gone. Of that watch there remained only its officer, Bully Hawes, and the man still clinging to the useless wheel.

Jordan was a good seaman. He was able promptly to size up, to accept and to act on any situation. He saw at once that the brig must break up, and soon. Of the boats, but one remained—that carried on stern davits and used for general utility. It was a small affair, and it was very doubtful if it would carry all his men: indeed, if it could survive at all. Doubts have no place when there is no choice. There was here no choice, so Jordan did not entertain them.

The seas rolled down to engulf the ship and to pass on with a certain majestic and inexorable periodicity. Between onslaughts, the draining lull was almost a calm. During these intervals the men in the watch below, in ones, twos and threes, attempted the passage from the forecastle to the quarterdeck. They were sadly hampered by the receding wash. Some were swept overboard by the suction of these draining waters. Some were caught by the rush of the next wave. Of the ship's company, finally remained nine men: Captain Jordan, two of the mates—Bully Hawes and Tate—five seamen, including Bill Carden, and the Mountain Man, Bob Scarf.

They managed to get the boat into the water and to swing it at the end of its painter to the partial shelter of the ship's lee. This was a bit of work whose nicety Scarf could only partly appreciate. But he could admire the decision of Jordan's commands and the smartness with which they were carried out. Nor was lost on him the skill and judgment with which, then, the men were embarked and assigned places in the overladen boat. Discipline did have its use.

"Now, Scarf, in the bow!" snapped Jordan.

Bob started, came to himself. He lifted the corner of the tarpaulin, possessed himself of his weapons, and half slid down the slant of the deck to take his place. Relieved of the proximity of the deflecting metal, the needle of the compass swung. The lubber's point now stood at S.E.

III

By a miracle of careful handling and frantic bailing, the boat remained right side up as far as the break of the surf. There she upset, spewing her human contents into the wash and the undertow. All reached the beach, though it was touch and go with some, and Bully Hawes, with his arm still in a splint, would most certainly have been lost had not the Mountain Man himself plunged back into the sea to give him a hand; at which the crew, already safe, cheered wildly, with the facile emotion of the simple of mind. But Captain Jordan did not share this emotion. He was choking with rage.

"You wrecked my ship! You wrecked my ship!" he hurled at the dripping and astounded trapper, and would have attacked the latter blindly, had he not been restrained by Tate and one of the cooler-headed seamen, who saw Scarf's hand drop defensively to the weapons at his belt.

"I know nothing about compasses," disclaimed the latter, when finally he understood the purport of the captain's ravings.

So evident was his innocence of intent that at length Jordan regained command of himself and took charge. He summoned the men together and addressed them. Already he had made his calculations, and in his mind had corrected his course for the aberration of the compass, so he knew approximately where he must be. They gathered in a close knot to hear him. But Bob Scarf stood to one side. He had briefly satisfied himself that the rifle, to which he had clung throughout, had suffered no damage and that the cup of its hammer had protected its capped nipple; and now he leaned on its muzzle, listening in silence.

"Men," said Captain Jordan, "we are somewhere on the coast of Baja California. Cape St. Lucas lies somewhere to the south of us. We must make our way along the coast to a port where we can get a ship. So we will start south."

Bob Scarf spoke up unexpectedly.

"How you goin' to do it?" he asked bluntly; then, as Jordan turned on him, red-faced: "What you goin' to eat? Yo're thirsty now. What you goin' to drink? What'll you walk on when the rocks cut the shoes off'n yore feet? What you goin' to do when the Injuns git a'ter you? Or the yeller bellies—the Mexicans? We only licked 'em three years ago, and they ain't forgot. They'll kill you for yore shirts. It's a sight better to go toward the States than farther away from them. I'm a-goin' north."

"I'm in command," snapped Jordan. "You'll take my orders."

"You may be the old he-wolf whar it's wet," said Scarf, "but I'm my own boss whar it's dry."

"Seize that man!" ordered Jordan.

Scarf shifted the rifle to his hands.

"No," said he.

For a few moments, no one spoke or moved. Abruptly, the Mountain Man terminated the argument.

"You kin go whar you want," said he, "all except Hawes. He comes with me . . . Hawes, git a-comin'." He lowered the muzzle of the rifle. "Git a-comin'," he repeated mildly, "or take yore medicine what you stand. I'll shoot in his tracks the man who interferes," he added.

Fearful, half angry, half panicky, Hawes slowly obeyed.

"I'm coming too!" cried Bill Carden.

"Stand where you are, Carden!" commanded Jordan. "Mr. Tate, stand by!"

"Eff'n Bill wants to come, he kin come," observed Scarf placidly, and the muzzle of the rifle gave force to the remark. "Ary others?"

The remaining four men glanced at one another uneasily. But discipline and the attitude of the two ship's officers prevailed. After a moment, the Mountain Man motioned Carden and Hawes to precede him. The three disappeared, not up the beach but into the low hills.

IV

Captain Jordan, Tate and the four men started south along the shore. Within a very brief period, they found themselves in difficulties from which there seemed to be no escape. They were stout enough to have stood the travel, hard though it was, in yielding sands, around deep bays or inlets, through broken rocks, or even over laborious headlands where the beach pinched out. They might have made out well enough with mussels and sea urchins for food. But the human frame can get on only so long without fresh water. There was none. They interrupted their journey to search the back country. It was parched and brittle, and the washes were powder dry. In desperation they dug, but when they struck bedrock they must desist. The tortures of thirst aggravate rapidly, especially under the hot sun of those latitudes. Men's tongues swell, to protrude from their mouths. The blood thickening in their veins clouds the mind.

Hallucination overtakes them. They strip off their clothes, and, naked, perish. If sea water is near, they drink that, and die. By the end of the day following the shipwreck, Jordan's party hovered dangerously near that point. But just short of it Bob Scarf appeared among them. They thought at first that he, too, was a hallucination.

"You boys thirsty, by any chance?" asked Scarf.

"There's no water," croaked the captain.

"Plenty," returned Scarf.

He turned aside from the beach into the nearest of the steep-banked eroded barrancas that cut through the cliffs. The party staggered after. Still within sight of the beach, the trapper deftly clipped the top from one of the thousands of barrel cacti, plunged the blade of his knife again and again into the soft pulp. A milky liquid welled up.

"Thar's water," said the Mountain Man. "Help yourself."

He stood aside, watching them fall eagerly on the cacti round about, content to give them their heads, for the liquid came too slowly to permit them to harm themselves. But when they had revived, he called a halt.

"Thar's better yonder." He jerked his head toward the hills. "Come and git it."

"Where are Hawes and Carden?" Jordan's feeling of responsibility for his ship's company still survived.

"Carden's watchin' Hawes for me," said Scarf. "You comin'?" he asked the men. "Thar's meat. Unless," he added with a faint irony, "you'd rather have mussels."

"I think we'd better, sir," urged Tate, aside.

However, Jordan could not yet bring himself to the idea that he was no longer in command. He shook his head savagely. The demonstration of the barrel cactus showed him how to avoid death by thirst. That was all he needed. His strength was now restored by the life-giving liquid. He turned on his men with all his old domination.

But before he could speak, Bob Scarf intervened, and in his own voice now was the snap of authority.

"Stand back, boys," he ordered, "clear back—and fa'r play. The first man that offers to interfere, gits his . . . . I'm talkin' special to you, Tate." He raised his voice . . . . "You, Bill, plug anybody that leaves his place. Mind what I tole you."

"Aye aye, sir!" came Bill Carden's voice, so close at hand that all jumped with surprise. For the first time they noticed that the frontiersman was not carrying his rifle, the muzzle of which was now only too evident protruding from a crevice in the barranca wall so near that even a sailor could not miss.

"Now," observed Bob Scarf, leisurely approaching to front Jordan, "we're a-goin' to settle this." He addressed the uneasy and expectant sailors over his shoulders. "Fa'r play," said he. He touched the knife and tomahawk at his belt. "I'm not usin' these, though I mout, and no man could blame, things bein' as they are, but I won't. I'll just keep them by me, though, in case." His voice hardened, and they understood the threat to themselves. "Now," said Bob Scarf softly to Jordan, "you aim to be sensible, or have I got to whop you?"

Jordan reddened, struggling mightily with himself. Every instinct of lifelong habit arose belligerent.

"This is mutiny!" he cried.

Scarf's eye flashed whimsically.

"Now, my man," he drawled in relishing parody, "yo're a high private aboard this yere expedition. Eff'n you refuse duty, yo're goin' to have a taste of what to expect; and eff'n yo're no high private, you soon will be. Defend yoreself," he snapped suddenly.

But Jordan's common sense prevailed. By a mighty effort that brought him near to apoplexy, he choked back his anger. He yielded. "Lead on," he muttered. Bob Scarf's eye lighted with a sudden admiration. He knew that a man of Jordan's type had not yielded to fear of the personal consequences.

"Yo're a man, Jordan," he conceded.

V

The reunited party started north. No one challenged now Bob Scarf's right to command. They obeyed him without question; the men with that total relinquishment of all responsibility typical of those accustomed to be commanded; Tate still in the spirit of a good second mate carrying out his superior's intentions; Bill Carden, at first with the relish of a small boy playing a congenial game, later in the pathetic disillusionment of the same small boy who discovers that the game has miraculously turned into a hard and disagreeable job of work. The other two, Jordan and Bully Hawes, did what they were told sullenly, and because there was nothing else to be done. In the case of the mate, this attitude persisted. But gradually, as the days and then the weeks crept by, Jordan veered, at first to reluctant admiration, at last to genuinely hearty acquiescence in Scarf's right to leadership.

The little expedition retraced its steps. But it no longer either starved or thirsted. Bob Scarf found water. Jordan discovered that in the desert country, astoundingly, it was to be looked for, not in the dry water courses, as seemed sensible, but far up the sides of the mountains, sometimes almost at the tops. There were thousands of mountains, but Bob had an unerring eye for the small indications that told of its rare presence. He found it also in hollows in the rocks. There were millions of these hollows, dry as powder, but the Mountain Man seemed to know, without mistake, which one in the millions was tight enough of crevice and impervious enough of substance and sheltered enough from evaporation to have retained the precious fluid from the sparse winter rains of months ago. He called these receptacles *tenajas*, but he did not explain how he recognized them. Some showed faint indications of use by the desert's tiny animals, and by a robust exercise of his imaginative eye, Jordan was able to discern the faint trails of their approach—after he knew they must be there, not before. But others were so deeply caverned as to be inaccessible to animals. After a period of puzzlement, the seaman realized that the Mountain Man must find them by watching the flight of birds. But only of certain kinds of birds, and at a certain time of day.

And Bob Scarf found food. Sometimes with his long rifle he killed mountain sheep in the high hills. To do so, he made some terrific climbs, as Bill Carden and some of the sailors discovered when they were called upon to repeat the climb in order to carry out the carcasses; for Bob shot as many as he could, and showed them how to dry the meat that they could not immediately use. This was fat living. But the frontiersman also constructed various traps and snares, with which he caught lesser game. He despised nothing, even to the tiny desert pack rats. At first the sailors recoiled from these, as from certain lizards and other members of the reptile family, but Bob was firm against the policy of overlooking anything the desert offered. He would not permit them to eat the dried meat as long as anything else was to be had.

"We're savin' that," said he, "case'n she gits stingy."

He always referred to the desert as "she."

There were also various dry and distasteful beans from the scanty grouth, and knobs from certain kinds of cactus.

Thus, from the same country in which they had so nearly perished, they now were assured a sufficiency. Nevertheless, when the first novelty of thankfulness at survival had worn off, they found plenty to grumble at. That is human nature. Even Jordan's superior intelligence did not prevent him from chafing.

Scarf would not permit a fire during the day. He said that smoke brings Indians, and, though it was quite evident that the country was uninhabited, he would have no smoke. He moved too slowly; they would all die of old age before they could arrive anywhere. He spent an idiotic amount of time scouting inland, hunting in the mountains, looking ahead for the next water. He seemed to look on this as a pleasure excursion to be protracted as long as possible. The men wanted to get out. As Scarf never bothered to explain reasons for what he did, resentment grew. Occasionally, capriciously it seemed, almost as though maliciously to sweat it out of them, Scarf got them out early, and nagged at them all day and far into the night. The heat was intense. The men complained, lagged; one or two showed evidence of giving out, though more from loss of heart than actual exhaustion. He carried on; feeding, guiding, protecting, thinking, planning for them all. He was made of whalebone and leather and whipcord; tireless, unrelenting in his caution and in his demands on them. They did not understand; he did not explain. They hated him.

There was even some talk of mutiny, so that they might push on more rapidly. The journey must by now be nearly over. Bob paid them no attention. He might have been herding so many cattle through the desert mountains. In his eyes they were merely children for whom he must care.

Suddenly, at the hottest of noon, in mid-march, he called a halt.

"Git in among those rocks," he ordered curtly.

"Where's the water?" asked Jordan.

"No water," said Scarf.

The senselessness of a stop at this furnace spot, in the middle of the day, after only a three hours' march, added the last explosive grain to their resentment. They turned on him heatedly. A scattering burst of gunfire cut them short. Bullets puffed in the dry soil like grasshoppers. Bullets sang past their ears in the long crescendo shriek of ricochet. For an instant they stood, paralyzed with surprise. Then, with one accord, they dove for the shelter of the rocks, where they crouched, bewildered. The landscape was empty. There was no more gunfire.

They took stock. No one had been hit by any of the bullets. But Captain Jordan carried a feathered arrow through the fleshy part of his upper arm. In the confusion, they had noticed no arrows. Bob Scarf was not among them. Nor, when they peered cautiously from their shelter, could they see his body on the bare terrain. He had disappeared.

They crouched behind the rocks. The sun beat down on them as though it had solid weight. The soil and the stones were almost too hot to touch with the naked hand. They began to get thirsty. The gourds they carried had little water. Scarf had never been able to teach them to husband their supply. There was nothing they could do about it. A cautious experiment convinced them of that, for a musket roared instantly when a man exposed himself. The unseen enemy waited in savage patience. They were bewildered, uncertain, without expedient. Gradually it was borne in on them that they were lost, for there was nothing, absolutely nothing, they could do. And by now their suffering was genuine. They cursed Bob Scarf futilely. He could take care of himself. He was armed.

The day wore on. They came slowly to black despair.

Suddenly the firing began again. The beleaguered sailors pricked up their ears, for even their inexperience could distinguish the difference between the hollow roar of smoothbores and the sharp flat crack of Bob Scarf's long rifle. At times the latter was discharged with a rapidity astonishing for a muzzle-loader. Again for long intervals it was silent; only to sound at last from another quarter. The sailors sat up, their discomforts forgotten, listening, hopeful, and yet hardly daring to hope.

As abruptly as it had begun, the firing ceased. And then Bob Scarf was among them. He was drenched with sweat, and looked tired. But his energy was unabated. Before they had fully realized his presence, he was hustling them to their feet.

"Yaquis—Injuns," he vouchsafed. "We got to git. They's likely more. Ary one hurt?"

He looked briefly at Captain Jordan's arm, grunted, and started off at a swift pace up the rocky ridge. He did not look back. They could follow or not. They followed.

All the rest of that day, and under the moon until nearly midnight, the Mountain Man led the way without slacking pace. The route he chose was along a high rocky ridge. Cruel going, but it left no trail. These men's profession had not habituated them to walking; they were in dire distress from heat and lack of water; their feet became blistered from the hot rocks. When at last Bob Scarf called the halt, they dropped like logs, too done even to crawl to the little trickle of water which the mountaineer's strange instinct, or knowledge, had disclosed. It was Bob who brought the water to them, little by little, gourd by gourd, until they were sufficiently revived to help themselves.

Bob was tense, preoccupied. He brushed aside the details of the fight.

"Nothin' but Yaquis," he grunted with a certain contempt. "They don't know much. I've fit a heap more *sabe* Injuns than them. They was only a few of 'em. A scoutin' or huntin' party. But I couldn't quite get them all. The balance of the tribe will be a'ter us. Our easy travelin' is over."

Easy traveling! The men looked at one another. Someone groaned in despair.

"I'll git you thar," Bob Scarf answered this groan, "but you got to step smart and mind orders. It's a-goin' to be tough," said he, "and that I don't deny. We'll be travelin' in the high kentry from now on. We'll be movin' at night and lay bakin' out by day. There'll be mouty little water and less grub. Fat livin' done. See that?" He lifted the powder horn and shook it significantly. It was nearly empty.

"Wasn't there any powder on the Yaquis you killed?" asked Jordan.

Scarf grunted. "Like black sand," said he. "I wouldn't sile Betsy's bar'l with such stuff!" He brooded for a moment and looked up. "One thing," said he: "From now on I ain't got breath to argy who's boss. Eff'n they's any argyment, let's have it now." He looked at Jordan.

"You're skipper," said the latter promptly. "I thought you knew that."

Scarf nodded. "But I've been seein' and hearin' things I don't want to see and hear no more." He looked in turn at each of the exhausted men. "All right," he concluded. "Git some sleep."

"Don't we eat?" mumbled someone.

"A'ter you sleep," returned Bob Scarf. "Food don't do you no good less'n you can handle it."

Without further explanation, he threw himself prone, and appeared instantly to sleep. But in a moment he raised his head to address Bill Carden, who lay by his side. In the moonlight, the sailor saw the Mountain Man's face twist to a sardonic grin.

"Well, old-timer," observed Bob Scarf, "how you like Injun fightin'?"

Bill struggled through the half stupor of his exhaustion.

"Same's you do sailorin'," he returned with a flash of spirit.

The Mountain Man dropped back with one of his hearty but silent laughs.

"Fa'r enough!" said he.

VI

With the pueblo of San Diego in sight from the ring of southerly mountains, Bob Scarf eased up. He used a charge of the precious powder and brought in a sheep. They lighted a satisfactorily bright and heartening fire. The men's spirits relaxed. Subtly the essence of command began to set its return tide toward Jordan, though Bob Scarf continued still to conduct the party in all practical aspects. He recognized that this shift of allegiance was right and natural, now that the emergency was over; but both men knew that he, the Mountain Man, did not come within it. For the first time he and the captain met as equals, with neither as the over or the under dog. And they found that somehow each had the admiration, the respect and the liking of the other.

"You lost me my ship, Scarf, but I bear you no ill will for that," said Jordan bluntly; "and, since then, I'll admit that we would have perished without you."

"Well," retorted the trapper, "as for that, you lost me my hoss and possibles, for they're back thar in Monterey, whar I'll never lay eyes on 'em again. As for your ship," he continued shrewdly, "eff'n what I did lost her for ye, then you wouldn't have lost her eff'n I hadn't been aboard. And whose fault that I was aboard?"

The seaman laughed.

"I reckon you got me there. Reckon there ain't rightly nobody to blame. Let it go at that."

"Exceptin' a grampus," said the frontiersman, with some bitterness. Jordan looked surprised, but as Scarf did not explain he continued:

"What you going to do yonder?"

"I ain't goin' on no ship," said Bob.

Jordan laughed again. "But you've lost everything," he persisted. "How you going to get along?"

"So've you," countered the Mountain Man.

"But my firm, the firm that owns my ship, has a branch doing business here. They'll take care of me and my men. We're all fixed."

Scarf looked up.

"Wan't that yore ship?" he asked.

"No. I was merely captain. Hired."

"I'm mouty relieved to hear that," said the Mountain Man sincerely. "And don't you worry none about me. I'll get me an outfit eff'n thar's Yankees in the fur business thar. I've been grubstaked from nothin' more times than a rattler's got buttons."

"Well, I'm glad to hear that," said Jordan with equal sincerity. "I think it likely my own firm will fit you out."

"Fa'r enough," said Scarf. He slipped the tomahawk from his belt and filled its bowl. "I been savin'," he explained the tobacco, "fer a last medicine smoke, at the proper time." He puffed, blew the smoke successively straight up, straight down, to the four points of the compass, and passed the pipe to his companion.

"One thing I'd like to ask"—at length Jordan broke a companionable silence. "Why did you go back in the surf and pull Hawes out—at the risk of your own life? And why have you nursed him along so since? I should have thought you hated his guts."

Scarf looked at him with surprise.

312

"Why," he said presently, "you kain't lick a man with a broken arm. I had to save him till he got healed up."

Jordan threw back his head with a quick bark of laughter.

"Let me know when you get around to it, will you? I'd like to be there," he petitioned.

"I don't aim to have no interference!" warned Scarf.

"Lord love you, I wouldn't interfere!" cried Jordan.

"I'll let ye know," said Scarf.

He knocked the ashes from the tomahawk and strode abruptly to where Bill Carden sat apart from the others, mending his rawhide *botas*.

"Wall, Bill," said the Mountain Man. "we're nigh done with the expedition together. Soon we'll be partin'. Less'n you want to go with me and fight more Injuns?"

"Not me!" cried Carden fervently. "I'm a sailor!"

"Thought not. Wall, we got one more thing we must do, and as soon as we git it in we'll be about it."

"What's that?"

"You and me," said Bob Scarf, "are goin' out together on a hunt. Yore goin' to help me kill myself a grampus, and I'm a-goin' to help you trap yoreself a weasel. Them two critters sure done us a lot of dirt. We got to play even!"

TEXT CREDITS